CELESTIAL MONSTERS

★ "Thomas unravels a plot that is as riveting as it is terrifying, as . . . Teo teams up with the other semidioses to save the world they all know and love, regardless of class difference. Fans of the Hunger Games and mythology will revel in this energetic, well-wrought adventure."
—*Booklist*, starred review

Praise for CEMETERY BOYS

"Detailed, heart-rending, and immensely romantic. *Cemetery Boys* is necessary: for trans kids, for queer kids, for those in the Latinx community who need to see themselves on the page. Don't miss this book."
—Mark Oshiro, author of *Anger Is a Gift*

"The novel perfectly balances the vibrant, energetic Latinx culture while delving into heavy topics like LGBTQ+ acceptance, deportation, colonization, and racism within authoritative establishments."
—*Teen Vogue*

★ "A romantic mystery as poignant as it is spellbinding, weaved in a mosaic of culture, acceptance, and identity, where intricately crafted characters are the pieces and love—platonic, romantic, familial, and communal—is the glue."
—*Publishers Weekly*, starred review

CELESTIAL MONSTERS

AIDEN THOMAS

FEIWEL AND FRIENDS
NEW YORK

A Feiwel and Friends Book

An imprint of Macmillan Publishing Group, LLC

120 Broadway, New York, NY 10271 • fiercereads.com

Our books may be purchased in bulk for promotional, educational, or business use. Please contact your local bookseller or the Macmillan Corporate and Premium Sales Department at (800) 221-7945 ext. 5442 or by email at MacmillanSpecialMarkets@macmillan.com.

Library of Congress Cataloging-in-Publication Data is available.

First edition, 2024

Book design by L. Whitt

Interior art by Mars Lauderbaugh

Feiwel and Friends logo designed by Filomena Tuosto

Printed in the U.S.A.

ISBN 978-1-250-82208-6 (hardcover)
ISBN 978-1-250-37069-3 (special edition)

1   3   5   7   9   10   8   6   4   2

TO ALEX ABRAHAM, WHOSE VOICE, HUMOR, AND GENIUS CAN BE HEARD IN EVERY PAGE. THIS BOOK WOULDN'T EXIST WITHOUT YOUR HELP.

AND TO HOLLY WEST AND EMILY SETTLE, FOR MAKING MY DREAMS COME TRUE.

PROLOGUE

Not all gods were created equal.

First, Sol shaped the Golds, who were powerful but ruled by vanity.

Second, Sol crafted the Jades, who were kind but ruled by duty.

Third, Sol forged the Obsidians, who were clever but ruled by cruelty.

Finally, Sol made humans, who were mortal but capable of boundless joy and passion.

Reino del Sol was bountiful with love and light.

It didn't last.

Sol tasked their godly children to watch over the mortals, to help them thrive.

They distributed gifts from fallen stars.

In one particularly trustworthy Jade, Sol placed the power of Good Fortune—

the ability to turn the tides in his favor.

The god, Suerte, worked with Sol and their beloved, Tierra,

to shape the world of humans.

Suerte showed Agua where to carve the rivers.

He guided the Estaciones into periods of sun and rain to nourish the crops.

He helped Maize teach the mortals to farm, to use the land Tierra provided them.

He created a paradise for Sol's mortal children, and for a time, all was good.

It didn't last.

The Obsidians grew bitter in their temples of black stone,
festering in their resentment of Sol's favoritism to the mortals,
and the imbalanced delegation of godly gifts.
They planned to enslave their human wards,
to steal Sol from the Earth, and rule over the chaos that remained.
They brought forth great creatures to terrorize the land
Suerte had worked so hard to protect.
All he had helped build was brought to ruin.
And so,
   Fortune
    fell.

A new god rose from the ashes—Mala Suerte
Bad Luck.
A deity made to fight back.
He rode out with the Golds in battle
and razed the Obsidian cities to the ground.

When Sol gave their life to trap the traitor gods beneath the earth,
the Golds and the Jades devised a system to keep the stones of Sol's
  flesh lit.
They would call it The Sunbearer Trials.
It was a chance for children of the gods to show their worth.

It didn't last.

CHAPTER 1
XIO

"Don't you get it?... I don't need *your help, I don't want you to save me! I am Obsidian, and this is our revenge!"*

Xio spat his final declaration as he was swallowed by the nebulous dark Caos had conjured. The rush of wind howled in Xio's ears as he flailed, untethered and falling endlessly. The air was sucked from his lungs and for a brief, disorienting moment, Xio thought he might suffocate—and then it was like someone flicked on the lights. He landed hard on his back.

He had a second to register their new location—wet stone soaking into the back of his shirt, the smell of damp moss and the relieving cool of being deep underground, the throbbing in his right hand—before the world exploded with movement all around him.

Ocelo was the first to launch, their claws extended and aimed directly at Venganza's face. The tall, goat-headed god sighed as though he found this all incredibly dull, and flicked his wrist, backhanding Ocelo with such force it sent them flying head over heels.

Auristela shouted. Unlike Ocelo, she had taken a moment to assess her surroundings before charging into action—which,

Xio reflected, was to be expected. Her gold jewelry sparked in firelight as she sent a massive wave of flames careening toward Venganza, Caos, and Chupacabra from behind.

Xio hadn't spent months of his life learning all her tricks to fall for that now.

"Watch out!" he cried, scrambling to his feet. But he didn't need to.

Caos threw out their midnight blue hand and Auristela's fire went out—disappearing in a puff. Auristela snarled, and Xio was pretty sure he heard a chuckle echo from Caos's shrouded, featureless face. The hem of their dark robes hovered above the ground, their exposed midnight blue skin dancing with moving constellations.

Xio crouched, readying himself to be the target of the Golds' rage, but they didn't seem to even notice him.

The semidioses put up a good fight, throwing all of their best moves at the three gods. Still decked out in their gaudy regalia, the Golds looked out of place. They were supposed to be parading around Sol Temple, gleaming alongside all the opulence and grandeur. Instead, they were in dank, wet darkness.

Xochi's thorns were out in full force, ready to shred whatever she struck with her vines. Marino used high pressure streams of water powerful enough to cut through wood, an advanced move he used so rarely that Xio had only ever seen one video of it on TúTube. Atzi tossed lightning, not at all weighed down by her ruffled dress. Earsplitting cracks filled the room as the bolts missed their targets and ricocheted off the walls.

Dezi, fast as a hummingbird, dodged around the others, trying to get within reach of one of the gods, but it was no use. They were disorganized and sloppy, frantic instead of calculated.

Xio relaxed. He wasn't in any danger.

For once, the Golden children of the dios were outmatched. And, damn, did it feel good to watch.

Xochi moved in again and this time Xio exhaled a laugh, shaking off his nerves.

"Seriously?" he asked aloud. "Just give it up before you—"

BOOM.

Searing electricity contracted every muscle in Xio's body, locking his legs. It lasted only a moment before he was staring up from the floor again. Everything hurt, from the top of his head and down his spine to his butt. Xio groaned, ears ringing and skull throbbing.

Atzi stood to his left, looking smug. She flipped Xio off before Caos snapped his fingers and bound her arms in ropes.

Cheeks hot, Xio struggled to his feet and tried to ignore the tingling of his skin, like ants were crawling all over him. He should have been keeping an eye on Atzi—he knew what she was capable of. He looked to Venganza for any trace of embarrassment or disappointment, but found none. The Obsidians seemed more amused by the Golds fighting back than anything else—but Xio knew they couldn't let their guard down.

He'd studied the Golds. He knew their strategies, their go-to attacks, and most importantly, their ultimate moves that they only used in the most dire circumstances.

That was why, when he saw Auristela pressing her flames between her palms, sweat beading her forehead as they changed from orange and red to bright white, Xio called out to the Obsidians, "Watch it!"

Venganza's goat head snapped to Auristela, horizontal pupils spotting her attack. He twisted out of the way, narrowly avoiding the blast before it careened into the wall and exploded on impact. The burst of heat hit Xio in the face, the worn stone floor trembling beneath his feet.

"Whoa," Xio breathed, squinting through the smoke where there was now a massive, scorched hole blown into the limestone. "Explosive Fireball Blast," he murmured to himself, updating the database of Gold Heroes in his head. Xio hadn't known that was a move Auristela was even capable of. He wished he had his binder to take down notes.

"I think that's enough playtime for now," Venganza said, pinching out a smoldering tuft of fur near one of his horns.

In a blink, something large streaked across the room and next thing Xio knew, Auristela was dangling in midair, her wrists trapped in Chupacabra's clawed hand. The diosa's skin was covered in fur, her head like a wolf's, and she walked on hind legs.

"That's a neat little trick, diosita," Chupacabra said, letting out a terrible laugh. Her eyes—scarlet pupils set in venom yellow sclera—danced with delight.

Auristela flexed her fingers, but the flames spluttered, unable to catch no matter how many sparks she flicked to life. Xio knew she couldn't create fire big enough to cause damage without full use of her hands, and the Obsidians knew that because he'd told them.

But that didn't stop Auristela. She fought back hard—thrashing, swearing, and kicking Chupacabra, who just laughed until Auristela landed a kick to her ribs.

Chupacabra grabbed Auristela's hair knot and gave it a hard yank, snapping her head back. Auristela let out a pained shout.

Ocelo roared. They charged at Chupacabra, muscles still swollen and fangs elongated, claws unsheathed from their fingers.

In a blur of movement too fast for Xio to track, an obsidian dagger appeared in Chupacabra's hand, held to Auristela's neck.

"Down, kitty," Chupacabra warned, her wolfish face twisted in terrible glee.

Ocelo skidded to a stop. Auristela stopped thrashing. The others froze. Frightened silence filled the room.

Ocelo's snarl twitched, fear behind their slitted pupils as their eyes danced between Chupacabra and Auristela. The edge of the glassy black blade hovered over the pulse of Auristela's neck.

"One wrong move and this will cut through her pretty semidiose skin like butter," Chupacabra teased in a singsong voice. "Your little semidiose healing won't do much good against pure obsidian—isn't that right?" she said, her attention swinging to Xio.

The haze of adrenaline cleared and Xio suddenly remembered dragging the ceremonial dagger across his palm. He looked down at his hand. It was a clean cut, black blood spilling freely like a weeping eye. There weren't any signs of healing yet, but he couldn't heal as quickly as other semidioses, and the obsidian of the blade didn't help. Blood slid between his fingers and dripped onto the dirty stone floor.

The Golds stared in horror and confusion.

On instinct, Xio hid his hand behind his back.

Auristela glared at Chupacabra like she was trying to set her on fire with just her mind. "I'd turn you into a pile of charred bones before you even got the chance," she seethed through clenched teeth.

Chupacabra let out another shrieking, feral laugh. She leaned her face close to Auristela's, her long tongue slithering out to lick her salivating jowls. "Want to bet?" With the lightest press, golden blood bloomed against the blade, trickling down Auristela's neck.

Auristela stilled, but her eyes blazed with violence as her friends pleaded with Chupacabra to stop.

Xio's heart leapt into his throat as the other semidioses cried out. Part of him said, *Who cares what happens to her? She's a Gold. She's the Gold, Her Royal Highness Auristela, pride of Reino del Sol and all their crooked gods.* Killing Golds had always been part of the plan.

You can't have a rebellion without slitting a few throats, Venganza had told him during the trials, using their secret method of communication—the stone on Xio's azabache bracelet. Venganza had been Xio's only *real* ally throughout the trials, the only person who gave a shit what happened to the low-blooded, powerless thirteen-year-old everyone else regarded as the obvious sacrifice.

Well, not *everyone.* But Xio didn't have time to think about that right now.

"Now, now, let's come to our senses," Venganza said. "There's no need for all this."

Relief crashed over Xio as Venganza stepped forward. Being near Chupacabra was like being stalked by a predator—you had to be constantly on guard, perpetually in fear of being attacked. Chupacabra was unpredictable and violent, but his father was levelheaded.

"Just be obedient and there will be no need for unpleasantness," he explained calmly, looking at each semidiose in turn.

Marino signed what Venganza said to Dezi while the other Golds exchanged uneasy looks. Except for Auristela, who was still locked in a staring contest with Chupacabra.

Venganza turned to Xio. "Oh dear." He *tsk*ed. "Come, let me see your injury."

Xio lifted his chin and approached his father. He laid his hand face up in Venganza's enormous, godly palm.

"Caos, if you wouldn't mind," Venganza said.

With a *snap*, a cloth appeared in his hand. It was dark, the deep purple-blue of midnight, and stitched with silvery constellations that undulated. Carefully, Venganza wrapped it around Xio's hand with his long fingers before tying it in place.

It was like holding the night sky in his palm. Like he could reach through the fabric and into the stars.

Venganza smiled down at him. "It'll certainly leave a scar, but it will at least heal with some time."

Xio did his best to smile back and ignore the fluttering of his pulse. This was his father, not someone to be afraid of. He just needed to get used to Venganza, his goat head and large teeth, and the pulse of vengeful energy that poured from him. While his father seemed calm and collected, Xio could feel the raw power Venganza held contained just below the surface.

"You've done so well," Venganza said earnestly, pressing a hand to his chest before placing it on Xio's shoulder. "I am proud to call you my son."

Xio released a shaky breath, the reassurance hitting him so hard his knees almost buckled. He puffed out his chest as he looked up at his father. He didn't even flinch when Venganza's nails bit into his shoulder as he gave it a squeeze.

"*What?*" Auristela hissed.

The Golds stared at Xio, a mixture of confusion, betrayal, and fear.

Xio stared back and soaked it in. For once, they were taking him seriously.

For once, people were afraid of *him*.

Except for Dezi. After Marino signed to him—the taller boy not taking his wide eyes off Xio as he did—Dezi turned to Xio. His eyebrows drew together, his features softening. Dezi's eyes held Xio's gaze and there was sadness behind them. And it wasn't for himself. It was for Xio.

And Xio hated it.

"We should secure the prisoners before they try anything," Xio said, turning away from Dezi's pity.

Auristela tugged against Chupacabra's grip again, earning another cut, but she didn't seem to care. All her rage was on Xio, eyes blazing dangerously as she snarled, "When I get my hands on you, I'm going to melt your eyes from your skull—"

Xio stepped back, bumping into Venganza.

"Caos," Venganza said politely, speaking over Auristela.

With a *snap*, Auristela's mouth snapped shut. Her jaw flexed and strained, but it was like her lips had been glued closed.

Xio forced the muscles in his face to calm as Chupacabra howled with laughter.

He wasn't *scared*. He wasn't even angry like some combustible little princesses. He was above that. And he wouldn't ramble any excuses out, either. This was the smart thing to do. He was composed. He was powerful. He was in his element. He was home.

When Xio opened his eyes, he found Atzi staring at him intently, her pretty mouth curled in disgust. Xio glared back.

"I think that's enough for now," Venganza announced, turning to Caos and Chupacabra.

Chupacabra put her dagger away, which seemed to let everyone relax a little.

"Junior's right, we'll have plenty of time to play later," Chupacabra cooed, dragging Auristela along so the diosa could give Xio a condescending pat on the head. He resisted the urge to bite her hand.

Xio had to dodge a kick from Auristela, but Chupacabra yanked her back.

"Let's make our guests more comfortable," Venganza said, turning to Caos.

They snapped their fingers. Gold bracelets, armbands, rings pulled free from the semidioses' regalia, landing in a heap. Xio's own jade-and-gold chest piece hung heavy around his neck.

"Hey!" Atzi tried to snatch back the large Tormentoso pendant around her neck, but she wasn't quick enough. All the jewelry landed in a heap at Caos's feet, including Ocelo's jaguar teeth necklace and the polished seashells from Marino's.

The fresh flowers were ripped from Xochi's dress by invisible hands, leaving her clutching its tattered black skirts with tears in her eyes. Then there was Auristela, who looked oddly plain after removing all the glitzy jewelry she was usually covered in.

"Let me *go!*" she snarled.

Chupacabra turned to Caos and raised Auristela in the air by her wrists as she continued to thrash. "Could you do something about this?"

Snap.

Auristela went limp.

"NO!" Ocelo cried as the others panicked, staring in horror as Auristela's motionless body swung from Chupacabra's grip.

"STOP." Venganza's voice boomed, echoing off the walls and reverberating down Xio's spine. The Golds fell into stunned silence. Venganza cleared his throat and put a pleasant smile on his face. "Your friend is fine, only sleeping," he told them gently.

It was true. Xio could see the slow rise and fall of her chest.

The Golds started asking questions all at once, signing wildly as they spoke.

"What did you do?" Xochi demanded, trying to look brave.

"What's going on out there?" Atzi asked.

The desperation was clear in Marino's voice when he said, "What do you even want with us?"

Dezi was on guard, intently watching. Xio could see the cogs in his head working on a plan, which wasn't good.

"What were those things falling out of the sky?"

"Where are our parents?"

"Where are *we*?"

"What *are* you?" Ocelo said in disgust, staring at the black blood smeared across Xio's hand.

Xio tensed and glared at Ocelo, unable to find his voice.

Venganza put his hands up, and the semidioses immediately stopped talking. This time, it wasn't one of Caos's tricks.

Venganza grinned at their obedience. "We have only done what Sol forced us to do," he said. "We were here for the creation of the world. We belong in Reino del Sol just like any other diose, semidiose, or human," he reasoned. "But we couldn't return under Sol's watchful eye. In order for us to come home, Sol's light needed to be snuffed out, so we had to put an end to that annoying little ritual of yours.

"Instead of that yummy golden sacrifice that was meant to recharge the Sol stones and keep us caged for the next decade, we fed the earth the rich obsidian blood of my son."

Here he turned to Xio with a knowing grin. "Without the sun in the way, Xio here was able to summon us home."

"Those *things*," he continued with distasteful emphasis, "are Celestials."

The Golds broke into hushed chatter.

"There's nothing to be afraid of." Venganza chuckled. "They're our creations." He gestured to himself, Chupacabra, and Caos. "I'm sure your parents told you they were monsters, but they're much more like pets. *Very* obedient."

Xio smirked. Venganza was downplaying how dangerous the Celestials really were. And the semidioses were likely desperate enough to believe him.

"The cosmos is a dark, cold, and terrible place," Venganza continued. "They were banished with us. We couldn't just abandon them out there." He gave a nonchalant wave of his hand. "They're finally getting some much-needed time to stretch their legs."

"Do you really think our parents will let you get away with that?" Atzi asked sarcastically as she glared at Venganza. Xio couldn't decide if she was brave or foolish. Either way, she definitely had a death wish.

Venganza's goat lips stretched into a smile. "No, that's why I stole their favorite children as collateral."

Chupacabra howled with laughter. "I mean, seriously, the *Sunbearer Trials*? Why not just put all your most talented and *special* children in an open field with a sign that says 'Please Kidnap Me!'? The Golds have always been so *arrogant*." She laughed again, but Xio could see the barely restrained rage twitching in her wolfish face.

"We weren't all Golds," Marino said hesitantly.

Venganza nodded at Xio. "Obviously."

"That's not what I mean," Marino said. He took in a deep breath and puffed out his chest with a defiant look. "The Sunbearer this year was a Jade."

A stabbing pain hit Xio in the chest, but it had the opposite effect on the Golds.

"Teo!" Xochi said, looking around like she'd just realized he wasn't there.

"That's right, and no one saw him coming," Atzi said, like it was some kind of threat.

"Including the dioses," Ocelo added gruffly.

Dezi nodded fervently.

"It's true, we didn't see that twist coming, either," Venganza admitted. "But that's not a complication. In fact, it made things much easier for our dear Xio. It was going to be a lot of work for him to throw the closing ceremony as an observer of the trials." Venganza chuckled. "Not only did Sol put him directly into the trials, but the Son of Quetzal did all the hard work of throwing the sacrifice for us, as well. It was too easy."

Venganza presented the Sol Stone. With the light gone, Sol's golden skull was barely visible through the smoky glass. "The dioses and Heroes will have their hands full with the Celestials, and the Sun Stones protecting the cities will go out in a matter of days," he went on. "Without this"—he rolled the Sol Stone between his fingers—"it will be impossible for the Golds to stop us. We'll remake Reino del Sol as it was meant to be: not dioses serving the humans, but humans serving their dioses." Venganza smiled. "All we have to do is wait."

When the Golds broke out in a panic and started to argue, Xio wasn't surprised, but it *was* embarrassing to watch.

"Like I said," Venganza told them slowly, his voice booming above the rest. "If you cooperate and do as you're told, no harm will come to you."

Everyone turned to Dezi as he started to sign. Mala Suerte had always prioritized learning accessible languages, so when Xio caught *bird* and *brother*, his stomach dropped before Venganza interrupted.

"Ah-ah," he said, waving a finger and chiding Dezi. "None of that."

Dezi jumped as ropes bound his wrists together. He turned to Venganza, staring at him in disbelief.

"Don't do that!" Marino said, with more backbone than Xio had seen since they arrived in Los Restos. He frantically signed reassurances to Dezi.

Venganza quirked an eyebrow at that, and then all the Golds' wrists became knotted in rope.

Xochi was bewildered. "We can't communicate with him without our hands!"

"Do you have any idea how hard it is to read lips, asshole?!" Ocelo fumed, throwing their whole body into trying to wrench themself free.

"Ooh," Chupacabra cooed. "Look how smart they are, Venganza!"

"I know exactly what tricks Amor's children can get up to," Venganza agreed. "I think it's better for all of us if we eliminate any opportunities for *problems*."

Xio had to look away from Dezi's pleading eyes—it was cruel, yes, but Xio trusted that Venganza had his reasons. Venganza had never lied to him, never made him believe he ought to be something he *could never be*.

Chills ran up Xio's spine as disembodied laughter filled the air. Caos appeared between the other two Obsidians in a wisp of indigo smoke. "Are you still sore about that little thing with Amor, Venganza?" Caos said in their strange way of talking, like multiple voices speaking at once, echoing from down a long hallway. "It's been, what, a few thousand years?"

Chupacabra shrieked with laughter, only to be cowed by a single look from Venganza. Xio didn't miss the way she and Caos retreated from his father. They were all scary-powerful in their own right, but Caos and Chupacabra knew who their leader was. Venganza commanded respect, and a healthy amount of fear.

That was what Xio wanted.

He looked back at the bound Golds. Angry tears gathered in Xochi's eyes and Marino stood between Dezi and the Obsidians, even though Xio could see the tension threading the cords of his neck. Atzi and Ocelo practically had smoke coming out of their ears.

"Caos, would you ready our guests' accommodations?" Venganza asked.

The skin of Caos's featureless face twisted and stretched into something that might have been a grin. Indigo tendrils of smoke unfurled from their robes before they sank and disappeared through the floor.

"Now, come along," Venganza instructed, walking down the hall.

The Golds exchanged looks, like they didn't know what to do. Xio wondered if that had to do with the fact that Auristela wasn't there to lead them, since she was still unconscious in Chupacabra's grip.

Chupacabra sprang into action, circling the semidioses like a dog herding sheep. Or, rather, a wolf hunting its prey. If someone fell behind, she was there, snapping her teeth until they huddled tightly together. All the while, Auristela was still draped over Chupacabra's shoulders, facedown and limbs dangling.

"Look what's become of your temple, Venganza," Chupacabra growled, nose twitching and lips peeling back in distaste. "It's a disgrace."

The ruined temple was a labyrinth of broken limestone and decaying vegetation, interrupted by dead ends of collapsed rubble. The floors were cracked and uneven, broken up by wandering tree roots. Water plinked down from the canopy of overgrown ferns that filled caved-in portions of the ceiling. Intricately carved walls were worn away and stained by moss and mildew.

"It *has* been sitting untended for a few thousand years," Venganza reminded her dryly.

The slap of their footsteps against the cold, wet stone floors echoed in the empty space. Cobwebs—and worse things Xio was trying not to notice—hung from doorways, and a thick coating of grime colored the whole temple in dull, muted grays.

Xio remembered the first time he'd found this place. The day everything changed, the day he'd learned the *truth* about where he came from—so different from the lies Mala Suerte had given him.

He couldn't remember the first time he ran away—he'd done it too many times. What he did remember was that by the time he felt guilty enough to turn around and go home, no one had even noticed he was gone yet. Mala Suerte's temple was too full, too hectic for one missing kid to stand out. So, running away became Xio's new favorite thing. For a few hours, or sometimes even a couple of days, just to get away from people. To not feel them staring, to not constantly feel on edge.

At first, the priests would panic and summon his dad—who was always able to find him—but then it happened often enough that he was just labeled as a flight risk, expected to eventually return, and the priests just let him run.

Xio found himself wandering closer and closer to the edge of town, past where Los Restos lay. He was drawn to the jungle. When he got close, it set his skin buzzing with electricity.

Everyone was warned of the dangers of Los Restos. The

former territory of the Obsidians was said to be cursed and full of bloodthirsty monsters. Sometimes he could hear movement and see glowing eyes in the shadows, but none of the creatures of Los Restos ever bothered him.

Maybe that should've been a hint.

Even now, a year later, he could still feel the horror of his first period when he looked down to find rivulets of black running down his legs and circling the shower drain. Terrified, he tried to clean it up, to make it stop, quick, before anyone could see—of course, Renata had heard him crying through the door and run for their father right away.

When Mala Suerte realized what was happening, he told the curious group of siblings and priests to leave and locked the door behind him. Xio clutched a towel, tears streaming down his face, trembling. Mala Suerte couldn't lie to him anymore because the truth was spilled across the white tile of the floor.

The dios he thought was his father had taken Xio to the observatory at the top of his temple. As they walked slowly around the room, Suerte revealed the real story of the war of the gods. After Sol banished the Obsidians, the Golds and Jades took it upon themselves to make sure no Obsidian could threaten Reino del Sol again. It wasn't enough to banish the gods alone—they had to wipe out their descendants, too.

Xio's mother had died shortly after he'd been born, but it wasn't simply bad luck. She'd been slaughtered by the gods as they burned Obsidian cities to the ground, searching for children of Venganza, Caos, and Chupacabra. Mala Suerte had been part of it. He didn't even try to deny it.

Thousands of years later, his dad said, something kept pulling him back to Los Restos. It was just after the last trials, when Suerte should have been preparing for the new Sunbearer to come and recharge Ciudad Afortunada's Sun Stone. Instead, he'd gone wandering Los Restos. He found the remains of Venganza's temple, nothing more than a pile of rubble, but he stumbled upon something strange.

In the ruins, Mala Suerte found a large orb of obsidian, covered in thousands of years' worth of dust, grime, and moss. When he touched it, the orb opened to reveal a small child, wrapped in soft blankets, fast asleep and unharmed. That was when the lies and charades began.

His dad tried to explain, but Xio couldn't hear him.

"Why am I here?" Xio demanded. "How can I exist?"

Suerte had only shrugged. "Sol willed it."

Xio still thought that was a bullshit answer.

That night at dinner, his siblings were kind and gentle with him. They thought he was struggling with the dysphoria of his first period—he'd only started using new pronouns a few months before, and they just wanted to help. But their sympathy only made him feel worse—maybe, if he were who he'd always thought he was, dysphoria would be his biggest problem right then. Instead, he was coming to terms with the fact that his entire life had been a lie. That he was one of the monsters children told stories about around the campfire.

His whole life, he'd felt like there was something wrong with him.

His whole life, Mala Suerte had known.

Mala Suerte made Xio vow not to tell anyone the truth about his parentage. The Golds would surely have him killed. Xio could only stare back at his pretend father, speechless.

That night, when he ran away, he had no intention of coming back.

He went to Los Restos, seeking out Venganza's temple. It was like a voice calling through the jungle. Xio found the ruins of his home city, Venganza's temple waiting for him at its center. He found the massive, destroyed glyph at the altar.

That was when Venganza found him.

He spoke to Xio through the glyph. Xio learned about what had happened to their people. How they'd been attacked and hunted down for no other reason than the color of their blood. Venganza warned him about the Golds and promised Xio a future where he had a family—his *real* family.

All it took was a little bad luck.

Lost in thought, Xio's pace slowed, until he walked side by side with the captured semidioses. He couldn't bring himself to look in their direction, but when a rat scurried across the path, he could hear Ocelo's growl of disgust and couldn't stop himself from smirking.

Niya would have loved to make fun of the meathead cat for that one.

Stop it, Xio chastised himself. He wasn't supposed to think of Niya or Teo or any of the time they'd spent together during the trials. Their friendship had been a farce, all a part of Xio's plan. And if he had enjoyed it—well, that was in the past.

Besides, Niya, Teo, and Aurelio had all managed to escape their trap. They were probably already working with the Golds to organize an attack against the Obsidians. This was war, and they were on the wrong side. Xio wouldn't waste time thinking about two inconsequential Golds and a Jade.

They reached a doorway that opened onto the landing of a long spiral staircase. It went up higher than Xio could see and disappeared into the darkness below. Chupacabra practically skipped down into the dungeon, Auristela's body jostling on her shoulder.

At the bottom of a set of pitted stairs, a large stone archway waited for them, yawning open like the mouth of a beast. Beyond it was pitch-black. Xio strained his eyes to see into the dark, but it was impossible.

"Ah, here we are," Venganza said. His voice echoed in the cavernous void when he called out, "Caos, do you mind?"

Xio watched as the Gold's faces drained of color. Dezi frantically looked to Marino, then the others, but their hands could not lift into any reassuring signs.

Snap.

All six vanished in wisps of smoke.

Xio whipped his head around. "Where did they—?"

Venganza chuckled and reached down, placing his massive hand on Xio's back. "Come, let me show you," he said with an encouraging nudge.

Xio glanced at the doorway again. He hadn't gone this far down into the temple during his own exploring. This deep underground, the cool, musty air slid across his skin, bringing with it the stench of mold and rot. In the dark, strange sounds echoed.

He forced himself to follow.

CHAPTER 2
TEO

On the long list of Teo's recent fuckups, accidentally triggering the apocalypse had to be number one.

The Sol Stone was destroyed, Luna was dead, and the sun—*the literal sun*—was gone. He had fucked up so completely that the strongest young Golds in Reino del Sol had fallen into the hands of the Obsidians who, until now, had been locked up in the stars. And all because Teo couldn't follow the rules.

In spite of all that, Teo knew if he could go back and do it all again, he'd still refuse to kill Auristela. Hell, he'd even still try to catch Xio before he fell.

Xio, Son of Venganza.

Betrayal, embarrassment, and heartache stormed inside Teo, filling up his chest. How had he not seen it? Every moment he, Niya, and Xio were together—talking about how they were the underdogs and needed to stick together, laughing over breakfast, combing through Xio's dorky trading card collection to memorize stats on the competition—flashed through Teo's head. He had known something was wrong before the trials ended, but he'd never imagined *Xio* had been behind it all.

Niya and Auristela fighting on the jungle floor. Ocelo, constantly trying to set Teo off. And Auristela, just before she blew the final trial and cost herself her life—their eyes had all been black. They'd all been acting so *angry*, so—so vengeful.

Teo thought about the story Xio had told, about the girls in Xio's class who'd gotten lice after bothering Xio about his own hair. *Bad luck*, Xio had said.

No, Teo realized now. *Revenge. All this time, Xio was plotting the Obsidians' revenge.* How could he have missed that?

And now all of Reino del Sol was paying for Teo's mistakes.

But they still had a chance. All Teo had to do was get through Los Restos, sneak into Venganza's temple, steal the Sol Stone back, and then summon the gods to resurrect Sol.

What could possibly go wrong?

Teo changed out of his now dirty and tattered ceremonial regalia, abandoning the feathered cape and Sunbearer crown in his room. He changed back into his Academy-designed uniform and couldn't help feeling like he was starting the trials all over again.

Huemac and the Sol priests brought essential supplies as Teo, Niya, and Aurelio packed their backpacks. Teo carefully wrapped Fantasma's used tapered candle into the sleeve of a jacket. He couldn't figure out a safe place for the iridescent feather his mother had pulled from her hair. Summoning the dioses when they were ready was a vital part to the success of their mission, so it needed to be close, easy to reach.

When she saw him struggling, Niya bounded over. Using some gold from her bangle, Niya fashioned an earring with a small chain and attached the feather by pressing another bit of gold around the quill. The soft feather tickled the side of Teo's neck when he put it on.

Aurelio had the tiny vial holding the Elixir of Charming tied around his neck with a leather cord, and the Decanter of Endless Water was tucked into a side pocket, but Teo noticed he'd stuffed the Scorching Circlet into the depths of his bag while they were packing. Meanwhile,

Niya was still wearing the Ring of Shielding with the Unbreakable Blade clutched in her hand. He knew she was going through it when she didn't make a single joke as she packed up Tormentoso's Bag of Winds and Primavera's Gem of Regeneration.

Teo struggled to heft his pack onto his back while Niya and Aurelio slung theirs over their shoulders like they weighed nothing. At school, his wings were always bound so he could wear a normal backpack over them with mild discomfort. But now that they were free, he needed a special bag to accommodate them.

Luckily, the Sol priests had made him one for the trials that he didn't end up using. It was a pear-shaped backpack that hung just below his shoulder blades and wings. In addition to the shoulder straps, there was another across Teo's chest to keep it secured when he was flying, and each strap was fitted with quick-release buckles.

Teo, Niya, and Aurelio followed Huemac down the broken steps of Sol Temple, lit by torches in the perpetual night.

"You have two weeks before the Sun Stones go out and leave the cities entirely defenseless," Huemac said as he led them through the streets of Sol City with surprising swiftness. "Without the Sun Stones, there will be no way to resurrect Sol and banish the Obsidians back to the stars." As if Teo could forget.

"Either we'll pull it off, or Reino del Sol will be swarmed by celestial monsters and turned to rubble, and all its people along with it," Niya confirmed, trying to sound confident but failing miserably.

Usually, Teo would be physically restraining Niya from chasing down the Obsidians and seeking her revenge. But now, she kept staring up at the night sky looking ... lost.

"No pressure or anything," Teo said, stumbling to keep up with Huemac and desperate to gauge what his mentor was thinking.

Teo couldn't get a read on him. Ever since the ceremony, Huemac had been in emergency response mode—focused, rushed, and wearing a somber expression that was hard to decipher. His curt intensity was making Teo's skin crawl. He couldn't tell if Huemac was mad at him, if he thought Teo had messed everything up.

If he thought Teo had made the wrong choice.

Aurelio was even quieter than usual, which, for him, was saying a lot. He hadn't said a word to Teo since they'd been ushered into their rooms to get changed. A deep frown had taken up residence on his handsome face, bunching his brow and sending the muscles in his jaw jumping as he tapped his fingers on one of his gold armbands.

When they reached the docks, Huemac pointed. "Take the trajinera," he said. Every other boat was long gone, leaving a lone white-and-gold Sol City trajinera. It bobbed silently in the dark water as the sounds of distant shouts and sirens echoed from beyond the protective rings of mountains surrounding Sol Temple.

The gods had jumped into action right away, retreating to their cities to protect their people. Their children and priests had followed. They all seemed to know exactly what they had to do, but Teo felt like a little kid lost at a street festival.

"It only took us, like, half a day to get to Les Restos for the fifth trial," Niya said before turning to Teo with large, hopeful eyes. "So, this should be easy, right?"

Teo realized with a jolt that she was waiting on him. This was his mission to lead.

"Longer than that," Aurelio finally said, his voice tight like each word took a concerted effort. "The fifth trial was on the outskirts of Los Restos—Venganza's temple is in the heart of it."

Huemac nodded. "He's right. It's a much longer journey, and trajineras aren't known for their speed, especially without a child of Agua at the helm," he said. "You'll need to use the smaller rivers and canals to get there. It will be difficult to navigate."

A thought popped into Teo's head. "We need to find Mala Suerte first."

Huemac, Niya, and Aurelio turned to look at him. Teo tried to swallow, but his throat was too dry.

"We need to know what the hell went down with Xio," he explained. "There's no way Mala Suerte raised Xio without knowing his true identity, but he ran off as soon as the Obsidians showed up. If we're going to stop the Obsidians and get everyone back, then Mala Suerte needs to cough up some answers."

"Coward probably ran home with his tail between his legs," Niya huffed angrily.

There was a distant *boom* as the earth shuddered below their feet.

"There's no time to waste," Huemac said, waving them forward. "Hurry."

It was time to say goodbye, but Teo wasn't ready. His heart rammed in his chest as he hesitated by the dock while Niya and Aurelio went on ahead.

When Huemac noticed, his eyes locked on Teo, a question wrinkling his brow.

"I'm sorry!" Teo blurted out, wringing his hands as his wings fluttered nervously. "For—for—" He gestured vaguely. Anything. Everything.

A surprised laugh jumped in Huemac's chest, catching Teo off guard. The old man sighed deeply, slumping his shoulders as he shook his head. "Teo, Son of Quetzal." Huemac's warm, calloused hands held Teo's upper arms. "I have never been more proud of you." He smiled, wrinkles creasing around his shiny, dark eyes.

Teo froze, shocked, as Huemac pulled him into a tight embrace. It took Teo a second to snap out of it before he squeezed Huemac back, his wings enveloping them both. The relief that Huemac wasn't mad at him—was *proud* of him, even—made his knees buckle.

"Now, finish what you've started," Huemac said, breaking the hug before clearing his throat. "I'll be here when you return."

Teo nodded fervently, blinking his burning eyes. "I won't let you down."

Huemac grinned. "I know." With that, the Quetzal high priest turned back to Sol Temple and disappeared into the shadows.

Once he'd gotten his emotions back under control, Teo wiped his nose and turned back to his friends waiting for him. "So, by boat it is?"

"I don't care how we get there, I just want to get there!" Niya announced. "Xio's little ass is going *down*."

"We have to be careful how we navigate," Aurelio pointed out. "The closer we are to the cities, the more monsters there will be."

"I can't wait to get my hands on that little twerp," Niya grumbled to herself, wringing the hilt of her sword with both hands.

"And the closer we get to Los Restos, too," Teo guessed with a groan. "I'm gonna *grab him*—"

"If we avoid the more densely populated areas, we'll have fewer obstacles and be able to move faster," Aurelio confirmed, but he didn't sound happy about it. Obviously Aurelio wasn't keen on the idea of avoiding people who needed help.

"And I'm gonna *shake him*—" Niya continued, pantomiming in the background.

"We can take the canals as close to Afortunada as we can, find Mala Suerte, and then head for Los Restos," Aurelio said, looking to Teo for confirmation.

"Until his stupid little head *pops off*—"

"What about sleep and, you know, rest?" Teo asked, feeling a bit desperate.

"I'm doing fine!" Niya said. "I've got another day in me, at least."

Teo balked. "*What?*"

"It's only been—" Aurelio glanced at his watch and then paused. He straightened and gave Teo a questioning glance. "Are you tired?"

"You're not?" Teo shot back.

"They train us to stay awake for long periods of time at the Academy," Aurelio explained slowly. "In an emergency, we can stay up for seventy-two hours at a time—"

"I can do eighty!" Niya interrupted with a proud tilt of her chin.

"Great," Teo said, trying to swallow his pride.

He was exhausted, but if Aurelio and Niya weren't too tired to keep going, then he wouldn't be, either. It was bad enough he'd gotten them here in the first place. He refused to slow them down because he was a Jade who didn't have as much stamina or training as a Gold.

Teo was determined to keep up.

"Anyone know how to steer a trajinera?" Teo asked as they stood on the dock, staring at the flat-bottomed boat.

Aurelio sighed. "I do," he said, cautiously stepping on board. Teo was pretty sure the last thing Aurelio wanted right now was to be surrounded by water, but he didn't complain.

Instead, he turned back to Teo and held out a hand. "Are you ready?" Aurelio asked, his steady, smoldering gaze on Teo.

Teo's heart clenched, the sudden gesture leaving him lightheaded. A grin tugged Teo's lips at the flush creeping into Aurelio's cheeks.

"Thanks!"

Aurelio started as Niya took his hand and pulled herself onto the boat.

"Come on, Teo!" She turned, grabbed him by the front of his shirt, and unceremoniously dragged him onto the boat. "The sooner we get going, the sooner you can get a nap!" Niya added affectionately.

"Thanks, Niya," Teo said sarcastically as he got his footing. He glanced in Aurelio's direction and rolled his eyes. Aurelio exhaled a soft laugh.

Maybe this mission wouldn't be entirely awful.

Aurelio took up steering from the back of the trajinera, expertly using the pole to move away from the dock and toward the enchanted waterfalls to make their exit from Sol Temple.

Teo and Niya sat at the long table, the empty chairs around them an eerie presence. Usually, boarding the trajineras meant fanfare and flamboyance, but now it was just the three of them.

All three took refuge under the curved roof as they slid through the first waterfall, plunging into darkness as they entered the cave. With a snap of Aurelio's flint-tipped glove, fire sparked to life in his hand, dousing them in a warm glow.

At the end of the cave, the waterfall split open. Without the shelter of the thundering water and echoing caves, screams and the sound of distant *somethings* rumbled through the air. Reino del Sol stretched out before them. Fires flickered in distant streets, reflecting in the dark water as plumes of smoke twisted into the inky sky.

"Whoa," Niya breathed, her eyes wide.

Even Aurelio's voice quaked, barely above a whisper. "It's chaos."

Teo swallowed the panic rising in his throat. "It's the end of the world."

The boat pitched, knocking Teo off-balance as Aurelio rushed to the bow.

"What happened?!" Teo asked, tripping over himself to catch up.

Aurelio stood rigid, his hands clenched tightly at his sides. Copper eyes bulging and lips falling open, Aurelio's expression caught somewhere between shock and horror.

"What is it?!" Teo pressed. He tugged on Aurelio's arm, but the other boy didn't even react.

"Oh no." Niya had appeared at Teo's side, her fingers pressed to her mouth. "It's San Fuego."

Teo followed their gazes. On the eastern shore, a large Gold city rose into the night sky. Fires licked up the sides of glass buildings, poured from broken windows, and flared in the streets below, spewing smoke into the air. A cacophony of shouts, crumbling stone, and monstrous shrieks echoed across the water.

San Fuego, Aurelio's home, was under attack.

CHAPTER 3
TEO

A chill ran down Teo's spine as he watched San Fuego burn. If this was what the Obsidians could do to one of the most powerful cities in Reino del Sol, then what fate awaited them in Los Restos?

Teo scrambled to the stern without hesitation, tripping over a couple chairs along the way. He grabbed the single long oar and haphazardly started pushing it back and forth, attempting to steer them toward San Fuego.

"How the heck does this even work?!" he grunted in frustration.

Teo looked up to find Niya and Aurelio still at the bow, staring at him.

"What are you doing?" Aurelio asked, his heavy brow knitted.

Teo exhaled a sharp laugh. He was scared to make the wrong decision, but this was an obvious choice. "It's not like we're just gonna stand here and watch, right?"

Niya's mouth curved into a smile. "Damn right!"

Aurelio blinked, the muscles in his jaw slack. A second later, his pale face lit with a flush. Something burned behind his flinty eyes that sent Teo's stomach tumbling. "Right," Aurelio agreed, a little breathless.

Niya looked between the two of them with an amused grin before turning back to San Fuego. "Let's go kick some monster ass!" she exclaimed as she grabbed an oar from storage and started rowing toward their destination.

Teo hurried into position beside her—brushing past Aurelio as he took over steering—and together they rowed with all their might. So much might, in fact, that Teo had to tell Niya to ease off before her powerful strokes sent them in circles.

The fires from San Fuego grew larger with each passing moment, as they kept pushing forward through the choppy current.

Flickering torchlight lined the hilly streets below towering buildings engulfed in flames.

The sounds of destruction and devastation reached out to them in the dark across the water, growing steadily louder. Sirens wailed and acrid smoke burned Teo's nose.

"I can't tell what's supposed to be on fire and what's not," Teo puffed, the muscles in his arms burning.

Lumbre's temple sat high in the middle of the city, shining gold and dotted with burning braziers. Small fires lined the massive steps that led to the altar at the top, where a cauldron blazed. Teo could just make out the Sun Stone hovering above it, barely more than a glimmer anymore.

He jerked his chin toward glass guard towers around the city. Each had a large, colored fire that blazed in the night with matching pigmented smoke. "What are those?"

"San Fuego uses smoke signals for emergencies," Niya told him.

"What do the colors mean?"

"Red means danger, blue means it's a safe place to seek shelter," Aurelio said. The distant lights sparked in his wide eyes as he frantically searched the streets of his home city. Teo thought he might dive into the water and swim for it before they could make it to shore.

The skyline was covered in streaks of red and very little blue. But it was pillars of white smoke that dominated the sky. Even as Teo watched, red and blue fires turned ivory. "What about white?" he asked.

Aurelio swallowed. "Help."

Teo rowed harder.

They hit their first problem before they even reached land. As they got closer, the true chaos of what was happening came into view. The docks were overrun with people trying to escape.

They passed by small dinghies, large fishing boats, and even a couple yachts loaded to the brim with refugees. There was nowhere for them to go except the lake surrounding Sol Temple and nothing to do but watch in horror as their city was destroyed by *things* that Teo, Niya, and Aurelio couldn't even see yet.

There were too many people and not enough boats. The people of San Fuego were dressed in fine linens and absolutely covered in jewelry. It was a sea of gold bands, copper hair ornaments, pearl chokers, and amber earplugs. The melodic tinkling of polished metals and precious stones was an eerie addition to the sound of voices screaming, praying, and pleading ringing out from the city burning behind them.

The frantic crescendo swelled, drowning Teo's own thoughts. This was a Gold city. These people were used to luxury and comfort—they'd never had to deal with an inconvenience, let alone monsters. Now the sun was gone and the gods were busy.

As vessels pulled away, some tried to leap on board out of desperation, and many fell into the dark water, weighed down by their adornments. When they got close enough, Niya and Teo abandoned their oars to help.

Niya grabbed them by their clothes and easily plucked them out of the water before dumping them onto the trajinera. Teo used his oar to reach others and pull them aboard as well. But once they neared the dock and people saw the empty space on their boat, things quickly went south.

Teo and Niya rushed to help, but before they could do anything, they were swarmed by a wave of bodies. It was a mass of panic—a blur of arms and legs pushing, pulling, clutching, and clawing. Teo cursed under his breath, trying not to lose sight of Niya as he was jostled and shoved.

"There's too many!" Aurelio called, gripping the oar as the trajinera pitched dangerously back and forth.

"WE'RE TRYING TO HELP YOU!" Niya shouted, but it was no use. There was no way to control the situation.

"Let them have it!" Aurelio yelled back.

Teo didn't need to be told twice. He quickly put on his backpack and fought his way through the crowd to Niya. "Swim for it!" he told her, shoving her pack into her arms.

Niya balked. "Seriously?"

"Yes!"

Niya threw her head back and released a frustrated growl, but she hefted on her pack and dove in.

Aurelio shot him a startled look from the helm.

"Come on!" Teo said, tugging Aurelio's arm before using a toppled chair to climb up onto the trajinera's curved roof.

Aurelio looked dubious, but complied. "What are we doing?" he asked, hoisting himself up after him.

"I need room!" Teo knew better than to drop the Son of Lumbre into a large body of water. And if they weren't going to swim for it, they'd have to fly.

Aurelio jumped out of the way, narrowly avoiding getting knocked over as Teo's wings shot out. With a powerful flap, Teo launched himself into the air. From up there, he could see how vast and sprawling the devastation was, but he had other problems to deal with first.

Teo banked, swooped back down, and grabbed Aurelio's outstretched arms. Teo's fingers clutched at Aurelio's golden armbands, and Aurelio's warm hands gripped him like a vise. Aurelio's legs dangled above the crowds as Teo flew them to shore. Gracefully, Aurelio dropped to his feet. Teo landed next to him, rolling and falling hard on his ass in a tangle of limbs and feathers.

"Ouch," Teo groaned. Aurelio was at his side in a blink, pulling him to his feet. "Thanks," he grumbled, shaking out his wings.

"You're the one I should be thanking," Aurelio replied with a self-conscious quirk of his lips.

"OH, FINE! I see how it is!" Niya came stomping down the dock, dripping wet. "Aurelio gets an airlift but I gotta swim?!" she demanded, wringing out her braids.

"We've got bigger problems, Niya!" Teo shot back.

Aurelio was silent beside them. The light of the fires illuminated his pained expression as he stared out over San Fuego.

Teo glanced back. Their trajinera, their way of getting to Los Restos the fastest, was long gone. "What do we do now?"

Aurelio squared his shoulders. "Whatever we can."

Niya clapped her hands and rubbed her palms together. "Welp, into the fray, boys!"

As they entered the city streets, they passed people fleeing to safety. San Fuego was unlike any other place Teo had seen. Unlike Quetzlan, where nature was slowly reclaiming the city, everything in San Fuego was shiny metal and reflective glass, illuminated by the burning fires.

The architecture was modern and sleek, linear and geometric—a true display of industry. Panels of stylized sunbursts and Lumbre's fire glyph hung above entrances, around windows and along roof edges.

The sidewalks were lined with gold and shimmery crushed quartz. Abandoned charcoal street artist stands were knocked over, their smudgy portraits littering the road. A steam-powered trolley had been knocked off its tracks and lay belly-up on a corner.

Posters of Aurelio and Auristela were still plastered everywhere and it seemed like every few blocks there was a golden statue of a Child of Lumbre Sunbearer. The news played on large screens built into the facades of skyscrapers. They flipped between shaky shots of the failed Sunbearer ceremony, the Obsidians returning, and the following destruction all over Reino del Sol. Verdad in her power suit and Chisme still dressed in gold were superimposed in the corner, reporting but impossible to hear. Marquees instructed people to shelter in place or find refuge.

Some people hid while others searched for loved ones they'd lost during the chaos. Teo noticed many had injuries that needed medical attention, but there was no one to offer it. Whatever was happening in the rest of the city was keeping emergency services busy.

"The heck is *that*?" Niya shouted, pointing.

Up in the hills, at the base of Lumbre Temple, huge swaths of fire were extinguished, like someone blowing out candles.

"My mom," Aurelio said through a tight jaw.

"Sol's sake," Teo said, staring in awe. He'd never seen Diosa Lumbre in action before, and, even from this distance, it was clear she was considered one of the most powerful dioses for a reason. Teo had only ever seen Aurelio's control when putting out fire, and that was just a room. Lumbre was extinguishing whole city blocks. She was too far away to see, but easy to track, especially when balls of fire flared, followed quickly by inhuman screeches echoing in the distance.

"We are *not* going over there!" Niya said.

Whether it was to avoid Lumbre or whatever she was fighting, Teo never found out because they rounded a corner and came face-to-face with a giant serpent slithering toward a group of people.

Teo didn't think.

"Move it!" Teo shoved a couple out of the way as the giant snake lunged for them, smashing teeth first into the side of a car. Its massive body wrapped around the sedan, coiling and crumpling it like a piece of paper. The creature thrashed wildly, ripping the door off its hinges and sending it flying across the street.

The monstrous snake turned on Teo, revealing several rows of venomous, dripping fangs. For a moment, Teo was too shocked to move. The snake's body was undulating with swirls of midnight blue and deep plum, dotted with glowing stars. Crimson feathers framed its head like a mane and its acid green eyes locked on Teo. It hissed—no, not hissed, it *screeched*, sending its feathers shaking.

Run, run, run! a voice screamed in Teo's head.

He ran down the street in the opposite direction from where people were taking refuge in a library. He sprinted over broken glass, ducking under a toppled telephone pole. Teo could feel the monstrous snake behind him, hear its body dragging over asphalt, and feel its hot breath tickling the back of his neck.

Terror shot up his spine, making him move faster than he thought himself capable. He jumped onto the hood of an abandoned car and scrambled to get onto the roof. When Teo turned, the snake was hot on his heels. It lurched forward and Teo launched himself into the air, his wings shooting him above the snake's head, but it wasn't enough. The snake coiled itself tightly into an *S* shape, its eyes locked on Teo, ready to strike.

Teo's stomach dropped, ice rushing through his veins. He tried to fly higher, wings frantically flapping.

But then the snake struck, fangs snapping, body stretching, stretching,

stretching. It unhinged its jaw, ready to swallow him whole. Teo could smell the sharp stench of its breath as its forked tongue lashed. A strangled shout ripped through Teo's throat. In vain, he tried to shield himself with his arms.

A wall of flame erupted between Teo and the beast.

The shock of it knocked Teo off-balance and he landed hard. He stumbled, trembling legs giving out under him.

The creature hissed, twisting toward the attacker.

When the flames receded, Aurelio stood before Teo, shielding him.

Aurelio held his hands out at his sides, flames dancing in his palms, licking its way up his golden armbands. Teo could feel the intense heat radiating from him, not just from the fire but from *him*. Glistening sweat covered Aurelio's exposed skin, a small line of it trickling down his lower back. Every muscle in Aurelio's body was taut and poised as he waited for the snake to make a move.

"Aurelio?"

"It's Aurelio!"

Cheers filled the air.

"Thank Sol!"

"He'll save us!"

Bystanders, who should've been running for their lives, stopped to stare. Dirty, tearstained cheeks lit with relieved smiles. The fear and panic was momentarily lifted, replaced by a glimmer of hope. Even though their city was being destroyed around them, Aurelio's presence—their Golden Boy, their Hero—brought them some comfort. He was the sun peeking over the horizon after an endless night.

Teo understood the sentiment all too well.

Aurelio tilted his head toward Teo, keeping his burning eyes on the monster. "Help them!"

The snake snapped its fangs, sending venom flying like spittle, but Aurelio refused to give it an opening. With a *whoosh*, the flames in his hands expanded. The monster reared back.

Teo didn't need to be told twice. He scrambled to his feet. "Get inside! Take cover!" he shouted, directing people to stores and apartment buildings where others were already crowded in lobbies and ducking behind grocery store shelves.

He ushered a family of three into the open doors of a clinic, but just as they reached the threshold, a chunk of the facade crumbled. Teo's wings instinctively shot out, shielding the three from the falling debris as he pushed them inside.

Teo cursed under his breath, panting. That was definitely going to leave some bruises, but it could've been way worse. Teo shook out the dust from his feathers and turned to the family. "Are you guys okay?"

All three members of the family looked back with blank stares. Teo realized their eyes were fixed not on his face, but his wings.

He didn't notice the murmurings at first, but then the voices got louder.

"Is that him?"

"Is that the Sunbearer?"

"Look—his wings!"

Teo spun around, hands lifted as if to say, *It's okay, I'm here to help!* But the voices only got louder, and now he had attracted a crowd.

"What are you doing here? Haven't you done enough?"

"This is your fault!"

"Where is Xio hiding?!"

Dread dropped into Teo's stomach. "I don't know, I—" he tried to explain, but the crowd was surging forward now. They looked *so* angry.

"Please," Teo rushed. "It's not safe here, you all need to head for the river—"

"Teo!" Niya materialized in the angry crowd. She pushed everyone out of the way and grabbed him. "Are you okay?!" she demanded. Her eyes were wild, frantically searching Teo's face, their hazel shade so bright he could've sworn they were glowing. Her bulging muscles strained under her sweaty, dirt-streaked skin. Her braids were a tangled mess, and a thin line of golden blood trailed down her temple from a cut.

Teo didn't like being reminded that even Golds—even Niya, Daughter of Tierra—weren't invincible. There were limitations, including monsters and obsidian sacrificial blades.

Teo nodded weakly, holding Niya's wrist tightly as she held him practically off his feet.

"Yeah," he managed to squeak out.

Niya's eyebrows tipped in relief, but it was short-lived. Her attention went to the angry bystanders. "HEY!" her voice boomed over the crowd. Some of the crowd parted to let her through. "Leave him alone, he's *helping*, you fools! Go find somewhere safe to shelter!"

"Of course Tierra's brat is on his side!" someone shouted.

"They're barely Golds themselves! She was probably in on this whole plan!"

"I saw her on TV during the trials, she was friends with the Obsidian boy, too!"

For once, Niya was rendered speechless, her face a mix of shock and hurt. She shot Teo a confused look, her eyes asking, *What do we do now?*

But Teo didn't know what to say. He was rooted to the spot, so Niya surged forward and grabbed him by the back of his shirt. She jumped back, pulling him along with her, and transformed one of her bangles into a large oblong shield.

He was risking his life to help these people, but they were so furious with him that Niya had to hold them off with a shield.

"Get back and head for the boats, you idiots!" she shouted. "You can yell at us later!"

That seemed to do the trick. As Niya forced through the mob, people began breaking off, angry expressions replaced with fear as they took in the severity of their surroundings.

"Keep it moving!" Niya barked. Then, over her shoulder, she shouted to Teo, "I got this! Go see if anyone else needs help. And be careful, for Sol's sake!"

As if on cue, three children darted across the street, screaming and pursued by a—

A rooster. A normal, everyday-looking rooster.

A laugh jumped in Teo's chest. Maybe he wasn't entirely useless after all.

"Hey, leave them alone!" Teo shouted, chasing after it.

The rooster skittered to a stop. It turned to face Teo, its beady black eyes looking up at him. Its star-spotted, black iridescent feathers ruffled. When it opened its glittery beak, it bellowed in the most horrifyingly demonic voice Teo had ever heard.

YOU DARE CHALLENGE ME, GODLING?

Teo reeled to a stop. "Holy *Sol*—"

TREMBLE BEFORE MY POWER.

The tiny terror stretched out its wings, eyes blazing violent red. It tilted its head back, spewing angry flames into the air. Teo whipped around, searching desperately for any confirmation that this was really happening.

I AM CHAOS, WRATH, VENGEANCE. AND I AM YOUR EXECUTIONER.

With an angry crow, a fireball ignited in the rooster's mouth and shot straight for Teo.

Strong hands grabbed him. Niya threw him to the ground and out of the way as Aurelio redirected the fireball to smash into an abandoned newspaper stand.

TEST YOURSELF AND BE ANNIHILATED BY MY—

The rooster suddenly choked and the fire went out, like it had been sucked from its lungs.

"Dammit, Teo!" Niya barked. "Don't try to make friends with evil roosters!"

"I *wasn't*, it was *monologuing*!"

Aurelio appeared in the middle of the street, palms held out.

The angry creature coughed up a tiny cloud of smoke before letting out a wretched squawk.

Teo threw up his wings to protect himself. Aurelio adjusted his stance. Fire gathered in the rooster's beak again and—

And Aurelio paused.

Teo didn't understand what he was doing, but before anything else could happen, a stranger's booted foot made contact with its side, punting the creature several streets over with an explosion of feathers. Its enraged crow faded into the distance.

The woman turned to face them with a perplexed and amused look. "What are you three doing here?" she asked, one hand propped on her hip.

Teo gaped up at her from the ground.

It was Brilla, Daughter of Lumbre, the previous Sunbearer and Aurelio's older sister. She wore a uniform similar to the crop top and fitted pants that Aurelio and Auristela wore, but instead of Academy black, it was mostly gold with accents of red. Brilla's hair was styled just like Aurelio's and Auristela's—an undercut with her hair knotted at the back of her head, and she and Aurelio shared the same wide nose.

Aurelio offered Teo his hand. "Are you okay?"

"Yes," Teo replied gruffly, letting Aurelio pull him to his feet. Aurelio's palm was calloused and hot. "Are *you* okay?" Teo shot back, looking pointedly at the other boy's red, angry hands.

Aurelio shook them out. "I'm fine" was his curt reply.

Teo wasn't convinced, but he decided not to push it. Aurelio, who was not fireproof, knew what his limits were, and Teo wasn't going to bring it up in front of Niya and his sister.

"Shouldn't you three be halfway to Los Restos by now?" Brilla said, looking between them.

"We *were*," Teo said.

"We got a bit sidetracked," Aurelio added tersely.

"Yeah, people *stole our boat!*" Niya lamented, throwing her hands in the air and gesturing wildly. "And Teo made me swim, and then we had to deal with a snake, and that evil *rooster*—!"

"We were trying to help," Teo explained.

Niya and Aurelio helped, anyway. Teo didn't feel like he was contributing much, and the people of San Fuego did *not* want him there. He wondered if that was how the rest of Reino del Sol felt, too. Teo did what he thought was right, but was it the right thing to do for everyone? Had he saved one person's life just to put the whole world in danger?

A flush creeped up the back of his neck, frustration rippling under his skin.

He was the Sunbearer, but what did that even matter now? He'd worked so hard to prove himself to everyone else, only to get crowned and immediately trigger the apocalypse. Tradition, sacrifice, and the will of the gods had kept them safe and protected for thousands of years, just for Teo to show up and ruin everything in a matter of minutes.

Brilla laughed. "Always to the rescue, huh, Relio?" She rubbed the top of Aurelio's head affectionately, causing locks to escape from his hair knot. Aurelio scowled.

Teo held back a grin.

"Why are there so many of these assholes?" he asked, changing the subject.

"And why are they so much scarier?" Niya demanded, annoyed as she looked around the torn-up street. "We fight monsters all the time but these ones are way stronger! And shiny!"

"These aren't regular monsters—they're Celestials," Aurelio said. "They're the original monsters the Obsidians created, the ones all the other monsters that now roam Los Restos originated from. They're more powerful and harder to beat, and they have that starry sheen."

Niya's shoulders slumped. "Oh yeah."

"Which is exactly why you should be avoiding them—not chasing after them!" Brilla chided, but not unkindly.

"We appreciate the help, but—" She turned and cut her arms through the air, snuffing out not only the newspaper stand but the fires down the rest of the block as well. Brilla threw them a grin over her shoulder. "I think we've got it under control."

Teo exhaled a laugh. He thought Niya and Aurelio were as strong as any Gold got, but that wasn't true. They were still just teenagers—they weren't even official Heroes yet, like Brilla.

"You three focus on getting the Sol Stone so we can put a stop to this once and for all," she went on, her eyes dancing in the firelight. "Us Heroes will save the cities, you save the world."

She was right. The three of them couldn't stop to rescue everyone in every city they came upon. They didn't have the skills or experience—especially Teo.

The tension in Teo's chest slackened. Instinct told him to dive in headfirst and help people in need, even at the cost of his own safety, but the trio wasn't doing this alone. It wasn't just him, Niya, and

Aurelio against the Obsidians. They had all the dioses and semidioses on their side, too.

If Brilla trusted him to do his part, then he needed to trust her and the other Heroes to do theirs.

"We should cut through West San Fuego and head south toward Afortunada," Aurelio said, ready to continue on their mission.

Brilla walked over to Aurelio, and pulled him against her side. Even at six foot four, the top of his head only reached Brilla's shoulder. "Go bring back our sister, okay?" she said, giving him a little squeeze.

Aurelio nodded, his jaw working. He seemed to hesitate. In a sudden move that startled everyone, especially Brilla, Aurelio threw his arms around her in a tight hug.

A surprised laugh jumped in her chest as she squeezed him back. "We'll take care of things here until you get back," she reassured him. As quickly as it had started, Aurelio let go and headed south without another word.

When Teo moved to follow, Brilla stopped him.

"Hey," she said, stepping into his path.

Teo stared up at her, feeling downright puny next to the powerful Daughter of Lumbre.

Brilla's expression softened just a touch. "I understand what you've been through, and I know you're scared," she said, in a tone that made the back of Teo's throat burn. "But you're also incredibly brave— braver than any other Sunbearer who came before you, myself included."

Teo blinked up at her. He didn't know what he expected her to say, but it wasn't that.

"You were under an enormous amount of pressure to complete the sacrifice, but you stood by your morals," Brilla went on.

"I also triggered the apocalypse," Teo pointed out weakly.

Brilla chuckled. "You did," she agreed. "But there's still time for us to stop it." She stood upright and put her fists on her hips.

"You're the Sunbearer, right?" Brilla asked.

"Yeah," he said, uncertain.

Her face lit up with a dazzling smile. "So, go bring the sun back!"

A surprised laugh eased the tension in Teo's chest. "Thanks for your help," he said as he took off after Aurelio.

"Bye, Brilla!" Niya waved cheerily at his side. "Don't tell your mom we said hi. I don't like her!"

Brilla chuckled and waved back before heading off down the smoke-filled street.

CHAPTER 4
XIO

Temples in Reino del Sol didn't usually have anything beneath them. Some, like Diosa Agua's, had been built over natural caves and cenotes, but the expanse of tunnels that ran under Venganza's temple had not been there naturally. Someone—maybe Caos, maybe human laborers—had dug out this space below the earth. As Xio walked, he felt the specter of a civilization long dead filling the void around him.

Like Mala Suerte, Venganza had once ruled over an entire city. Priests had tended the temple—had they used these tunnels? What was life like in Los Restos all those years ago?

In the periphery of Xio's mind, like an image he couldn't yet see clearly, there was the awareness that—had things gone differently—this would have been where Xio grew up.

Several torches along the worn stone walls ignited at once. Xio's eyes adjusted to the warm light. Cells lined the corridor on either side, each holding one of the Gold semidioses behind glass walls enchanted with force fields that rippled faintly like heat waves.

"Caos did some renovations to the tunnels," Venganza explained. "Per your guidance, of course," he added with a toothy grin.

The uneven floor was covered in dirt and rocks that crunched under Xio's shoes as he walked by the cells. "Whoa," Xio breathed, taking it all in.

Xio had used his binder full of trading cards, stats, and news articles to learn the Golds' weaknesses. Then, he spent hours making notes and sketching out designs for prison cells. Each was carefully planned to neutralize a semidiose's powers. It seemed to be working.

Xochi was in the first cell on the left. Even though they were underground, the three non-glass walls, ceiling, and floor were encased in gray cement, making it impossible for Xochi to grow anything. In addition, there was no sun to grant her energy, so it was just a matter of time before she'd be too weak to do anything. By the way she searched her cell, tears cutting lines down her fierce expression, it was clear Xochi knew it, too.

Next to Xochi was Marino. The muscular boy stood in the middle of a room made of metal. The walls were lined with heating elements that worked as giant radiators. Metal fans hummed on the ceiling, circulating the air and removing moisture. Xio's plan wasn't to roast Marino, but to slowly dehydrate him into a weakened state.

"You can't just keep us in here!" said Marino, still in disbelief as he wiped away the sweat already beading on his forehead.

Xio rolled his eyes and ignored him. They absolutely could, and would. While he was still sweating, Marino was dangerous. With enough of it, he could use his own sweat as a weapon, but once he ran out, it would be easy to keep him contained. Even then, Xio made sure that Caos knew to make the metal walls several inches thick so it would take time and effort to use water pressure to cut through it.

On the other side of Marino was Ocelo. Their cell was the smallest, especially while Ocelo was hulked out like they were now. It was barely wide enough for Ocelo to lie down, which meant there wasn't enough room for them to get the sort of momentum they'd need to slam through the walls.

Ocelo threw themself against the glass over and over again, but the force field did nothing but ripple where they hit. They shouted in anger, muscles bulging and fangs extending, then switched tactics and started clawing the walls, leaving huge gashes in the stone.

"Hmm."

Xio jumped, Caos appearing at his side. "That's annoying," they said in their strange voice. With a snap of his fingers, the walls repaired themselves, leaving no sign of damage.

Ocelo roared viciously.

Warm, delicious satisfaction settled into Xio's stomach.

On the other side of the corridor, Atzi's cell was closest to the entryway. She stood in four inches of water and was surrounded by copper poles sticking out of the floor.

When Xio came into view, Atzi immediately threw a bolt at him. It bounced off the barrier with a *crack*, then struck the lightning rods and scattered over the water's surface in all directions.

Xio'd had the most trouble figuring out how to contain Atzi and spent far too long researching conductors, but he was satisfied with his work. The rods attracted the lightning and dispersed it harmlessly underground, making it impossible for Atzi to aim. As a young semidiosa, only thirteen years old, Atzi still had years before she would be able to operate at her full potential. Until then, energy depletion would always wear her out quickly, especially if she tried any big moves.

In the cell next to Atzi, Dezi stood in an empty room. The walls were plain and gray without seams or cracks. Unlike the other cells, the force field door undulated with navy blue smoke, nearly obscuring the view inside. Dezi turned in slow circles, his brow puckered as he looked around.

Directly across from him, Marino jumped in place and waved his arms, trying to get Dezi's attention, but his eyes slid right by him.

"He can't see you," Xio said.

Marino's attention swung to him. "What?"

"He can't see you," Xio repeated. When Marino didn't get it, he explained. "On the inside, it just looks like an empty room. You can see him . . ." Xio glanced back.

Dezi approached the door and cupped his hands around his eyes, trying to squint through the barrier.

Xio turned to Marino. "But he can't see you."

Finally, it sank in.

Marino's jaw clenched, his sweaty face twisting in anger.

The worst thing to do to a Son of Amor was to lock him in a room alone where he didn't know where his friends were or what was happening. And the second worst thing to do was to make the boy who loved him watch.

Chupacabra scampered to Dezi's cell. "Woo-hoo!" she sang, waving her hands at Dezi, who remained oblivious. Chupacabra snickered and pressed her face to the glass, her jaw hanging open to reveal black gums, sharp teeth, and a crimson, dripping tongue.

She tapped the wall with a clawed finger, and the blue smoke of the enchanted glass disappeared, making the wall completely transparent.

Dezi leapt back so fast he tripped over himself and fell to the ground. Chupacabra cackled as Dezi scrambled away from her. His chest rose and fell in sharp breaths as he stared up at her, frightened.

Dezi's eyes slipped past her, searching for his friends.

Chupacabra began tapping repeatedly on the glass. "There's your friends!" she chanted before tapping it again, blocking Dezi's view. "Oops, now they're gone! There they are again! Now you see them! Now you don't!"

"Leave him alone!" Marino shouted.

Xio felt a stab of something deep in his chest. Was it . . . guilt? No. Of course not. This was what the Golds deserved. They had taken *everything* from him, locked his real father away, and left Xio to die. And the Jades, Mala Suerte—they were just as bad. Complacent in the violence and tyranny of the higher class.

Xio remembered the looks on everyone's faces when his black blood had spilled onto the stone that morning. Their screams echoed in his ears. *Good.*

Bad luck, that was what they had always called him. Well, he was about to show them just how bad he could be.

Xio was pulled out of his thoughts by a sudden shout.

"You freaky little demon spawn!"

Auristela was awake.

Farther down on the right, she was trapped in an oversized icebox. The walls were covered in frost and Auristela was in the center, encased in a sphere of ice up to her neck.

"Is this your sick, fanfic torture dungeon?" she snarled. Her words came out in cloudy wisps as steam poured from her skin. Droplets of water trickled down the sides of the ice prison, pooling on the floor. "How long did you fantasize about locking us in here during the trials, creep?"

Xio felt a wave of fury wash over him—*stupid Auristela, always has something nasty to say, can never just admit defeat*—but his father was watching, and Venganza was always so levelheaded in the face of adversity.

So, channeling some of that energy, Xio fixed his mouth into his best approximation of a sneer. "Aw, Auristela, it's cute how even on that side of the cage, you somehow think you're better than us."

Auristela seethed. "That's because we *are* better than you, Xio."

Xio shrugged. "Yet, I'm not the one trapped in ice."

Chupacabra howled with laughter at that. "*Oh!* Careful, everyone, Junior's got a mean bite."

Xio flushed. He couldn't tell if it was out of embarrassment or pride. Maybe some weird mix of both? He'd made someone as terrifying and ruthless as Chupacabra laugh—that was probably a good sign. They were on the same team, after all.

"How did you get these cells ready so fast?" Xio asked.

"Creation comes from chaos," Diose Caos said, their words quaking and tumbling in multiple voices at once. "In order to create discord, I must understand order."

Xio squinted. That didn't answer his question, but okay.

"It's one of their many talents," Venganza provided.

"I have some ideas for improvements," Xio told his father. "We should—"

"Your passion is appreciated," Venganza said, cutting him off with a smile. "But unnecessary. Caos has a certain . . . *talent* for this kind of work. These children won't be a problem."

Xio wasn't sure. He'd seen all six in action firsthand, and they weren't the top students at the Academy for no reason. But maybe Venganza was right. They *were* only half gods. There was no way they stood a chance against three Obsidian dioses.

"They'll be fine on their own until you come down to check them—"

"Me?" Xio balked. "Why do I have to?" He was the Son of Venganza, why did he have to babysit a bunch of prisoners?

"I could do it!" Chupacabra offered, horrible eyes wide and mouth salivating.

Xio paused. There were thousands of terrible fates he'd wish upon the Golds, but even he wouldn't release Chupacabra on them.

"I'll do it," he grumbled, much to the diosa's disappointment.

"Shall we, then?" Venganza said, gesturing to the doorway.

The captive semidioses glared as the Obsidians passed by.

All but Atzi, whose eyes were trained unblinking on Xio.

For a moment, their stares locked. Xio immediately diverted his gaze, then cursed himself for the cowardice. Who was Atzi to judge him? Just another Gold loser, a child of the very beings who had subjugated and imprisoned his Obsidian-blooded ancestors. What right did she have to make Xio feel ashamed?

None. None at all.

✳

It was a long journey to the altar atop Venganza Temple, but Xio would take the burning in his calves over Caos's nauseating tele-portation any day. Venganza led the way, Chupacabra at his side while Caos floated along behind and Xio took up the rear.

Xio already knew the state of Venganza's altar from when he first came to Los Restos. The ancient gray stone was polished smooth from centuries of rain. The structure itself was unlike any other he'd seen in Reino del Sol. From the outside, the altar looked like a crown surrounded by flying buttresses. Sharp spikes of obsidian topped its spires, like spears aimed at the sky.

Unlike the Gold and Jade observatories, there was no opening to welcome in the sun. The structure was entirely closed off to the outside other than the main entrance and sections of the building that had been destroyed during the war with the dioses. Towering above the jungle below, it stood out like a jagged mountain among the deep green canopies.

The inside of the altar was in worse shape. The high ceiling stretched so far that Xio couldn't even see where it ended in the darkness. Fingers of roots climbed in through large sections of wall and ceiling that had collapsed. Between puddles of standing water, chunks of obsidian and the bones of small creatures were scattered among debris blown in from outside. It was hard for Xio to imagine what it had looked like before.

What he *did* like was the abundance of natural obsidian protruding from the craggy walls and ribbony veins in the floor. It reminded Xio of Tierra's temple, minus the dizzying colors. A crumbled throne and Venganza's broken glyph sat in the middle of the room on the dais where Xio had originally made contact with his father. He still wore the piece of obsidian he'd swapped out for the jet fist on his azabache bracelet.

Venganza looked over the crumpled remains of his altar, face pinched with disgust or disappointment—Xio still found him hard to read.

From all the impassioned speeches Venganza had given him, Xio was surprised the dios was so relaxed now. Ever since he'd gotten his hands on the Sol Stone, an eerie peace had settled over the vengeful dios's face. Xio couldn't help feeling like it was the calm before a storm.

Especially since that was how his own anger acted, too. Xio's temper was just another mystery from his upbringing that snapped into perfect clarity the moment he learned the truth about his parentage. Xio often felt like his anger was teetering on the edge, just one perilous moment away from consuming him entirely. He had to actively push it down into himself, where it festered and churned restlessly, ready to burst out of his skin.

Venganza kicked the knocked-over candles surrounded by wax drippings. The squeak of an agitated bat sounded from somewhere above.

The dios clicked his tongue in disapproval. "Well, first things first." He reached out with his knobbly, crooked fingers and the walls groaned around them. Xio had to steady himself as the temple floor trembled under his feet.

Two large slabs of obsidian pulled themselves free from the walls and Venganza guided them to the floor. Unblinking, he curled his fingers. Chunks broke off the first slab as if by an invisible sculptor. Large statues of the three Obsidian dioses erected themselves around the room. Venganza's massive square glyph, adorned with his goat head, was reborn in the center of the room.

Xio stared in disbelief, an exciting trill racing up his spine. Could *he* do that?

Behind the glyph, a throne appeared from the second chunk of obsidian, ornamentally carved with three-dimensional figures. Humans kneeled around the base, cupped hands held up. Xio wasn't sure if they were giving offerings, or begging for mercy. Above them, set into the base and arms of the chair, the celestial monsters twisted through stars and squared-off clouds. Venganza's head was on the high back of the chair, surrounded by rays as it eclipsed the sun behind him.

Chupacabra picked up an old woven reed mat and placed it on the seat of the throne. "Practically good as new!"

"Nearly," Venganza declared, gliding up the stairs of the dais to take his seat. Chupacabra giggled disturbingly, perching herself on Venganza's left side like a dutiful hound. "Would you mind?" he asked Caos, who was lingering at the center of the throne room.

Caos's hands moved, and the temple shuddered again, repairing itself as stones lifted into the air and fit back into the walls. It was like watching the room get destroyed in reverse. Glass flew through the air and reassembled itself into arched windows. Vines and branches retreated. Decorative arches and intricate moldings moved back into place. Even the candles stood upright and lit themselves, surrounding Venganza's throne and glyph.

Xio hurried up the steps, two at a time. "Da—F-Father," he began, wringing his hands anxiously.

Venganza turned to him, fingernails drumming on his armrest. "Yes?"

"What exactly—" Xio faltered, worried the question might come out wrong. "Er, what I mean is, you're the God of Vengeance."

Venganza paused before answering. "Astute, my son."

Chupacabra snickered, but Xio ignored her. And the burning in his cheeks.

"But you can control obsidian?"

"Ah." Venganza sat up a little straighter, a pleased look curling his features. "You are curious about your godly inheritance, yes?"

"It's just that, with Mala Suerte, I always thought..." Xio trailed off again. He hated talking about Suerte in front of the Obsidians. He felt ashamed. "He said my powers caused *bad luck*. But that wasn't the truth."

Venganza nodded. "There is much the dioses would have kept from you about the nature of obsidian blood and the powers it grants our offspring. I think it would be fit for me to offer you some training in these matters. Do you agree, Chupacabra?"

Chupacabra, who had been picking her nails, snapped up. "Hm? Oh, sure! We could use some well-trained soldiers in our new army. *My* children were once considered to rival those of Guerrero in combat," she said proudly.

Xio tried to imagine what the half-mortal children of Chupacabra might look like—would they transform, like Ocelo? Would they also have freaky wolf heads?

Then again, it wasn't like Xio had a goat head or horns.

Oh gods, was he going to grow horns?

To his father he said, "I would be honored."

Venganza's approving look made warmth radiate through Xio's chills.

"I think you've earned a title befitting a Son of Venganza," he announced, gesturing for Xio to step closer.

Pieces of discarded obsidian on the floor flew to Venganza's open hand. They fused together into a sharp tangle, forming a crown.

Xio held his breath as Venganza placed the crown on his head. He wanted to touch it, but the razor edges would slice right through his fingers if he wasn't careful. The crown was heavy, but he refused to show any discomfort. Instead, he stood taller, hoping to exude confidence and strength.

"You shall be known as Xio, Son of Venganza, the Nightbearer," Venganza declared, motioning for Xio to step back. "And with your training, you shall become a valuable asset to our family and our cause."

Xio's heart swelled with pride. A sense of purpose ignited inside him. This was his destiny, his path. For once in his life, he felt like he *belonged* somewhere.

"Thank you, Father," Xio said, bowing his head respectfully. His voice was steady and resolute. "I accept my new role."

Chupacabra cackled. "Well, aren't you just adorable?"

"Good," Venganza replied, a wicked grin spreading across his face. "Together, we shall bring vengeance upon the gods."

A fierce resolve surged through Xio. He had spent his life hiding from the dioses, concealing his true nature, fear twisting his every decision. But he was an Obsidian, and he would no longer cower in the shadows.

The dioses had spilled the blood of their kin, and Xio would make them pay.

"Teach me," Xio urged, the fire inside him now blazing. "Teach me how to make them tremble."

"Patience, my child," Venganza said, his voice a low, approving rumble. "In time, you will learn to harness your power and exact the vengeance we so rightly deserve."

CHAPTER 5
TEO

The burning fires of San Fuego faded behind them, nothing more than a faint orange smudge in the distance. Neighborhoods gave way to rolling, rocky hills as Teo, Niya, and Aurelio headed south. The ground sloped toward the Casa de Corazón desert. Spiky agave, craggy boulders, and sharp rocks dotted the desolate landscape like the feathers of a spotted owl. The ground was loose and gravelly, shifting under Teo's shoes in a way that made him worried about rolling an ankle.

To Teo, it was like being on a totally different planet.

Unlike the unrelenting humidity of Quetzlan, the dryness here seemed to suck the moisture from his lips, leaving them chapped and cracking. The heat refused to cool, even with the sun gone. Quetzlan was a city slowly being consumed by the jungle. There, Teo's clothes always felt damp with his own sweat, but in this strange place, he felt like his skin was covered in a layer of salt.

Teo was used to city lights and the constant hum of traffic, to being surrounded by big buildings and even bigger trees. But outside the city limits of San Fuego, nothingness stretched around them, quiet as the dead and darker than Teo thought possible. Stars and the glow of their suits lit the trio's way as they passed abandoned coal mines, their entrances like crooked mouths plunging into the dark depths of the earth.

It was too dark, too quiet, too creepy.

"Do any dangerous animals live out here?" Teo wondered, searching the small circle around him illuminated by their suits.

"Nothing too scary!" Niya said behind him before casually listing off, "Just snakes, scorpions, venomous Gila monsters, bobcats—"

Every muscle in Teo's body tensed. "*Bobcats?*" he squeaked.

"Don't worry, they're only twenty-five to thirty pounds," Aurelio offered.

If that was supposed to comfort Teo, it didn't. "At least there's no jaguars," he muttered. He considered forcing himself to pick up his pace to get out of this creepy area, but it wasn't like safety lay ahead of them—only more darkness.

"Can we stop somewhere soon?" Teo asked. His shoulders, wings, and legs *seared* with exhaustion.

Aurelio glanced back. His copper eyes gave Teo a once-over and then he frowned. "Are you okay?"

No, was what he wanted to say, but Teo's ego was currently too fragile for that. "Could use some rest and food," he went with, trying to not sound out of breath.

Aurelio checked his Academy watch.

"Aren't you guys tired?" Teo asked, looking at Niya.

She just smiled and shrugged. "I'm fine!"

Teo's shoulders slumped in disbelief. "Seriously?"

"I'll find a place for us to stop for the night," Aurelio announced, leading the way.

After passing a herd of curious donkeys, Aurelio directed them to an abandoned stone cabin slumped against the side of a hill. The wood floor was rotten and covered in debris, but there was a sturdy table and a fireplace that Aurelio cleared out and lit a fresh fire in. There was a small shrine set up on the mantel. A nicho had been painted white and yellow. Sunbursts and stars radiated from a golden silhouette of Sol, their hands pressed to the center of their chest.

Teo undid the clasps of his backpack. As soon as it dropped to the ground, his wings immediately shook themselves out. It took effort to lug his bag up onto the table. Niya easily tossed hers next to it with only two fingers looped around a strap.

"You're acting like that thing weighs nothing," Teo grumbled, his voice echoing in the empty building. The air was cool and had the faint smell of wet stone.

"Well, I'm stronger than you," Niya said. Not unkindly, just matter-of-fact. "And like, one-third of this thing is just Takis, so it's pretty light to begin with," she added, giving the stuffed bag a slap.

"Do you have enough emergency supplies?"

"Uh, *yeah*, Teo," she said, annoyed. "What do you think the Takis are for?"

Teo patted his own pack. "I've got enough nutrition bars for a couple days. I hope."

"I've got plenty of camping supplies so we can cook our own food," Aurelio added, always the practical one. "That, along with our sleeping bags and Agua's Decanter of Endless Water, means we should be prepared for the worst."

At least one of them had their shit together. Teo had never even been on a hike until he was thrust into the Sunbearer Trials. While Aurelio pulled out a small pot filled with tiny bags of ingredients with Niya hovering over his shoulder, talking a mile a minute about nothing in particular, Teo decided to see what exactly Huemac had added to his own bag.

There were several sets of clothes, a flashlight, and first aid supplies suitable for a semidiose. Huemac had even thought to pack a tooth-brush, thank Sol, so Teo didn't have to worry about his breath smelling rank the whole journey. When he pulled out his sleeping bag, something rolled out onto his lap.

Teo sucked in a breath. It was Tuki, his stuffed toucan. Huemac had given it to him when he was just a baby. The plush was well-loved. Its ratty white-and-orange fur was stained and had been rubbed threadbare in places Teo had worried at as a child. Tuki had two different-shaped beads for eyes since his mom had had to replace one after Teo accidentally swallowed it in first grade. One of the bird's little yellow feet was missing and his right wing was overstuffed from all the times Huemac had had to repair it.

He'd hidden it in the depths of his backpack before he left to attend the Sunbearer Trials. Huemac must've found it and packed it with his things.

Tears prickled behind Teo's eyes as he ran his thumb over Tuki's beak, wishing more than anything that he was back in Quetzal Temple with Huemac and his mom.

"What is he doing?"

Teo jumped. He stuffed Tuki back into his sleeping bag before spinning around.

Niya was at the window, hands cupped around her eyes as she squinted through the dingy, cracked glass.

"Who?" Teo asked, his heartbeat suddenly in his throat.

Niya scoffed. "Aurelio, obviously!"

Teo exhaled. "Right."

"I'm going to investigate!" she announced, her bare feet stomping to the door.

Teo followed. There was no way he was going to be alone in an abandoned shack-place-thing in the middle of nowhere without his very strong and brave friends.

Outside, Aurelio stood staring up at something looming just outside of the light.

"What *is* that?" Teo asked as they drew closer.

"It's a cactus!" Niya said, like she was scolding him. "Haven't you seen one before?"

"Of course I have!" Teo snapped back. "But not that big!"

It was more than fifty feet tall, and Teo had to crane his neck back to get a full look at it. The cactus was wider than Aurelio with several thick, reaching arms. Plump white flowers grew at the ends in clumps, like they were holding bouquets. The light from the shack sent its shadow stretching out into the darkness. Spines covered its green flesh in thick vertical rows. They reminded Teo of the barbed-wire fences surrounding Quetzlan High School, which he'd ripped his clothes on more than once.

"It's a saguaro cactus," Aurelio explained. "They're the biggest in Reino del Sol, and the flowers only bloom at sunset and stay open for less than a day." He tilted his head at a curious angle. "I guess the lack of sun has confused them."

"They smell like melon," Teo said, the sweet aroma filling his nose as he stepped closer.

"What's so interesting about a big-ass cactus?" Niya asked, sizing it up.

Aurelio pointed up. "Fruit."

Sure enough, a cluster of ruby red fruit about the size of an avocado sat at the top of the cactus's thickest stem.

"Thank Diosa Guanabana," Teo said, sending gratitude to the Jade goddess of fruit.

Niya gasped. "Dessert!" she cheered, her hazel eyes dancing. "Fly up there and grab some, Teo!" Niya said with an encouraging nudge.

"I'm not doing that," Teo said flatly. "I'm not that coordinated yet," he admitted. "One wrong move and my ass would be impaled on those spines and *you* guys would have to get me out of it."

Aurelio searched the ground. "If I can find a long stick—"

Before he could finish his sentence, Niya scooped up a big rock.

"I've got this!" she announced before chucking the stone. It flew up and knocked into the side of the cactus with a dull *thud*.

Hey! A sharp voice rang out in a melodic *whit-wheet!*

A bird with a compact body, long tail feathers, and short wings appeared from the clump of fruit.

I've got a nest up here! she shouted down at them, hopping angrily. *This is my fruit! If you want to take it you'll have to come up here and fight me for it!*

"Oh shit," Niya murmured to herself with a small chuckle before adding louder, "My bad, birdie!"

Teo winced and stepped forward to translate. "Sorry, we didn't see you up there!" he called out to the curve-billed thrasher. They were known for being very territorial and prone to aggression, so Teo tried to be as respectful as possible. "We weren't trying to mess with your nest or steal your fruit, we just—"

The bird hopped onto one of the saguaro fruits and peered down at Teo with a golden-yellow eye.

Who are you?

"What's it saying?" Niya asked in a stage whisper while Aurelio's gaze flicked back and forth between Teo and the bird.

Teo ignored Niya for now. "I'm Teo—" he started before the curve-billed thrasher gasped.

Son of Quetzal! she finished for him. *What on earth are you doing here?! Does Diosa Quetzal know where you are? This is no place for a jungle fledgling!*

Teo exhaled a laugh. "It's a long story, but we're on a very important mission and just passing through."

Oh dear, oh dear, she tittered, clicking her bill. *Out here all on your own!*

"We were hoping to get some fruit," Teo went on, "but we can find a different cactus—"

That won't be necessary! the bird told him, shaking out her feathers. *I thought you were a snake or something trying to get to my eggs! I'd be honored to share my cactus with the Son of Quetzal,* she sang.

Without further prompting, she swooped to one of the lower branches and used her sickle-shaped bill to saw through the stems of the fruit. Aurelio managed to catch three out of the air with one hand while Niya chased down the ones he'd missed.

You're the only one who's ever been polite enough to ask! the bird explained to Teo as she snipped off more ripened fruit. *If it's not snakes trying to steal my eggs, it's tortoises, bats, and javelinas coming through and eating up all my fruit!*

Teo bent down and scooped up the one that had landed by his feet. The ground was littered with the remains of squished and rotten cactus fruit.

"Thank you for sharing with us," he said, relieved.

The curve-billed thrasher trilled a happy *whit-wheet!*

Anything for a Son of Quetzal!

She vowed to keep a lookout and to alert Teo if she saw anything dangerous come through before shooing him and his "featherless friends" back inside.

"Mmm, these smell *so good,*" Niya said, holding the fruit up to her nose as Aurelio set up his makeshift kitchen.

"Can I help?" Teo asked, taking a seat next to him.

Aurelio was already deep in thought and cast Teo a wary glance. "No, thank you," he said.

Teo chuckled at his bluntness. "Fine, then I'll just watch."

It was the best source of entertainment Teo'd had in days.

Aurelio used one of the sharp sepals from the cactus fruit to slice it open. He cut out a few chunks for Niya and Teo to try. Teo thought the consistency was similar to figs, but it was juicier and had a hint of strawberry that deliciously quenched his thirst.

The pulp Aurelio scraped out of the cactus fruit was an even darker shade of ruby and filled with large seeds that reminded Teo of a watermelon's. Aurelio's fingers became stained red as he separated out the seeds from the pulpy flesh. After some badgering and with a lot of instruction, he eventually let Teo help him with this stage.

Next, Aurelio tossed the fruit into a small pot with some sugar over the fire. While that cooked down, he rinsed the seeds and laid them on a flat slab of rock to roast them. When they were properly dried out, Niya ground them into a powder with a chunky rock.

Teo was mesmerized as Aurelio combined the ground cactus seeds and flower with water, oil, and salt into a wet paste. With his large hands and long, deft fingers, Aurelio kneaded it into a hunk of dough. In what felt like no time at all, Teo, Niya, and Aurelio sat down to eat.

The protein bars lay forgotten as the trio tore off pieces of cactus-seed bread and dunked it into the still-warm pot of dark red, syrupy compote. The bread was dark and pretty tough, but it had a pleasant nutlike flavor and the fruit spread was the best thing Teo had tasted in days.

"It's so *good*," Niya moaned, shoving another piece into her already full mouth.

"It's seriously incredible," Teo agreed before turning to Aurelio. "How did you learn to make this? TúTube?" he guessed teasingly.

"Dezi," Aurelio said, helping himself to another piece. "We had a training camp in the desert, and at the end of it, Diosa Amor invited us to her temple for dinner. She, Dezi, and his mortal mom cooked everything by hand. Cactus-fruit jam and seed bread is a staple in Casa de Corazón."

"I almost forgot about that!" Niya said, smacking the table with her palm. "Oh, Teo, it was so much fun! The food was so good, and Diosa Amor is so *nice*! We stayed up super late just talking and eating and having a great time!"

A tired smile curled at the corner of Aurelio's mouth as he stared down at their spread. "Dezi showed me how to make it and I wrote it down in my phone to remember."

"That sounds really nice," Teo said, also smiling. He liked the mental image of Niya, Aurelio, and all the others—Auristela, Ocelo, Marino, Dezi, Xochi, and Atzi—sitting around with Diosa Amor, eating and talking. It seemed peaceful, which seemed like something the Golds didn't get a lot of between their grueling schedules at the Academy and, you know, saving the people of Reino del Sol.

"Oh my gods, *yes*! You would've loved it, Teo!" Niya shouted. "They have quarries full of this special pink sandstone that they turn into adobe and make their buildings with! So everything in the city is a rosy pink color!"

"I'm not sure I could handle that much heat," Teo confessed. "I haven't spent much time in the desert, if that wasn't obvious."

"The adobe keeps the houses surprisingly cool," Aurelio explained. "The walls are thick and absorb heat during the day, and release it during the night when it's cooler. Pretty much everything except for Diosa Amor's temple is on one level. The roofs are flat and have rounded edges, and there's reservoirs for collecting rainwater." He looked impressed when he said, "It's basic technology, but functional. Pretty brilliant in its simplicity."

Teo grinned. He loved hearing Aurelio talk about something he found interesting. He always used so many words.

"And everyone wears pretty clothes, too!" Niya said wistfully, gesturing with her hands. "It's all *flowy* and *pretty*—"

"The layers help protect your skin from the sun."

"And so *soft*—"

"Linen and cotton, so everything's breathable and keeps you cool."

"It sounds great," Teo agreed. His dream to see all of Reino del Sol bubbled up. There was still so much of the world he hadn't seen yet, and a pink city sounded pretty magical—even if it was in the middle of the desert.

She slammed her fists on the table. "We should go!"

Teo wasn't exactly ready to be making any plan for when—*if*—they managed to stop the world from ending, but he didn't want to burst Niya's bubble. "Sure," he said, "maybe after we've stopped the Obsidians—"

Niya cut him off. "No, I mean *now*!"

Aurelio frowned at her. "*Right* now?"

She let out a frustrated noise. "Not *right* now, but next!"

Teo and Aurelio exchanged doubtful looks. What was she thinking?

"What do you mean?" Teo prodded.

"Casa de Corazón is a big place!" Niya began. "They don't have big, tall buildings, so everything is super spread out! We could go help Diosa Amor, kick some Celestial butts, and then go on to Laberinto!"

Teo balked. "*Laberinto*? But that's all the way on the east coast—"

Niya kept going excitedly like she hadn't even heard him. "Casa de Corazón, Laberinto, Lago Relámpago," she listed off on her fingers. "If we follow the main roads, we can hit all the major cities and smaller towns along the way to Afortunada! We can help rescue people and fight the monsters!"

"That's completely out of the way," Aurelio said, stepping in with a firm tone. "Afortunada is southwest of where we are now, just across the Río Serpiente. Casa de Corazón and Laberinto are all east. The journey alone would take days, plus all the time we'd waste in each city."

"Helping people is *not* a waste of time," Niya shot back angrily.

"We should stay out of big cities to avoid running into Celestials," Aurelio said, fidgeting with his armbands.

Niya balked. "Sol only knows how many monsters are out there attacking our cities and our people! We're supposed to be the Heroes of Reino del Sol," she reminded him. "We should be fighting the Celestials, not avoiding them!"

"If we have to stop and fight a monster on every block, we'll never make it in time," Aurelio said tersely.

They both turned to Teo. His stomach dropped.

Teo had never been the source of brawn in this operation. As a Jade, he wasn't as strong or as fast or as durable as the Gold semidioses— but he *could* bring the brains. A lifetime of pranking and troublemaking had turned him into a clever planner.

At least, that was what he used to believe.

When he didn't respond right away, Aurelio stepped in. "We should go whichever way is the fastest and most efficient," he said, drawing a line from just below San Fuego to Afortunada. "If we keep following this road, we'll cross the Río Serpiente and avoid Lago Relámpago, and Afortunada should be waiting just on the other side."

"But you saw what your home city was like!" Niya argued.

Aurelio's posture tensed.

"It was crawling with monsters and those humans couldn't defend themselves!" Niya said. "The people need our help!"

Both Niya and Aurelio turned to Teo again, waiting for him to say something.

Teo's mouth went dry. He was uncertain about his ability to make any plans with his most recent, and catastrophic, failure being so fresh.

"You're both right," Teo said after a moment. "But we can't stop the Obsidians without the Sol Stone. That should be our main focus." When Niya's mouth popped open to argue, he rushed to add, "We can't help *everyone*, but we can help whoever needs it along the way. We'll leave the big jobs to the dioses and the professional Heroes, like Brilla and your brothers."

Aurelio nodded in agreement, but Teo could see Niya warring with herself as she sat there scowling.

"Right?" Teo prompted her.

"Yeah, I *guess*," she finally conceded, crossing her arms.

Aurelio gave her a look. "Do you really want to travel all the way across the desert to get to Casa de Corazón?"

"*Yes*," Niya shot back tersely.

One of Aurelio's dark eyebrows arched. "In the dark?"

Niya paused, unblinking.

"Without any daylight?" Aurelio added.

Teo watched a shudder roll down Niya's spine. "Good point." She sniffed. "I've changed my mind."

Aurelio seemed satisfied.

Confused by the sudden shift, Teo looked between the two. "That's it? Problem solved?"

"You ever been in the desert at night, Teo?" Niya asked, dunking another huge piece of bread into the compote.

"No . . ." he said slowly, unsure.

"I suggest we keep it that way," Aurelio said, carefully spreading more fruit on his bread.

"What's up with the desert?" Teo poked because he couldn't help himself.

"Things, Teo," Niya told him. Her voice was hollow and far away. "*Things.*"

It wasn't like Teo was used to a life of luxury, but his sleeping bag provided little cushion between his wings and the cold, hard floor, and without a pillow, he already had a crick in his neck. He was up against a wall, tucked next to Niya while Aurelio was on her other side. Both of them fell asleep easily, leaving Teo to lie awake, toying with his mother's feather in his ear while he stared at the holes in the tin roof.

Niya's snores filled the small cabin, but Teo kept jumping at every sound. Wind barreled down the mountains, howling through gaps between the piled stone slabs of the walls. Things skittered over the dilapidated tin roof, and Teo's skin crawled as he thought about all the bugs that had probably already climbed into his sleeping bag.

Outside, something rustled.

Teo sat bolt upright, clicking on his flashlight. "What was that?!"

Niya remained dead to the world, but Aurelio got up. "What's wrong?" he asked groggily, squinting as he shielded his face from the light.

"I heard something," Teo whispered, shivering so hard his teeth clacked together when he spoke.

Aurelio eyed the flashlight rattling in Teo's grip, and then the stuffed toucan tucked in the crook of his arm. Teo braced himself, expecting Aurelio to laugh at him, or the very least be annoyed. Instead, he shuffled over in his sleeping bag, making space between Niya and himself.

Teo took the silent invitation. Still wrapped in his sleeping bag, he crawled over and hunkered down between the two of them.

Silently, Aurelio dug out his phone and pulled up TúTube.

"I thought you said there was no reception here?" Teo asked.

"There isn't," Aurelio mumbled sleepily as he scrolled through a playlist. "I downloaded some videos before we left the Academy." Aurelio lay back down and balanced his phone on his chest, angling it so Teo could see.

A video of someone making pastries started to play, showing only a pair of hands as they measured ingredients and poured them into bowls while classical music played in the background.

Teo grinned, his cheek nestled against Tuki's soft fur. "Baking videos, of course."

"She's my favorite," Aurelio said through a yawn. He tucked his free hand under his head, his heavy eyelids already drooping. Teo took the opportunity to slide in closer.

Heat radiated off the Son of Lumbre, soothing Teo's nerves and warming his frozen bones. He curled into it, letting his temple lean against Aurelio's chest. The familiar, faint scent of campfire and cinnamon teased his nose.

Snug, warm, and safe, Teo drifted off to the sound of Niya's snores, the soft hum of a stand mixer, and the light plinking of piano keys.

The next morning, Teo found Aurelio was packed and ready with protein bars before Niya even woke up.

Teo went to heave his pack on and nearly chucked it over his head. It was stuffed full, but way lighter than it had been yesterday. "What happened to my bag?" he asked, frowning.

"I repacked so the heavier supplies are in our bags, and the lighter ones in yours," Aurelio said. Teo wanted to object, but Aurelio cut in before he could. "We're still carrying equal loads, yours just weighs less."

Teo snapped his mouth shut and exhaled through his nose. He wanted to argue, but Aurelio already had a counter. And, to be honest, it'd be nice to give his back a break.

"Thank you," Teo grumbled.

Aurelio grinned, satisfied.

They spent a few hours hiking south before the terrain became less rocky and dry. The air got thicker with humidity while cacti and dry shrubs turned to tall grass and bushy palms. Finally, they crested a hill to face their next challenge: Río Serpiente.

The river stretched out to the east and west. Starlight reflected off the surface of the water as it curved back and forth like the body of a glittering black snake.

"Really wish we still had that boat," Teo said, rubbing his sore shoulders.

Aurelio stared silently at the river, his lips pressed into a grimace.

"Should we just swim for it then?" Niya asked.

Aurelio certainly couldn't, and Teo doubted he'd fare much better with his wings. "No," Teo sighed, already hating his solution. "If we can find a narrow section of the river, I could fly you guys over, one at a time."

Aurelio turned to him. "Are you sure?"

Teo rolled his eyes. "*Yes*. And don't look at me like that, or I'll drop you in the water."

With the help of Aurelio's map, they found a nearby section that Teo thought he could reasonably carry a demigod-sized person across. Large boulders had gummed up river flow enough that they were able to hop across, leaving only about five hundred feet of open water to traverse.

Teo took Aurelio first. Aurelio instructed him that the safest hold was for them to grip each other's forearms, just below the wrist. Teo did what he was told, and a few seconds later, they were up in the air.

Aurelio's warm hands were slick with sweat, but his terrified grip was like a vise. Teo tried to fly as quickly as possible, but he wasn't the most coordinated flier. He felt how hard Aurelio was trembling, his wide eyes glued to the dark river down below. After he deposited Aurelio safely on the opposite riverbank, Teo went back for Niya.

Her sheer size and muscle mass was way more difficult to carry.

"I saw you guys last night."

"What are you talking about?"

"You and Aurelio!"

"Shut up."

"I had to pee in the middle of the night and you two were all cuddled up, snoring together and looking all cute."

"Niya," Teo warned.

She cackled, her voice too loud and carrying out over the water where Aurelio could probably hear her. "Did you guys hook up?"

"No!"

"Did you kiss? Did you get a little smooch?"

"I'll literally drop you into the river."

"Maybe got a little handsy under those sleeping bags?"

"Shut up!"

It was no use, she was on a roll.

"Oh, Aurelio, you're so strong and handsome!" Niya said in a nasally voice that Teo found both rude and inaccurate. "Teo, you always make me smile even though I'm a big grumpy grump with mommy issues."

Teo started to laugh. "*Niya!*" He tried to warn her, but it was too late.

They had to stop on the other side of the river so Niya could wring out her braids and change into a dry set of clothes. When Aurelio asked what happened, Teo just said she lost her grip.

That was the start of what would end up being several days of traveling by foot through the countryside between Río Serpiente and Lago Relámpago. The farther south they went, the more humid it got. There were long stretches of empty fields and oak woodlands.

With nothing to look at, Teo's only source of entertainment was Niya's stories of her various adventures in Hero-ing. Aurelio was in his own world, constantly checking the map and double-checking the supplies in his bag whenever they stopped.

Finally, Lago Relámpago came into view in the far-off distance. Tormentoso's city was named after the large lake on the western side of the city. The largest and oldest lake in Reino del Sol, it was known for its daily thunderstorms, with lightning strikes that could occur upward of two hundred times an hour.

The people of Lago Relámpago affectionately called the perpetual, swirling storm the Eye of Sol.

It was a wonder to see, even from a distance. Flashes of lightning illuminated the mass of dark storm clouds through sheets of rain as the sound of thunder rolled over the hills. They were bright and occurred often enough that it made seeing their surroundings easier. Teo was thrilled for a change of scenery.

Until the rain hit.

The storm raged with Dios Tormentoso's fury and grief as he protected his people. Lightning streaked through the sky. Loud cracks split through Teo's ears, echoing across the countryside. The wind howled, slinging raindrops sideways so violently it hit Teo's skin like needles. He had to keep his wings tucked, afraid a strong gust would send him flying Sol only knew where.

It was miserable. The trio changed into rainproof clothing, but it did little to help as they trudged along. The hard-packed earth turned to slippery, muddy sludge. Teo lost track of how many times he fell.

Aurelio seemed to be suffering the most. He was bundled head to toe, desperate to keep the rain out. For a solid two days, the most Teo saw of Aurelio was his strong nose and the hard line of his mouth poking through the cinched hole of his hood as he marched ahead, back bent and shoulders hunched against the storm.

Sleeping was even worse. They had to use their hammocks to avoid the muddy ground, and the rainfly and bug nets did little to keep out the bitter cold.

At least Niya seemed to be enjoying herself. She loved the slick earth beneath her toes and made impressed sounds whenever there was a particularly brilliant blast of lightning. She didn't even seem to mind being wet.

Finally, after no signs of civilization for days, Dios Tormentoso's city came into view.

Lago Relámpago sat upon the hills on the eastern bank of the lake. Buildings stood in clusters of tall, white concrete columns with geodesic roofs. The lack of corners let hurricane-level winds slip right through them without knocking them over or uprooting them from their foundations.

Dios Tormentoso's temple was set between the edge of the lake and the sprawling city. Storm clouds swirled around the observatory, lightning leaping and thunder crashing as the god fought to defend his city. The temple's tiers were rounded, made of the same sturdy concrete, inlaid with silver and gold designs. Teo couldn't make out what they were from so far away, but they sparked with each lightning strike.

It seemed like Tormentoso and his Heroes had things well in hand, so Aurelio took them on a path around the outer edge of the city to avoid any fighting. It took a full day of hiking before they made it to the southern edge of Lago Relámpago. The rain let up to a drizzle as they left the storm behind them.

Teo's fingers and feet had been so wet and so prune-y for so long, he thought it was only a matter of time before the skin just sloughed off entirely. The chill was bone-deep, living in his marrow.

Teo broke first and asked if they could find somewhere to stop and recover for a bit.

He expected Aurelio to push back, but after a moment of searching the distance, Aurelio grumbled, "Let's find somewhere to dry off and make coffee."

"*GREAT!*" Niya shouted, rolling the R enthusiastically. She knocked shoulders with Aurelio as she bounded off. "I'm gonna look around!" she announced, smiling her big, goofy Niya smile. It was her best defense against a tense social situation. Aurelio's expression didn't even crack as he set down his pack, his jaw tight as he gazed out into the night.

Without Auristela, it was like Aurelio was an unrooted plant withering in the sun. He was pulling into himself, retreating to the quiet and unreachable Gold he had been at the very start of the trials.

And Teo didn't know how to help.

Taking a breath to ground himself, Teo sidled up to Aurelio and let their knuckles brush together. He totally did *not* take it personally when Aurelio didn't take the hint to interlock their fingers. Aurelio didn't look well. The color of his skin was off—paler—and he kept sniffling like he had a cold.

"Hey," Teo said, careful to keep his voice low enough that Niya wouldn't overhear. "You okay?"

Aurelio looked up at him, startled. Like he hadn't noticed Teo and was suddenly yanked back into reality. "What? Yes—I mean, *no*." At least he was being honest. "Are *you* okay?"

Teo let out a little huff that, with a little imagination, could have been a laugh. "No, I guess not. I'm sorry."

Aurelio gave him a puzzled look. "Why are you sorry?"

Teo didn't know how to respond to that, so instead, he paused and undid the straps of his backpack. "Here," he said, pulling out a fleece sweatshirt. "Put that on."

Aurelio's hands remained at his sides. "Don't you need it?" he asked.

Teo shook his head. "My wings are basically a down comforter attached to my back," he said. "You take it." He chucked the sweatshirt at Aurelio, forcing him to catch it.

Aurelio looked like he wanted to argue, but eventually he just murmured a shy, "Thanks."

Aurelio removed his rain jacket and tugged the sweatshirt over his head.

Teo burst into laughter.

It was way too small. The material clung to his torso and barely covered his navel. The sleeves didn't even reach his golden armbands.

"It doesn't fit," Aurelio said, looking disgruntled.

"Obviously," Teo agreed, chuckles shaking his voice. "But it'll keep you warm, and no one is going to see it under your jacket, anyway."

Aurelio grumbled unintelligibly, tucking his nose into the neck of Teo's sweatshirt before pulling his jacket on over it.

"AYO, I FOUND A SWEET SPOT OVER HERE!" Niya's voice ripped through the air, startling several *things* in the nearby underbrush.

Teo heard a particularly unhappy spotted owl let out a screeching *AAAH!*

"*Niya!*" Teo hissed, rushing after her. "Don't be so loud, you're freaking out the birds!"

They cut through a line of trees to find Niya in a clump of white oaks. Their dense, dark green leaves provided decent coverage from the rain.

Niya swerved around to face them, looking confused. "What?"

Teo pinched the bridge of his nose. "I said *keep it down!* Who knows what's lurking around out there that could hear us. We're trying to keep a low profile, remember?"

And some of us are tryna sleep! another bird shrieked from the tree line.

Teo winced and called back a quiet "*Sorry!*"

Niya and Aurelio blinked at him.

"What?"

"Nothing," Niya said, shaking her head as she swung her backpack around to the ground. "I just keep forgetting you can do that."

"Talk to birds?"

"Yeah. Do the birds out here speak the same language as the birds back home?"

"Um." Teo fidgeted uncomfortably. He'd never paid much attention to the *how* part of his bird-speaking abilities. "I guess so? Different species have different accents, but they mostly just ... do bird talk."

"But what's bird talk? Like what would it sound like to us?"

"It would sound like birds, Niya."

"You *know* what I *mean!*" she huffed, stomping her foot. She turned to Aurelio. "What do you think?"

Aurelio could not have been less prepared to be dragged into this debate. He shot Teo a beseeching look, one that asked, *Is it really going to be like this the whole time?*

Teo clapped him on the shoulder as if to say, *Unfortunately.*

A shrill *chi-dit* cut through the air and a second later, a tiny *something* burst through the trees overhead.

Son of Quetzal!

The bird dashed through the air excitedly, more a blur than anything else, until it came to a stop before Teo. Broad-billed hummingbirds were easy to spot by their bright red bills. His wings were metallic green with white undertail coverts and a brilliant blue throat.

There you are!

"Hello," Teo greeted as the hummingbird flitted around their heads inquisitively. He wasn't sure how the small bird recognized him since his wings were tucked under his clothes.

I heard you were flying this way!

Teo frowned. "You knew we were coming?" he asked, giving enough context for Niya and Aurelio to understand the one-sided conversation.

Oh yes, news spreads quickly through the flocks! the hummingbird said in rapid *chi-dit*s. His wings were a blur of green and made an insectlike, metallic trill. *Diosa Quetzal asked us to keep an eye out for you!*

Teo exhaled a laugh through the pang in his chest. His mom was still doing her best to take care of them, even from so far away. Teo sent her a silent thanks.

There's a little neighborhood nearby if you need some shelter! the hummingbird said, practically tripping over himself to be of assistance. *Unless you like being in the rain,* he added with an uncertain tilt of his head.

"No!" Teo nearly shouted, startling both the hummingbird and his friends. "I mean—" He cleared his throat. "I think we would very much like some shelter," Teo corrected himself, giving Niya and Aurelio pointed looks.

"GODS, YES," Niya groaned dramatically.

Aurelio nodded, just a stiff jerk of his chin.

"If you don't mind showing us?" Teo added.

The hummingbird released a happy string of *chi-dit*s. *Of course! Follow me, please!*

Their new friend led the way, chirping rapidly about how excited he was to meet Teo, and how scary his little home in the white oaks had gotten since the sun went out. When he led them to a road, Teo's stomach gave an uneasy churn.

"What's up?" Niya asked, bumping him with her shoulder. "You look all stressed and freaked out."

Teo tightened his grip on the straps of his pack. "The last city we were in didn't go super great," he said, thinking about all the accusations slung at him by the people in San Fuego. "I'd rather not get chased out of town."

"Pft!" Niya waved him off. "It'll be fine! Aurelio's people are a bunch of stuck-up snobby babies," she said, before adding to Aurelio, "*Full* offense intended, dude."

"I understand," was Aurelio's hollow reply.

Niya continued, "I bet the people of Lago Relámpago are way more chill!"

The rain clouds cleared as the hummingbird brought them to a main road that led into town before bidding the trio farewell. Unlike the tall buildings they'd seen from a distance, this seemed to be a more suburban neighborhood with squat, dome-shaped homes. Wide gutters ran along the streets in rows, dotted with storm drains to accommodate all the rain.

Two blocks in, Teo realized that, even though there were many homes and shops lining the streets, there wasn't a single soul to be found. Storm shutters covered every window and door they passed.

Niya cupped her hands around her mouth. "Hello?" she called. "Anybody home?"

Her voice echoed down the street. There was no response.

"Weird," Teo said, trying to ignore the goose bumps prickling his arms.

He and Aurelio followed Niya deeper into town, both their heads on a swivel while Niya merrily stomped through puddles. The end of the street opened up into a small town square, illuminated by silvery starlight.

A fountain with a massive, golden statue of Dios Tormentoso— the gods really loved a statue of themselves—stood on a grassy knoll with some trees and a few boulders that Teo assumed were meant for people to sit on. There were food carts, trucks loaded with rotting produce, and stalls displaying handmade crafts.

Everything was abandoned.

CHAPTER 6
TEO

"Where is everybody?" Teo wondered, peeking into the open door of an abandoned car. Someone's purse was still sitting in the passenger seat. "It's like they all just disappeared."

Niya shrugged. "Sleeping?"

"They probably retreated to Tormentoso's temple where he and his Heroes could better protect everyone," Aurelio murmured, carefully taking in their surroundings.

Teo thought that was a good point. There was no sign of any Heroes—let alone the storm god—in this part of town, but there weren't any monsters, either.

"The heck is all this?"

Teo looked up to find Niya pointing at one of the boarded-up buildings.

There were deep gashes cut into a wooden door.

Teo backed up and looked around. He hadn't noticed it before, but there were similar markings gouged into the sides of buildings, revealing white stone under a layer of paint. They were in the pavement, too.

"Claw marks," Aurelio said, verbalizing the fear that had pooled in Teo's throat.

"What came through here?" Teo wondered out loud.

"No idea," Aurelio said, deep lines pressed into his forehead. "But whatever it is, it's probably why all the people abandoned the town."

Niya moved to Teo's side immediately, her head whipping back and forth as she searched the square. "Do you think it's gone?" Niya asked, mostly to Aurelio.

"It looks like it, but I'm not sure," he said, almost reluctantly.

"Maybe just a quick pit stop," Teo suggested. His wings twitched in protest. "Just to eat a snack and drink more coffee," he added. "Then we can find somewhere less creepy to sleep."

Aurelio still seemed uncertain, but Niya was apparently comforted by Teo's words.

"Great!" She flung out her arms and collapsed onto one of the large rocks in front of the fountain. "These boulders are perfect for lounging on! Aren't they nice?"

Teo wrinkled his nose. "I guess." Sol only knew what kind of creepy-crawlies were waiting to invade his personal space the moment he sat down, but he supposed it was better than the hammocks. He pressed his hand against the damp stone and was surprised to find how warm it felt against his palm.

Teo gathered some wet magazines from a newsstand for kindling and brought them to Aurelio while Niya went to chop up discarded planks for firewood, the *thunk* of her Unbreakable Blade following her into the distance.

Crouched by one of the boulders, Aurelio attempted to start a fire, with little luck. He kept snapping his fingers, sending sparks flying from his flint-tipped gloves, but the damp paper refused to catch. His brow furrowed in deeper concentration as he tried again and again, but the wet kindling only spluttered and hissed.

"Uh, do you need help?" Teo asked, but what could he possibly offer a Son of *Lumbre* when it came to fire?

"I can't get it to light," Aurelio mumbled, a sheen of sweat prickling his brow.

Teo wanted to hit himself. *Why did I bring him wet paper?* He looked around frantically for an alternative but everything had been left out in the storm, and he couldn't search the insides of any buildings because they were boarded up tight.

Aurelio dropped the useless kindling and shook out his hands. "When we did drills at the Academy and got dropped into the jungle, Auristela made the fire and I cooked the food," he explained, the frustration in his voice quickly turning to defeat.

He picked up another magazine. When he tried to tear it in half, it just turned to sopping wet mulch in his hands. Aurelio huffed. "What am I supposed to do with this? How did Stela ever even—?"

His mouth opened and closed, like he had more to say, but the words never made it out.

Teo wanted so badly to say or do the right thing. But he had no idea what that would be.

Why was this so *hard*?

"I got wood!" Niya announced, followed by a chuckle as she stomped back into the clearing, a pile of haphazardly chopped planks in her arms. "That's what—"

"No fire this time," Teo said, cutting her off. "Everything is too wet to light."

Niya's face scrunched up in confusion. She tipped her head toward Aurelio. "What's this guy for then?"

Aurelio turned his face away, his shoulders bunching up to his ears.

"We'll figure it out later," Teo shot back, exhaustion fraying his nerves. "This is only a quick pit stop, anyway."

"But I—"

"No fire!"

"UGH, FINE!" Niya groaned dramatically, dropping her five minutes of hard work on the ground.

Teo yanked open his pack and pulled out some bolillo that Diosa Pan Dulce had baked for them. "Sit down and eat some pan."

They moved to a cluster of three boulders and Teo unpacked the tiny jars of jam and butter Pan Dulce had neatly wrapped in brown paper and tied with twine. When the lids popped off, the smell of guava and butter tickled Teo's nose in a way that made him feel painfully homesick.

"Let me see those," Niya said, flapping her hand at Teo until he passed over the rolls. Using the boulder as a table, she sliced them open with the blade of her sword. "Can you toast these?" she asked, turning to Aurelio.

His brow puckered. "How do you want me to do that?"

Niya reached out and grabbed his wrist, giving it a shake over the halved bread. "How do you turn this thing on?"

Aurelio caught Teo's glance and gave a slight roll of his eyes, but ultimately snapped a small flame to life in his palm. Niya cheered and proceeded to unevenly toast the rolls.

Teo handed her the jar of butter, but instead of using one of the utility knives, she conjured up the sword again.

"You're gonna mess it up if you keep using it for everything like that," Teo said.

Niya scoffed as the tip of the very large sword rattled against the very small mouth of the jar. "It's an *Unbreakable* Blade, Teo."

When Niya was done with the preparations, all three dug in.

Teo took a bite, his teeth sinking through the toasted crust into the warm bread. The guava jam was sweet and flowery with just a hint of lime. A wave of satisfaction that could only come from food prepared with love spread through him. Teo, Niya, and even Aurelio let out a collective sigh of contentment. It was like Pan Dulce was there, wrapping them in a warm hug.

When they were done with their snack, Teo packed the jars back into his bag while Niya stretched out on a rock and Aurelio went to the fountain.

Teo watched from the corner of his eye while Aurelio slipped off his gloves and rinsed his soot-stained hands in the cascading water, which was probably a good idea. All three of them were looking raggedy. Niya had at least three different kinds of foliage stuck in her braids and Teo could practically feel the sweat and grime caked on his own face.

Aurelio reached up and untied the strip of red leather, letting his hair loose.

Teo's heart jammed itself into his throat.

It spilled down to his shoulders, silky and straight. It softened Aurelio's appearance in a way that reminded Teo that he wasn't *just* a Gold, born and bred to be a famous Hero of Reino del Sol, but that he was also a teenage boy like Teo.

He was disappointed when Aurelio gathered his hair, twisting and looping it around his hand like rope before retying it into a knot again.

Niya nudged Teo's shoulder with her own, cocking an eyebrow in Aurelio's direction.

Teo blushed and tried to make himself look busy rearranging his backpack into a makeshift cushion. Niya cackled, but she managed to do it softly enough that Aurelio didn't hear.

Part of him wanted to call Aurelio over and suggest the other boy set up his pack beside Teo's so that they could lay side by side for a bit. The thought of resting of course led to thoughts of sleeping, and thoughts of sleeping sort of collapsed into thoughts of . . . other horizontal activities.

That was what regular teenagers did on a camping trip, right?

Snuggle up "for warmth" and spend the night grossly, adorably wrapped in each other's arms?

But Aurelio had never been a "regular" teenager. And this wasn't just a camping trip—this was a *Finish the Mission or Everyone Dies* trip, which sort of killed the vibe. Despite everything at stake, though, Teo couldn't help the knots of anxiety and frustration coiling in his gut.

Teo opened his mouth to say something before he lost his nerve, but just then, Aurelio threw his things down beside Niya and collapsed in a heap on her other side.

"Fifteen more minutes of rest, then we should head out," Aurelio said, making himself comfortable.

Niya looked over at Aurelio's back, then to Teo, her eyebrows pressed together in confusion. She mouthed, *What's that about?*

Teo tried to mouth back, *I think he misses Auristela,* but that turned out to be too many words for Niya to lip-read. She blinked, slowly, and waited for a better answer. Teo sighed and went for a simple, *Don't worry.*

He had learned the hard way that making assumptions about Aurelio's behavior usually led to unnecessary miscommunication. Aurelio had been raised to put his mission before his feelings. He struggled to open up, especially when it came to family matters. But Teo was confident he could get those walls down again—it would just take patience, and a gentle touch.

Teo lay back down on his makeshift pillow, staring up at the thousands upon thousands of stars in Sol's sky. He cursed the universe for giving him the ability to talk to birds but not boys.

Aurelio sat up suddenly.

"What?!" Teo asked, jumping to his feet.

"I saw something," Aurelio said, keeping his voice low. His eyes were glued to a nearby house.

"Where?!" Niya demanded, searching.

He pointed to one of the front windows. "Someone's inside."

Time stretched as Teo held his breath, his eyes watering as he stared at the window, too afraid to blink.

Then, a whisper.

Teo turned. A pair of eyes stared at him through a cracked-open door.

At first, a scream rose in Teo's throat, but then he noticed how wide open the set of eyes were, the white sclerae visible around dark pupils. He knew that look—terror.

"Are you okay?" Teo asked, trying to sound reassuring even though his knees and wings quaked.

Niya and Aurelio closed ranks beside him. They spoke again, but Teo still couldn't hear. He took an apprehensive step closer.

"I can't hear you," he said gently, trying to be quiet.

The sound of shuffling feet distracted him. Niya's elbow dug into his side.

"Look," Aurelio breathed.

Teo followed his intense gaze. It took him a second to notice several other sets of eyes watching them through cracked-open doors and peering through windows.

They weren't alone. They were surrounded.

"What's happening?" Teo asked, trying to keep his voice low as the rapid pulse of his heart pounded in his ears.

The door creaked as a young woman opened it a mere inch wider. She licked her full, trembling lips and whispered shakily, "*Help us.*" Tears welled in her pleading gaze. "*Please.*"

Teo's blood ran cold in his veins. The ground beneath him shuddered.

Behind him, something groaned.

Niya and Aurelio were immediately at the ready, searching the area for threats like they'd been taught their entire lives.

"Earthquake?" Aurelio guessed.

Niya shook her head. "No way—I know what an earthquake feels like, and this ain't it," she said, shifting her bare feet against the pavement.

Overhead, the clouds blotted out the rest of the sky, hiding the stars and plunging them into darkness.

But Teo was still able to see the boulders by the fountain move.

"Guys!" Teo yelped.

Fire sparked in Aurelio's hands, the flames just large enough for them to see the stones shift and stretch. Large paws reached forward as rock cracked and scraped, reshaping itself into large creatures. Their stony pelts were dotted with rosettes that glittered like stardust between patches of moss. The hulking forms grew thick tails and heavy square heads. Feline eyes made of moonstones opened and sparked in the firelight. Their rattling snarls reverberated through Teo's chest.

Their movements sounded like a molcajete—stone grinding against stone as they stalked toward the trio. Their heads hung low, watching the semidioses with intense curiosity and hunger, their massive claws scraping over the pavement, their low growls like echoes in a cave.

"Nice kitty," Teo said, tripping over himself as he backed away.

Niya and Aurelio immediately stepped in, placing themselves between Teo and the jaguars.

"They're stone jaguars," Aurelio said, muscles taut and body poised to fight. His eyes darted between the three beasts. "Starlight keeps them from turning into jaguars, but when it gets cloudy—"

"They come alive," Teo guessed, realization dropping into his stomach.

"What do they want?!" Niya demanded, white-knuckle gripping her Unbreakable Blade in both hands.

"Dinner, probably!" Teo squeaked as the jaguar stared at him with those large, blank eyes. His wings gave an unnerved shudder as the jaguar's tongue licked its lips. Teo could practically see little cartoon roasted chickens dancing around its head.

Niya swung her blade down hard against the jaguar's rump, only for it to glance off with a spark, the rebound jolting up her arms. "Okay, well, what's the plan?!"

"Why do I always have to have the plan?" Teo snapped.

"Because you're the Plan Guy!"

The jaguar took another step toward Teo. Moving faster than he could think, Teo leapt and shot himself into the air just as it attacked.

The loud crack of stone sounded below him as the jaguar slammed into the building he now knew people were hiding inside. Panicked screams sounded behind the door.

Niya appeared holding a shield. The jaguar lunged, slamming into it. Niya strained under the weight. Teo had nearly forgotten about Guerrero's Ring of Shielding.

"Careful, Teo!" she shouted, trying to shove the jaguar back as it swatted at her. "These things will crush your hollow little bird bones!"

Teo didn't need to be told twice and flew away. The jaguar jumped after him, but Niya shoved her full body weight into her shield, knocking it off course.

Teo circled around the middle of the square, a safe distance away. The fighting down below was pure chaos. Niya fought back relentlessly, striking at her opponent with sword and shield. The terrible sound of clashing metal and stone made Teo's teeth hurt.

Meanwhile, Aurelio fought off the other two creatures with a lot less confidence. His face screwed up in concentration as he threw balls of fire left and right. This wasn't the Aurelio Teo had seen battling in the trials. Instead of advancing, he was retreating to the buildings as the Celestials advanced, looking for holes in his defenses. Whenever one lunged at him, Aurelio shifted and used fire to block, only for the second jaguar to edge in on the other side.

He couldn't keep up. Aurelio's movements were sloppy, distracted. As bottled-up as Aurelio had always been, it had never stopped him from fighting like an absolute terror. Teo used to think it was annoying, Aurelio's ability to stay cool during a fight.

But now, the dread was clear on his face as the jaguars inched closer.

Panic clawed up Teo's throat as he tried to think of something. With another powerful flap of his wings, he shot higher into the air. The stars weren't out to help, but the golden glow of Aurelio's and Niya's suits along with the flashes of fire were enough for Teo to track the action.

Just in time to witness Niya trip on a gutter.

She pitched forward, slamming facedown into the ground and sending her blade clattering out of reach.

The jaguar reared back, ready to lunge.

Teo screamed, "Niya, YOUR SHIELD!"

In one swift move, Niya was up, planting her feet and bracing herself behind the shield a split second before the stone jaguar crashed into her. The sheer terror that gripped Teo was enough to seize his wings and send him dropping several feet before he caught himself.

The jaguar recalculated and knocked her onto her back again. This time, she tucked her knees to her chest and braced her bare feet against the jaguar's stomach. Niya then used the momentum to roll back and shoved the jaguar with her feet and shield, throwing the monster across the square as she did a somersault.

The jaguar went flying, its heavy body plowing through a food cart.

Niya was immediately upright, smudges of muck on her cheeks and eyes blazing. The jaguar shook itself off and turned back to Niya, a little dazed but extremely pissed off. Its roar seared through Teo's ears. Niya snarled back.

She shifted her grip on the shield and with a twist, slung it like a discus. It crashed into the jaguar's side, knocking it into one of the trees with a splintering *crack*.

"Bring it on, kitty cat!" Niya shouted, grabbing her blade and shield from the ground as she advanced on the stone jaguar.

Once again, Teo was blown away by how brave his best friend was. Even when looking danger in the face, she never backed down. While Niya was holding her own again, Teo turned to see Aurelio was now backed into a corner.

He was pressed to the line of trees as the stone jungle cats closed in, flanking him on either side. In rapid succession, Aurelio slung fireballs, sparking a new one to life as soon as he threw.

The jaguars let out angry bellows, moonstone eyes flashing and ears flat. They shrank back from the flames, huge paws swiping, but as soon as the fires went out, they advanced again with nothing more than scorch marks left on their rocky pelts.

Suddenly, Teo had an idea.

"Aurelio!" he shouted, swooping forward. "We need light!"

"I can provide light or I can fight, but you have to *pick one!*" Aurelio growled through gritted teeth.

"If you can make the fires bigger and brighter, it'll drive them away! You're a Gold, right?" Teo called down.

Aurelio gave a short, jerky nod.

"So, act like one! Manipulate the shit out of that fire!"

Aurelio squared his shoulders and lifted his chin, every muscle in his body taut. He threw a ball of fire on the ground between the two jaguars. It sparked and spluttered, unable to catch the damp earth and rotten leaves.

But then before it could go out, Aurelio held his hands palms out at his chest, his thumbs and pointer fingers pressed together. He set his jaw, drew in a deep breath, and thrust his hands forward.

Whoosh.

The small fire blazed into a towering inferno, spitting embers into the air that Teo had to dodge.

For a moment, Teo could see everything clear as day. Aurelio, sweaty but determined, as the two jaguars scrambled away from the burning light.

"YES!" Teo crowed, but the triumph was short-lived.

As soon as the fire went out, one of the jaguars charged for Aurelio. He spun toward it, pelting it in the face with a handful of fire. It roared and reared back, shaking the sparks from its eyes.

Distracted, Aurelio left his back open and unprotected. From the way he stepped to the side, it was like he expected someone to step in and cover him.

But there was no one there to defend Aurelio against the second jaguar.

Searing fear tore through Teo's veins as he saw the jaguar lunge at Aurelio's back.

Impulsively, Teo dove and twisted, colliding into the jaguar's side feet-first, knocking it off course. The force jolted up Teo's shins, rattling his knees. He hit the ground hard, cement dragging painfully against his wings. But Aurelio wasn't a pile of golden guts, and that was all that mattered.

"TEO! GO BACK UP IN THE AIR!" Niya shouted. "THE GROUND IS VERY DANGEROUS!"

"Yeah, I can see that!" he called back.

A ring of fire ignited, forming a barrier between them and the jaguars. Aurelio stood with his arms out, hands shaking as he fought to control the wall of waist-high flames.

"I can't hold them off for long," Aurelio said tightly.

On the other side of the licking flames, the three jaguars paced impatiently back and forth. Teo swore loudly. Nothing seemed to work against the Celestials, and even Niya and Aurelio were fading fast. They needed a permanent solution.

"The fire's not doing any damage, and Niya's blade isn't making a dent," Teo said, wracking his brain for *something*.

"Well, I'm TRYING!" she said, angrily brandishing her blade and shield. "But they just keep *bouncing* right off! These bastards are hard as rocks!"

Teo's heart leapt. He and Aurelio spun to look at Niya at the same time.

She blinked back. "What?"

Teo grabbed her shoulders and gave her a shake. "*Rocks*, Niya! They're *rocks*!"

"*So?*"

"So, they're made of earth!" he said. "You should be able to kick their asses with your bare hands, you don't need fancy weapons!"

Niya just stared at him, confused. "But—" The bangles on Niya's wrists jangled together as she lifted her blade and shield. "I've never done anything like that before!"

"I've literally seen you split a boulder in half!" Teo pressed, his words frantic as the jaguars moved in again, testing Aurelio's strength.

Niya frowned and gave a slight shake of her head. "But the Unbreakable Blade—"

"It's not working!" Teo shot back. "We don't need fancy Gold weapons—we need *you*—Daughter of Tierra!"

Niya's eyes darted back and forth between Teo and the advancing jaguars, mouth moving but no words coming out.

"Niya, you have to *try*!" Teo pleaded, giving her arm a squeeze.

"*Shit*—okay, *fine*!" She let out a frustrated growl and stomped her foot.

The ground quaked.

With a flick of her wrist, the shield turned back into Guerrero's ring, and the Unbreakable Blade morphed and turned back into a dark metal bracelet.

Niya stepped forward, firmly planting herself between Teo and the fire. Excited by the sudden movement, the jaguars closed ranks, tripping over each other as they paced back and forth. Hunger shone in their moonstone eyes.

"Put the fire away, Aurelio!" Niya told him. She planted her feet wide, fists coming up to guard her face like a boxer. "It's my turn!"

Exhausted, Aurelio dropped his hands to his sides and the fire went out.

The first jaguar charged, releasing a terrible, sawing roar.

Teo backed up into Aurelio, who caught him, his hands practically burning Teo through his clothes.

Niya shifted her footing and drew back her left fist. Focused and unflinching, she kept her eyes on the jaguar. A split second before they collided, Niya twisted her hips and with the full force of a mountain, punched the jaguar in the face.

The stone exploded under her fist. The jaguar went flying, its face crumbling. Shattered pieces of rubble flew in all directions, crashing into buildings.

Teo threw up his wings to shield himself, flinching as he got pelted by bits of stone.

"Oh my gods!" Niya gasped, clamping her hands over her mouth in shock.

The stone jaguar's limp, headless body collapsed, motionless for a moment before disappearing in a burst of stardust.

"That was scary!" Niya squeaked.

"That was *awesome!*" Teo crowed.

"Watch it!" Aurelio yanked Teo back violently as another jaguar lunged.

Teo tumbled head over feet a safe distance away. He got up as quickly as he could, thinking he was moments away from becoming cat food, but the scene had changed.

Now Niya was on a rampage.

She'd gotten the upper hand on one of the jaguars and was proceeding to punch and kick any piece she could get her hands on. By the time the creature was missing its jaw, tail, and one leg, Niya actually seemed to be enjoying herself.

"Okay, this *is* awesome!" she said with a triumphant grin, pinning the creature to the ground with her foot. Niya brought her knee up and slammed her heel down.

The jaguar cracked into a million pieces before shattering into stardust.

Teo whooped, punching his fist triumphantly in the air. For once, things were working out for them. Not only that, but the clouds were starting to thin out again. The starlight let Teo see what was going on without having to strain his eyes. If they could hold them off for a little while longer until the clouds cleared and the rest of the jaguars turned back to stone—

"TEO!"

Aurelio's shout—sharp and fearful—made Teo's heart lurch to a stop.

He turned.

The third jaguar was mere feet away, claws extended. Its moonstone eyes were wide and frenzied.

Teo leapt into the air, flapping his wings as hard as he could to get away. He was up, up, up, but not fast enough.

Claws caught the meat of Teo's calf. Pain seared his leg.

Teo slammed back to the ground, face-first.

The jaguar landed on his back. Its massive paws and heavy weight pressed the air from his lungs. A rattling growl spilled hot breath across his neck, reeking of rotten leaves and soil.

This is seriously how I die? he thought distantly. *We've not even made it to the jungle. It's like dying in the first level of a video game.*

Teo shouted in pain as the jaguar's claws dug into his wings—excruciating.

There was a sudden wave of heat and a flash of orange light. The jaguar let out a terrible howl, but Aurelio's fire didn't work this time. The Celestial lifted a paw, and Teo was certain his head was seconds from being squished like a grape. Niya screamed.

But the jaguar's movements stuttered to stop. Time froze for a terrible moment before the jaguar's body shuddered and cracked. Returned to stone, the jaguar crumbled, pinning Teo underneath. Grit and dirt choked him, filling his nose and mouth. He thrashed, desperately trying to free himself as the last bit of air was crushed from his lungs.

"TEO!"

Niya's scream was muffled, either because he was buried alive or about to pass out. Suddenly, the weight of the shattered jaguar pieces disappeared, followed by a series of meaty *thunks* and cracking wood.

Teo gasped, air filling his aching chest.

Before Teo could piece together what was happening, strong hands grabbed him and yanked him up off the ground. His vision blurred with the sudden motion. Aurelio's face came into focus, illuminated by the lights in his suit. His coppery eyes were wide—panicked. A thin line of golden blood trailed from a small cut on his cheekbone.

"Are you all right?" Aurelio demanded, like an order.

Teo was able to enjoy five uninterrupted seconds of staring at that beautifully creased brow and chiseled jaw before Niya yanked him to her chest.

"ARE YOU HURT?" she shouted right into his ear, her arms locking around him so tight that several pops ran up his spine. "DID YOU HIT YOUR HEAD? DO YOU KNOW WHO I AM?"

"Niya, you're smothering me—" Teo used what little strength he had to push himself away from her chest.

Disoriented, Teo looked around the square. There were no jaguars in sight, just scorch marks and dwindling embers. But what really startled Teo were the huge shards of rocks sticking into the ground and impaling the sides of buildings and nearby cars.

It was like the jaguar had *exploded.*

"*Gods*, Niya, did you do that?" he asked.

"I thought it crushed you to death!" she said. "Do you have all your limbs?!" Niya smoothed her hand down Teo's arms, frantically looking him over. "YOUR LEG!"

His pant leg had been torn to shreds where the jaguar sunk its claws into him. There were large gashes in his skin from knee to ankle, jade green blood trailing down his leg.

Teo winced. "I'm *fine*," he told her. "Thank Sol the stars came back out, otherwise we would've been screwed." It hurt like a bitch and looked disgusting, but the sharp pain was already dulling into a throbbing ache. If he weren't a semidiós, things would've been a lot more dire.

Teo tried to put his weight on it but his knee immediately buckled.

Niya grabbed him again. "*They mangled you!*"

Niya's chest rose and fell in shallow, rapid breaths, and the tendons running down her neck flexed. She was so worried about Teo it was like she hadn't even noticed all the dirt and cuts that covered her exposed arms, chest, and even stomach. They glittered with gold in the starlight.

"It's okay," Teo tried again, this time in a gentler voice.

"What if it's infected?!"

"It's not."

"What if we have to amputate?!"

"*We don't.*"

"Where'd our stuff go?" Aurelio snapped, cutting off Teo and Niya's argument.

They blinked at him, then looked around. In the midst of all the chaos, they had lost track of their things.

"We need to find our stuff," Aurelio said, like this was the biggest issue they were being faced with. He squinted, searching the ground. "If I don't find my bag—"

"What we *need* is to use the gifts the gods gave us!" Niya snapped, clenching her hands into shaky fists. "We aren't strong enough to fight these monsters on our own. Teo could've gotten killed!"

Aurelio jerked back, startled.

"Niya," Teo hissed, taken aback by her sudden anger.

Ignoring him, Niya stepped closer to Aurelio, pointing a trembling finger at his chest. "Where's the Scorching Circlet your mom gave you?!" she demanded. "Why don't you have it on?"

To his credit, Aurelio didn't back down, but at the mention of his mother, his expression shuttered. "It's in my bag," he said, void of emotion.

"Then use it!" Niya snapped. "I haven't let my dad's sword out of my sight for a second. The circlet is *your* responsibility. Your mom gave you that power so you could *use it*. To protect your friends!"

"My mother gave me that circlet to save my sister, because she didn't think—" Aurelio blinked, like he was surprised at the words that almost spilled out of his mouth. After a moment of stunned silence, he folded his arms across his chest. "It doesn't matter."

"It *does* matter!" Niya shouted. "Look what happened to—!"

Teo couldn't take it anymore.

"*Niya!*" he snapped. "I'm not made of glass! And despite what you seem to think, I'm capable of holding my own in a fight. It was a dumb fumble, and it hurt, but I'm *fine*. It's not Aurelio's fault."

Niya's face fell, hurt and confusion clouding her eyes. When she spoke, her voice was softer than Teo could ever remember hearing it. "I didn't mean it like that, I just . . ." She trailed off, biting her lip. Then she cleared her throat. "I'll find our bags."

She stalked away, head down like a kicked puppy.

Teo felt like an asshole. He hadn't meant to scold her like that—everything was just escalating so quickly. But he also knew Niya well enough to know there was something else going on beneath the surface. Something that was making her so reactive.

Not to mention whatever was bothering Aurelio . . .

"Aurelio?" Teo tried, but the other boy wouldn't meet his eyes. He just stood there, frowning at the ground and looking downright miserable.

Teo didn't know what to do. Aurelio was acting so strange, and Niya was so angry, and the world was ending, and their friends were in danger, and Teo didn't know how to solve any of it. He just wanted to scream.

Niya returned with their backpacks slung over her shoulder, looking shame-faced. "Found them."

"Thank Sol," Teo sighed.

"I'm sorry I yelled at you," Niya blurted out, looking miserable as she handed Aurelio his bag.

He took it quickly, but managed a quiet, "It's okay. I understand."

Teo was impressed. Usually he, or Huemac, had to tell Niya when she owed someone an apology.

Niya yanked open her own bag and rummaged through it, sending bags of Takis flying.

Aurelio watched her with a curious tilt of his head. "I thought you were joking about the Takis."

"I don't joke about Takis," Niya replied curtly.

Aurelio glanced at Teo, and he returned it with a tired shrug.

"Here!" Niya pulled out a brilliant green stone—Diosa Primavera's Gem of Regeneration. "Leg, Teo!"

Teo did as he was told and sat on a curb. Niya squatted down in front of him.

"How does this thing even work?" she asked, waving it above Teo's injured leg.

"I've got it." Aurelio shifted his bag. He pulled out Diosa Agua's Decanter of Endless Water and unclipped a collapsible cup that was attached to a side pocket. After pouring some water into the cup, he held out his hand. Niya reluctantly handed it over.

Aurelio dropped the gem into the cup and gave it a swirl. Green light shone, dancing across the lines of his focused expression. Aurelio kneeled down and propped Teo's foot on his knee. The touch was so gentle and soft, it sent Teo's stomach tumbling.

Carefully, Aurelio tipped the cup and let the water dribble over Teo's leg.

Teo sucked in a breath but the sharp sting quickly cooled, soothing the hot, angry cuts.

"Is it working?" Niya asked, anxiously twisting her bangle.

"Yes," Aurelio answered. The jade blood washed away, leaving behind angry gashes in Teo's skin. As Aurelio continued to pour, Teo watched in amazement as his skin began stitching itself back together.

Niya crinkled her nose. "Gross."

A relieved laugh jumped in Teo's throat. "Super gross," he agreed. "But it's definitely working." Teo took the cup from Aurelio and cleaned off the rest. By the time the cup was empty, there were only jade-colored scars left. "Practically good as new!" Teo said, showing Niya.

Her shoulders slumped. "Thank Sol," she said with a heavy sigh.

"Wait," Teo said, holding up the cup. "Don't you guys need it, too?"

When Aurelio gave him a confused look, Teo gestured to the cut on his cheek. Aurelio reached up and wiped the line of golden blood away, revealing untarnished skin. Niya grabbed what Teo was pretty sure was a pair of underwear from her bag and wiped off the bloody marks on her arms and stomach, which had likewise already healed.

Teo's heart sank. "Oh, right."

He pushed himself onto his feet and Niya immediately grabbed his arm. "Let me help you!"

"I can stand up on my own," Teo said with a tired grin. "But thanks for looking out for me," he added, not wanting to hurt her feelings.

With a sheepish look, Niya released him but stuck close to his side. "Is it safe?"

Teo nearly jumped out of his skin.

Shutters slid open as people peeked through windows and hovered in doorways, taking in the scene.

"Are they gone?"

Teo looked around the square. Pockmarks from the shrapnel dotted walls and sidewalks. Shards had even buried themselves into the handful of trees in the small park. The statue of Dios Tormentoso was now missing an arm.

"Pretty sure!" Teo called back. "You can come out now!"

Slowly, people stepped outside of their homes. Everyone was disheveled, with wrinkled clothes, tousled hair, and a distant, frightened look in their eyes. Several people had scratches and bruises. It looked like the stone jaguars had caused a good amount of damage before Teo, Niya, and Aurelio had showed up.

"Is everyone all right?" Aurelio asked in his authoritative Hero voice.

"We've been trapped inside for days!" said a man, a toddler clinging to his leg.

Niya stayed by Teo while Aurelio used the decanter and gem to heal the more serious injuries.

"No one has come to save us," an older woman lamented as Aurelio dabbed at a gash on her forehead.

Teo looked around at the crowd, perplexed. The residents of Lago Relámpago seemed lost and completely defenseless. At least the weatherproofing of their buildings had provided them with somewhere to hide.

"You have nothing to protect yourselves with?" Teo wondered aloud.

What would've happened if they hadn't come through?

"The Heroes are supposed to protect us!" a tall man snapped.

Teo reeled back.

"This is your fault!" someone else shouted, pointing a finger directly at Teo. "You're the one who caused all of this to happen by releasing the Obsidians!"

His chest tightened, his heartbeat spiking as sounds of agreement swelled in the crowd. They closed in around him. It was San Fuego all over again.

"Now our city is in ruins!"

"We have no way to defend ourselves!"

"No Heroes have come!"

Teo tried to back up and bumped into Niya. She stepped in front of him.

"We're leaving!" she announced, grabbing Teo's arm.

The crowd began to panic.

"No!"

"You have to stay!"

"You and Aurelio have to protect us!"

"We need you!"

Niya was seething and seemed on the verge of cussing everyone out.

Aurelio stepped forward. "We can't stay, we're on a mission," he said, trying to be reasonable.

"We're going to fix everything," Teo rushed to add. "We have a plan, we can—"

The crowd wouldn't let him finish.

"It's already too late!"

"You have to save us!" they pleaded with Niya and Aurelio.

Teo didn't know what to do.

Niya, on the other hand, was fed up. "HERE." She snatched the Gem of Regeneration and stomped over to the fountain. She stuck her hand in the water and swished it around until it glowed with green light.

"There!" she barked, stomping back to Teo's side. "Fix yourselves up—or don't and die! I don't care!" Niya added, angrily heaving her pack on. "C'mon, Teo!" she said, tugging his arm. "HURRY UP, AURELIO," she added when he didn't immediately follow.

Teo was more than happy to go with her, but Aurelio hesitated.

"You should retreat back to the temple," he told the crowd. "Dios Tormentoso can provide you protection—"

"And abandon our *homes*?" someone shot back.

"You have to stay!"

"We need you!"

Guilt churned in Teo's stomach as he and Aurelio followed Niya away from the square, angry shouts and hurled insults following them. He knew they had to keep going, and yeah, the townsfolk were being assholes, but they also had no autonomy. Clearly, Reino del Sol's system of Heroes only worked so well. For larger-scale disasters, there clearly weren't enough gods and Heroes to keep everyone safe.

Which was why they needed to leave. The sooner they stopped the Obsidians, the better.

"I want to put as much distance between us and this place as possible," Aurelio said, leading the way. "If there's more of those stone jaguars around, I don't want to find out."

"I've changed my mind about helping people," Niya grumbled as they started down the road headed south. "I don't like them anymore."

Aurelio excused himself for a bathroom break, leaving Teo and Niya by the side of the road. Teo watched Aurelio's retreating form while Niya paced back and forth.

Aurelio's behavior was getting under Teo's skin. He was running so hot and cold, Teo didn't know what to make of it. After all they'd gone through together during the trials, he'd expected—well, he didn't know what he'd expected, but it wasn't this.

"Is it just me, or is he acting weird?" Teo asked out loud. When he turned to Niya, he found her standing rigid, face red. She looked at him with a pained stare, tears welling in her eyes. Any thoughts of Aurelio were quickly pushed aside.

"Are *you* okay?" Teo asked, going to her. As soon as he gently touched her elbow, Niya burst into tears.

"Niya!" Teo said, a jolt shooting through him. "What's wrong?"

"I thought you died!" she wailed, tears streaming down her dirty cheeks.

"Hey, it's okay, I'm fine!" he said, rubbing her back. "My leg already feels better!"

"It's all my fault!"

"What are you talking about?"

Niya shook her head viciously, angrily wiping her tears. "I—I'm not strong enough! Stupid Xio got away! I couldn't save *anybody*! I could barely hang on, I nearly l-lost you!" The words spilled from her quivering lips, interrupted by hiccups. "I'm not strong enough!" she repeated.

A surprised laugh jumped in Teo's throat. "Niya, you are *literally* the strongest person I have ever met!"

"I've b-been training at the Academy since I was little, b-but this is real life! It's so much harder! And scarier!"

Teo didn't know what to say. He'd never seen her like this. Since when was Niya afraid of anything? Usually, Niya would just wake up, drink water, and believe in herself, and she could take on the world. But now it was like she'd lost her confidence.

"I don't want to go into Los Restos!" she cried, breaking into a fresh wave of sobs. "I w-wasn't strong enough t-to save the others. Wh-what if something happens?! What if I'm not strong enough to protect you?!"

"Niya, that's . . ." Teo trailed off, not entirely sure *what* it was. *Ridiculous, not your job, more than I deserve after landing us here in the first place.* He settled for placing a hand on her shoulder and gripping tight. "Okay. It's all okay."

Niya looked down at him incredulously. "*Nothing* about this is okay!"

Teo sighed and nodded. "I mean, yeah, you're right. But *we're* okay. And we're gonna be okay. No matter what. You and me, right?"

Niya didn't seem convinced, but the tears had at least stopped for the moment. "Yeah, but—"

"No *buts*, dude. I mean it," he said firmly. "No matter what happens, we're gonna do what we have to do to fix this. This is *my* mistake. I'm the one who was supposed to make the sacrifice, I'm the one who let Xio trick me into—"

"Xio tricked *us*," Niya corrected him, a bit of fire back in her voice. "That little brat. When I get my hands on him—" She made a strangling motion with her hands and snarled.

Despite the bone-aching exhaustion and blood loss, Teo managed a smile. "Attagirl. And listen, I'm not trying to say that your fears aren't, like, valid, you know? I get being scared, especially after all that went down. But we gotta keep going. And you really are the strongest person I know."

Niya averted her eyes, playing bashful. "Oh, stop it."

"The way you crushed those jaguars?"

"Teo, knock it off—"

"The way you swing that sword?"

"Okay, I get it, thank you very much—"

"And girl, those *biceps*?" Teo whistled, and Niya smacked his arm, laughing. Right then, it was the best sound in the world.

CHAPTER 7
XIO

The decaying temple was starting to mess with Xio's head. It was so dark and massive and *empty*, a stark contrast to Afortunada, or anywhere else in Reino del Sol. He spent hours wandering, followed by the slow, rhythmic drips of water, the lonely moan of wind through the halls, and the echoed taps of his own footsteps like someone was following him.

Xio decided to check in on the prisoners. Not because he cared about their well-being—he was just bored and had nothing better to do.

And maybe he wanted to rub it in their faces a bit.

For Xio, capturing them was the endgame. He had been so focused on the closing ceremony for the Sunbearer Trials that he hadn't put much thought into what happened after that.

And, okay, maybe he felt a little bad for them. But it didn't last long.

Muffled voices drifted down the hall as Xio descended the stairs.

Someone whispered, "Did you hear that?"

"Shh, someone's coming."

They quieted as he approached the tunnel. When Xio stepped

inside, he could feel it—the desire for vengeance billowing off the captives. Like a fog, it crept toward him, seeking him out. Hate, anger, and desperation.

Satisfaction warmed Xio's skin. Good. That was what he wanted. Xio held his head high as he stopped at the first two cells and surveyed his prisoners.

Little sparks of lightning danced over Atzi's skin before harmlessly skittering across the water at her feet as she glared at Xio. Marino watched him, his heavy brow casting his eyes in shadow. No longer hydrated and glowing, Marino's dark skin was turning gray around his nose, lips, and elbows.

On his right, Xochi stood frozen, staring at Xio with her hands pressed against the cement wall. On the other side, Dezi remained curled up on his side with his back to the glass.

Xio frowned. What was he doing?

Suspicious, Xio approached Dezi's cell and tapped the enchanted glass, making it transparent. Dezi's head snapped up to look at him with surprise, and then relief.

Xio ignored him and instead searched the small room, trying to spot anything out of place—

"Hey."

Xio turned to face Marino. He started to sign before he spoke, reminding Xio that Dezi could see, but before Xio could tap the glass again to hide Marino from Dezi's view, Marino's question distracted him.

"What's on your head?" he asked, jerking his chin at the obsidian crown.

Xio threw his shoulders back. "A gift from Venganza," he said. Marino squinted in distaste. "But why?"

Next to him, Ocelo pressed themself against the glass to get a better look.

Doing his best to mimic his father's deep voice and air of grandeur, Xio announced, "Because I'm the Nightbearer."

The words hung in the air for a long moment and Xio soaked it in, basking in their silent reverence.

Until Xochi's snort broke the spell. "*Nightbearer?*" She spelled the word out with her hands.

"Booo," Ocelo jeered from down the hall.

Xio's confidence popped like a bubble, anger fast on its heels.

"What's he wearing?!" Auristela demanded from her cell. "I can't see! Xochi! Describe it to me! I want to picture how stupid he looks in my head!"

"Okay, so from this angle," Xochi said. "It looks like a tiara—"

"It's not a tiara!" Xio snapped.

"It's *absolutely* a tiara," she said dismissively before going on. "With these pieces of obsidian fanning out around his face. They're taper-cut and polished, but the edges are *completely* unfinished—"

"That's because—"

Xochi ignored him. "It's kind of like the Sunbearer crown, but way uglier—"

"ENOUGH!" Xio's booming voice echoed down the hall. Xochi, Marino, Ocelo, and Atzi watched him from their cages before Auristela broke the silence.

"Well, it sounds *ridiculous*."

Xio's fingers twitched, itching to tear the crown off his head.

"Careful, Stela," Ocelo droned. They leaned against the glass, watching Xio with hungry jaguar eyes. "You're gonna hurt the eighth grader's feelings." The stone walls around them were covered in gashes and streaked with gold from their torn fingertips.

It sent a shiver up the back of Xio's neck. He reminded himself that *they* were the ones locked up in cages. They weren't the threat, *he* was.

When Xio looked at Atzi, she turned away from him with her nose in the air. It pissed him off for reasons he refused to process.

Auristela shook her head, blinking rapidly. "I can't *believe* I got captured by a little twerp!" she said, a delirious laugh bubbling in her throat.

"How did you even trick us into believing you were a Jade?" Marino demanded.

"It was easy," Xio told him. "You guys don't even look at anyone who isn't a Gold. The only reason you noticed me at all was because I got picked for the trials. We've been attending the same events, the same ceremonies for thirteen years—did any of you know my name before that?" he asked, spinning to look at each of them in turn. "Or did you not even recognize me when that crown appeared on my head?"

They exchange uneasy looks, except for Auristela, who continued to stare him down.

Xio let out a sharp, bitter laugh. "Exactly."

How had he idolized these people for so long? He'd spent years collecting their trading cards, watching news specials about them, even following them on social media just to get a glimpse of what it was like to be one of the chosen few. Xio had held them to such a high standard, just to find out they were the vapid offspring of violent, narcissistic gods.

It was pathetic. *He* was pathetic. But now he knew better.

"Even during the trials, you guys only went after me because you couldn't stand the idea of a Jade becoming Sunbearer," Xio fumed.

"I didn't go after you!" Xochi said, offended.

"Yeah, that was mostly Ocelo and Auristela," Marino agreed.

Ocelo bellowed, "AND I'D DO IT AGAIN."

"In a heartbeat," Auristela hissed through her teeth.

"How do we even know *you* didn't *make* us go after you, huh?" Ocelo pressed, bumbling through their own logic. "Teo said you were messing with our eyes and—and—making us be angry and mean to each other!"

The mention of Teo sent Xio's skin crawling. The memory of that dinner was carved into his mind. Teo's frantic desperation. The nauseated fear that filled Xio's throat. That night, Xio thought Teo had figured him out. That the dioses would grab him and cut him open right there on the table to see what color his insides were.

"He said it was an entourage!" Ocelo added.

"Sabotage," Xochi corrected.

"A sabotage!" they repeated.

Xio scoffed. "I can't amplify vengeance if it isn't already there," he said. "The hate has to already be in someone's heart." It was an important distinction. "Whatever the reason was—fame, glory, payback—you all were ready to destroy each other from day one. I barely had to give you a nudge before you were at each other's throats!"

Xochi huffed. "That's not true!"

"Ocelo trying to squash me with a boulder, Atzi roasting Teo out of the sky," Xio listed. "*You*, Xochi—nearly squeezing Marino to death!"

She winced in response.

"Auristela with the nest, Auristela during tag, Auristela *several* times over but especially when she almost smashed Teo's brain in with the fake Sol Stone!" Xio sucked in a breath. "I barely did any of that!"

Marino craned his neck toward Auristela. "Hey, why *do* you try to kill him so much?"

Auristela's rage tugged at her pretty face. "He made my brother sad."

Marino squinted at her. "Are you serious? Is she serious?"

Dezi, who had been watching Xochi interpret, nodded in solemn understanding.

"When it came down to it," Xio said loudly to regain their attention, "you'd all turn on each other without me doing shit." He paused and breathed in deeply. The scent of leather, tobacco, and hot asphalt stung his nose.

Xio exhaled a laugh. "Even now, you all reek of anger and revenge."

Well, that wasn't entirely true.

"Except for Dezi," he added, glancing back at the semidiós alone in his room. He'd always been impossible to crack.

"How did this even happen?" Marino asked with a spike of renewed frustration. "How can you be Venganza's kid if the Obsidians have been gone for thousands of years?"

"And what about Mala Suerte?" Xochi added. "Was he in on it, too?"

Xio's annoyance flared. "Mala Suerte wanted my secret to die with me."

"Then how have you been working with Venganza this whole time?!" Auristela snarled.

"I swapped out the jet fist for a piece of obsidian from my father's glyph," Xio said, holding up his wrist where the glassy stone still dangled.

Mala Suerte had given Xio an azabache bracelet when he was just a baby and warned him as a child never to take it off because the jet and coral would keep him safe. As it turned out, it was everyone else who needed protection from him.

"It was like a cosmic cell phone. Venganza and I could communicate through it. We came up with a plan and I followed it through," Xio told them.

When he returned to Afortunada, his entire worldview had shifted. At school, he had to sit through history lessons about Obsidians. How evil they were. Betrayers, they called them. Monsters. People spoke about ridding the world of Obsidian evil, but the history books never talked about how the gods slaughtered his people. His family. Entire cities. What about them?

He'd seen the rubble. He'd relived their deaths in his dreams. He knew what happened when the ruling class decided someone was dangerous.

"How did you manipulate the trials?" Marino pressed.

"All I had to do was stop the sun and release the Obsidians," Xio replied. "You all were so busy fighting tooth and nail to become the Sunbearer, it should've been easy to come in last. I threw every trial—acted helpless on the Tepetl, pretended to lose my alebrije, not completing the temple in time . . .

"*I* was supposed to become the sacrifice," Xio said. "But Auristela beat me to it."

"I'd be happy to kill you myself if you have an unfulfilled death wish," she offered.

Xio couldn't help laughing. "Teo even suspected something was going on the whole time, but you wouldn't listen to him! I nearly shit my pants when he spelled it out for you during the banquet! But you refused to listen to him because he was a Jade!"

"Maybe," Marino shot back. "But you're the one who betrayed him and Niya. How is that any better?"

Xio paused. He hadn't seen Teo and Niya coming. He hadn't

wanted to make friends during the trials, but they didn't give him much of a choice. He didn't expect them to get in the way, and he definitely didn't expect them to risk their lives to keep him safe. He was confused every time they stuck up for him and tried to protect him.

It was fucked up. Xio had been longing for someone to connect with, for a friend who understood him. He had grown up so isolated, so used to hiding who he was and avoiding attention. There was no place for him, an Obsidian, in the world of Golds and Jades. He was alone. An outsider looking in.

Then Teo and Niya opened the door.

Suddenly Xio wasn't the only one who felt like an outcast. It was like he'd finally found people to belong with, but it was always destined for disaster. They couldn't stop what was coming, and neither could Xio. It was too late to change his mind.

He was haunted by the look on Teo's face as he *still* tried to save Xio, even after he released the Obsidians. The way Niya's terrified scream echoed in his head after he went through Caos's portal . . .

Xio shook himself. "Vengeance is the name of the game," he said, shuttering his guilt behind a well-crafted facade. He crossed to Dezi's cell and tapped the glass, blocking out the boy's dismayed face. "We'll make you and your parents pay for what they did to me and my people." With that, Xio turned to leave.

"How did you rig the selection ceremony?!" Auristela screamed after him. "HOW DID YOU TRICK SOL INTO CHOOSING YOU?"

Xio didn't look back. "I didn't."

CHAPTER 8
TEO

Aurelio reached the top of the hill first and came to an abrupt stop, making Niya bump into him.

"Thank Sol," Teo sighed under his breath, jogging the last few steps. But when the city came into view, Teo's heart plummeted. Nestled in the valley below sat Afortunada.

And it was worse than he could've imagined.

Teo wasn't sure what he'd expected Afortunada to be like, but—if he'd been a little less distracted by the whole "Obsidians are back" thing, not to mention the hordes of celestial beasts or the cute boy brooding beside him—he probably would have imagined it to be more like a goth version of Quetzlan.

What he was *not* expecting was a whole-ass dumpster fire.

Afortunada was a disaster zone. Buildings that looked like they had once been tall and proud now seemed on the verge of caving in on themselves. The streets were crooked and cracked, windows in buildings were marked with *X*s in tape, and people ran through the streets, shouting above the cacophony of sirens and car alarms. The streetlamps didn't quite penetrate the endless night, so everything was washed in a shadowy gloom. It was like the apocalypse had done a speedrun through here on its way to everywhere else.

"Sol's *sake*," Niya cursed as they jogged through the streets. The two Golds had slowed their pace to match Teo's. They were bumped and jarred by people hurrying past who didn't even seem to notice them. "What *happened* here?"

"I imagine it has something to do with the *apocalypse*," Teo said as he took in the mess.

"No, this is how it usually is," Aurelio said, eyes scanning their surroundings as they went. The jet-and-coral eye of Mala Suerte's glyph watched them from nearly every doorway they passed.

Teo shook his head. "It's usually *falling apart?*"

"Well, it's usually not *this* bad," he reasoned. "But, yeah."

Teo looked around. Brick buildings with rusty fire escapes were covered in scaffolding. Wooden walkways detoured around half-collapsed buildings surrounded by yellow caution tape. A lot of the destruction had been there much longer than just a few hours, when the Obsidians released the Celestials.

"This is a border city," Aurelio explained. "Los Restos is just over the river, so they get a decent number of monsters to begin with. Not to mention, Afortunada has the most densely occurring natural disasters in all of Reino del Sol. The vibes are . . ." He squinted, trying to come up with the right word.

"Unlucky?" Teo guessed.

"I mean, it's called *Afortunada*," Niya agreed.

But Aurelio shook his head. "No, no, that's not what I mean. Stela and I hardly ever come here—actually, Stela refuses to do it anymore—refused to—refuses to—" Aurelio took a deep breath. "But the people of Afortunada rarely summon us for help."

"Why?" Teo asked, still confused. He looked over at Niya and found his own expression mirrored back.

"It's—Hang on," Aurelio said, sidestepping a pickup truck full of water barrels at the last possible second. Niya and Teo squeaked in harmonious surprise, tumbling back into each other and nearly landing flat-assed on the sidewalk. Luckily, Niya was strong enough to set them both upright before anything too embarrassing happened.

The beat-up truck pulled to a stop outside one of the bigger fires. Three mortals in fireproof clothing spilled from the cab and began pulling a firehose from the back and racing for a fire hydrant.

Without thinking, Teo rushed over to help.

"Is there anyone inside the building?" he asked, letting his heavy pack fall to the ground.

"Holy shit, it's the Sunbearer!" someone cried from the crowd.

"The *Sunbearer*?"

"It's Teo, Son of Quetzal!"

If he was being honest, Teo was surprised to be met with smiles and astonished looks.

That was when Teo realized—the tattered posters hanging on the stained brick walls of nearby buildings were of him and Xio. There were the awkward studio photos they'd posed for with Chisme, action shots taken from the trials, and even ones with both Teo and Xio together with the words HEROES OF REINO DEL SOL! above them. Xio smiled like he was in pain as he looked up at Teo from an abandoned newsstand. Guilt sank into his gut.

There had finally been two Jades competing, and one of them had been made Sunbearer. The people of Afortunada had been celebrating the Sunbearer Trials—celebrating Xio and Teo—when the Celestials attacked. A breeze swept fallen posters and green pieces and purple pieces of tissue paper into piles in corners and gutters. Broken glass and charred, discarded sparklers were strewn about the streets and sidewalks like confetti after a parade.

"Are you okay?" a woman asked, looking him over.

"Shouldn't you be in Sol City?" a man wondered, confused.

"What happened after the broadcast cut out?" a kid Teo's age blurted out.

A young man with deep circles under his eyes squeezed Teo's arm. "Is Xio all right?"

Teo's thudding heart choked him. He assumed everyone hated him, considering that what he'd done had been broadcast live to all of Reino del Sol—not to mention the angry mobs they'd run into in San Fuego and Lago Relámpago.

But the people of Afortunada were not only glad to see him, they were relieved to see he was okay.

And they were still worried about Xio.

"Hey, hey, hey!" Niya shouted. "Focus! Burning building! Is there anyone still inside?"

"I was trying to tell you—" Aurelio started as he came up behind Teo's shoulder, but before he could finish, an older woman in the crowd stepped forward.

"You honor us, Sunbearer, but please, don't trouble yourself!" she said, flapping her hand dismissively. "We've already evacuated the offices—and the volunteers are here to stop the burn. Please, let us deal with this. We'd hate to bother you."

Even though she was smiling, and seemed to have a generally friendly demeanor, it was clear to Teo that he was being dismissed.

Teo blinked. "Oh, uh...okay..." He trailed off, not knowing how to react.

Aurelio sighed. "This is exactly what happened last time."

Teo pulled on his backpack again and dragged Niya and Aurelio back to the curb and out of earshot as the group of Afortunada volunteers dug through smoldering ash to make sure the fire was fully extinguished.

"That was weird," Teo whispered, pulling the other two closer.

"This is what I was trying to tell you," Aurelio said.

"But—but we're Heroes! Everyone needs us!" Niya said, looking around in confusion.

"Afortunada is known as a safe haven for mortals. Mala Suerte takes in humans who are down on their luck," Aurelio explained patiently. "He provides protection, support, and resources until they can get back on their feet. Most people leave, but a lot of people stay."

This was wildly different from what Teo had expected. He'd figured that, since Mala Suerte was the god of bad luck, no one would want to live in Afortunada. He'd pictured it as a city falling apart and in turmoil—which, to be fair, it was, but it wasn't devolving into chaos.

The streets, while cracked and full of potholes, had been packed by someone with coarse gravel or dirt. Teo realized now that the tape Xs in the windows were to protect the glass and keep it from shattering and harming passersby. And the people weren't running around shouting in fear and taking cover like in San Fuego—they were coordinating with one another.

The smell of exhaust burned Teo's nose as beat-up trucks and sputtering cars passed by, full of people. Leaders in orange reflective vests instructed others to go from building to building, reinforcing doors and windows with plywood and passing out five-gallon emergency tanks of water. Shoes clapped against the sidewalk as people ran to their positions.

These weren't Heroes in shiny outfits, but civilians in everyday clothes saving their city alongside Mala Suerte priests in purple robes. It reminded Teo a little of home. Quetzlan wasn't the shiniest or fanciest city in Reino del Sol, but the people loved it and took care of it.

"If you think about it, Mala Suerte's people are better equipped to handle the end of the world than anyone else," Aurelio said, watching as the small group doused the fire with surprising efficiency.

"Well, that's great for them," Niya snapped. "But what about *us*? What are we doing here if they don't need saving?"

"Looking for Mala Suerte," Teo reminded her gently.

"Oh yeah!" Niya shouted with a bubble of laughter before getting serious again. "Where's he at? I have a few choice words for that betrayer-raising grease bag!"

"'Grease bag'?" Teo repeated.

"Have you seen his hair?"

Teo shrugged. "I dunno, I kinda like his hair—"

"You *like* his hair?!" she gasped.

Aurelio sighed. "*Guys.*"

"Sorry, you're right." Teo forced himself to focus. "First things first, we need to find Mala Suerte and figure out what the hell Xio did to make the sun go out. We should probably find his ... temple?" Aurelio nodded encouragingly, so Teo went on. "And uh, that is ... at the center of the city?"

"Why would it be at the center of the city?"

"Because that's where temples go, Niya!"

"Says who? My dad's temple isn't at the *center* of La Cumbre, that'd be dangerous! The center of La Cumbre is in a volcano!"

Aurelio pinched the bridge of his nose.

Teo tried again. "We could find a priest? Ask for directions?"

"Great idea, Teo!" Niya praised him. "Where do we find a priest?"

The three of them turned their heads in all directions. One benefit of the multiple fires burning down the city block was that they made for exceptional lighting amid the all-encompassing dark of the Sol-less world.

Suddenly, Niya jumped. "*Ooh, there, there!* Mortal girl in purple robes!" She waved her pointer finger in front of her to where a Mala Suerte priestess was tying off a splint on a large man who seemed otherwise unharmed.

Teo led the way across the street. "Excuse me, could you help us?"

The priestess glanced up, did a double take, and then shot up from where she'd been kneeling on the opposite sidewalk.

"Oh my gods!" she exclaimed. She turned back to the man, who gave her a thumbs-up before shuffling away. "It's the Sunbearer! And Aurelio and Niya?" Flustered, she tried to pat down her tousled short hair. "What are you doing here?"

"We're here to save you!" Niya announced, proudly brandishing her sword for emphasis.

The girl's eyes went wide. "Wow! That's so kind of you," she said, a bit sheepishly. "But we've got things under control here."

Niya's shoulders slumped, the Unbreakable Blade dropping to her side. "You do?"

Teo balked. "But what about the monsters?"

"Oh, there were a couple, but we took care of them."

"Only a couple?" Aurelio pressed, frowning.

"There was an iguana that kept trying to swallow cars." Her eyebrows pinched. "I think it was confused, probably thought they were livestock or something. The other one was an axolotl covered in flames. She kept setting little fires everywhere, as you can see."

She gestured around at the scorch marks and steaming wet patches on the sidewalks and buildings.

"It was hard to get her because she was so small, but someone tossed a bucket of water on her and after that it was easy to get her to the jungle and send her on her way. We managed to herd them out of the city and they seemed happy to flee to Los Restos. Our city borders the Obsidians' jungle," she explained. "So, when we saw things go south on TV"—her eyes momentarily flicked to Teo—"we mobilized."

"How did you get them to leave?" Teo asked.

She laughed. "Turns out they really hate light! The headlights on cars seemed to do the trick. They slunk into Los Restos and disappeared. We've got people patrolling the border and keeping an eye out, but so far none of them have tried to come back."

"Should've killed more of those jerks back in Lago Relámpago when I had the chance," Niya grumbled under her breath, nudging a broken piece of concrete with her foot.

"But we passed at least ten on our way here," Teo said, not understanding how Afortunada could only have *two* when Lago Relámpago was infested.

She shrugged with a pleasant smile. "Just lucky, I guess!"

Teo looked to Aurelio for some kind of explanation.

"Maybe it's because this is a Jade city?" Aurelio guessed.

Teo was immediately irritated. "So, what, not even the Obsidians thought the Jade cities were important enough to attack with full force?"

Aurelio rubbed thoughtfully at his chin. "They might have an especially big grudge against the Golds?"

Even at the end of the world, Jades were still being overlooked and underestimated. The one upside, Teo supposed, was that if the Obsidians didn't think the Jades were enough of a threat to send their biggest, baddest monsters after, maybe that meant Quetzlan would be able to hold it together until he and his friends put an end to this.

"I'm sure there are plenty of other cities that need your help," the priestess gently nudged Teo.

"We need to speak to Mala Suerte," he told her. "Do you know where he is?"

"Of course!" she said, her smile back in place. "He's at the temple, I can take you to him."

CHAPTER 9
TEO

The priestess, whose name turned out to be Ana, led them through the streets of Afortunada to where Mala Suerte's temple loomed. The facade was black, deeper even than the perpetual night, surrounded by smoldering fires. When they got closer, Teo saw the entire building was actually covered in large pieces of jet. Polished red coral and amethyst were fashioned into large eye-shaped mosaics, looking out over the city below.

They reached the temple and found white pop-up tents administering first aid to those who needed it. The crackle of radios cut through the din of paratransit buses dropping off denizens of Afortunada who needed help. There was even a line of food trucks that had pulled up to donate their supplies.

When they started their ascent up the main steps, the ground groaned and shuddered under them.

Teo stumbled and Aurelio caught him by the arm. Teo clutched him back. "What was that?!"

Ana stopped and glanced back. "What was what?" she asked.

The ground shook again.

"*That!*" Teo squawked, widening his stance in an attempt to stabilize himself.

Niya was unfazed. "Earthquake!" she announced, smiling down at her bare, filthy feet.

"Oh, that! Don't worry, that happens all the time." Ana laughed, pressing her hand to her chest in relief. "I don't even notice it anymore, to be honest."

Niya wiggled her toes and chuckled. "Tickles."

Teo was not reassured. Especially when a low *crack* sounded and both Teo and Aurelio had to leap out of the way as one of the jet steps splintered under their feet.

"Is this safe?" Teo asked, staring up at the long path of stairs ahead of them.

"Very!" was Ana's nonchalant reply as she stepped over another broken chunk of jet. "The temple is doing her job! The jet wards off bad luck and evil." She affectionately ran her hand over the brittle, soft stone.

Aurelio touched the same spot. When he withdrew his hand, there was a black smudge across his palm.

"It's like coal!" Niya exclaimed.

"It breaks when under attack—physically and metaphorically—so we thank her for protecting us and replace the broken pieces. Although—" Ana shrugged sheepishly. "In light of... *recent events*, we've fallen a little behind on the upkeep."

At the top of the steps stood the observatory—or, that was what Teo assumed he was looking at. Unlike the Quetzlan observatory, which was open-air for the birds to fly in and out, Mala Suerte's was a solid dome covered in jet, with another coral-and-amethyst eye watching them from above the doors.

"Mala Suerte has not strayed far from the Sun Stone since his return," Ana explained, lifting the hem of her robes as she scampered up the steps. Ana gestured for the others to go through the door ahead of her, head bowed reverentially.

Entering the observatory was like stepping into a room made of shadows. The soft blackness enshrouded them. Teo looked up at the domed ceiling and an icy trill ran across his skin. More red coral and amethyst had been used to create a large eye staring down at them. There was a cutout where the pupil would be, presumably where Afortunada's Sun Stone should've beamed out. Instead, the night sky stared down at them, stars winking like they knew something Teo didn't.

At the center of the room on a raised dais was a throne made of jet with purple velvet cushions. Next to it sat a bowl of polished jade that was filled with small azabache charms. Tiny pieces of jet had been fashioned into small fists, circles, and squares, each accompanied by a piece of red coral and a gold loop. In the same way his mother handed out feathers from her beloved quetzals, Teo assumed the azabaches were how Mala Suerte gave out his blessings.

Seeing them made Teo's chest ache. He couldn't escape thoughts of Xio, fiddling with his azabache bracelet, smiling through his unkempt curls at the breakfast table.

He betrayed you, Teo reminded himself. *He threw himself and the Gold semidioses into a giant pit.*

Behind the throne, Mala Suerte's eye glyph was carved into a huge chunk of jade, surrounded by candles and tokens left by visiting humans. Hovering above it, Afortunada's Sun Stone faintly shone. Without the Sunbearer's sacrifice to repower them, every Sun Stone would only continue to fade until the light went out entirely. Teo tore his gaze away.

Along the walls was a mosaic that reminded him of the murals in Luna's office. But instead of telling the story of Sol and the creation of Reino del Sol, its gods, and its people, this one showed the battle of the Jades and Golds versus the Obsidians.

It was unlike any of the other revolutionary-era art that Teo had seen. Rather than the usual iconography of Lumbre and Guerrero leading the Golds to victory against the Obsidians, this mural began with a lone man twisting tendrils of gold and orange together, dressed in white. His hands were positioned palm out by his waist, his lips quirked into a grin like he was welcoming the beholder. Gifts spilled from his hands, surrounding him. Grain grew thick and lush, and on the horizon was the outline of a village.

As Teo scanned the wall from right to left, the flourishing field transitioned into darkness. Black clouds speckled with stars rolled across the field, the village, and the man.

For an entire plane of the wall, there was only darkness.

Then, a figure rose from the ruin. The man's white clothes were stained dark from the Obsidians' rush. Two polished pieces of coral now represented his eyes, a harsh spot of red amid the colorless landscape. The man's hand was raised, and the Obsidian forces fell back on themselves, curling back across the wall.

At the end of it all stood the man—now recognizably Mala Suerte—standing alone over a blackened field. In the distance, Gold and Jade figures celebrated in the sky, but Mala Suerte's gaze was turned toward the horizon, where the village once had been.

Something heavy sank into Teo's gut. A faint itch tickled his palm.

"I hate my nose in that one," said a familiar voice from behind, causing Niya, Teo, and Aurelio to jump nearly out of their skins.

Teo spun to find Mala Suerte himself gazing back at them. He had one shoulder against the doorframe, hands tucked casually into the pockets of his slacks. "But otherwise, not a bad likeness." He nodded toward the final mosaic. "What brings you kids to my temple?"

Ana bowed her head a bit. "Forgive me for intruding, Dios Mala Suerte. They were looking for you down in the city. This was the first place I thought to look."

Mala Suerte shook his head, dark eyes trained on Teo. "Nothing to forgive. Ana, be a dear and check on my children, won't you? I told them to stay in their rooms until things calm down, but I don't trust them to obey those orders without a fight," he said with a tired grin.

"Of course," Ana agreed, nodding vigorously. "Very wise, sir. I'll go to them now."

And with that, Ana scampered off back down the steps with the same frenetic quickness she'd had when leading the trio to the temple.

Once she was gone, Mala Suerte's face hardened, cold as stone. "I assume this is about my son."

Aurelio looked at Teo. By the way he stood, back rigid and hands clenched into fists, Teo realized Aurelio wasn't sure if Mala Suerte was a friend or foe.

At this point, Teo wasn't entirely sure, either. He opened his mouth to respond, but Niya was too quick.

"You mean *Venganza's* son?" Niya demanded with a scowl. "Wanna explain how *that* happened, Mr. I-adopt-a-thousand-kids-but-never-bothered-telling-y'all-that-one-of-them's-an-OBSIDIAN?"

Mala Suerte winced, though whether it was because of Niya's words or her volume, Teo couldn't tell.

Mindful of using his inside voice, Teo added, "We could really use some answers here, man."

Mala Suerte ran a hand through his (admittedly, kinda greasy) hair, sighing heavily.

"Are you working for the Obsidians?" Aurelio asked in a tone Teo had never heard from him before—firm, sharp. Too much like his mother's.

But Mala Suerte just laughed, bitter and unkind. "How poorly you must think of me, Son of Lumbre," the god said, approaching the Sun Stone in the middle of the room.

"I was just as shocked as the rest of you when Xio seized that dagger. I never thought, not in a million years..." Mala Suerte dragged his hand down his face before taking a steadying breath. "My greatest fear throughout the trials was that Xio would be exposed, whether by injury from another competitor or as the sacrifice in the end. I never imagined this would happen..."

With great strength of will, Teo swallowed a thousand snarky comments and forced the conversation back where they needed it to go. "But *why*? Why did you raise Xio in the first place? Where did he come from? *How* is he an Obsidian? They've been banished for thousands of years!"

Mala Suerte approached the start of the mosaic story. He gestured to the field of wheat. "Did you know I worked with Maize back in the day? He got all the credit, of course, but he didn't come up with *farming* all on his own—"

"What does this have to do with Xio?" Aurelio interrupted.

Teo was surprised by how angry he sounded. Something was simmering beneath the surface of Aurelio's calm exterior, and Teo feared the amount of strength it must have taken the other boy to keep himself together.

"I'm getting there," Mala Suerte assured them.

Niya let out an exasperated sound and began wandering around the interior of the observatory. *Sitting still* had never been one of Niya's strong suits. Neither had *listening*, and Mala Suerte seemed to be gearing up for a long bit of monologuing.

Teo sympathized with Niya's plight. He certainly wasn't the god's biggest fan at the moment—but part of him was curious, too. Why was this the version of the war Mala Suerte decided to cover his walls with? And why had Teo never heard it before?

"Not all gods are created equal," Mala Suerte began. "You all know the stories. First, Sol made the Golds—"

"ACTUALLY," Niya called from across the room, hovering over the bowl of azabaches, "*first*, Sol made my *papi*," she said with a proud lift of her chin before plunging her hand into the charms.

"*Niya*," Teo hissed.

"What? This feels *awesome*!" She lifted up fistfuls of azabaches and then let them fall back through her fingers over and over.

Aurelio seemed shocked and gave Mala Suerte a nervous glance, but the dios looked more amused than anything else.

Teo sighed loudly. "I know it's been a long day, but I need you to rein it in. They're *good luck charms*, not a sensory bin!"

Niya made a face, up to her elbows in azabaches. "Why would the god of bad luck be handing out *good* luck charms?"

Now it was Mala Suerte's turn to look perplexed. "Why would I hand out *bad luck* charms? Who would want those?"

Aurelio nodded like that made perfect sense. Niya only shrugged and continued playing with the stones.

"Niya!" Teo pleaded.

"Okay, okay, I'm sorry," Niya relented. She wiped her hands off on her shorts and turned back to the group. "Go ahead, Mala Suerte," Niya said, flapping her hand at him.

Eyebrows still dangerously low, Mala Suerte picked up where he'd left off. "Like I said, Sol decreed it would be the duty of the gods to safeguard their human children. This was when we took on the aspects we still wear to this day, when we became Golds and Jades as you know us."

Putting on his usual air of mild disrespect, Teo interrupted, "Yeah, yeah, yeah, and the Obsidians were jealous and created their own divine monsters to destroy the humans and subjugate them all into worship machines, we know, we know—"

"No, you *don't* know," Mala Suerte snapped. His voice was just loud enough that it echoed off the black walls of the dome.

Teo watched as Niya and Aurelio both stilled, eyes wide. But instead of scolding them, Mala Suerte only shook his head and took a deep, calming breath, then continued.

"Sol made me their Dios of Fortune, a steward to pass down their blessings to the mortals. I worked closely with Sol and Tierra to create a home for humanity here—and the Obsidians destroyed it.

"These were the darkest times. With the Obsidians and their monsters on the loose, it seemed all but certain that our world—and everyone living in it—would be destroyed. I had grown to love the mortals just as much as Sol or Tierra. But watching the celestial monsters wreak havoc broke something inside of me. I realized that Sol, in all their wisdom, had made a great oversight. I was the dios of fortune, but fortune alone cannot protect the vulnerable. There was no diose of fairness, of justice, of equity. I could no longer focus on the blessings in life, not when our world was being torn to shreds. Good fortune wasn't enough to protect the humans. If I wanted to end the warring, and save any of the brightness still left in our world, I had to give up who I was and what I stood for. I had to fight back."

Mala Suerte's hands clenched into fists at his sides. "The Obsidians had temples, once. Priests, patrons, mortal subjects, just like any other gods. What you know as Los Restos—ruins abandoned in a jungle—were flourishing cities devoted to the Obsidian dios."

Mala Suerte stopped himself short, eyes locked somewhere in the distance. Silence hung heavy beneath the vast dome of the observatory. Teo couldn't help glancing back at the mural on the wall—the empty field, the missing village.

"What happened to them?" Teo asked, breaking the silence. "The humans, I mean."

A mirthless smile curled Mala Suerte's lips. "Fortune turned its tides on them. In order to fight against the Obsidians, I had to become a dios who could fight the Celestials alongside the more powerful, combat-oriented gods like Guerrero and Lumbre. Instead of bringing good luck and prosperity to the humans, I turned into a dios of wrath, no better than the Obsidians we were fighting against." Mala Suerte winced. "I never *wanted* to wipe out the Obsidian cities, but I compromised my morals because I believed it was the only way. And I hated myself for it—every waking second of my immortal existence, I regret it."

Teo's stomach gave an uneasy twist.

In every corner of Reino del Sol—from La Cumbre down to Quetzlan—the war against the Obsidians was celebrated as a triumph of good against evil. They learned about it in school. It was retold every opening ceremony of the trials. Any chance they got, they would sing praise to the gods for defeating the Obsidians.

Teo had been taught that Sol sacrificed themself for the good of the world—but was it really the good of the world, or just the good of the gods?

"Where does Xio come into all of this?" Aurelio asked, redirecting the conversation.

"Thirteen years ago, I ventured into Los Restos and returned to the ruins of Venganza's temple. Something drew me back, I don't know what or why. It was strange, the sense that something had . . . *shifted.* I found Xio among all the bones and broken stone, inside an orb of obsidian that slid open when I approached. He was inside, wrapped in a poncho and fast asleep."

"Hang on," Teo interrupted, holding his hands up. "Does that mean Xio is, like, *from the past*?"

Mala Suerte nodded gravely. "To this day, I don't know how Venganza managed it. But Xio survived the slaughter of his people, frozen in time until I found him."

"Wait, so that means he's like—like . . ." Niya squinted one eye shut as she attempted math. "A *bajillion* years old."

Aurelio's eyebrows pressed together. "That's not a real number."

Niya *tsk*ed at him and said, "It may not be real in *fact*, but it's real in *feeling*," which Teo thought was a very good point.

"I'm so glad the fate of the world lies in your hands," Mala Suerte deadpanned. "It inspires such confidence."

"But why would you keep him?" Niya asked, frowning at Mala Suerte. "The Obsidians hurt you, they destroyed everything you cared about—"

"But *Xio* didn't," Mala Suerte said, unwavering. "I couldn't change the past or what I had done, but I could take in this child, an innocent who had done nothing wrong other than being born with the blood of Venganza. I believed Sol had led me to him for a reason. But I knew if the other dioses found out he lived, they wouldn't see it my way. They would look at a poor, forgotten creature lost in time and see nothing but a weapon. I wanted to give Xio a chance. I wanted him to make his own life."

Niya tipped her head to the side. "So you went all creepy and evil to protect some random baby?"

"I'm not—" Mala Suerte stopped, his attention on her. "You think I'm *evil*?"

Teo and Niya exchanged looks.

"Well, yeah, kinda," Niya admitted with a shrug.

"Your name is *Mala* Suerte," Teo pointed out.

"Your city is literally the capital of the *downtrodden*—"

"They are not downtrodden because they *live here*, you fools," the god snapped. "Did you listen to a word I said? I don't curse my people with bad luck, I keep bad luck away. They live here because they were outcasts everywhere else. Here, they make their lives. Here, they are treated with compassion again.

"When Sol created me, I was only Suerte. After the fighting was over, I was changed. I wanted nothing to do with the Golds, or even the other Jades. I couldn't go back to being the same Suerte. I didn't have it in me. Over time, I got a reputation. I embraced the *bad guy* image they were painting of me—"

"Is that why you wear black all the time?" Niya asked. "Because you want to look all tough and scary?"

"I wear all black because it looks *good on me*—" Mala Suerte took a steadying breath, physically turning his head away from Niya and her nonsense. "*They* called me Mala Suerte. I was Bad Luck and I let that become my reputation. If I let everyone think the worst of me, then they'd stay away from my home, my people, and those I cared about."

So you pushed everyone away, Teo thought, and suddenly, hundreds of little moments over the years began to piece themselves together. His strange moodiness at the godly gatherings, the way he seemed hell-bent on making others uncomfortable, even his fellow Jades. Why he'd adopted so many kids only to keep them locked away in his strange, forgotten city, where the greatest threat he had to worry about was himself.

It struck Teo that, of all the gods he'd met, Mala Suerte was the most human.

The god released a sad sigh. "Xio deserved a chance at life, just like anyone else, Obsidian or not."

"Yeah, great job with that one," Niya muttered under her breath.

Mala Suerte turned his attention to Teo. "Xio was never meant to escape the wrath of the Golds the first time," he said, glancing at the mosaic. "They destroyed three cities in an attempt to wipe out all trace of the Obsidians, with no regard for the humans living there."

"It's not like the rest of the dioses do," Teo quipped. "Every ten years they let one of their own children be slaughtered. How is that okay with any of you?"

Mala Suerte was quiet for a moment as he stared down at Teo thoughtfully. "A sacrifice is still required, it's true," the dios admitted. "A long time ago, Diosa Quetzal once told me if human life was fleeting, she'd do everything to pack as much love and joy into her children's short lives as possible."

Teo's heart ached. He thought of his childhood. Of all the time his mother spent with him and Huemac at Quetzal Temple. The first time she flew Teo over the coast, wrapped safely in her arms. How she played silly games with him and Aurelio in Sol City. How she shielded Teo from witnessing the sacrifice at his first Sunbearer ceremony. He thought of his sister, Paloma, and how it must've broken his mom's heart that her daughter's life was cut so short.

Teo was lucky to have her as his mom and, right now, he wished he was enveloped by her wings more than anything.

"When the Golds show up to deal the final blow, they won't take mercy on Xio," Mala Suerte said. "Enough innocent blood has been shed to keep our world safe. You are the Sunbearer, and a sacrifice is still needed to resurrect Sol."

Mala Suerte looked at each of them in turn before settling on Teo. "When the time comes, will you spare Xio?"

A delirious laugh bucked in Teo's chest.

"I'm not killing Xio!" he nearly shouted. "I'm not killing anybody! I couldn't do it the first time, remember? That's how we got here in the first place!"

He looked to Aurelio and Niya, desperate for confirmation.

"In order to stop the apocalypse," Aurelio said slowly, "there still needs to be a sacrifice."

Teo's heart sank. He turned to Niya.

She stood to the side, pissed off with her arms crossed. "Listen, I don't want the little turd to die!" she barked. "But Sol *is* dead, and we need a sacrifice to bring them back to life!"

"Gods don't *die*, least of all Sol," Mala Suerte said. "They gave up their physical ties to the mortal world to keep us safe, but that doesn't mean they're gone. They're still here. You can still feel their presence all around us."

It might have been Mala Suerte's voice, but it was Luna's words Teo heard.

"Not anymore, though," Aurelio corrected him. It caught Teo by surprise that Aurelio would speak to a dios so brazenly.

Urgency and desperation propelled Teo forward. "But we can get them back!"

"Your dad seems to think so," Mala Suerte said, his gaze swinging to Niya.

She nodded vigorously. "And he's never wrong!"

This made Mala Suerte grin. "You'll spend the night here," he said, allowing no argument as he led them out of the observatory. "I'll have Ana show you to the kitchen. We'll make sure you get a warm plate of food and set you up with some beds.

"One more thing," Mala Suerte said, stopping Teo with a hand on his shoulder. The dios's eyes softened as he looked down into Teo's. "Xio shouldn't have to deal with the consequences of my failure to protect him. My actions sent Xio down a dangerous path, but there's still good in him. He's just lost. Bring him home." Mala Suerte was so earnest it was hard for Teo not to look away. "Please. Surely, if anyone else in those trials could understand Xio's resentment of the Golds..."

It's the other Jade everyone else wrote off from the start, Teo silently finished. He hated the pang it caused in his chest—mostly, because Mala Suerte was spot on. Teo had entered the trials with nothing but resentment for the Golds, Aurelio most of all. And look how wrong he'd been.

Teo could also feel the anguish in Mala Suerte's voice. Teo understood the pain of what Xio had done, and he also blamed himself for a lot of it. If he was this torn up about it, he couldn't even imagine what Mala Suerte was going through. He wanted to believe that the Xio he once knew—and Mala Suerte still believed in—wasn't completely gone.

He was glad at least one of the gods was thinking rationally.

"I'll try," Teo said, finding his voice again. "But I can't force him—he has to want to."

Mala Suerte smiled, a glimmer of hope in his eyes. "I always liked you," he said.

Teo let out a dry laugh. "Even though I'm a troublemaker?"

Mala Suerte's smile curled into a mischievous grin. "*Because* you're a troublemaker."

The dios led the way out of the observatory. "Ana is downstairs waiting for you. She will set you up with food and accommodations," Mala Suerte said, standing at the entrance of the observatory. "Rest up. You still have a long journey ahead."

"Thank you," Aurelio said, giving Mala Suerte a solemn bow of his head.

"We'll catch you later!" Niya added, tossing the god a lazy salute before starting down the stone steps, Aurelio right behind her.

But Teo hesitated.

"Wait a second," he said when Mala Suerte turned to go back inside the observatory.

Niya and Aurelio stopped. Mala Suerte paused and glanced back.

"What do you want us to call you?" Teo asked.

Mala Suerte arched an eyebrow.

"Suerte or Mala Suerte?" Teo clarified.

The dios paused for just a moment before giving Teo a withering look. "I'm not concerned with what gods or mortals call me, Son of Quetzal."

Niya huffed. "Well, I wouldn't want people calling me *Bad Niya*!"

"We gotta call you *something*," Teo said.

"I've long since given up on being understood by others," he said dryly.

Teo nodded. He knew what that was like.

"We won't let you down, Suerte," Teo said.

Suerte rolled his eyes at the earnestness. "See that you don't," he said before turning away, but Teo caught the grin on his face before he disappeared back into the observatory.

Once they started down the steps, Niya turned to Teo and Aurelio with a self-satisfied smile. "Well, well, well," she said. "That sure was *lucky*, eh?"

She was locking eyes with Aurelio in particular, waiting for some kind of response. Aurelio returned it with a long-suffering stare before turning on his heel and continuing down the stone steps.

Teo arched an eyebrow at his best friend. Bad puns weren't exactly out of character, but the sudden interest in Aurelio's reaction was new.

"I thought you didn't like him?" Teo asked with a grin.

"I didn't!" Niya said, falling into step next to him. "But now that you two are dating—"

Teo choked on his own breath. "We're not—"

Niya continued like she hadn't heard him. "—Aurelio's been promoted to second-best friend!"

Teo's instinct was to push back, but what was the point in denying what he felt for Aurelio? If the world really was ending, why not just go for it? It was a surprisingly freeing thought. "So, that's how it is, huh?"

Niya nodded and draped her arm across his shoulders. "Yup!" With a tilt of her head, she gave Teo an affectionate head bump. "Whether he likes it or not!"

Aurelio stopped to turn back from several steps below. "Are you guys coming?"

"GODS, AURELIO! WE'RE HAVING A MOMENT, DON'T INTERRUPT!" Niya shouted, making the other boy jolt.

Aurelio shot him a puzzled look, but Teo laughed—the open-mouthed, unrestrained kind that lightened his chest and momentarily released the tension knotted in his nerves. Aurelio rolled his eyes, but before he could turn away, Teo caught a glimpse of his lips curling into a smile.

Niya crossed her arms with a satisfied grin, watching Aurelio's retreating back. "It's gonna feel good when he finally warms up to me."

Teo couldn't think of any two people he'd rather spend the end of the world with.

CHAPTER 10
XIO

Xio stood alone at the top of Venganza Temple, working up the nerve to go inside.

Just be brave and be confident, he said to himself. Head high and back straight, Xio entered the room where Venganza sat on his throne, in conversation with Caos and Chupacabra. When he walked up to the altar, they stopped talking.

"Xio, my son," Venganza said with a reserved smile.

Xio gave an awkward wave and immediately regretted it. Any plans of being brave or confident were quickly abandoned. "Heeey . . ." He trailed off awkwardly. He tried to add *Dad* but his tongue refused to work.

Venganza lifted his brows. "Is there something you need?"

"Did Baby have a bad dream?" Chupacabra cooed. "Want us to check under your bed for monsters?" Tickled by her own joke, she shrieked with laughter.

Caos's strange laugh sounded like someone sawing through violin strings.

"Uh, no . . ." Chupacabra was annoying as hell and twice as condescending, but she was also unpredictable and blood-thirsty. Xio valued his life too much to be snide.

"I was just wondering if you could, or were interested, I guess, in showing me how my powers work?" Xio flashed Venganza a hopeful smile, his face on fire.

"How your powers work," the dios repeated flatly.

This was a terrible idea.

"Yeah—I mean—I know how they *work*," he corrected. "But I can only do basic Emotional Manipulation, with a specialization in vengeance, of course," Xio rattled on. "I was wondering if you—or, if *we*, I guess—could do Emotional *Energy* Manipulation, too? Can you manipulate emotional energy to manifest it in a physical way? Like, Emotional Energy Waves, Blasts or Beams? Maybe Emotional Energy Absorption—?"

Venganza's expression finally cracked, only to reveal dry amusement. "My, my, how *clinical* the verbiage has gotten."

Xio rushed on, tongue tripping. "I mean, I've just never met someone else with influence over vengeance, aside from you of course. So, uh . . . I guess I just wanted to learn?" Xio asked, lacing his fingers together. "I thought it'd be useful if you guys needed me—"

Chupacabra barked a laugh. "What makes you think we need *your* help?"

Xio winced. He wasn't sure what he'd been expecting. Venganza certainly wasn't a toss-the-ball-around-after-dinner kind of father—it was like he expected Xio to know everything already. And it wasn't that Xio had expected personal lessons per se, but even the smallest bit of guidance would have been nice.

Luck was abundant for the children of Suerte. If you told his sister Renata about a nightmare you had, she could keep it from coming true. If you gave Dani a coin, she could squeeze it in her palm and give you good luck for thirty minutes. But Xio wasn't like them. He had never been gifted with *good* luck.

When he was younger, Xio had begged his sisters to help him learn to control his power, but even they were at a loss. Things always went *wrong* around him, like the girls who teased him about his hair and got such bad lice, they'd had to shave their heads. Or the boy who tried to drop a spider down Xio's shirt, only for it to turn around and bite his own hand, sending the kid to the hospital. He'd spent so many afternoons in the principal's office, crying and insisting he hadn't done anything to them. Whatever made Xio's magic tick, it just wasn't the same as the rest of his siblings.

Fortune is a coin toss, Suerte would say. *Your sisters represent only one side of my power—you are the other. It's just the way things are.*

The way things are, my ass, Xio thought bitterly, as if the memory could hear him. What other lies had Suerte fed him over the years?

Suerte had always told him that his mother died shortly after he was born. *Wrong place, wrong time*, Mala Suerte had said. *Bad luck.*

Later, Xio found out that this was only half a lie. His mortal mother *had* died as the result of some incredibly bad luck: having Xio as her child.

Xio had heard of semidioses who were raised mostly by their mortal parent, but Mala Suerte acted as the primary caretaker for all his children, including the mortals he adopted—at least, as far as Xio knew. He used to spend so much time staring at his semidiose siblings, searching for any trace of resemblance that could tie them together. A handful of them had inherited Suerte's strong jaw, others his perfect teeth. Even the kids with no diose blood seemed to take after Suerte more than Xio.

You've got your father's eyes, a priestess told him once, and Xio felt weightless with joy. Now he could only laugh at the memory, an icy twinge in his chest.

It turned out Xio was just one of many strays the god of bad luck had taken in over the years. Suerte had raised many orphaned mortals who had been abandoned on the temple steps. But Xio couldn't have passed for mortal, with his enhanced demigod durability and superhuman reflexes.

Xio just felt lost. He was an Obsidian by blood, but he'd only been taught the Gold-approved version of their history—and he had no idea where he fit into their story yet.

It's okay if you haven't figured yourself out yet, Teo had told him once. Xio had to stop himself from physically recoiling at the unwanted voice in his head. Why the hell was he thinking about Teo at a time like this?

Probably because Teo and Niya were the first real friends you ever had, said the annoying little voice. *They were the first people to really* listen *to you.*

Venganza was always calling him "my son," but what if he wasn't a son at all? What if the words he thought he'd grow into never actually fit?

Pull it together, he reminded himself. Now was not the time for a full-on gender crisis. "I just thought," Xio said finally, "I ought to learn to use my birthright."

This got Venganza's lips to curl into a disturbing approximation of a smile. "That's a wonderful idea."

Xio blinked. "Really?"

"Of course!" Venganza rose from his chair and met Xio at the base of the dais. "You are my son. I should impart upon you my fatherly wisdom." He clapped his large hand against Xio's back.

Son, son, son, the word ricocheted through Xio's body. But he was finally getting what he wanted.

A huge smile split Xio's face. He ignored Chupacabra rolling her eyes behind Venganza's back.

"Why don't we start with something simple, like conjuration." Venganza's eyebrows ticked upward expectantly.

Xio nodded, hoping that successfully hid how little that meant to him.

"Our first step is to call upon the power from within our body," Venganza told him.

Xio's mouth twisted. "Yeah, that's the part I don't know how to do." Xio couldn't bear the disappointed look on Venganza's face. It felt like the walls of his body were caving in.

"Not even with your hands?" Venganza asked with a withering disbelief.

Xio held his hands in front of his chest, fingers curled to create a round, empty space. He tried to pull everything from within him into that void, or at least to keep his hands from shaking. He gritted his teeth and thought he might have seen a gray wisp start to form, but it flickered out once sweat formed on his brow.

Venganza sighed. "No."

Xio's heart raced, his chest tightening. Training with the Obsidians—this was what he had been yearning for. He *had* to get this right.

"More like *this*."

A fathomless black aura seeped from Venganza, crackling around him. The hazy darkness shivered and grew, each spindle thickening into tendrils, ends reaching outward from his body. The ball of writhing shadow grew at the center of his chest and then—

BOOM.

It shot across the room, blasting a perfect hole in the wall. The room shook, dislodging chunks of stone.

Xio beamed, absolutely delighted. "Yeah, like that! How do I do *that*?" With a signature move like that, he'd rival the strongest semidioses, including Auristela.

"We can't just jump ahead," Venganza said with a chuckle. "You'd likely knock yourself unconscious. Let's take another step back: discovering the power before we draw upon it. Why don't you tell me how you feel when you try to call upon that darkness within you?"

It was difficult to hide the disappointment on his face. But Xio was here to learn, and just like every prodigy and mentor he'd seen on TV, they needed to start with the basics before the epic epiphany. This was the beginning of his training arc.

"Well, I can feel vengeful energy," Xio began, choosing his words carefully. "It's like a weight or force in the air around me. Kind of like being in water and getting bumped by the current? And it's got a pulse, too."

The truth was, Xio could always feel the power of vengeance stirring inside him. When he was younger, he thought it was a sense of misfortune—an ability passed down from Mala Suerte.

The outbursts of his power constantly got him in trouble at school—Suerte's priests would come and retrieve him from the principal's office, keeping him at arm's distance, like that would somehow protect them from picking up some of Xio's bad luck.

And even though Xio had never wanted to hurt anyone, he was rarely sorry for it, either. Those kids'd had it coming.

When he said as much to his father, Suerte had been worse than angry. He'd looked disgusted. Well, at least now Xio knew why.

If he wasn't watching for it, low levels of vengeance in people around him could go overlooked. The more vengeance held in their heart, the more noticeable it was. And if he focused on it, and tuned in to it, he could feel it entirely.

It was similar to listening to music while he studied for class. If he wasn't paying attention, he didn't even notice it. But if he listened for it, he could hear the music and understand the lyrics.

"How have your gifts manifested in the past?" Venganza asked, a contemplative hand to his furry chin.

A memory surfaced—fourth grade, jungle gym. An older boy had pushed Xio off the top. Xio landed hard on his back, the wind knocked out of him. He stared up at the boy, whose face was twisted with laughter as Xio struggled to catch his breath. Anger flared in Xio's gut, and through his spotty vision, he saw it happen—like an invisible hand shoved the boy back, his spine arching, his eyes flying open just a second before he crashed to the ground with more force than his mass alone should have allowed.

Thanks to his semidiose durability, Xio walked away without a scratch. But the other boy's forearm snapped in half.

The sharp *crack!* of it reverberating across the playground still appeared in Xio's dreams some nights. That was the first time he'd really *hurt* someone. And it had felt . . . good. Right.

"People—bullies," Xio corrected himself, "would get hurt when I was around. Everyone thought it was just bad luck."

You're the reason I'm like this! he had shouted at Mala Suerte, more times than he could recall. *This is* your *power I'm cursed with!*

Of course, Suerte already knew what Xio hadn't learned yet— his power wasn't related to luck at all.

His real father smiled. "Good. That means you are already very attuned to your own hunger for vengeance. Can you feel it in others?"

Xio nodded. What he now understood to be vengeful energy

had different characteristics depending on the person, but two things were consistent—a change in air pressure, and a pulse. Sometimes it was just a shifting of air, like feeling someone come up behind him. When it was more intense, it made his bones ache and his blood pressure jump.

The rhythm of vengeance he felt could range from a faint heartbeat to a subtle vibration. Strong feelings of anger, revenge, and a hunger for justice literally pushed against Xio. He was constantly getting shoved around by Ocelo's bad attitude.

When he was younger, it had made him moody and stern. Other kids at school avoided him like a mariposa de la muerte—a bad omen. By middle school, he had decided to lean in. If everyone was going to insist he was a troublemaker, then he might as well act like one.

During the trials, Xio really honed his emotional manipulation skills. When he sensed vengeance in another person, he could coax it bigger, like stoking a fire until it took over. Once their eyes turned black and they were consumed by their need to seek vengeance, there was no stopping it. Either a greater force needed to interrupt it, or it just had to run itself out.

"Now, focus on feeling the vengeful energy in this room," Venganza instructed.

Xio nodded and closed his eyes. The Obsidians' thirst for vengeance plowed into him like a truck.

He stumbled back, gasping as a headache squeezed his brain like a vise. Xio's ears popped, every joint in his body aching. It was unlike anything he had ever experienced.

The Obsidians' pulses pummeled him. Chupacabra's shuddered and lashed out like a rabid dog, barely contained. Caos's was especially odd. It felt . . . playful. Instead of powerful strikes, it rolled over him like tumbling waves.

Venganza's was the worst. It was sharp and steady, like hundreds of nails pushing into his skin with every pulse.

Xio crouched over, pressing his palms to his throbbing temples.

Venganza's face curled into a smile. "Excellent."

Just as quickly as it had come, Xio was released. He collapsed forward onto the cold floor, panting and covered in sweat. The searing pain in his head dulled to a thumping ache.

"H-how did you do that?" Xio choked out, staring up at Venganza. His chest heaved as he wheezed.

"I'm Venganza, Dios of Vengeance," he said, as if it were that simple. "There's many things I can do that you'd never be able to manage.

"You seem well-versed in manipulating it in others," Venganza continued as Xio tried to catch his breath. He held out his hand and a ball of crackling black energy bloomed in his palm. "But to be a real wielder of vengeance, you need to perfect the art of channeling the vengeance inside of *you* into a weapon."

Xio perked up and struggled onto unsteady feet. "I've seen other semidioses do that!" he said, eager to show off his knowledge.

"Of course," Venganza said. It wasn't completely dismissive, but enough to give Xio a pang of disappointment. "But vengeance operates differently. Positive emotions aren't as strong as negative ones. Vengeance is infinitely more powerful. What was it you wanted to learn?" he asked. The ball of energy in his hand shrunk and disappeared. "An energy wave, I think you called it?"

Xio nodded vigorously. "Yes!"

Venganza's aura crackled to life around him. With a single gesture, chunks of obsidian—each of a similar size and shape to a mortal human—detached themselves from the walls and formed a circle around Venganza.

A new ball of energy formed between the god's hands. His knobby fingers flexed. A strong force slammed into Xio as the orb burst, sending out a crackling shock wave. The makeshift dummies exploded on impact, pieces scattering across the floor.

Xio had to move quickly to avoid getting hit by any of the shards. "Whoa," he breathed.

Venganza glanced over his shoulder at Caos. With a snap of their fingers, the dummies flew through the air and put themselves back together.

"Thank you, Caos," Venganza said. Caos gave them a small bow.

"You asked to see your father's power, but all you care about is breaking rocks?" Chupacabra snorted.

"A raw obsidian edge is the only thing sharp enough to cut semidiose skin. It can even harm dioses if we're not careful," Venganza spoke in a slow, gentle voice that irritatingly reminded Xio of Mala Suerte.

"I know that," Xio said, with more defensiveness than he meant. "But doesn't that make it an even more powerful weapon?"

"Sure, junior. Bring a rock to a divine power fight," said Chupacabra. "Let's see what happens."

Caos giggled. "I think playing with obsidian makes a delightful party game. Toss a piece back and forth, anyone who loses a finger is out."

Even Chupacabra grimaced at that.

"That is beneath you, son. Any fool or mortal can wield a sharp edge. You hold a gift the likes of which is unfathomable to your enemies." Venganza laid a heavy hand on Xio's shoulder. "Now, conjure your power."

Xio focused on the energy streaming through his veins. Felt the familiar prickle of the skin around his eyes.

"Begin by harnessing your emotions," Venganza instructed.

Eyes closed, Xio searched within, seeking the raw energy that fueled his powers. Moments of anger and betrayal bubbled up, memories of feeling like an outcast. Hands trembling, he struggled to control them.

"Channel it," Venganza urged. "Shape it."

A faint flicker of darkness formed around Xio's fingertips, then dissipated just as quickly. Frustration gnawed at him, but he refused to give up.

"Again," Venganza commanded.

Breathe. Focus. Xio dug deeper into the well of his emotions, willing the shadows to dance at his command. This time, the darkness swirled, growing stronger and more tangible.

"Good, Xio," Venganza said, satisfaction creeping into his tone.

Xio couldn't help smiling, a surge of pride.

He needed this. He needed to prove he belonged here.

"Remember," Venganza said, "control comes with practice. You'll master it in time."

In that moment, Xio decided to trust him. The Obsidians were all he had now. Maybe he could finally find a sense of belonging among these misunderstood gods.

"Again," Venganza said. "This time, condense it into a ball."

Brow furrowed, Xio tried to gather the energy pulsing in his chest. It buzzed and grew, a pressure in his chest. But the bigger it got, the harder it was to contain. Sweat prickled on his upper lip. When he tried to press the energy into a tight ball, it quaked.

"Focus," Venganza encouraged him. "Use yourself as a conduit."

Xio took a deep breath. It had never been bad luck following him around, but the power of vengeance protecting him. That was why people stayed away. It was like they could smell it on him, like rot.

But it kept him safe when no one would, stuck up for him when no one would speak on his behalf. It curled around him and lashed out when someone with ill intent got too close, but now, Xio was old enough to control it on his own. He just needed to practice.

It took all his concentration to keep it contained.

"And release it."

Xio had no idea what that meant, but the shuddering energy grew more persistent, trying to escape. If he didn't do something, he'd lose control of it. So Xio did the only thing he could think of and threw his hands forward, like he was chucking a soccer ball.

The vengeful energy dissipated. When Xio opened his eyes, he found the stone targets untouched and his father watching him. After a long pause, Venganza asked, "What was that?"

Chupacabra burst into yipping laughter.

Humiliation seared Xio's cheeks. "I—I was trying to throw—"

"I said *release*," Venganza said. "Not throw. Try it again."

Xio shook out his arms and exhaled a breath between pursed lips. *Release*, repeated in his head. *Not throw.*

This time, Xio kept his eyes open as he conjured another ball of energy. He almost lost it immediately, distracted by the aura radiating from him. Like Venganza's, Xio's was velvety black, but, unlike Venganza's, it also crackled with neon purple energy.

"*Focus,*" Venganza reminded him.

Determined, Xio gathered the energy between his hands, pressing it into a ball. The blackness got darker as it condensed. The purple energy crackled and sparked between his fingers, fighting to escape. When it felt strong enough, and Xio thought he could contain it no longer, he did what his father told him and released the ball.

It burst and sent out a shock wave. Instead of obliterating the chunks of obsidian, it only knocked them over. "*Yes,*" Xio couldn't help hissing under his breath, triumphantly squeezing his hands into fists.

Venganza nodded his approval. "Much better."

"Ooh, such a quick learner!" Chupacabra said with a hungry look in her eyes.

Xio puffed up his chest, unable to hide his grin. It wasn't as impressive as Venganza's, but it was a start. He wondered if this was what it would've been like at the Academy. He imagined himself standing in a fancy gymnasium, training among the Golds. Becoming a Hero of Reino del Sol.

But vengeance wasn't exactly a good guy move, was it?

Xio tried it a few more times, the strength of the blast growing steadily stronger until the targets were chunks of rubble.

"Do you know how to turn it into a beam?" Xio asked. He was too excited to care about his growing headache or the soreness of his joints.

Venganza sniffed. "Of course."

Xio looked up at him with wide eyes. "Will you show me?"

"Unlike a wave, where the physical force of the emotional energy rapidly expands, like an explosion," Venganza said, "a beam is a concentration of that energy shooting in a specific direction. When you focus the energy, instead of releasing it, aim it."

"Got it," Xio said, and it was only half a lie. The terminology made sense. He always did well in physics, and semidiose powers were a subject he was well-versed in, but theory and practice were very different.

Concentrating as hard as he could, Xio gathered the crackling ball in his hands. But he didn't know *how* to shoot it, and the longer he hesitated, the less control he had. So, Xio did the first thing that made sense and threw his arms out at one of the targets, leaning into it with all his might.

And the ball disappeared in a spark of purple. Xio righted himself and stared at his hands. What happened?

Across the room, Venganza pinched the bridge of his nose. Caos's head swiveled back and forth.

"Was that a practice shot or something?" Chupacabra asked, scratching the side of her neck.

Venganza's brow was furrowed. "Push it," he reminded Xio. "Don't throw it."

Xio clenched his jaw. How the hell was he supposed to know the difference? Stubbornness wouldn't let him give up, so he tried again.

The second time, Xio kept his hands at his chest and focused on pushing. The beam of black and purple shot out from his chest like a fire hose. The kickback knocked him off his feet, right onto his ass.

This time, Venganza said nothing. He only sat on his throne, one leg crossed over the other, and waited to see what Xio did next. Next to him, Chupacabra hopped from foot to foot and clapped her hands, mouth stretched in a twisted smile.

The muscles in his arms trembled, but Xio pushed his sweat-dampened curls out of his face and tried again. He did his best to ignore his own labored breaths as he focused on condensing the energy once again. This time, he changed his stance, mimicking what he'd seen in TicTacs of semidioses showing off their special moves.

Xio rolled his shoulders back to engage his chest and planted his feet solidly on the ground. He tightened his stomach muscles to stabilize his core and made sure his arms were bent at his sides. Before the energy could break free, Xio braced himself and shoved the power forward.

A steady beam of black and purple blasted from his chest. He was so relieved to see it cut through solid stone that it took Xio a few seconds to realize his aim was off. He tried to direct it away from the wall and at one of the obsidian targets but overshot and blasted through three of them before he ran out of juice.

"Better" was the only feedback Venganza gave him.

Xio took a second to catch his breath. He didn't have much left in him. He was plagued by fatigue, his muscles weak and unsteady. It was annoying because Xio wanted to keep trying. He wanted to perfect his skills and show the Obsidians, and especially his father, that he was an asset, not just some weak kid following them around. He was desperate for their approval, but they didn't need to know that.

Squaring his shoulders, Xio tapped into his power again, but his well of energy was nearly empty. He didn't think he could even concentrate it into physical form, let alone create a focused beam.

So, what options did he have?

Xio remembered the strength of the Obsidians' powers he'd felt earlier. He went looking for it again and this time he was prepared for their vengeance. The stench of leather, tobacco, and hot asphalt assaulted Xio's nose. The three distinct pulses pushed and prodded.

If he had used up all his energy, maybe he could borrow some of theirs.

Xio focused on Venganza's needling power and reached out with his mind to tap into it.

A ragged gasp sawed through Xio's lungs. A swell of power surged through his body. His aura expanded into twisting black wisps and purple electricity, licking at his skin. His hair stood on end and it felt like his bones were vibrating, his muscles tensing around them.

Venganza's voice boomed. "NO."

It scared the shit out of Xio, breaking his concentration and severing the connection to Venganza's power source.

Venganza was on his feet, eyes blazing.

Xio shrank back, shoulders hunching to his ears. His whole body quaked. "S-sorry," he stammered. "I was just—I don't know—I—" His thoughts were incoherent, tumbling over themselves in his foggy brain.

Venganza took a deep breath. After a moment, his face relaxed. "That was very dangerous," he said, stern but calm. "You can absorb vengeful energy from others and use it as a weapon, but never from a dios. And especially not from me. You can't handle my power. You wouldn't survive it. Do you understand?"

Xio nodded quickly. "Sorry, I didn't know—"

Venganza held up a hand to stop him. "I understand, but you need to be careful." He reached down and gave Xio's trembling shoulder a squeeze. "I don't know what I'd do with myself if something happened to you."

Xio nodded again, trying to calm his body down. Every nerve in his body felt fried and raw. "I'll be more careful," he promised.

That seemed to appease Venganza. "I think we should stop for now," he announced. "Fatigue is a very serious side effect for young semidioses. Why don't you go rest and recover?"

Xio nodded, but he couldn't help feeling disappointed. He turned to leave, but Venganza stopped him.

"Xio," he said in a disarmingly gentle voice, "I'm very proud to have you by my side."

Xio froze. "I . . ." He didn't know how to respond. He cleared his throat. "Thank you, Father."

Venganza nodded and smiled.

Xio walked out into the night air, high above the jungle. He swayed dangerously on his feet, lightheaded. A maelstrom of emotions clawed their way up his guts. Was this what it felt like to get everything he wanted?

He had done it. He had resurrected his *real* family and caused the sun to disappear from the sky. He would finally see the end of the Golds and the Jades with all their ceremonies and finery and hypocrisy. He was learning to control more power than he could ever imagine wielding. His father was *proud* of him.

So why did he feel like shit?

CHAPTER 11
TEO

Mala Suerte Temple ended up being a lot cozier than Teo expected. A whole floor had been converted into something like a dorm. There was no special treatment for Golds or Sunbearers here. They were given the same accommodations as everyone else. There were bunk beds with mismatched linens, shared bathrooms, and stockpiles of travel-sized toiletries to go around.

Teo didn't know if it was just exhaustion, or the weight of the impending end of the world, but Aurelio was being quiet, even by his standards. Something about the conversation with Suerte had clearly upset him, but as hard as Teo tried, he couldn't think of *why*.

Now wasn't the ideal time to try to get the stoic boy to open up. Teo wanted to talk to Aurelio, see what was going on in his head, but he was bone-tired and in desperate need of a shower. He dragged himself into the tiny bathroom and let scalding hot water pummel his back until the aches and pains in his body eased. When he was done, Teo stared at his reflection in the mirror and was startled by what he saw.

It was like Teo had aged several years in only the last few days. There were dark bags under his eyes and pink, mostly healed scratches on his skin, and his shoulders were hunched by the weight of exhaustion. It was like looking at a different person. The only things that felt reassuringly the same were his iridescent black hair, jade-green top surgery scars, and, of course, his wings.

Teo gave himself his testosterone shot, hoping that would help him feel more like himself.

He toweled off and barely had enough energy to put on the purple cotton pajamas Ana had given them. They were a little scratchy, but clean.

By the time Teo got Niya to settle down for bed—"I'm too excited to sleep! Is this what summer camp is like?"—Aurelio was curled up against the wall with his back to the room, presumably asleep. When Teo finally lay down, he stared at Aurelio's back, trying to come up with something to say to make him feel better. He fell into a deep, dreamless sleep before he could.

What felt like five minutes later, Teo awoke to a warm hand gently squeezing his shoulder.

"We need to get going," Aurelio said into his ear.

Teo groaned and rolled over. According to his watch, it was 6 a.m. What he wouldn't give for just a few more hours of sleep. Or days.

Aurelio was already dressed, backpack on and ready.

"I tried to wake up Niya, but . . ." Aurelio glanced to where she was still snoring in a tangle of sheets.

Groggily, Teo forced himself upright. "I've got it." He gave the arm thrown across her face a shake. When that didn't work, he tried calling her name once. And then twice.

And then he grabbed Niya's pillow and bopped her in the head.

With a sharp snort, she sat upright. "Wha' happened?" she mumbled, squinting into the room.

"Time to get up," Teo said, grabbing his uniform from his bag. "We've got monsters to fight."

Niya stretched her hands above her head and smiled, letting out a happy, sleepy noise. "Yay!"

They grabbed some breakfast from the kitchen where Afortunada priests and local vendors had volunteered to cook and hand out food. The trio—but especially Teo—got a lot of stares as they sat down to eat. People craned their necks to get a look at the semidioses, smiling and whispering.

It was hard to eat with all those staring eyes. It made his skin crawl and his stomach clench. Aurelio and Niya seemed unbothered, but they were used to being the center of attention, and Teo definitely wasn't. He was used to being ignored.

Teo did his best to take a few more bites, but then he gave up and went looking for Ana.

Since the boat they'd gotten in Sol City had been *commandeered* in San Fuego, they needed a new one. A few minutes later, Ana showed them to the docks behind Suerte's temple, where an old deck boat waited for them.

"Sorry," Ana said with a nervous smile. "All the other boats are being used, so it's kind of slim pickings right now."

"Our last one didn't have a motor, so this is already an upgrade," Teo replied.

After exchanging goodbyes with Ana, Niya marched onto the boat. Teo started to follow, but stopped when he noticed Aurelio hadn't moved. He stood there gripping the strap of his pack, a troubled expression on his face. Teo could tell by the look in his eyes that Aurelio's thoughts were a million miles away.

Or rather, in the heart of Los Restos with Auristela.

Teo also knew Aurelio wasn't stoked about being on a boat again. After what had happened last time, he didn't blame him.

"It'll be okay," Teo said, low enough that Niya couldn't hear. "You said we need to get going, and a boat is way faster than walking, right?"

Aurelio only hummed in response.

"Can't be any worse than wandering through a jungle full of Celestials." Teo nudged him.

Aurelio sighed, snapping himself out of his trance. "I wish you hadn't said that."

Teo bumped him with his shoulder. "Come on. If shit goes south, I'll just fly you to safety again," he teased.

Aurelio rolled his eyes, but even in the dark Teo caught the red blooming in his cheeks. "Eventually you won't just be able to charm me into every situation," he muttered. "It'll wear off." He straightened his posture and started down the dock.

"Wait a second!" Teo chased after him. "What's that about me being charming?!"

The boat bobbed as Teo plopped down onto the cracked beige upholstery that lined all the benches, opposite Niya. Aurelio busied himself messing with the controls at the captain's chair. The engine spluttered to life, spewing exhaust. They pulled away from the dock, leaving Afortunada behind them.

"If we follow this river south, we'll eventually reach the lake we have to cross to get to Los Restos," Aurelio said, checking the compass on his watch as he consulted his paper map.

As they got farther from Afortunada, the landscape changed dramatically. Sparse trees became dense jungle that seemed to close in around them. The sounds of bugs and howler monkeys drowned out the engine. Teo heard things climbing through the branches overhead and slithering through the underbrush along the banks.

It was like the worst ambient noise playlist imaginable.

With any trace of Afortunada—or civilization, for that matter—hours behind them, the river felt endless.

"Are we there yet?" Niya whined, half-heartedly polishing her Unbreakable Blade on her shorts.

A ball of fire danced in Aurelio's palm. "To Los Restos?" he asked, scanning the river. "No."

"It feels like we've been out here forever," Teo agreed. With the perpetual night and lack of sleep, time seemed meaningless.

"It's been seven hours," Aurelio clarified.

"SEVEN HOURS?" Niya's screech carried through the trees, pausing the buzz of insects for just a moment before they started up again.

"*Niya,*" Teo snapped, searching the trees and straining his ears for any sound that could be a Celestial on the prowl.

Suddenly, the engine spluttered and spewed one last huff of exhaust before cutting out.

"What happened?!" Teo asked Aurelio as he crossed the deck again, unscrewing the ventilation cap of the fuel tank.

"We're out of gas," Aurelio murmured, a deep frown set into his features.

Teo fought the urge to groan. *Great.* "Maybe there's more on board?"

All three searched the boat.

"I found some old fishing gear," Teo said, pulling out a rusty metal tackle box.

"I've got some propane lanterns!" Niya added, holding one in each hand.

She bounded over to Aurelio, sending the boat rocking. Aurelio white-knuckle gripped the gunwale.

"Niya!" Teo snapped.

"Sorry—I didn't mean to!" Niya said with an apologetic smile.

Aurelio tried to muster up a brave face. "I'm fine," he said. He lit the lanterns with his flint-tipped gloves and hung one on either end of the canopy, making it easier for them to see, at least.

"No gas, though," Teo said, looking around. This was the very last place he wanted to get stranded. And if they had to walk the rest of the way to Los Restos, Teo might just sacrifice *himself*—

"OH, OH, OH!" Niya pulled something from a storage bin under one of the seats. Teo's chest lifted with hope, but when she revealed a dingy, sun-bleached life jacket, it plummeted back down. "Here!" she said, chucking it at Aurelio.

He easily caught it out of the air. "I know how to swim," he said flatly.

"Sure you do!" Niya said, like she didn't believe him. "But this way you're safer!"

It was a nice gesture, but Teo didn't think Aurelio was used to being anxious, or weak. Especially in front of other people.

So when Aurelio insisted, "I'm *fine*," and set the life jacket on the bench, Teo shook his head at Niya as she opened her mouth to argue. She just huffed and threw herself down on the bench, giving the boat another good jostle.

Aurelio sighed. "I can at least use this to steer," he said, pulling out a weather-worn oar.

Teo shifted in his seat. Not having a working motor in a motorboat seemed like an issue, but he tried to be optimistic. "Might be better than running a noisy motor, right? Less chance for something to hear us?"

Aurelio considered this for a moment. "I suppose," he decided. "But we'll be at the mercy of the current."

"That doesn't seem so bad!" Niya said, leaning over the edge of the boat to dip her finger in. "We wanted to go downriver anyway, right?"

"It *is* the direction we want," Aurelio said, taking a seat near the engine again, oar laid across his lap. He pulled out a laminated map from his pack. "Just not as fast as I'd like." Aurelio threw Teo a pointed look.

"Hey, it's still faster than walking!" he objected. "And we get to rest our feet, which is a nice break."

Niya kicked her dirty feet up on the bench. "I'm enjoying it!"

Aurelio made a displeased noise at the back of his throat.

"You know, you're gonna get wrinkles if you keep frowning like that," Teo said.

But all Aurelio did was frown deeper and rub his forehead.

As they got settled in, Teo couldn't help feeling like he was reliving the boat trip they took to the final trial. Had it really only been a few days? It felt like a lifetime ago. That sinking feeling crept back into his stomach. With all the chaos, it was easier to push everything to the back of his mind. The trials. Teo botching the sacrifice. Xio's betrayal.

Xio. That part stung the most.

Teo shuddered, feathers ruffling. He wrapped his wings around himself, snuggling into them like they were a blanket and doing his best to ignore the queasiness in his stomach. And the flash of eyes peeking at them from the depths of the jungle as they floated down the river.

Aurelio decided he would take the first shift. Teo figured it was because Aurelio didn't trust him or Niya, which was fair, but Aurelio would need to rest at *some* point, even if Teo had to bully him into it.

Niya fell asleep across one of the benches almost immediately, but Teo had a harder time. He was too amped up, and between Niya's snores and the cacophony of howler monkeys, frogs, and buzzing insects, Teo couldn't coax himself to sleep.

Instead, he discreetly watched Aurelio steer the boat as the river pulled them along. He finessed the oar like someone who *wasn't* afraid of water. Probably another skill he'd picked up at the Academy.

The slow-moving current meant they weren't being quick, but it was at least easier for Aurelio to navigate around the rocky boulders breaking the water's surface.

The smell of wet earth and clean water in the thick night air was occasionally cut by the sticky sweetness of overripe fruit. Spiderwebs stretched between branches and hanging moss, catching droplets that sparked like diamonds in the lanterns' light. The shrill echolocation of bats bounced between trees, accompanied by the errant *splash* of a fish feasting on bugs and the *plop* of a startled turtle diving back into the water.

The *clink* of metal brought Teo's attention back to Aurelio. He was hunched over and fiddling with something, the rusted tackle box open in his lap.

"What are you doing?" Teo asked, propping himself up on his elbows.

Aurelio had set up a couple of fishing rods in the holders on the sides of the boat. When the light caught them just right, Teo could make out the thin lines stretching into the river.

"I figured I'd get these set up and see if we catch anything on the way," Aurelio murmured, his attention focused on tying an iridescent yellow jig to the end of the line.

"You know how to fish?" Teo asked, impressed.

Aurelio shrugged and cast the line. "Not really, but I've watched videos on TúTube before."

Teo exhaled a laugh. "TúTube. Of course. You never cease to amaze me with your many talents."

Aurelio grunted and dipped his chin to his chest, but even in the darkness, Teo was certain he was blushing. "I just like learning stuff."

Satisfied, Teo grinned. He'd need to compliment Aurelio more often.

"You know," Teo said, sliding down the bench until he was right next to Aurelio, "I've always wanted to see all of Reino del Sol—"

"I know," Aurelio said a little too quickly, like he was worried Teo thought he wouldn't remember.

"But definitely not like *this*," Teo finished, gesturing around. "I mean, this place probably looks pretty in daylight or whatever, but I'm starting to think I don't like the outdoors."

"That tracks," Aurelio agreed as he adjusted their course with the paddle.

Teo scowled. "What's that supposed to mean?!"

"You're not exactly the outdoorsy type," Aurelio said, far too reasonably. "You really didn't like sleeping in the cabin, or on those boulders—"

"Yeah, and those boulders turned out to be monsters! Clearly I sensed it!"

Teo caught the amused tug at the corner of Aurelio's mouth. "Have you ever been camping?"

"I grew up in a city!" Teo spluttered, a hot flush rushing to his cheeks. "Also, it doesn't make any sense to *pay money* to sleep outside without a real toilet and cook your food over an open fire!"

"You also have very soft hands," Aurelio added, enjoying himself now.

Teo smirked. "When exactly did you notice I have soft hands?"

Aurelio's stunned expression was so satisfying that Teo decided to let him change the subject.

"It's not a *bad* thing," Aurelio said, fingers tapping the handle of the oar. "Auristela isn't outdoorsy, either."

Teo placed a hand over his heart in faux surprise. "Noooo, that can't be! Little Miss Instagrafia Influencer? Her three-inch acrylics just scream, *I love hiking!*"

Aurelio chuckled. "Our mom never let us take time off from training, but when we were eleven our dad convinced her to let us go camping for a weekend in the monarch butterfly cloud forests north of San Fuego. She only agreed because he works at the Academy as a survival instructor, so he presented it to her as a field trip. Stela was pissed because she wanted a real vacation, and she hates camping. She can also be pretty hard on our dad. We never got to see him much when we were growing up—which was Mom's decision, but Stela always says if Dad really *wanted* to see us he'd find a way or—whatever, sorry. Anyway, she refused to help with anything—finding food, shelter, any of that. She just sat on a rock and pretended she had a phone signal to text with while my dad was trying to help me get better at starting fires with my flint gloves. I don't think she said two words the whole day until it started getting dark, and our dad still hadn't come back from searching for more dry wood for me to practice on. I got scared and couldn't focus enough to spark a fire to go looking for him.

"When Stela realized I was crying, she jumped right into action. Grabbed my hand, set a whole branch on fire to light our way, and stomped through the woods, yelling obscenities. Stela was convinced it was some terrible training exercise meant to frighten me, but we found our dad with his leg trapped between two felled trees. Looking back, it was pretty funny to see my angry eleven-year-old sister throw a grown man over her shoulder and then lecture him for the hour it took to hike back to the car. She didn't let go of my hand the entire time."

Teo had never heard him say so many words at once.

"She's always been a little overprotective of me, acts like the older one even though we're twins. I think it probably started when we were younger and I had trouble making friends, and then—" Aurelio stopped. He seemed almost surprised by himself, like he'd said more than he meant to.

Teo's chest tightened. "You're worried about her."

"Yes," Aurelio admitted, which surprised Teo. Then he exhaled a small laugh. "But then I remember who she is and feel a little less worried. I half expect to show up to Venganza's temple and find Auristela has already rescued everyone and burned the place down."

"Honestly, I'm shocked they haven't sent her back yet," Teo said, grinning. "I bet she's giving them a whole lot of trouble."

Aurelio's smile was soft and affectionate. "Absolutely."

Splash.

Teo yelped at the small noise, his wings shooting out and knocking one of the fishing rods overboard. "What was that?!" he gasped.

Unfazed, Aurelio leaned over the side of the boat.

"Be careful!" Teo snapped, grabbing his arm.

Aurelio blinked, his copper eyes pinging from Teo's face to his hand. "I'm pretty sure it was just a fish."

"No, it wasn't!" Teo said, but only because he wouldn't be able to survive the humiliation if it was.

Aurelio looked over the side of the boat again. The corner of his mouth twitched as he motioned for Teo to move closer. "Come see."

Hesitantly, Teo scooted closer to him and, holding the gunwale in a death grip, peeked over.

A school of fish swirled and twisted in the water. They were round, about the size of Teo's fist, and absolutely dizzying. They glowed like gems in kaleidoscopic hues of turquoise, ruby, and amber. There were even some iridescent white ones that reminded Teo of opals. Some were solid while others had spots and stripes.

"Discuses." Aurelio leaned in. "And they're *glowing*. They must be a unique species native to Los Restos."

"Are they safe?" Teo asked, mesmerized.

"I mean, probably," Aurelio said with a hint of amusement. "They're just fish."

"Listen—I've had a rooster spit fire at me and then got attacked by a pile of rocks, so forgive me for being a bit suspicious of wildlife at the moment," Teo grumbled.

To prove his point, Aurelio removed his glove and slid his hand slowly into the water.

The fish swarmed, and for a brief moment of terror, Teo thought they might attack and pick his bones clean like piranhas. But all they did was inspect Aurelio's hand with their tiny round eyes and maybe give an experimental nudge before continuing on their way.

Teo stole a glance at Aurelio from the corner of his eye. He gazed down into the water, dark lashes brushing the tops of his cheeks. The light reflected off fish scales and sent undulating colors dancing over his deep brown skin. Aurelio grinned—tired but peaceful—and warmth flooded Teo's stomach.

"Fine, I'll do it!" Teo announced with a huff. "I'm not gonna let some goldfish make me look like a coward!" Especially not in front of Aurelio. Teo gingerly dipped his hand into the warm river water—but like in a confident way, not a shaky, hesitant way—and held his breath.

At first, the fish ignored him, apparently too enamored with Aurelio—relatable—but an electric green one with white squiggly lines swam over to check him out, quickly followed by a second and a third. Teo leaned back as far as he could without taking his hand out of the water as they got closer.

In a matter of moments, a whole crowd of luminescent fish lit up the water. They brushed up against Teo, their delicate fins tickling his fingers.

"Not so bad, huh?" Aurelio said in a soft voice.

"Just because they haven't gnawed off my hand *yet* doesn't mean they *won't*," Teo replied, keeping a close eye on them. "Probably just trying to lure me into a false sense of security."

Aurelio let out a surprised laugh and when Teo looked up, he was gifted with the full brightness of Aurelio's smile. The kind that crinkled the skin around his eyes and showed off his perfect teeth.

Teo could feel how goofy the big smile plastered across his own face was, but he had no control over it. Aurelio was so pretty, it was almost unreal. Starlight danced across his warm brown skin and twinkled in his copper eyes, illuminating his features so powerfully it was almost as if the stars themselves had come down to dance around Aurelio's gorgeous face—

Only, hang on. The light *was* dancing around Aurelio's face. Teo blinked, letting his eyes refocus.

"Uh, do you see those, too? Or am I hallucinating?" Teo asked, mesmerized, as the tiny yellow-green lights bobbed around the boat.

Aurelio's brow lifted. "You mean the luciérnagas?"

"Ooh, is that what they are?"

"Wait, you've never seen luciérnagas before?"

"I've seen them in, like, cartoons and stuff."

"Seriously?"

"I'm an indoor guy!" Teo said defensively. "The closest thing I've seen to luciérnagas are the headlights of cars from the top of Quetzal Temple. And even if we did have any, the birds would probably eat them all!"

"Birds don't usually eat fireflies. They taste bad."

"How do you know that?"

Aurelio cocked an eyebrow. "How do you *not* know that? You're the one who's part bird."

"Okay, but that doesn't mean I go around *tasting bugs*—"

"I've seen you eat a bug—"

"WE WERE SIX."

Aurelio laughed again, and Teo's next argument died in his throat. He didn't even care what they were bickering about, he just wanted to keep Aurelio smiling.

And now—gods, now they were just silently staring at each other. How long had it been since they'd spoken? A minute? A year? If this were a movie, this would be the moment one of them leaned in and ...

Teo waited, but Aurelio wasn't leaning in. Did that mean *he* was supposed to lean in? Who decided which one of them was supposed to initiate? What if Teo went in at the wrong angle, and they bumped noses? Aurelio had such a cute fucking nose, Teo would hate to cause it harm.

Or what if Aurelio wasn't even *trying* to put out his cool, sexy, broody hero vibes? What if he was just living, and the romance of the situation was all in Teo's head? What if, gods forbid, Teo leaned in, and Aurelio pulled away?

Aurelio's eyebrows creased—*Fuck, did I say that out loud?*—and his eyes drifted from Teo out to the river. "Did you hear that?"

Teo was struck silent, but after a moment, he managed, "Wuh?"

Suddenly, the luciérnagas blinked out. The fish shuddered and quaked against Teo's fingers, sending goose bumps up his arm before they all scattered in a flash of scales. Both Teo and Aurelio wrenched their hands from the water.

"Uh, is that normal?" Teo asked.

Aurelio was alert, carefully scanning their surroundings. "No."

"Where are they running off to?"

Fire sparked to life in Aurelio's palms. "What are they running *from*?"

They both froze and listened. For a moment, it was eerily quiet, nothing but the gentle rush of the current and Niya's rattling snores. Teo had just enough time to think, *Maybe it's nothing,* before a soft cry carried on the wind.

Teo strained to hear over the heartbeat thudding in his ears. "Is that a fucking baby?"

"Why would there be a baby?" Aurelio muttered, leaning toward the sound with a puzzled look on his face.

It was getting louder, like whatever was making the noise was moving toward them in the dark.

Bubbles erupted in the water around them.

"What is that?" Aurelio leaned farther over the edge of the boat, trying to get a better look.

Meanwhile, Teo leaned as far away as physically possible. "Absolutely not!" He didn't know what was going on there, but he did not like it and was not interested in finding out.

There was a time and a place to be a Hero, but stuck in a tiny boat in the dark with creepy baby noises was not it.

Something big and heavy flew out of the water, slapping Aurelio square in the face. Teo shouted in surprise. Aurelio jerked back, stunned into silence as a giant frog flopped into his lap and bellowed a low *WRRRBT*.

"What the—?" Teo's heart pounded frantically in his chest. A frog? Why was a frog throwing itself out of the water and *into* their boat like that?

Aurelio seemed to be equally confused because all he did was blink down at the creature. His face was completely blank like his brain just short-circuited. 404 error: Semidiós not found.

Suddenly, dozens of frogs leapt out of the water, hopping into the dense foliage of the jungle. It wasn't *just* the frogs, either. All along the riverbank, gem-bellied fish of all shapes and sizes were throwing themselves into the air, flopping and gasping, trying desperately to escape the water.

"Why are they doing that?" Teo asked, squinting into the darkness, before adding with a nervous laugh. "Is this another wild animal thing I don't know about?"

"No," Aurelio said curtly. "We need to get out of here."

As if pulled by the same strings, Teo and Aurelio jumped to their feet.

Teo nudged Niya awake.

With a violent snort, Niya shot upright, one of her braids obscuring her vision. "I'm up!" she exclaimed. "What's going on?!"

"We need the other oar," Aurelio instructed, yanking open a storage cabinet.

"Oar! Got it!" Niya hurriedly dug through another cabinet, tossing life jackets and rope as she searched. "Oar, oar, oar," Niya muttered. More supplies went flying. "Okay, *it's not that big of a boat*! Where is it?!"

Teo winced as the crying crescendoed to shrill wails.

Niya's head popped up, cocking to the side like a dog's. "Wait—is that a *baby*?"

"That's what I said!" Teo exclaimed, ready to crawl out of his own skin. "If this is some La Llorona bullshit, I swear to Sol—"

Niya was on her feet again. She flicked her wrist, and the Unbreakable Blade materialized from her bracelet.

"You gonna row with that?!" Teo demanded.

"No—I don't know!" she shouted back, gesturing wildly with the blade. "What am I supposed to do?!"

"You hear a baby crying and your first instinct is to pull out a *sword*?"

"IT'S ALL I HAVE, TEO. WHAT DO YOU WANT FROM ME?"

A small splash sounded behind them. Teo raised his hand for quiet, and Niya let the sword drop to her side. There was something there, just beyond the edge of the boat. Teo bent over the side to look—there was a hand, tiny and human-shaped, frantically waving from the depths.

Terror sliced up Teo's spine. "*Holy shit.*" Teo surged forward, but Niya caught him by the back of his shirt.

"That doesn't look right, Teo! Is that *fur*?!"

Teo tried to wrench himself free of Niya's iron grip. "Just because it's an ugly baby doesn't mean we can let it drown!"

"It's an ahuizotl," Aurelio said, like Teo was supposed to know what the hell that meant. But judging by the alarmed expression on Aurelio's face, it was bad. Very bad.

"Well, what the f—"

WHAP!

With a horrifying dexterity, what looked like a furry tail ending in a monkeylike hand whipped out of the water. Before Teo could react, it snatched him by the wrist.

Niya screeched.

Teo gagged. "GET IT OFF—"

In one swift movement, Aurelio yanked the furry hand free and set it on fire. With another terrible wail, it disappeared into the river.

"Are you all right?!" Aurelio stood over Teo, concern twisting his face. He reached down to offer Teo a hand up. "Do you—"

Before he could finish his sentence, Teo heard a wet *slap.*

For a moment, everything slowed. He heard Aurelio suck in a gasp. Saw the tail wrapped around his neck. Saw his brown eyes grow wide between the splayed, fur-covered fingers gripping his face.

Then everything sped up. Before Teo could even think, Aurelio was yanked off his feet and dragged overboard.

"Aurelio!" Teo stumbled to dive in after him, but Niya's arms tightened around his waist like a vise. In one movement, she yanked him back.

"*Stop!*"

"He can't be in the water!" A burning pain shot through Teo's heart. "*He's gonna drown!*"

"AND SO WILL YOU IF YOU GO AFTER HIM!" Niya shouted back, towering over him. She was so angry and frightened, her breaths sawing between her teeth.

In a sudden burst, Aurelio popped up out of the water, gasping and flailing. His eyes darted frantically, disoriented. Teo had never seen Aurelio—who was always so stoic, so calm—look panicked. It made him sick to his stomach.

Teo threw his arm out as far as he could, but he was still a few feet out of reach. "Aurelio!"

Teo had nearly gotten himself killed, and Niya was so obsessed with protecting him that neither of them had been looking out for Aurelio.

"*Where did the life jackets go?*" Niya exclaimed, diving for the storage lockers.

When he finally spotted Teo, Aurelio's eyelids fluttered with relief. His frantic movements settled and he swam for Teo, slicing through the water with practiced precision.

But he wasn't fast enough.

Bubbles gurgled in the river. Wakes rippled through the water, heading right for Aurelio. Two fins cut through the surface—no, not fins, but pointed ears with notches missing, covered in slimy fur. As they got closer, something dark rose from beneath the surface.

Teo stopped breathing.

"Oh *shit*," Niya hissed.

The creature was canine and grotesque, its fur a slick black marbled with ribbons of stars and milky white eyes that reflected like twin moons. As it got closer, its jaw opened, revealing several rows of sharp teeth.

The chilling cry of a baby gargled from the back of its throat.

"*Hurry!*" Teo shouted.

Aurelio glanced back over his shoulder. His precise strokes became frantic, his eyes bulging as he swam for his life.

"Stay out of its whirlpool!" Niya yelled, but it was too late.

The water churned and swirled around Aurelio, pulling him toward the ahuizotl. It drew him in faster than he could swim. He tried to kick the beast's head, but its tail whipped out again. The monkeylike hand clenched around his wrist, its tiny fingers digging into Aurelio's skin and pulling him down as he fought frantically to escape.

Teo caught one last glimpse of his terror-stricken face before he went under.

"RELIO!" Teo screamed, rushing to go in after him, but Niya slammed him back onto the bench.

"NO!" Niya said, her trembling fists at her side. "I'll save him! That's my job!" Before Teo could do or say anything else, Niya plunged into the river headfirst. She wasn't as fast as Aurelio, but her powerful kicks sent water spraying into the air as she swam into the whirlpool.

Teo searched desperately, but there was only the churning water, picking up speed as the boat started to drift toward its center.

If they weren't fast, they'd get sucked right in.

"*Niya!*"

Treading water and fighting the current, she twisted around, head on a pivot. "Where is he?!" she called. "Can you see anything?!"

Teo searched the dark water and finally spotted it—the faint golden glow of the Academy uniform. "THERE! HE'S THERE!"

Niya sucked in a breath and dove down.

Teo's wings twitched and flapped, panic rattling his bones. He fought against the urge to take flight and go after them.

After agonizing moments, Niya burst through the surface of the water, clutching Aurelio. She hooked her arms under his armpits from behind, pulling him to her chest as her legs kicked wildly, dragging him back toward the boat.

Teo's relief was short-lived, crushed by the realization that Aurelio wasn't moving. His head lolled as Niya fought to keep his face above the water while fighting the deadly current.

When they were finally within reach, Teo grabbed Aurelio and pulled with all his might. He'd almost gotten him back into the boat when the ahuizotl's tail shot out like a whip. Its freaky little hand grabbed Aurelio's ankle. It nearly yanked him back into the river, but Teo gripped tighter. Aurelio was cold to the touch and trembling. There was no way in hell Teo was letting him go.

If the ahuizotl wanted Aurelio, he'd have to take Teo along with him.

The side of the boat dug painfully into his hips, the only anchor keeping them from going overboard. With an annoyed wail, the ahuizotl pulled harder. The boat groaned beneath them, slowly tipping. "*Let—go—of—him!*" Teo gritted out. He tried to flap his wings to gain some traction, but all he did was rock the boat more perilously.

Niya appeared next to Teo, dripping wet and angry. With a grunt, she scooped both Teo and Aurelio into her arms and yanked them aboard. Before Teo could recover from being dumped on the floor, Niya was across the boat and digging in her pack.

"I've got an idea!" she said, tossing extraneous supplies as she frantically searched. "Where is it?!"

Teo scrambled over to Aurelio. "Hey, wake up!" he said, patting his cheek.

Aurelio's skin had paled to a sickly hue and purple tinged his lips, but the important thing was that he was breathing.

Niya let out a triumphant cry, thrusting a strange bundle of fabric up into the air. "I got it!" She stumbled over herself to get to the back of the boat, shouting at Teo, "Hang on to him!"

Teo hooked his arms under Aurelio's armpits and pulled him tight against his chest, hanging on for dear life.

At the back of the boat, Niya fumbled to untie the drawstrings of what Teo now saw was a bag. She wrenched it open, releasing an explosive gust of wind. The force of it shot them across the river like a skipping stone.

And straight into the bank. The boat came apart with a loud *crunch*, and all three of them got thrown onto the shore.

Teo spat some mud out of his mouth. "Are we alive?"

"I think so!" Niya replied, staggering to her feet.

"What was that?!"

"Tormentoso's Bag of Winds!" Niya exclaimed, clearly pleased with herself. The sack was still open, gripped tightly in her fist, spewing wind and tugging at her wet braids. She let out a low chuckle. "Heh. Bag of Winds."

Thunder crashed overhead, followed almost instantly by a flash of lightning. Niya's smug look disappeared.

"Close the bag!" Teo shouted.

Niya cinched it shut, but the damage was done. A split second later, a heavy blanket of rain fell from the sky in a torrential downpour.

And because the near drowning, crashed boat, and sudden rain weren't enough—the ahuizotl had to prove itself as deft on land as it was in the water. It emerged from the river and climbed atop the broken boat, perching easily on four catlike limbs, poised to strike. Its lips peeled back over its many rows of teeth and it let out a deep, gurgling growl as it stalked toward them.

Teo looked at his friends. Niya had already pushed herself too far—even as she braced her sword, he saw her movements were sluggish and stiff, dragged down by exhaustion. Aurelio was slumped on his side, face pale and chest rising and falling in quick, shallow breaths. Still, Niya staggered to kneel, bracing herself with her blade while determination blazed behind Aurelio's eyes as he tried to sit up. Teo moved to help brace him.

It was like the universe's worst game of rock, paper, scissors—Earth, Fire, Water. And the stupid demon dog was about to win.

Was the whole quest destined to be like this? Unbeatable monster after unbeatable monster, barely escaping with their lives, tipping ever closer to ultimate failure until—

"HEY, ASSHOLE!"

Teo figured he was hallucinating. Because why would a teenager be standing on the bank of the river, waving their arms over their head and shouting at him? They were human size, wearing a large raincoat with the hood pulled up and a pair of muddy boots. And they were, remarkably, real.

"What are you doing to that ahuizotl?"

"What are *we* doing to *it*?!" Niya demanded.

The ahuizotl's head snapped in the stranger's direction.

"Watch out!" Teo shouted, panic squeezing his throat.

But the person ignored them, rolled their eyes, and held something out at arm's length over the river. When they spoke again, their voice reminded Teo of the way his mother spoke to newly hatched chicks: "Look what I've got!"

Teo squinted in the dark. Held between their thumb and forefinger was a small, rose pink seashell.

"Go get it!" The stranger threw the shell into the river where it sank with a tiny *plop*.

Teo had no idea what was happening, and when he turned to Niya, she looked just as perplexed, her face screwed up in a way that would've been hilarious in any other circumstance.

The ahuizotl let out a wet huff through its nostrils before turning back to Teo and his friends. The new person's triumphant expression dropped.

"Damn it—" They dug in their pockets as the snarling ahuizotl stalked forward. "Here!" They tossed a handful of colorful shells into the river.

The ahuizotl didn't even glance at them. It crept toward Teo, tongue lolling and tail whipping back and forth.

"Got anything in there more helpful than seashells?!" Teo called.

The person made an aggravated sound at the back of their throat, yanked the backpack from their shoulder, and riffled around inside.

A second later, they started chucking fistfuls of sand dollars into the river.

Inexplicably, the ahuizotl paused and turned away from Teo.

"Do you like those?" the person asked. "What about these?!" They pulled out a massive, iridescent abalone shell.

The ahuizotl's ears perked up.

Teo had no fucking clue what was happening or why, but it seemed to be working.

The stranger smiled triumphantly. "I've got more!" Two more abalone shells plunked into the water. "Oh! Is that what you want?!" They pulled out half a dozen chunks of raw jade.

The ahuizotl's posture changed immediately. Its tense body relaxed and it trotted curiously toward the person. Before it got too close, they shouted, "Go get them!" and sent the jade flying into the river.

The ahuizotl let out a weirdly happy yip before running across the destroyed boat and diving into the river with barely a splash.

Teo blinked. "The fuck just happened?"

"We were saved by some feral jungle teen!" Niya exclaimed. She threw her pack over the side of the boat onto dry land and began examining the waterlogged contents.

The stranger eyed them, skeptical but maybe semi-entertained.

Teo had bigger things to worry about—namely, the half-drowned boy in his lap.

Aurelio looked up at him, dark circles under his eyes that looked more like bruises. He gave Teo a weary attempt at a grin.

Teo frowned and tried to suppress the anxious fluttering in his pulse. He reached for one of the backpacks, but Aurelio tugged it out of his reach, cradling it close to his chest even as his head listed, exhausted, to the side.

Teo rolled his eyes. "Can you stop being an ass and let me help you get your jacket on?"

Aurelio relaxed his grip and did as he was told. The rain jacket provided by the Academy was lightweight and waterproof and had a thermal reflective lining for keeping warm. Teo helped Aurelio into it and zipped it up all the way.

The collar covered Aurelio's mouth, but Teo could tell he was frowning.

"Don't complain," Teo told him sternly.

"I'm not," Aurelio grumbled.

Teo tugged his hood up for good measure. "Great." He then put on his own jacket. Niya seemed unbothered by the rain.

"Well, that could've gone a lot worse," the stranger said, stomping over to them in heavy work boots. She pulled down the hood of her jacket, revealing glasses and black hair shorn short on the side with a messy swath of curls on top. Hands on her hips, she observed the trio with an annoyed expression. "You're lucky you've still got all your eyes, nails, and teeth and everything."

"My *nails*?" Niya repeated, alarmed.

"How did you do that?" Teo asked, gaping up at them from the muddy ground as rain continued to pour.

"I've got better questions," the stranger replied. "Who are you, and what are you doing in Los Restos?"

CHAPTER 12
TEO

"You don't know who we are?" Niya asked, confused.

The stranger's wide brown eyes regarded them skeptically. "Am I *supposed* to?" she demanded.

"Not even this guy?" Niya added, hooking her thumb toward Teo. He waved awkwardly.

The stranger only raised an eyebrow.

If their faces weren't a dead giveaway, maybe she hadn't tuned in to the trials. After San Fuego and Lago Relámpago, Teo was actually relieved to run into someone who didn't know him.

"We came from Ciudad Afortunada," he offered. "We were headed south when that monster attacked us."

"You were headed south," the stranger repeated. "The only thing south of here is Los Restos."

"That's good, because that's where we're heading," Teo replied.

The girl gestured to the moonless sky. "In the dark. In the middle of the apocalypse."

"*Apocalypse* seems a bit harsh," Niya said.

"What else do you call it when the *sun disappears*?" the stranger demanded as she took a few wobbly steps down the slope of rocks. If she was going to help them, she clearly wasn't happy about it.

She offered a hand to Niya, who ignored it and stubbornly charged up the bank unaided. The stranger's hand hung there in the air for a moment, an annoyed look on her face, before she sighed and offered it to Teo.

"He needs more help than I do," Teo said, struggling to get Aurelio up and onto his feet. It was tricky work getting him up the hill. Teo slipped in the wet earth twice but managed to keep from falling on his ass.

"I don't feel so good," Aurelio murmured, barely awake.

"No kidding," Teo grunted, trying to support the muscular demi-god's full weight. Aurelio was shivering, his skin abnormally cold. Even his knot was askew, leaving escaped locks of wet hair stuck to his face.

It was freaking Teo out. If they didn't get him dried off and warmed up soon—he refused to think about it.

The girl's expression shifted to full-blown suspicion now that they were all standing up. "You're very tall," she said, looking between Niya and Aurelio. Then to Teo she said, "Well, you're kinda average."

"Yeah, I get that a lot," Teo said. His wings unceremoniously shook themselves out, flinging mud and river water.

The girl sucked in a sharp breath, eyes bulging. It took Teo a full three seconds to remember that most mortals had never seen a person with wings before.

"You have *wings*," she hissed.

Teo gave her a confused look. Why was she so angry? Did she recognize him?

"Yucca!" a new voice shouted out from behind the trees. "I heard screaming, but not your screaming. Is everything okay?"

The stranger—Yucca, apparently—slapped a hand to her forehead, annoyed. "*Fucking*—" She cut herself off before raising her voice. "Down here, Paz!"

A new figure came frolicking out of the woods.

Frolicking was the only word Teo could use to describe the way she moved. Like Yucca, this girl was another human teenager. If Teo had to guess, he would have said they were both about the same age as the semidioses, maybe a little younger.

Unlike Yucca, Paz had a friendly smile and rich brown skin. Her hair was done up in tiny front-to-back cornrows that fed into a bun of chunky twisted braids at the top of her head.

She took in the crashed boat, the drenched and battered trio, and Yucca. "The heck happened over here?"

"What part of *stay with the wagon* wasn't clear?" Yucca snapped.

Paz put her hands on her hips. "I'm supposed to just *stay with the wagon* when I hear screaming?"

"Yes!"

"What if you were in danger?!"

"I wasn't! I was helping these fools!" she said, gesturing to the trio. "They ran into another Original."

Paz whistled, impressed. "Which one?"

"Ahuizotl," Yucca said curtly. "I just threw some shells at it. Wasn't a problem."

"Uh, it was definitely a problem!" Niya said, wringing out one of her braids. Teo wasn't sure what good that would do, since it was still pouring rain.

Yucca's flat expression didn't change. "Where did you say you were from again?"

Teo was happy to answer, but Niya didn't give him a chance.

She crossed her arms over her chest, clearly trying to match Yucca's standoffishness. "Where are *you* from?"

Yucca quirked an eyebrow but offered no reply. "And the wings, where did you get those from?"

"My, uh, my mom..." Teo hesitated, bracing himself for her reaction. "Quetzal."

"I *thought* you looked familiar!" Paz chirped with a wide smile. "You're that Jade kid who just won the Sunbearer Trials, aren't you?"

"*What?!*" Yucca barked, at the same time Teo muttered, "Shit."

"You're a damn *Sunbearer*?" Yucca put her hands on her hips, and Teo was suddenly reminded of standing in the principal's office back at Quetzlan High.

"Ease up, Yucca—he's cool, I think!" Paz said, her words coming out too fast. "I was doing a supply run to Afortunada last week and saw posters of him all over the place! They were really rooting for him, 'cause he was gonna be the first Jade to win or something like that." She beamed. "He's a Hero!"

Teo's stomach gave a queasy twist. "I don't know about all that," he said, rubbing the back of his neck. He was distracted by the strange way Paz and Yucca were talking, like the trials were an entirely foreign practice. "What city are you two from?"

Paz laughed. "We're not from a city! We're from here!"

Niya blinked. "Here?"

Yucca slapped her hand on her forehead again. "Paz!"

"What?" Paz said defensively. "It's not a big deal!"

Except it *was* a big deal.

"You don't live in a city?" Teo repeated, his brain running a mile a minute.

"Technically it's a village," Paz corrected him. Yucca groaned at her side.

"You're out here by yourself?! With no one to protect you?!" Niya demanded, looking Yucca over. Her aggression quickly melted away to concern. "But you're so small!"

"I've never heard of a village on the Los Restos border," Teo said, genuinely confused. "Who's your patron?" Maybe there was a smaller, lesser-known Jade diose near Los Restos that he didn't remember.

"We don't have one," Yucca snapped.

It didn't make any sense. "How would the gods not know about that?"

Paz froze. "Mm," she hummed. "I shouldn't have said anything," she muttered to herself before adding louder to the others, "What are *you* doing out here? Shouldn't you be flying around Reino del Sol, lighting up your magic rocks and stuff?"

"We are on a *very* important quest to bring back the sun!" Niya divulged proudly without a second thought. More meekly, she added, "Which . . . we kind of messed up in the first place."

"Oh, great!" Yucca exclaimed, sarcastic. "Of course that was you guys!"

"It wasn't *us*," Teo corrected. "It was *me*."

"*Actually*, it was that little shit *Xio*!" Niya spat his name. "No more blaming yourself or I'll punt you back into the river." She turned her attention to Paz and started a rapid-fire explanation of the whole sequence of events. "Now we're on a quest to rescue our friends and bring back Sol to banish the Obsidians once and for all!"

Paz's eyes went wide, like all the pieces were falling into place. "*Oh*, so you're the *Sun*bearer, but you didn't bear the sun?"

Niya nodded vigorously. "*Exactly!*"

"And now everything is all perma-night and the Obsidians are back?" Paz guessed.

"You've got it!"

"Wild!"

"I know!"

Yucca elbowed Teo. "Did you get any of that?" she asked.

"Kinda," Teo said. "I'm only semifluent in this brand of ADHD."

Paz let out a low whistle and shook her head sympathetically. "Well, that *does* explain a lot. As soon as the Obsidians turned out the lights, all the critters at *our* borders started flocking to yours!" She said this with a little laugh, like it was a funny happenstance rather than the literal end of days. "Yucca, that must be where all the Originals came from, too!"

"Originals?" Teo repeated.

Yucca sighed. "Yeah, like that ahuizotl you just met. They're basically bigger, badder versions of the creatures that normally live out here. We call them *Originals* because, according to our ancestors, they were the first of their kinds."

"There are *more* of that thing?" Teo asked, squirming uncomfortably as he remembered the way it had wrapped its nasty little hand around Aurelio's neck.

Yucca waved him off, though. "Just little ones."

"Oh, cool, awesome," Niya muttered. "Just little evil-baby-hand-water-dogs. Great. Love that."

Yucca rolled her eyes. "Okay, well, this sure has been fun, but Paz and I need to be getting home now," she said, shooing them away. "Good luck on your godly quest, or whatever."

"C'mon, Yucca, we can't just leave 'em here," Paz said. She stood up from Aurelio's side. "They're all beat up from that fight, plus it's raining—"

"So?!" Yucca threw her hands around a lot when she spoke. "I can't control the weather, Paz!"

Paz gave her a disapproving look. "You don't seriously expect me to believe you're okay with *abandoning* these strangers who are cold and wet and hurt just because—"

Yucca huffed. "They're not strangers!" she insisted. "You said it yourself, they're the Sunburners—"

"Sunbearer," Niya corrected her. "And technically it's only Teo—"

"I don't care!" Yucca shouted. She pushed her glasses up onto her head and scrubbed her eyes. "We come from a place where there *are no dioses*, and we've worked *very hard* to keep it that way! We don't trust outsiders, especially not semidioses!"

"Whoa, whoa, whoa!" Teo said, raising an arm in surrender. "We're not going to hurt anybody—we want to *stop* the Celestials!"

Niya moved to his side, chest puffed up. "Yeah, we're the good guys!"

A sarcastic laugh bucked in Yucca's chest. "Oh, fantastic! In that case, please, come right on in!" she said, flashing a sharp smile as she opened her arms wide. "Infiltrate our blessedly diose-free village that's managed to live outside the power of your barbaric immortal parents for generations! Can I get you anything?" she asked with fake sincerity. "A healthy snack, maybe a nice blood sacrifice?"

Niya perked up. "Do you guys have Takis?"

Aurelio leaned toward Teo and Niya. "I think she's being sarcastic."

"I am *very much* being sarcastic, Man Bun!"

Aurelio jerked back, his hand going to his hair. Teo choked on a snort.

Yucca dropped the theatrics, carefully enunciating every syllable. "You are *just as dangerous* to us as Celestials."

Niya crossed her arms, spluttering unintelligibly.

"Okay, well, we're not here to harm you," Teo tried.

"It's more complicated than that! You heard Niya's stories!" Paz argued. "They didn't mean to shut off the sun, and they especially didn't mean to resurrect the Obsidians—that was their other friend, who turned out to be a *total* jerk—"

"He's not our friend!" Niya interrupted angrily. "We don't like him anymore!"

"And now they're trying to fix it!" Paz continued. "Doesn't that put us all on the same side?"

"No, Paz, it does not!" Yucca shot back, her face red with barely contained rage. "We don't have a side! Our side is *staying the fuck out of it*, remember? What if they call their gods here, and we end up like the Obsidian cities at the end of all this—massacred or left for dead?"

Paz's face became surprisingly stern. "They're trying to bring back the sun. That's a good thing for *all of us*, right?"

Yucca glared at her but eventually huffed. "I guess."

"Listen, Yucca, we completely understand your hesitation," Teo said, trying to sound diplomatic. "But if you could just bring us to whoever is in charge here to explain—"

"Wait, aren't you in charge?" Niya asked, pointing at Yucca.

"I'm fucking sixteen," Yucca deadpanned. "And we don't do *in charge*. Power in the hands of one or the few corrupts. We have your parents to thank for that lesson," she added bitterly. "Power needs to be spread across the many. We're a community—when we make a decision, we make it together. And we'd betray that rule by bringing you there."

Paz looked hurt, but she stood straighter. "I was raised to believe that *community* meant helping your neighbor," she said. "*They* are our neighbors."

"You know that's not what that means!" Yucca said with an exasperated groan. "They're not our neighbors, they're—they're—"

"Dioses?" Paz guessed. "But they're half mortal, too. Right?" she said, turning to Teo, Niya, and Aurelio for confirmation.

Yucca glared at them over Paz's shoulder.

Teo nodded emphatically. "Exactly." It was the best argument anyone had made so far, so he was going with it. "Listen, we're not trying to steamroll the thing you guys have going on here," he said. "We genuinely just need somewhere to rest and get our energy back so we can continue our mission to *fix the sun*. This isn't about us versus them—this is for everyone."

"Why don't you get rid of all the dioses while you're at it," Yucca growled under her breath.

"And we seriously *did* get our asses kicked by that Original ahuizotl," Teo added. "We're really not supposed to get him wet—" He jerked his head in Aurelio's direction.

The Son of Lumbre looked particularly pathetic, still damp and exhausted. All the talking over one another had clearly overstimulated him. Between that and being physically drained and processing everything they'd just learned, he was fully closed in around himself, shoulders hunched and arms crossed over his middle.

"It's only a matter of time before he's full on disassociating at this point," Teo said. "I *barely* know what I'm doing at any given moment. And Niya—"

She smiled. "I'm fine!"

"Okay, Niya's fine," he continued. "But we could *really* use a break." Yucca opened her mouth to argue, but Teo pressed on. "Plus, we're basically the only ones who can stop the world from ending."

Yucca pressed her lips into a hard line.

Teo exhaled a short laugh. "Look, I'm not happy about it, either, but we're kind of out of options and almost out of time."

Yucca looked over at Paz, who jutted out her bottom lip and made some very impressive puppy-dog eyes.

"Argh!" Yucca threw up her hands. "*Fine!* One night. We'll have some of our healers look you over—assuming human medicine works on your freak god bodies—but tomorrow you're gone. And you never come back, and you never breathe a word about us to your mommies. Got it?"

"I won't tell mine," Aurelio said, solemn and earnest.

"I don't even *have* a mommy!" Niya agreed pleasantly.

"We won't tell *anyone*," Teo agreed before adding, "I'm Teo, by the way."

"Niya," Niya supplied. "The angry one in need of medical attention is Aurelio."

"We have to keep moving—" Aurelio swayed on his feet, pale green washing over his face.

Teo tightened his grip on him. Aurelio was already getting worse. He was shaking so hard his teeth clacked together. "Hey, are you okay?"

When Aurelio turned to him, his gaze was unfocused. His eyes seemed clouded and dull, more a faded brown than their usual bright copper. Aurelio opened his mouth, probably to insist he was fine, only to swoon to the left.

"Relio!" Teo tried to catch him, but Aurelio was five inches taller and had about fifty more pounds of muscle on him. Luckily, Niya stepped in before Teo could be crushed.

"All right, then, no more walking for you!" she exclaimed, hooking one arm under Aurelio's knees and the other around his shoulders, bridal style.

"We've got a first aid kit back in the cart," Paz said, happily leading the way.

"C'mon, Teo!" Niya called back. "I'm not carrying your soggy boyfriend around the jungle all day! Or night! Whatever it is!"

Yucca was clearly uncomfortable with this development. She shared a wary glance with Teo before giving in and stomping after the other two. Teo followed.

Paz had left their cart and donkey a short distance from where she'd found them. The pair of humans led the way back, bickering quietly. Niya was clearly trying—and failing—to eavesdrop while she carried Aurelio. Teo hovered anxiously.

When they approached, the donkey—Louisa, according to

Paz—brayed nervously. Teo didn't blame her. Paz reassured Louisa with some scratches and a banana.

The cart itself was smaller than the luxurious bed Teo had had at Sol Temple, but bigger than his old twin back home. It had two big wheels and was packed with plastic crates full of food, some textiles, and several shopping bags from big department store chains. A wooden rod at each corner suspended a patchy green tarp to keep the supplies—and anyone sitting on the cart—mostly dry.

It was a group effort to lay Aurelio down between two crates of mangoes. Teo pulled out the Decanter of Endless Water with the Gem of Regeneration and made Aurelio gulp down as much as he could. At least that would jumpstart the healing process.

Yucca stood at the foot of the wagon, glaring.

"To be clear," she said carefully. "I do not trust you people."

"Well, we didn't trust you first!" Niya snapped back.

Paz went back to the front of the cart. "Niya, you can sit up front with me and tell me all about your fancy magic powers. Teo, you sit in back with Yucca and the sleepyhead. Make sure he doesn't puke—"

"*Hang on,*" Yucca demanded as Niya sprang into action. "We can't let them know how to find the village. They have to be blindfolded."

Teo blinked. "Seriously? We're in the dark in the middle of the jungle." He waved his hand in front of his eyes. "I can barely see as it is, let alone track wherever you end up taking us!" Teo glanced back. "Niya—do you know where we are?"

"Not a clue!"

He turned back to Yucca. "See?"

"Don't care!" Yucca sang. It was the happiest Teo had seen her.

She climbed into the cart and dug around in one of the boxes. She pulled out a roll of fabric, ripped off a strip, and gestured for Niya to step forward. She put up a fuss but let Yucca tie the fabric over her eyes.

Niya fidgeted. "This stinks. Literally." She sniffed. "Like fish."

"Perks of living on the river," Yucca said jovially, then motioned for Teo to step up next.

Paz took them each by the hand and guided them onto the cart. Teo clumsily found his way to Aurelio's side and sat down. He kept his thigh pressed against Aurelio's to make himself feel better. Usually, the heat that poured off Aurelio was scorching, but right now, it felt more like the embers of a dying campfire.

Teo clenched his fists in his lap as he sat in the pitch-blackness, willing Louisa to make quick work of their journey.

"So," Niya said conversationally, "do you guys just have monsters crawling all over the place in your village, too, or?"

Paz laughed. "Just the friendly ones." Yucca groaned, like an audible eye roll. "We're pretty good at keeping the troublesome ones out of our way, though."

"*How?*" Teo asked, remembering how calm and collected Yucca had been, even against the giant ahuizotl. "How do you know about Celestials—I mean, Originals?" he clarified.

"They teach us in, like, second grade about all that stuff with the gods and the Obsidians," Yucca said. "We also learn about how to deal with creatures like the ahuizotl, since there's so many roaming Los Restos. I'm surprised *you* don't know. You're half gods, aren't you?"

Teo was once again frustrated by the lack of real-world information he ever got in Quetzlan. Even someone from a border village in the middle of the jungle knew more about monsters than he did?

"Is it true you bleed rocks?" Paz asked.

"I mean, basically," Niya said before launching into a long explanation about jade and gold blood.

Paz and Niya spent the rest of the ride chatting like old friends. Niya even regaled Paz with some daring stories of her past heroism. Niya hadn't been able to show off in front of anyone since they'd left Afortunada, so she was desperate for attention that Paz seemed all too happy to give. Yucca spent the entire ride silent aside from a disgruntled hum every now and then.

Teo didn't blame her for not trusting them. He wondered what Reino del Sol must look like to a mortal who had grown up on the outside, fighting monsters left behind by careless gods after a war that—according to Suerte—had wiped out all the humans who had once populated Los Restos.

Did the dioses seriously have no idea there was a whole community of mortals living just beyond their borders? Or did they just not care? And what did it mean, to live in a place with no dioses at all?

Aurelio stirred beside Teo. He put aside all his complicated thoughts about gods and humans.

"Hey, can I take the blindfold off now?" he asked, blindly reaching for Aurelio.

"No."

Teo pulled it off anyway.

"Hey, put that back on!" Yucca objected.

Niya yanked hers off as well. "If Teo's not wearing it, I'm not wearing it!"

"You—"

"It's okay," Paz told Yucca, patting her arm. "You did a good job, and we're almost there, anyway."

Teo helped Aurelio get settled against some bags of feed. He looked better, but usually Aurelio was alert, his head on a constant swivel. Now he was near motionless, heavy eyelids drooping.

It was freaking Teo out.

Aurelio didn't even put up a fight when Teo settled in next to him and used his wing to shield them for added protection. The rain had stopped, but water still fell from the jungle canopy and plinked onto the muddy ground, pools of it gathering in the dips of the canopy and dripping heavily onto the tarp.

Up ahead, two lanterns came into sight, hung from posts at the beginning of a trail of planks. Louisa pulled the cart onto the boardwalk. The wheels turned much easier over solid wood than they did in the sticky mud. Gradually, the path inclined until it was a few feet above the water below. It reminded Teo of the fifth trial.

Around them, the jungle had changed. As the path snaked through the maze of woody vegetation, trees with massive fronds became sparse as the swamp took over. Mangroves and shrubs with dense tangles of prop roots looked like they were standing on stilts above the water.

Clouds of bugs flocked to the lanterns that lined the path every twenty feet or so. Frogs sat on tangled tree roots above the scummy water, their croaks in melody with the water dripping down black-trunked trees. Clumsy turtles parted overgrown reeds while lizards skittered up trees. Squeaking bats swooped under low-hanging moss, and in the distance, Teo could hear an owl.

The ambient noise mixed with the soothing sound of rainfall and Niya's stories must've created some kind of soothing ASMR for Aurelio. Teo sat with an amused grin as Aurelio's chin kept dropping to his chest. Eventually, Teo just gave his arm a small tug and Aurelio slumped against him. He could feel the slow rise and fall of Aurelio's chest against his side, his breath tickling Teo's neck.

Heat bloomed in Teo's cheeks. In the dark where no one could see them, it was safe for Teo to grin and enjoy the feel of Aurelio leaning against him. He shifted into a more comfortable position and adjusted his wing, careful not to jostle the sleeping boy. Teo snuck his arm around Aurelio—just to help hold him in place, obviously.

"We're here!" Paz called from up front. "There it is!"

Teo craned his neck to see. "It" was a massive fence made out of solid wood that stood at least three times taller than him.

"Damn, that's a big-ass wall!" Niya remarked.

Teo was distracted by the claw marks of different shapes and sizes that scarred the wood. At the very top, the fence pitched forward.

"Well, that's foreboding," Teo muttered to himself with a shudder. He assumed it was to keep out all the terrible monsters that roamed freely in the borderlands. But regardless, the farther they went from home, the closer to danger they'd be.

At least this place *had* a fence.

Teo gently shook Aurelio's shoulder until he opened his eyes. "Time to wake up, sleepyhead," he teased.

Aurelio sat up and glanced around. "Where are we?" he asked, squinting into the dark. He still looked like shit, but at least he was talking.

"At a secret village on the border of Los Restos," Teo said.

Aurelio stared at him and waited. When Teo didn't say anything, Aurelio said, "I don't understand the joke."

"I'm not being sarcastic this time."

"It's a lot prettier on the inside!" Paz assured them.

"I'm still not happy about this," Yucca muttered. She took a deep breath to steady herself, then marched up to the gate. A massive flood-light turned on, frying Teo's retinas. He threw up his hands to shield his eyes.

There was a loud *thunk* followed by clanking chains. Slowly, the massive door began to open.

Aurelio tried to get his bearings. "Where is this place?"

"End of the world, by the looks of it!" Niya said, far too cheerily.

Aurelio looked around the cart and frowned over at Teo. "Did I—"

"Fall asleep and curl up on me like a little cat?" Teo teased with a grin.

Aurelio's cheeks flushed.

Teo laughed. "Of course not! Aurelio, Son of Lumbre, would never be caught dead in such a compromising position."

"You snore like a little puppy!" Niya announced. "It's adorable!"

Aurelio's mouth opened and closed uselessly, which only made Teo laugh more. Honestly, after everything they'd been through it was nice to laugh about *something*.

Paz flicked the reins, directing Louisa through the gate with Aurelio in the back. The others hopped down to follow on foot.

Teo was immediately confused. He was expecting a village full of people, but instead they walked into a huge livestock area. The whole thing was on a raised platform above the swamp, but different areas were covered in sod, hay, and something that looked like sawdust. Various shelters had been built around the enclosure with slanted tin roofs that collected rainwater into barrels. More lanterns hung around the perimeter and along pathways.

Animals milled around in sectioned areas. There were goats grazing, ducks paddling around in what looked like a plastic kiddie pool, and pigs snuffling happily in a pen. There were even cows and a welcoming party of three donkeys that trotted over to Louisa.

"Uh, where are all the people?" Teo asked Paz, sending a nervous glance at the giant gate as it closed behind them.

Paz laughed like he'd just made a very funny joke. When Teo only blinked at her, she stopped. "Oh, you're serious!" Paz jerked her chin. "Look up!"

Teo, Niya, and Aurelio all tipped their heads back.

"*Whoa*," Teo breathed.

The village was at least a hundred feet above their heads. Structures had been erected around branchless tree trunks, above the mangrove roots but below the canopy. They were supported by massive stilts that plunged into the swamp below. Smaller platforms formed a ring around the livestock pen, and a much bigger one sat in the middle, directly above their heads.

From the ground, it was hard to see everything, but Teo spotted more lanterns hung around the railings, illuminating dozens of curious faces looking down at them. Adults spoke in harsh whispers while kids flocked to see what all the commotion was about.

Teo didn't really know what the protocol was in a situation like this, so he just awkwardly waved up at them.

Yucca was practically vibrating with anxiety. "We are in so much trouble," she hissed. "We have one rule. One rule! No outsiders. Especially no *semidiose* outsiders who just made the sun disappear."

Paz led them to a wooden elevator where they positioned the cart and released Louisa to her waiting donkey friends. The lift was run by a water mill. When Paz engaged a lever, a series of pulleys started, slowly raising the elevator with them on it.

"This is *so* cool!" Niya said, practically hanging off the side of the railing.

"Seriously," Teo breathed, trying to take it all in.

Paz puffed with pride. "We've worked hard at keeping our village functional by using what the swamp and jungle provide," she explained. "But we do need to go to the cities for more complicated things like batteries, medical supplies, and food to supplement what we can't provide for ourselves. And we're always looking for ways to improve!"

As they traveled up through the tree system, they passed precarious rope bridges that a group of teens raced along with impressive dexterity. There were also more plank paths with slightly sloped switchbacks and moving ropes with handles that someone in a wheelchair used, their companion walking along beside them.

"It's like a ropes course!" Niya laughed gleefully. "I want to try!"

When she hitched up a leg to climb over the *moving elevator*, Yucca let out a distressed cry. Teo locked his arms around Niya's waist.

"Niya, *no!*" he scolded, anchoring himself to keep her in place. "I don't think even your Gold body could take that fall."

Niya pouted.

"Oh, don't worry!" Paz said with a nonchalant wave of her hand. "We've got nets set up as safety precautions!"

Teo shot them a look. Keeping Niya safe from herself was a full-time job, and Paz was not helping.

But to his surprise, Niya scoffed, shoulders slumping. "Well, that's no fun," she grumbled, but a second later, she gasped. "Are those *slides?*"

Sure enough, they passed the unmistakable polished plastic of a tube slide curving around the lift.

"It's the easiest way to get down during an emergency," Paz said, pointing to where more of them twisted through the trees. "It's the quickest, most accessible option we could think of. And they're just *really* fun," she added with a bright smile.

Niya was downright giddy, and, maybe under different circumstances, Teo would be, too.

As they continued their ascent, the lift cleared the lower canopy, widening the view.

"Whoa," Teo breathed, gripping the rail a little tighter.

With the moon gone, it was starlight that danced along the top of the lower canopy. He couldn't see far, but the jungle they'd spent days navigating stretched seemingly endlessly to the north.

Beyond the river stood Los Restos. The jungle was a smudge of impenetrable black against the landscape. There were no lights, and Teo couldn't even make out the lines of the trees. It was like the darkness had swallowed everything up. Teo wondered where Venganza's temple stood, how far it was, and if Auristela, Dezi, Marino, Ocelo, Xochi, and Atzi were okay.

He also worried about Xio, but that felt in direct conflict with his worries for everyone else.

The lift shuddered to a stop.

"And here's the village!" Paz announced, throwing her arms wide.

The tree houses were all on one main level. There were platforms among the trees, set in a ring around the livestock area down below, which made a great vantage point for keeping an eye on the animals and surrounding areas. Groupings of small houses made out of interlocked logs and thatched roofs sat on each platform with an outdoor communal kitchen, complete with an adobe oven, at the center.

Paz led them to a large platform constructed in the center of everything that held one large, squat building. "This is the Great House!" she said. "It's basically our community center. We use it for gatherings, celebrations, a safe haven during emergencies, votes—"

"Figuring out what to do with random semidioses you found in the jungle?" Teo guessed.

"Well, this is the first time *that's* happened," Paz admitted. "But yeah!"

Yucca let out a strained noise.

Paz ignored her. "And it's where the council meets."

Teo felt the sudden urge to solidify their plan, before he charged into whatever *council* they were about to be presented to. "So, when we get in there, should I start at the *beginning* beginning, or just the part where Yucca saved us from that big monster?"

Hands on her hips, Yucca gave them a cross look. "First of all—we don't call them *monsters*. How would *you* feel if someone called you a monster, just because you're bigger than they are?" she asked, pointing up at Niya.

Niya shrank back. "I would feel sad," she agreed.

"The creatures from Los Restos have been here just as long as we have, maybe longer," Yucca went on. "Your dioses may get some twisted pleasure from slaughtering them for sport, but we don't do that here. Our policy is to capture and release back to the other side of the river."

Niya sighed and rubbed her forehead. "This is a lot to process."

"But how do you . . . protect yourselves?" Aurelio ventured carefully, like he, too, was afraid to incur Yucca's wrath.

"Just like Yucca did for you guys!" Paz piped in. "We lure them away, or distract them, or whatever. You said you went to school to learn how to fight, right?"

Aurelio and Niya nodded.

"Well, we learn how to . . . not do that!" Paz explained. "To build a different world, we needed different tools, so we learned how to deal with animals as peacefully as possible."

Yucca nodded in a very self-satisfied way as Paz spoke.

"So, you just . . . don't kill anything?" Niya asked, frowning like she was having a hard time understanding.

"We didn't say *that*," Yucca said, irritated. "Sometimes we have to use violence to protect ourselves, but we try to avoid it at all costs."

"How long have you been here?" Aurelio asked.

"Since the Dioses' War," Yucca replied. "We've spent centuries turning this swamp into our home, safe from you all, and we plan on keeping it that way. Which includes bringing you to the council so we can decide what to do with you, so come on," she said, ushering them toward the Great House.

Teo followed Yucca into the large tree house. Inside was an open space filled with people. Adults stood chatting while kids chased one another around tables and chairs. There were people with food and drinks, and groups of others mending clothes and nets.

Yucca headed to the back of the room, where two large wooden doors stood open, but they were quickly gaining attention. Niya and Aurelio stood a head above most, and there was the matter of Teo's bright green-and-blue wings that stood out like a beacon no matter how tightly he tucked them.

Conversations paused and kids toppled over one another to get a better look. Curious murmurings filled the air as Yucca brought them into the next room.

A dozen or so people sat around a massive circular table in its center, their conversation halting as they spotted Teo and his companions.

Yucca heaved a big sigh. "We've got a situation," she announced.

Friendly smiles rapidly turned to apprehension and confusion. Teo forced his mouth into an uncomfortable smile and held his breath. He had no idea what to expect from this council—if they would help them, or just kick them out like Yucca seemed to want.

Teo hesitantly stepped forward and explained that the three of them had been competitors in Reino del Sol's recent Sunbearer Trials when the ceremony was hijacked by Obsidians, resulting in the whole "the sun is gone" situation. Niya jumped in every so often to embellish the details, especially the heroic ones.

When Teo finished, there were shocked gasps all around the table.

"They wanted you to *kill* someone?" exclaimed one woman with gray hair and wrinkles around her eyes, horrified.

"That sucks!" said a teenager who looked barely older than Teo himself.

"And because you didn't... the sun has gone out?" a middle-aged man said, slowly trying to piece everything together as he bounced a toddler on his knee.

"What a fucking mess," a girl in her twenties said, rubbing her temples.

"Those damn dioses," grumbled an older man with a bushy gray mustache.

Teo was relieved by their reactions. He wasn't the only one who saw how horrific the trials were. The people in this village didn't even like harming monsters—of course they thought the idea of a human sacrifice was barbaric.

The old woman turned to them with a solemn expression and asked quietly, "What are you going to do now?"

Guilt sank into Teo's gut. A whole community had separated themselves from Reino del Sol to protect their people from the dioses, only to get dragged back into it by a wayward Jade.

It took Teo a second to realize the woman was talking to him, specifically, so he scrambled for an answer that would make him sound more heroic than he felt right now.

"We have a plan," he said firmly. "Venganza—the Obsidians—have the Sol Stone. If we can get to them in Los Restos, and distract them enough to get the Sol Stone, we have a chance to resurrect Sol so they can banish the Obsidians again."

"Sol?"

"Does this mean another war?"

Worried chatter broke out.

Right. Teo had forgotten that Sol wasn't the almighty savior to everyone.

"We're trying to *stop* a war from happening," Teo explained. "If we don't get the Sol Stone and resurrect Sol to stop the Obsidians, it will turn into an all-out war among the dioses."

Frightened voices rose.

Teo spoke louder. "But *we*"—he gestured at Niya and Aurelio beside him—"won't let that happen. I'm so sorry I brought you all into this. But I promise to do everything I can to make things right," he said.

Debates broke out immediately. Their presence, along with the loud voices, was drawing more people into the council room. Teo felt claustrophobic, trapped under the crushing weight of reality.

Yucca sighed and pinched the bridge of her nose. "This is going to take a while," she said, looking at Paz.

"Why don't I take you guys back to my place while they figure things out?" Paz offered the trio with a pitying smile.

"ALL RIGHT, LET'S BE CIVILIZED!" Yucca barked to get everyone's attention while Teo, Niya, and Aurelio followed Paz out. "I'd like to remind everyone that we have rules during a meeting! We can all sing together, but we all can't talk at the same time."

Paz led them to her home, and even though it was just the next platform over, it felt like it took forever. It felt like a parade, if anything. People stared as they walked past. It was weird to see Niya smile and wave while they received looks that ranged from curiosity to anger. Aurelio was entirely unfazed, just going through the motions like he had been this whole trip, and Teo was just too tired to care. At least Aurelio was doing better thanks to Primavera's gem.

Time was slippery without the sun to mark the hours, but Teo guessed it must be late into the evening by now. He wondered if the villagers had a way of keeping time, like the electronic clocks he'd grown up with in Reino del Sol. Their entire setup here was amazing, beyond anything he ever could have imagined lying just beyond the borders of his world.

Paz's home was small but cozy. She dragged out some extra blankets, and the trio took over the cramped living room. Aurelio and Niya set up camp on the floor, and Teo took the couch since he was the only one short enough to fit on it. Paz left them with some snacks before heading back to the Great House.

Showers were the first priority. Their suits were waterproof, but that was no help with being dunked in a river, not to mention the gallons of sweat from trekking through the jungle. Struggling to get his spandex pants up and down was like trying to wrestle his old binder on after a hot shower.

"We need dry, clean clothes for you to change into," Teo said, reaching for Aurelio's bag.

Aurelio took it. "I can manage that on my own," he said, sitting on the floor as he slid open the zipper.

Teo paced circles around Aurelio. "Get something warm!" he told him. Suddenly, Teo jumped. "Wait! Isn't water bad? Should you not even take a shower?!"

Aurelio glanced up at Teo with an amused grin.

Teo frowned back. "Will it make you worse?!"

When Aurelio snorted a small laugh, Teo threw his hands up. "Fine then, die! See if I care!"

Aurelio stood up, his clothes tucked under one arm. When he passed by Teo, Aurelio lightly touched the small of his back. "I appreciate your concern," he murmured in a low, smoky voice before disappearing into the bathroom.

From the corner of the room where she lounged on the floor, feet propped up on a coffee table, Niya coughed, "*Down bad.*"

"What?" Teo swiveled around to face her.

She stuck a fistful of chips into her mouth, feigning innocence. "I didn't say anything."

Teo stared absently at the bathroom door. He remembered the way Aurelio had stumbled during the fight with the stone jaguars. And again, with the ahuizotl. Like his movements were a half step behind.

All the pieces fell into place. "*Shit,*" Teo hissed.

Niya turned, brow knit in concern. "What?"

"Aurelio's slipups," Teo said. "You know how he kept hesitating with the stone jaguars? And back there with the ahuizotl?"

"Yeah, he really doesn't like being wet—"

"He's used to being half of a team," Teo pressed. Guilt and sympathy soured his stomach. "I don't think he's actually hesitating. I think he's instinctively waiting for Auristela to step in."

Niya's expression softened. "But she's not there."

Teo's chest ached. "Right."

The two of them sat in the uncomfortable silence that followed, listening to the muffled sound of the shower. Teo had spent so much time worrying about *getting* to the Gold semidioses, he hadn't any time to process that they were gone.

A few minutes later, Aurelio stepped out of the bathroom in a pair of clean shorts and another one of his slutty tank tops. Steam billowed off his bare shoulders and his skin had a healthy flush.

"Do you need to eat something?" Teo asked, following Aurelio around the living room. "Or drink? Tea?"

"I'm fine," Aurelio said, digging into his backpack.

Teo frowned. "You always say that."

"Well." He stood up and looped his long, wet hair into a rope before fastening it back into place. "This time I mean it."

"Oh, well, *that's* reassuring."

Aurelio huffed a laugh as he plopped down onto his nest of blankets. "I'm joking."

"No, you're not," Teo grumbled, crossing his arms and leaning against the doorjamb. "You don't even know how."

"Oh my Sol, would you two stop flirting!" Niya crooned through a mouthful of chips.

Teo's face burned red. He spluttered uselessly, refusing to look at Aurelio. Niya ignored him.

"AURELIO, SHUT UP AND SLEEP. TEO, GO TAKE A SHOWER, YOU STINK."

Teo tried to argue, but then Niya began hurling homemade tortilla chips at him until he left the room. The shower was basic—mostly just a bucket with holes drilled into the bottom and heated water that fed in through a hose. He washed his hair and wings three times with shampoo that smelled like papaya from a little tub. It felt amazing to be clean and have his aches and pains soothed.

He had no idea how long he'd been in the shower, but by the time he was done, Niya and Aurelio had completely passed out. Niya had fallen asleep with her legs still propped on the coffee table, the empty paper bag on her stomach and tortilla chip crumbs all over her white pajamas. Her mouth hung open and her sawing snores felt especially loud in the small room.

Teo had to hop over a sleeping Aurelio, who was curled up on his side with his back pressed against the base of the couch. His arms were wrapped tightly around one of the fluffy blankets as he held it to his chest, his face buried in the soft material.

Teo sat there and watched the slow rise and fall of Aurelio's breath, fighting back the urge to—well, he didn't know what. Lock him in a padded room where nothing bad could ever hurt him, and fill it up with sweets and all the fun things he hadn't been allowed to do before.

Perfect, golden-boy Aurelio, who had the power and the prestige to be exactly the kind of professional Hero Teo had always wished he could be—and who had known nothing but suffering because of it. Instead of empowering Aurelio, his mother and the Academy had only torn him down, made him feel inadequate, made him feel like he would never be enough. Teo hated that—hated all of them—hated the whole stupid system. And he couldn't stop thinking about the things Yucca had said.

We don't do in charge ... *We're a community.*

Teo thought he knew what that word meant, growing up in Quetzlan. But whatever the mortals in this treetop village had going on was entirely different from how things worked *anywhere* in Reino del Sol. It almost reminded him of Afortunada—the mortals there had rallied together to defeat the celestial monsters before the semidioses had even arrived. His entire life, Teo had felt resentful of the Golds with all their pomp and power, but maybe ... Well, maybe it wasn't just the *Golds* that were the problem.

For the first time since it all happened, Teo let himself remember the anger on Xio's face. "*Don't you get it?!*" the younger boy had screamed. "*I don't need your help, I don't want you to save me!*"

In Reino del Sol, they had all grown up with the story that Sol gave humanity to the dioses to protect—but had the mortals ever asked for that protection? The gods and their children reigned over the mortal cities—they kept the people safe and sheltered and fed. Every ten years, they sacrificed one of their own to keep the Obsidians away, because the Obsidians had tried to enslave all of humanity.

Right?

Yucca had said, *We'll end up like the Obsidian cities at the end of all this—massacred or left for dead!*

His mother's feather tickled his neck. Maybe Teo was just being paranoid. So what if a group of rogue mortals on the outskirts of Reino del Sol thought the dioses were the bad guys? None of them had actually been around during the war, not like Teo's mom or the other dioses. But then, there was also that mosaic at Suerte's temple...

Teo sat up and angrily fluffed up his pillow, scouring his brain for anything Quetzal ever said about the war. His memory came up blank. He wasn't sure his mom had *ever* mentioned fighting the Obsidians.

She'd never mentioned that Teo had an older sister who was sacrificed to the trials, either.

He wanted to believe that his mom would never do something so horrible—but then again, didn't *everyone* want to believe that about their parents? Niya certainly thought Tierra could do no wrong. But it wasn't hard to imagine someone like Lumbre, so cold and distant to even her own children, as the villain in Paz and Yucca's bedtime stories.

Teo sat up and pulled Tuki out of his pack before flopping back down on the couch. At this point, he didn't care if his friends knew about his stuffed toucan. He needed the comfort of home. Teo heaved a sigh as he rubbed his thumb over Tuki's soft bill. When had everything gotten so complicated?

Probably right about the time that stupid sunburst crown had appeared on his head.

Aurelio made a noise below, like a tiny snort. Teo couldn't help smiling a little, and as sleep clouded his eyes, he decided to push away all thoughts of Golds and dioses and humanity, and let himself dream about the cute boy asleep beside him.

CHAPTER 13
XIO

Xio stalked down the stairs, his footsteps echoing off the cold stone walls. He had a woven basket full of meager food, small cups, and a jug of water. The last place he wanted to be was in the dungeon with the Golds, but it was his duty to tend to the prisoners. Or, as Venganza put it, *make sure they're still breathing.*

When he got to the bottom of the stairs, voices floated down the tunnel.

"Stay awake, Marino!" Atzi urged.

Marino's weak voice trembled. "Is . . . is Dezi okay?"

Xio hesitated and peered around the corner into the dimly lit hall. The flickering torchlight cast eerie shadows on the Golds huddled in the dark.

Marino was on his back in the middle of his cell. His eyes were barely open, and his chest rose and fell in shallow, labored breaths. Xio wondered if Marino had moved at all since the last time he was down there.

"Of course he is," Xochi told Marino, even though she was in the cell directly next to Dezi's and thus unable to see him. She was pressed against their shared wall again, tapping her fingers experimentally against the cement. "You just worry about yourself for now, all right?"

Curiosity piqued, Xio slid inside the corridor, pressing against the wall to avoid being seen.

Auristela muttered something in response that Xio couldn't make out. He watched as Xochi rolled her eyes, clearly annoyed, but replied with a surprisingly gentle "Okay, Auristela."

"I miss the cubs," Ocelo said miserably, kneading their balled-up cape in their lap. Their roots were growing out, leaving a shadow beneath the dyed jaguar spots of their buzzed hair. "I was teaching them how to swim before we left for the trials."

Xio had a hard time picturing Ocelo gently guiding jaguar cubs into a pool of water. It was a stark contrast to the angry, violent Ocelo that Xio knew.

"I'm sure you're a wonderful teacher," Xochi reassured them.

"Maybe," Ocelo conceded, a bitter smile tugging at the corners of their mouth. "But it doesn't matter now, does it? They won't remember me, and I'll never see them again."

"Hey," Atzi interjected, crouched against the glass wall of her cell. "That's not true. We'll find a way out of here, and you'll be reunited with the cubs. You'll teach them how to swim again and, I don't know, whatever else baby jaguars learn how to do—"

"Yeah, like maiming," Auristela offered.

That seemed to cheer Ocelo up a little bit.

The sight of the once proud Golds, now reduced to pitiful, weakened versions of themselves, should've been invigorating. These were the people Xio had been taught to despise—the embodiment of what Xio hated about Reino del Sol—but all he saw now was suffering and vulnerability.

It was hard for Xio to even look at them in such a sorry state. This didn't feel like getting retribution against bullies. It felt like kicking an injured dog.

"Who's there?" Atzi's sharp voice sliced through the heavy silence, her eyes narrowing as she caught sight of Xio's silhouette in the darkness.

Xio stepped forward into the light.

"Come to gloat?" Ocelo spat. "Or did the Obsidians send you to finish us off?"

Auristela laughed with a vicious smile through chattering teeth. "Oh *please* let it be the latter."

Xio rolled his eyes. "Calm down." He moved through the tunnel, handing out stale pan and water. Just enough to keep the semidioses functional. Auristela couldn't use her hands, so Xio had the humiliating task of feeding her, which she never accepted. When he tried, Auristela snapped her teeth at his hand.

"Sol, get us out of here so I can bite this little twerp," Auristela prayed angrily. The ice sizzled and steamed against her skin.

"Starve, then," Xio barked before moving on to the next person.

"Wait!" Xochi called.

At first, Xio didn't understand what he was looking at. He tapped on Dezi's door and the opaque wall turned transparent.

Dezi was sitting on the floor with his legs crossed, looking at the ground with a small smile on his face. His hands were cupped around a small pink dahlia that had somehow grown through a crack in the cement.

Realization hit him. That was what Xochi had been doing when she was tapping on the walls—growing Dezi a flower? Once Dezi noticed the wall had become see-through, he jumped and moved quickly to hide it with a piece of torn cloth from what was left of his regalia.

While Xio was deciding what to do about this, Dezi's eyes drifted past him.

Dezi's mouth popped open in a gasp, anguish tilting his pretty features as he saw the state of Marino across the hall.

Despite his weakened state, Marino managed to lift his head when he saw Dezi. He smiled—weak but genuinely so happy— as shallow breaths shook his chest. Marino signed something Xio didn't understand.

Dezi nodded and pressed his forehead against the glass, his chin trembling.

Xio hated looking at it. Hated the guilty churn in his stomach.

Even though he was under explicit orders not to, he half-filled one of the small cups with water. Careful to leave the jug far away from Marino, Xio crossed the hall and, with a tap, opened Marino's cell.

Marino's expression changed to a glare as Xio stepped inside. It was like stepping into an oven.

He placed the cup on the floor, a few feet from Marino, before quickly stepping out and sealing the door shut again with a tap.

Marino released a mirthless laugh. "Are you serious?"

"Marino," Atzi warned, but he ignored her.

With effort, he pushed himself up to get a better look at Xio. "Do you know your body is sixty percent water?" Marino croaked, the dry air sucking the moisture from his throat. His lips were cracked and dotted with gold, the skin around his eyes hollowed.

Xio steeled himself and held Marino's gaze but didn't say anything.

"Your brain and heart are seventy-three percent, and your lungs are about eighty-three percent," he continued slowly. "Your skin is sixty-four percent water. Your muscles and kidneys are about seventy-nine percent. And even your cowardly little bones are thirty-one percent."

Marino paused to catch his breath. The muscles in his face twitched with barely contained anger.

"And I've got nothing but time on my hands. Once I figure out how to tap into it, you're done."

"I have never been more attracted to you than this exact moment," Auristela called.

"Yeah, I'm real scared," Xio said. The truth was, he was more than a little afraid. He didn't want to be on the receiving end of whatever Marino was capable of, even in this state. A once-proud Hero brought low by captivity yet still clinging to defiance. Inwardly, Xio couldn't help admiring his courage.

"Hurry up and drink that before I change my mind," he said, nodding at the cup.

Marino hesitated for a moment, like he thought maybe it was poisoned, but his thirst must've gotten the better of him. He snatched the cup and swallowed down the small amount of water like a shot.

"All right, Marino, lie down before you hurt yourself," Atzi ordered before turning on Xio. "So, what, have you come down here to watch us rot?"

Xio bristled. "*No.*"

"Oh my gods, is he *lonely*?" Ocelo exclaimed. "Aww, the widdle pwince of dawkness doesn't have any fwiends?"

Xio's flash of anger burned through his nerves. "Shut up! I'm not *lonely*—I've got real friends upstairs."

Now it was Auristela's turn to taunt. "Is that what you call them? Please. The Obsidians don't like you any more than we do."

As always, Auristela knew how to stick her perfectly manicured little fingers *right* into the heart of Xio's insecurities.

"Chupacabra is clearly only restraining herself from killing you because you're Venganza's brat. And Caos couldn't care less either way," she went on. "All you need is five minutes in the room with either of them to tell they couldn't be bothered if you live or die. And we all know Venganza's using you for his whole 'world domination' thing."

Xio was struggling to remember the pang of sympathy that had led him down here in the first place. He should just leave the Golds to rot until the war was over, then let Chupacabra have her fun.

"I just don't understand how you could do this to your real dad," Marino managed, his voice barely above a whisper. But Xio heard it loud and clear.

Before he knew what was happening, his fist collided with the wall outside Marino's cell, the stone cracking under the force. Purple fissures of vengeance magic dug deep into the wall, sparking softly in the low light.

Xio stared at what he had done. The room went quiet.

"Since when can he . . . ?" Ocelo asked. Auristela shushed them before giving Xio a carefully calculated unimpressed look.

Marino glared up at Xio from the floor, not a drop of that familiar friendliness in the boy's eyes. "You told us Mala Suerte lied to you, wanted to keep your obsidian blood a secret. Did it ever occur to you that he was *protecting* you from those monsters?"

Monsters.

Xio's blood boiled.

"He was *protecting me* from YOU!" Xio shouted.

It was like all the anger and resentment he'd caged inside during the trials was tearing its way to the surface in one violent burst.

"NONE OF YOU UNDERSTAND! You spent your whole lives never having to question your place in the world, never having to wonder if the people you loved—the people you *trusted*—could be lying to your face for their own benefit *because you're Golds*. You've never had to question your worth because from the moment you were born, everyone taught you exactly how worth*less* the rest of us are. Including the Jades. Including the humans you so *honorably* protect, sending the weakest link in your teenage army off to die once every ten years 'for the greater good.' It's all a fucking game. Lumbre and Guerrero and Agua and Tormentoso and fucking *all of them* are in on it. They are *no better* than the Obsidians ever were—you rule over the lower classes like it's your birthright and never once stop to wonder what makes you so different from the bad guys. The monsters you created in those stories? You can stand there and lie to me, tell me you don't think you're better than the Jades or the humans or even me, but the fact that you wake up every morning and proudly call yourself a Gold says otherwise. It's all one big hypocrisy," he spat.

"Your parents wiped out *three cities*," Xio stressed, trying to get it through their thick heads. "It wasn't just the Obsidian dioses—it was *people*! Humans, who you all have sworn to Sol to protect! Entire bloodlines disappeared overnight, and I would've been one of them. If anyone had found out who I was while I was with Mala Suerte, I would've been killed."

Xio turned back toward Auristela, waiting for her next smart comment. But the semidiosa just glared back, chewing her lip. He went down the line to Ocelo, Dezi, Marino, Xochi—staring them down, daring them to fight back. No one had a thing to say.

Silence stretched, interrupted only by the distant howl of wind rolling through the tunnels.

Then he locked eyes with Atzi.

"I don't think I'm better than anyone because I'm a Gold," she said. Her voice sounded so quiet compared to Xio's shouting, it made the space suddenly feel much smaller. "Not Jades, not even humans. I can do things they can't, sure—and yes, that's a privilege. And maybe we could all do a better job of recognizing that privilege at play. But *no one*—not Sol, not Luna, and least of all you, Xio—gets to tell me what I'm worth. And that would still be true if I was a human, or a Jade, or even an Obsidian."

In the next cell over, Xochi folded her arms over her chest, eyes cast down. "I would be lying if I said I never thought about it before. But I always thought my mother was a kind ruler, someone who respected her subjects, who did what was best for them."

"A ruler is still a ruler," Xio snapped.

Atzi's eyebrows shot up. "Hm, okay. Which would make Venganza . . . ?"

Xio froze.

Atzi's lips twisted, smug. "No, go ahead, Xio. Keep telling us about how fucked up the system is. I think you're really starting to get through to me."

"Atzi's right," Marino chimed in. "And—hell, maybe Xio's right, too, about some of it. When we get out of this, I'm going to have a serious conversation with my mom."

"Same here," Xochi agreed.

"Me too," said Atzi.

"Enough!" Auristela barked, her anger a palpable force in the air. The light treason of semidioses questioning the authority of their godly parents was clearly a sore subject. "This is all your fault, you know," she hissed, directing her venom at Xio. "If it weren't for you, we wouldn't be stuck in this hellhole!"

Xio flinched at the harshness of her words, but he couldn't deny the truth in them. He had played a part in bringing them all here, and now they were trapped like rats in cages.

And they had no idea what the Obsidians had planned for them. But Xio knew.

He threw his hands up. "Okay, fine—what would you do in my place?"

Xochi cleared her throat. "Well, I'd start by not locking all my friends in personalized underground prison cells—"

"We're not friends!"

"Whatever." She rolled her eyes. "And I'd probably have some questions for Venganza about what this whole 'new world order' is supposed to look like, because if the history books are anything to go by, I can't say I'm optimistic."

Xio shook his head. "Yeah, right. Like *any* of you have ever questioned your parents' leadership like that."

"I have," Atzi said easily.

"Like, all the time," Xochi added.

"My nini can be a little hotheaded," Ocelo admitted. "Sometimes I gotta talk them down."

"I do not," Auristela said firmly.

Atzi lowered her eyebrows. "You wanna talk about personal responsibility, Xio? Understanding why the world is fucked up isn't the same as making it better. Did you ever even stop to ask yourself what kind of new power structure you're creating? The Obsidians want to *enslave all the mortals.*"

Xio threw up his hands. "At least it'll be different! At least the Golds won't be in charge!"

Atzi's laugh was sharp. "I can't believe this! Are you hearing yourself?" she said, caught somewhere between anger and disbelief. "You're just proving our parents right, that Obsidians are all monsters!"

Even after everything, the word pierced through Xio's ribs. "You think I'm a monster."

"Look at yourself!" Atzi ordered. "Look at what you've done—*you*, Xio!" she pressed. "*Your* direct actions!"

Xio clenched his trembling hands into fists. His and Atzi's rage crackled in the air between them, that telltale scent stinging his nose.

"Leave it to a Gold to decide who the monster is, right?" Xio asked. "You can sit there and blame me for this all you want, but I'm not the one who ruined the sacrifice. I may be working with the Obsidians, but Teo is the one who let it happen."

Atzi let out another angry laugh. "You think you can turn this all on Teo? All he did was refuse to stab somebody—walk me through how that's a bad thing?"

"It was a *cowardly* thing," Xio insisted. "It went against everything we've been taught all our lives, that the Sunbearer must make that sacrifice."

"But you're so brave for turning on all of us, is that it?" Atzi asked, voice dripping with sarcasm. "When Teo does it, it's a problem, but when you bring back your evil ancestors, that's heroism?"

Xio balked. "*Turned on you?*" he repeated. "You all did nothing but make my life miserable during the trials!"

"What did I ever do to you?" Atzi shot back, stomping up to the glass. "I hardly *talked* to you during the trials! I was too busy trying to cover my own ass, because in case you didn't notice—*I was the underdog, too!* I'm *thirteen, too,* Xio!"

Xio tensed. It was hard to remember Atzi was the same age as him because of how advanced her skill set was.

"I didn't know what I was doing! I could barely keep my head above water! I came in last *twice!* I was so sure it would be me up there the day of the Ceremony, that I'd have to die before I got a chance to leave the stupid Academy, all because the gods decided my sacrifice was worth more than *my life*—"

Xio saw Atzi's bottom lip tremble for just a second before she turned away.

"Whatever, Xio. Maybe you're onto something after all," she said, angrily rubbing her eyes. "Maybe the Obsidians really should take over the world. I don't care about that. I care that me and my friends are stuck in this shitty prison, rotting away while you sit pretty with that stupid crown on your head and the people of Reino del Sol get rounded up for slaughter."

"I don't owe humans anything," Xio said, summoning as much apathy as he could. "And I definitely don't owe any of *you*"—he gestured to the other cells—"anything, either. Just because you weren't on Auristela's and Ocelo's level of bullshit doesn't mean you aren't just as guilty. *None* of you ever stood up for me, ever offered me a kind word—"

"Bullshit." Atzi defiantly held his gaze. "Maybe I didn't, but Teo and Niya sure did. *They* were your friends."

The words struck Xio like a slap across the face.

"And you repaid them by betraying their trust," she continued, taking her time with each word. "They risked their *lives* for you over and over again—"

"I never asked them to!" Xio snapped, trying to regain his focus. "When Venganza told me to sabotage the trials, I had no idea I'd be *competing* in them," he said, watching tiny bolts of Atzi's lightning dance across the water. "I had no idea if this was something my father had rigged, somehow, or if Sol just really wanted me dead. Everyone knew I was meant to be the sacrifice. But if that was what Sol wanted . . . fine. My black blood would spill on the stone either way. The Obsidians would still come back."

"You don't think all-powerful, all-knowing Sol might have seen that one coming?" Atzi said.

Xio finally looked up. "Why was I even chosen for the trials in the first place, huh? Luna says competitors are chosen by Sol's will, so why the hell would Sol put me in there? An evil Obsidian who should have died thousands of years ago with the rest of my people?"

"Maybe that's exactly why Sol put you in the trials," Atzi told him, even toned. "So you could fix them, so you could fix everything. Did you ever think of that? That just maybe, the person who created the whole damn universe thought there could be more to you than just some evil Obsidian who should be dead?"

It was like the floor had fallen out from under Xio, but he refused to let Atzi know how deep she'd hit. His voice was tight but level. "Well, then I guess I really fucked it up for them, huh?" It was hard to get the words out around the lump in his throat.

Atzi hesitated. She squinted at him, eyes narrowed like she was trying to read his mind. Xio stared back, not knowing what exactly she was looking for.

After a moment, she heaved a big sigh, her brow still creased. "Maybe there's still time to make it right again."

Xio couldn't believe it—was she really suggesting he undo what he had done? He'd brought the apocalypse to Reino del

Sol. He'd released the Obsidians. No matter what he did, nothing was ever going to change that fact. What was even the point?

Xio needed to snap out of it. Atzi was getting into his head. This had been Xio's idea to begin with. This was what *he'd* wanted. This was *his* plan. He wasn't looking for an out or a redemption arc.

"I get it, okay?" Atzi said. "It sucks that you got pulled into this situation and now everyone hates you for it."

Xio felt sick to his stomach. He didn't want to be there anymore.

"But if you don't try to fix it, then nothing will change at all and your situation will stay the same forever. So, why not just try?" she asked, searching his face. "Even if it feels pointless, at least you can say that you tried—that has to count for something."

Xio glared at her, but he couldn't exactly argue. His cheeks flushed as he struggled to find the right words. "You don't understand. I've been trying to prove myself my whole life, and now . . ." His voice wavered. "I don't even know who I am anymore."

"Maybe that's because you're too focused on proving yourself to others instead of figuring out what *you* actually want," Atzi shot back. Xio could've sworn her voice softened just a touch.

Xio raked a hand through his dark, curly hair. "You're infuriating," he told her.

"Likewise," Atzi replied with a sarcastic smile.

Their banter felt oddly familiar, like the teasing exchanges Xio used to have with Teo and Niya. A pang of longing tightened Xio's chest.

A soft giggle echoed through the tunnel. "Aw, you two are so cute," Xochi cooed, her face pressed against the glass wall of her cell.

Xio jolted. "What are you talking about?" he asked, his voice embarrassingly high-pitched.

"Please." Xochi rolled her eyes, somehow managing to look both innocent and smug. "It's obvious you're into each other."

"Xochi," Atzi warned.

"Right, right. Sorry." Xochi smirked, clearly not sorry at all.

"Be serious," Atzi snapped, glaring at Xochi. "He's such a douche!"

"Uh, actually," Xio said, "I was thinking about giving they/them pronouns a shot."

Xio hadn't planned on saying that, it just came out. They couldn't believe they'd just said something so personal that they were still figuring out in front of the Golds, of all people. But maybe it was easier to tell people who didn't like them— there wasn't as much pressure or dread.

Atzi blinked, processing the request for barely a second before nodding. "Okay, fine. *They're* such a douche," she amended.

A surprised laugh bucked in Xio's chest, their uncertainty suddenly overwhelmed with gratitude.

"Thanks," Xio said, shifting their weight between their feet. Even though it was coupled with an insult, they still appreciated it.

Atzi rolled her eyes, but Xio didn't miss the hint of a smirk. The air between them felt charged, crackling with a strange energy. Xio couldn't deny the strange sense of camaraderie that was beginning to form between them and Atzi. It was a far cry from the connection they'd once shared with Teo and Niya, but it was something.

And right now, in the midst of this dark, twisted world they found themself in, Xio clung to that something like a lifeline.

"I can't take this anymore," Auristela complained from her cell, her voice sharp with annoyance. "Are you all hearing yourselves?

You're making nice with *the enemy*. Xio is an Obsidian—even if they hadn't trapped us all down here, it's our duty as Golds to stop the Obsidians from returning. We *failed*."

"Stela, did you *want* to be sacrificed?" Xochi asked earnestly.

"Of course not! But if it's my duty to die for Sol, then that's how it should have been. *This* is why low-blood Jades shouldn't even be allowed to compete. Look what happened!"

Ocelo shifted uncomfortably in their cell. "Well, sure, but . . . I'm not *mad* Teo spared your life."

"*How could you say that?*" Auristela demanded. Her voice was starting to get louder, and tension prickled in the other cells. "You *know* how it works. The blood of the sacrifice feeds the Sol Stone, and we are safe from the Obsidians for another ten years—"

Xochi scoffed. "Okay, but, like, does that even matter now? The trials are over, the Obsidians are back. We can't go back to the way things were—"

"*So?*" Auristela seethed.

"*So*, maybe there's a bright side to all this!" Xochi shouted, throwing her hands up. "*Excuse me* for trying to be an optimist!"

"Leave it to the Daughter of Primavera to try to see the literal apocalypse through rose-colored glasses," Auristela snapped. Xochi's eyes flickered with anger—ideological debates were one thing, but going after someone's godly parent was crossing a line, apparently.

"Back off, Stela," Ocelo warned.

"No, let her talk," Xochi goaded. "What else do you have to say about my mom? Because I've got a few bones to pick with Lumbre, while we're at it—"

"Ladies, please," Marino said, attempting to intervene. "There's no need to—"

"You're so lucky I'm stuck in this block of ice, or I'd—"

"What? You'd *what*, Auristela?" Xochi snapped, her frustration bubbling over. "Burn me? Make something explode? Because that always worked out *so* well back at the Academy."

"I liked you better when you kept your mouth shut."

"I liked you better when you weren't such a brat."

Auristela's already pink face went, somehow, pinker. "Well, I liked you better when you didn't go around befriending *monsters* who locked us all up in a torture dungeon!"

Their bickering went on, with Ocelo and Marino occasionally jumping in to try to quell the rising tempers.

Xio's hands shook, clenched into fists at their sides as they struggled to reconcile the image of the person they thought they were with the reality that now stared back at them. Seeing Auristela turn against her own friends under duress made them realize, maybe for the first time, what little consequence her jabs actually held.

She had always been horrible to Xio, but she was horrible to everyone. Here, now, when it really mattered—the others were willing to hear Xio out. Maybe they had been willing all along.

How much had Xio missed, just because they weren't willing to see?

Quietly, they said, "I'm not a monster."

Only Atzi heard them. She sighed. "You're only a monster if you choose to be. Right now? I think you're just . . ." She shrugged. "Lost."

Xio shook their head, trying to physically fling the thought out of their mind. "Okay, I see what you're doing and it's not gonna work. You're not tricking me into helping you out of here."

Hurt flickered across Atzi's face before her expression shuttered. "Oh, don't worry," she reassured them, the sarcasm back in full swing. "I know that when I get out of here, it'll be no thanks to you. And I'm really looking forward to knocking your teeth out when I do."

"Now you sound like Auristela."

Atzi looked them up and down. "There are worse things to be."

Like an Obsidian monster, Xio's brain supplied.

Atzi turned away. "When all this is over, and we're dead or whatever happens next, you can look out from your little tower and take in the new world—alone."

Xio turned on their heel and left.

CHAPTER 14
TEO

Teo woke up to the sound of low voices and the rich smell of roasted coffee beans. For a blissful moment, he believed he was back home. That he'd slept too late and Huemac was there to give him a stern look and a cup of coffee before rushing him out the door. But when he opened his eyes, he remembered.

Pushing himself upright, Teo rubbed the sleep from his eyes.

Paz and Aurelio stood at the sink, Paz smiling and talking animatedly while Aurelio washed dishes in the sink, nodding along.

"Morning, sunshine." Yucca stood leaning against the counter, arms crossed and scowling.

"Uh, hi," Teo said, clearing his throat. He grabbed his pillow and tossed it at Niya's head.

She startled awake with a loud snort, sitting bolt upright. "Wha' happened?"

"Time to get up," Yucca said.

Teo just grumbled, muscles aching as he pushed himself off the couch.

Niya was immediately on her feet. "Man, I slept like a rock!" she announced, all smiles as she stretched her arms over her head. "When's breakfast?"

"It's being served at the Great House!" Paz said.

"Thank Sol," Teo said, searching for the shoes he'd kicked off the previous night.

"No, no, no, timeout!" Yucca interrupted, making an X with her arms. "Paz was kind enough to let you crash at her place, but we've tolerated you long enough—"

Niya's shoulders slumped. "I thought we were having a nice time together."

"And you three have an apocalypse to stop." Yucca arched a thick eyebrow. "Remember?"

Annoyance sparked under Teo's skin. "*Yes.*" Being tired and hungry was not putting him in a good mood.

"But I'm starving!" Niya complained.

Paz placed her hand on Yucca's shoulder. "They've got such a long way to go, don't you think—?"

"No, I don't!" Yucca barked.

"If you wouldn't mind…" Shocked silence fell over the room as everyone turned to Aurelio. "It would take more time if we had to eat on the way," he said, methodically drying his hands with a dish towel. "We'd have to stop, unpack, cook something, then break everything down again. If we could refuel here, we'd save time and be able to cover more ground today. If you don't mind," he said before rushing to add, "Please."

Yucca stared at him for a long moment before saying, "That's more words than you've said the entire time you've been here."

Aurelio glanced at Teo, like he didn't know how to answer that, which further irritated Teo. If anyone was gonna tease Aurelio for being the way he was, it was *Teo*.

"That's very sound logic," Teo told him, which seemed to ease some of Aurelio's distress.

"It really is," Paz agreed with an enthusiastic nod.

"Can't stop bad guys without feeding the girls," Niya said, slapping her biceps.

By the look on her face, Teo was sure Yucca was going to kick them out right then and there, but then Paz made that sad face at her again. "URGH!" Yucca scrubbed her hands over her face. "A quick breakfast and then you're gone!"

"*Yes!*" Niya tripped over herself in a rush to drop trou right in the middle of the room and change into a fresh uniform. Aurelio lowered his gaze and busied himself with folding the dish towel while Yucca let out an irritated growl and Paz's eyes went wide, a blush creeping across her cheeks.

"You have to be on your best behavior!" Yucca warned. "Don't bother anyone, don't break anything, and don't get into trouble."

"She reminds me of Huemac." Niya chuckled as they followed Yucca and Paz out the door.

"She's acting like we're gonna burn the whole village down or something," Teo grumbled.

"I would not let that happen," Aurelio said, adorably earnest.

Teo laughed. Aurelio was making it hard for him to hold on to his bad mood. "I know you wouldn't," he said, knocking his shoulder into Aurelio's.

"She is also much shorter and angrier than Huemac," Aurelio added, which made both Teo and Niya break into a fit of laughter.

Despite Yucca's stern commands, Paz took the long route and gave the trio a small tour of their village in the trees. Yucca followed begrudgingly.

"It's safer for us up here than on the ground," Paz explained as she led them over a suspended bridge. "We don't have to worry about floods, we can see if any creatures approach the fence, and we're low enough beneath the upper canopy to see anything coming down."

Teo's chin jerked up instinctively. He couldn't see any monsters getting ready to drop down on them, thankfully.

"We use palmetto trees for the buildings because they're resistant to decomposition," Paz went on, pointing out a nearby cluster of houses. One man stoked a fire while another passed pillowy mounds of dough into the open mouth of an adobe oven. A gaggle of little kids surrounded a woman with a braided mohawk tending to a grill covered in sizzling meats. "We use the leaves for thatching and weaving, and the drupes and palm hearts are edible!"

"Are those chinampas?" Aurelio asked. He was facing east, a gloved finger pointing at something in the distance. Even in the dim light, Aurelio was already looking way better than the night before, which was a huge relief.

"Good eye!" Paz replied, delighted.

Teo moved to Aurelio's side to get a better look. In the distance was a large clearing, dotted with hundreds of lanterns. It was a patchwork of thin, rectangular strips of land that reminded Teo of the meticulous farmland in Maizelan. But instead of walking paths between them, water reflected silvery starlight and the warm glow of the lanterns.

"Floating gardens!" Teo realized out loud. Chinampas were made by weaving reeds and sticks together to build a giant raft, then piling them with mud, soil, and manure to grow crops. He'd learned about them in school, but it was so long ago and had seemed so insignificant, Teo hadn't retained much. Here, each one was anchored to mangrove trees at every corner and lined with canals for people to pass from garden to garden by canoe.

"That's where we grow our crops," Yucca told them, adjusting her glasses. Teo could tell she was reluctantly proud of how mesmerized they all were. "Maize, beans, squash, tomatoes, chili peppers, rice— we've even got flowers!"

Aurelio's brow creased. "But the salt water—?"

"We built aqueducts and canals to siphon fresh water from a nearby lake," she explained.

Aurelio's eyebrows lifted. "Impressive."

Teo fought back the urge to call him a nerd and nodded along. So did Niya, even though he knew good and well she was just as clueless as he was.

"Of course," Yucca added, a bit of that unfriendly bite back in her voice, "without the *sun*, our crops aren't doing great at the moment."

Paz smiled back at the trio apologetically.

Teo crumpled under the weight of his responsibilities. "Sorry about that," he murmured, rubbing the back of his neck.

"It's okay!" Paz said, for some reason trying to cheer *him* up even though this was clearly his fault. "You guys are going to stop those jerks and get the sun back soon, right? Then everything will be back to normal!"

"Yeah!" Niya agreed enthusiastically.

"*Yeah,*" Yucca echoed, the word dripping with sarcasm.

Aurelio uncomfortably shifted his weight between his feet.

"Right," Teo said with a forced smile.

They *had* to. There was no other choice.

"Do you use hydropower to run everything?" Aurelio asked, maybe to change the subject but maybe because he was genuinely interested in that stuff.

"About half," Yucca replied. "We've got water mills along the river." Far below to the south, the dense foliage of the swamp came up against a wide river. "The turbine system feeds power lines that we run up the trees to provide electricity to the entire village. It depends on the flow of the river, obviously—"

"Obviously," Niya agreed.

"So we usually supplement with solar power. Of course, now—"

Teo's heart sank deeper into his stomach. "There's no sun to power them."

Paz winced with an uneasy smile. "Yeah."

The Great House had a communal kitchen and a large dining room filled with long wooden tables. Niya ran so fast toward the food, Teo could practically see the cartoon dust cloud in her wake.

They were laid out family style with large bowls, reusable plastic containers, and platters laden with food. Each table had a big clay pot full of café de olla or masa-based champurrado to go with piles of tamales. The air was filled with the mouthwatering aroma of tortillas, beans, eggs, cheese, peppers, and salsa, all the makings for huevos rancheros or chilaquiles.

Teo grabbed a random assortment of anything that looked good before wandering back to the table Yucca and Paz had picked out in the middle of the room. He slid into the spot next to Aurelio. Teo's plate of mostly pastries and tetelas was a stark contrast to Aurelio's, which had been carefully portioned with protein, grains, and steamed vegetables.

Villagers of all ages filled the tables, chatting and laughing. A group of kids stared at them as they ate, and as soon as Niya offered them a friendly smile, they swarmed the trio. Some of the little girls doted on Niya, complimenting her on her cool outfit and pretty braids.

Teo had his own audience who were keenly interested in his wings, how he got them, and how they worked. They even *asked* Teo if they could touch his wings, although he politely declined and, instead, pulled a couple feathers out for them to keep. Aurelio was joined by a toddler who just stood there, staring up at him with wide eyes. Whenever Aurelio awkwardly glanced in his direction, the little boy burst into gleeful laughter.

As much as it pained him to think about, it reminded Teo of home. How everyone in the community seemed to know and look out for one another. The Golds—and the trials, too—turned acts of good-will into competitions, concerned only about the ego of heroism. Even Niya, whom he loved deeply, was guilty of it.

The Golds were so focused on the performance of being Heroes, Teo was starting to doubt they even really cared about the people they saved. How could they if they never descended from their ivory tow-ers to get to know humans?

Aurelio and Auristela came and put out the fire in Quetzlan, but did they care about Veronica and how she was recovering? Chavo had a whole altar in devotion to Dios Tormentoso and his daughter Lluvia to thank him for saving him and his family during the hurricane that tore through their city, but did Lluvia even remember them? She was Chavo's savior, but did she ever even give them a second thought?

Did the people of Reino del Sol mean *anything* to the Golds?

Maybe the people here had the right idea.

Out of nowhere, an alarm blared.

Aurelio and Yucca were immediately on their feet while Teo nearly toppled off the bench. The earsplitting siren let out three sharp bursts then a short pause before cycling through again. Bright lights flashed from every corner of the room.

"What the hell is that?!" Teo shouted, covering his ears as his heart rammed against his ribs.

"Security breach!" Yucca said, eyes darting around the dining hall.

"The fence?" Paz guessed, gripping Yucca's arm.

"*Shit,*" Yucca hissed, scrambling out from behind the bench. "Stay here!" she told Teo.

But as soon as Yucca bolted, Aurelio charged after her. "Let's go!" he called over his shoulder.

"But!" Poor Niya had three plates balanced on one arm and a half-eaten bigote in her hand.

"You heard him, Niya!" Teo shouted over the alarm as people ran to evacuation points.

Niya looked down at her full arms, clearly conflicted, before finally giving in. She dropped everything and ran after Teo.

Outside, it was organized chaos. The siren continued to blare and emergency lights flashed from railings and through windows. Elders, kids, and people who had trouble getting around quickly filed into orderly lines to seek refuge in the Great House while the others flocked to their stations.

"What's going on?" Teo asked as he and Niya joined Yucca and Aurelio on a rope bridge facing south.

Yucca dragged a hand over her face. "Didn't I tell you to stay?"

"Your fault for not tying us down," Niya told her. She gestured to the crowd that had gathered. "What gives?"

"There's something in the river," Paz said, pointing down below.

Teo followed her finger and squinted into the darkness. At first, he didn't see anything, but then he noticed the wakes rippling out from a dark spot slicing through the water.

"What is it?" Teo asked, the hairs on his neck prickling.

Yucca shook her head. "We don't know yet."

"Something big," Aurelio said.

A shiver ran down Teo's spine, sending his feathers ruffling. "Maybe it'll just keep going down the river."

As if on cue, it made a wide arc and headed right for shore.

"Oh, fuck me," Teo growled under his breath.

Whatever it was disappeared behind the lower canopy that blocked their view of the riverbank. They waited and watched, the silence eerie below the drone of the alarm. Teo's eyes burned from not blinking.

Distant shouts floated up to them, but Teo couldn't make out what they were saying.

Niya leaned over the railing and pointed. "There!"

Down below, the canopy leaves rustled. Something cut through the trees, parting them like they were little more than blades of grass. The haunting groan of wood filled the air, accented by the occasional crack of a splintering branch.

Finally, a voice broke through all the noise.

"Cipactli!"

Yucca's jaw clenched, color draining from her face. Niya let out a low whistle, but it was Aurelio's expression—how hard he was trying *not* to look frightened—that sent adrenaline flooding through Teo's veins.

"Is it that bad?" Teo asked, his voice tight. He could only watch the trees bow one by one as the thing headed straight for the clearing. When it reached the edge, Teo held his breath.

From the tree line, a crocodile emerged, but it wasn't just any crocodile.

"It's huge!" Teo said, hardly believing his eyes.

"It's the Original cipactli," Paz said breathlessly, more in awe than anything else.

The giant cipactli had a pointy snout and strange rear legs that bent like a frog's, but hopefully couldn't jump like one. Its jaw opened, revealing thick, pointy teeth and a mouth wide enough that Teo could easily walk right into it without ducking. With its nose in the air, the cipactli's head swiveled back and forth.

"Is it *sniffing*?" Niya wondered, confused.

"It's after the livestock," Aurelio blurted out.

Sure enough, the cipactli crawled toward the enclosure, dragging its belly through the swampy muck. When it reached the fence, it reared up and attempted to climb it, its sharp nails dragging gashes through the wood.

"Does that fence hold up against cipactli?" Teo asked.

"Yeah, against *normal* cipactli!" Yucca snapped. "Not a thirty-foot Original!"

"You don't have any other security measures?" Aurelio asked.

"Well, usually it's an *electric fence*, but since we use solar power and SOMEONE TURNED THE SUN OFF—" She closed her eyes and took a steadying breath. "No, we do not."

The words hit Teo like a punch to the gut. He'd fucked up, and now the rest of the world was paying for it, even this village of people who tried so hard to stay out of the gods' trouble. It was fucked. Like, *majorly* fucked, way beyond what Teo and his friends were capable of fixing. The world was bigger and more imbalanced than he could've ever comprehended.

As if on cue, the fence splintered and caved under the cipactli's weight.

Teo dragged his eyes away from the monster and turned to Yucca. "What do we do?"

"Kick some ass!" Niya announced, a dangerous, excited grin on her face.

Niya leapt over the rail to the next level below. Aurelio only hesitated for a moment before chasing after her.

"HEY!" Yucca shouted after them, but it was too late.

Teo moved to follow, but she threw out her arm and stopped him. "DON'T! Just stay here, out of the way!" she told Teo.

He tried to object, but she ignored him and turned to Paz. "Make sure everyone is up in the trees." Paz nodded and took off.

Teo wasn't about to let Niya and Aurelio take that thing on by themselves. Against Yucca's orders, Teo took to the air and dived down into the action, leaving her angry shouts behind him.

Down below, goats screamed and cows waddled for their lives as people tried to herd them out the gate. Meanwhile, the cipactli crawled over the broken fence and into the enclosure. It wasn't particularly fast, or maybe this nice bowl of meat was too convenient for it to move with any sense of urgency. It seemed to almost take its time as it headed for the pigs trapped inside their pen.

The poor animals screeched and tried to escape, but the sturdy log fence didn't budge and their short legs wouldn't let them hop over.

The mottled pattern of the cipactli's deep cobalt and phthalo green scales had a black shift when it caught the light of Aurelio's flames. Fishlike fins ran down its spine and fanned out from its tail. They were a translucent, electric blue and sparked with stardust when it slung its tail at Aurelio.

He tried to leap out of the way, but one of the fins caught his ankle and sent him tumbling in a painful-looking somersault before slamming onto his back, the wind knocked out of him. The cipactli advanced. Aurelio managed to sling another round of fire as he struggled to his feet.

"ROAST IT!" Teo shouted as he circled above, trying to figure out something he could do to actually help.

Now the monster was *really* pissed off. It snapped at Aurelio, its teeth nearly sinking into his thigh before he tumbled out of the way again. Aurelio blasted fire into its open mouth and straight down its throat. The cipactli released an agonized screech. When the flames receded, it slammed down on its front legs and bellowed.

Determination burned in Aurelio's eyes as he stared down the beast. But when it charged at him again, Aurelio hesitated. Hands up and at the ready, he took a step to his left and then—

He did nothing. Aurelio paused, waiting for a combat partner who wasn't there.

Teo's heart crumpled. He tried to rush forward and fill that space, but he was too far away.

The cipactli swung its head into Aurelio's side, sending him flying. He tumbled and landed in a heap, extinguishing his hands.

Teo did the only impulsive, reckless thing he could think of.

His wings snapped closed against his back and he dropped through the air, landing feet-first on the cipactli's snout before launching himself back into the air like a springboard. The force slammed the cipactli's chin into the ground, rough scales dragging over hard dirt, its momentum pitching it forward.

Hovering in the air, Teo got two full seconds to feel proud of himself before the cipactli spun toward him with surprising speed.

One of its eyes locked on him, acid green with a spiral galaxy instead of a pupil. Its gaping maw opened wide, revealing a purple tongue and lethal set of teeth. A rattling hiss sounded deep within its chest, sending the gills on either side of its head vibrating. Teo nearly gagged on the hot wave of breath that reeked of rotting meat.

Its tail came flying through the air. Teo dropped to avoid it, but he was too low to the ground. He landed hard and pinwheeled as he stumbled, trying to keep his feet moving so he didn't trip.

A strong hand gripped him by the arm, tugging him back into balance.

"Keep running!" Aurelio told him, pushing him toward the collapsed fence. Yucca was there with some others, shouting something that Teo couldn't make out.

The cipactli released an angry roar. The ground shuddered under Teo's feet as the crocodile charged after them, tail whipping.

"I think you pissed it off!" Aurelio called out.

"You think?!"

The cipactli's tail lashed out. It knocked them over and sent them sprawling to the ground in a tangle of limbs. Aurelio quickly got back to his feet, tugging Teo up along with him, but the cipactli was already on them, all teeth and claws. Then—

"PICK ON SOMEONE YOUR OWN SIZE!"

Niya appeared and quickly broke into a fit of coughs. "Oh my Sol," she said, face screwing up in disgust. "Why does it smell SO BAD?"

The cipactli lowered its head, jaw wide open in an impressive show of teeth. It let out a long, low hiss as it slowly shuffled back from Niya, tail flicking.

"WAIT!"

Teo turned to see Yucca sprinting toward them, waving her arms over her head. Aurelio shot him a confused look.

"*Niya!*" Teo called, trying to get her attention, but she'd already gone after the cipactli.

"I've always wanted to wrestle a crocodile!" she said, closing in on it. Before Teo could yell at her to get away from it, the monster lunged forward, snapping its vicious teeth.

In the most unhinged act of bravery Teo had ever witnessed, Niya lunged back.

The two collided, rolling, thrashing, and snarling. Teo was too stunned to do anything but watch.

Niya managed to get behind its head and straddled the base of its neck. She threw herself forward onto its head and locked her arms around its snout, trapping its jaw shut. When it thrashed more wildly, Niya dug her knees into its gills.

The cipactli let out a terrible screech.

Niya laughed. It was the one Teo recognized that she did when she was about to win dominoes and spend the next three years bragging about it.

Yucca skidded to a stop between Teo and Aurelio. "WHAT ARE YOU DOING?" she shouted, looking on in disbelief.

"I'm saving you!" Niya called back.

Yucca shook her head, eyes wide with terror.

Cold fear dropped into Teo's stomach. "Niya, get away from it!"

Her triumphant look turned into one of confusion. "But I'm winning!"

While she was distracted, Niya's grip loosened. With a violent twist, the cipactli rolled, tossing Niya to the ground. Teo and Aurelio rushed forward to pull her onto her feet while the cipactli righted itself.

For a moment, Teo didn't understand what he was seeing. Every joint on the cipactli's body—its shoulders, its elbows, its knees—split open into red gashes. At first, they looked like wounds, but instead of revealing blood and flesh, something slimy wriggled out.

The gashes were mouths, each with sharp teeth and long, lashing tongues.

"Oh shit," Teo said weakly.

"DUCK!"

Aurelio dragged him to the ground as Yucca tossed what looked like a whole rack of raw beef ribs over their heads. It landed with a wet *thud* before the cipactli. The creature's nostrils flared. With a quick snap, it snatched up the offering and tipped its head back, letting the meat slide down its gullet.

"Over here, big guy!" Paz called. She held up a raw turkey and wiggled it back and forth. "We've got some nice treats for you!"

Teo, Niya, and Aurelio quickly backed out of the way as the cipactli changed course and crawled toward Paz. When it was close enough, she tossed the meat.

The cipactli snatched it in midair, crushing bones in its powerful jaws. A pleased rumble sounded deep within its chest.

Yucca sprinted to a waiting wheelbarrow loaded with more meat. She grabbed the handles and quickly walked backward toward the hole in the fence, keeping an eye on the cipactli as she went.

Teo could hardly believe his eyes. The beast had been beyond pissed and ready to turn them into snacks, but now gleefully waddled after Yucca, following the trail of animal carcasses.

"Are you seeing this?" Aurelio asked in a hushed tone.

"Yeah, but I don't really believe it," Teo replied.

Niya was struck silent, her face screwed up in confusion as she watched Yucca reach the gap in the fence. A woman rushed forward to help her navigate the wheelbarrow over the broken fence.

The semidioses trailed behind at a safe distance, watching as Yucca and the woman kept tossing pieces of meat. The cipactli followed along, gobbling the food as they led it through the mangroves. When the tree line ended, Yucca turned the wheelbarrow around and jogged to the river's edge. An inflatable raft piled with a random assortment of thawing meat sat on the shore, where it was roped to a team of three people in a fishing boat.

Another woman helped Yucca dump what was left from the wheelbarrow into the raft and then they quickly moved out of the way. When the monster emerged from the tree line, the boat took off, dragging the raft along with it.

The cipactli flopped onto its stomach and slid into the water. It followed the raft up the river from where it'd come. They watched as the cipactli, with just its eyes and snout gliding along the surface, disappeared into the night until the sound of the boat's motor faded into the distance.

"Well, that was exciting!" Paz said with a huff, joining the trio.

"How did you do that?" Teo asked, bewildered.

Paz shrugged. "It was just hungry!"

"But how did you *know*?" he pressed.

"It's a cipactli!" Yucca barked, making Teo jump. She stomped toward the group, positively fuming. "Insatiable hunger—that's their whole deal! If you just lead them away with food, they'll leave you alone!"

Teo turned to Niya and Aurelio. "Did you guys know that?"

"I forgot," Aurelio said, embarrassed.

"There's a lot of monsters we have to learn to fight, Teo!" Niya snapped moodily, crossing her arms over her chest. "I'm sorry I didn't remember *every* detail about *every single one of them*!"

"Dude, chill," Teo said.

"I AM CHILL."

"What if it comes back?" Aurelio asked.

"Then we'll deal with it again!" Yucca said, pushing past them to march back to the village.

"If you'd just let me kill it, you wouldn't have to worry about it coming back!" Niya shouted after her.

Yucca spun on her heel, seething. "We don't kill things just because we're frightened of them!" she shouted back. "But I wouldn't expect a bunch of *semidioses* to understand that!" With that, she spun back and disappeared into the trees.

"But they're monsters," Aurelio said quietly, his brow all bunched up.

Paz lifted one shoulder in a small shrug. "They're just animals." When it was clear that Aurelio still didn't understand, she added, "Like, you wouldn't call a scorpion a *monster* because they're dangerous and scary, right? You'd just call it a scorpion."

Weirdly, that made a lot of sense to Teo. It reminded him of something his mom had said about Suerte.

If people treat you like you're bad for long enough, I imagine you start believing it.

Teo's mind wandered to Xio, but he immediately pushed it back.

"Whatever," Niya grumbled, walking back to the village. Most of her fight was gone, but she was clearly bothered.

"She'll bounce back," Teo told Paz with an apologetic grin. "She always does."

"Same for Yucca. She tends to lash out when she's scared," Paz said with a smile. "Most things do."

The trio had just finished repacking their bags when Paz and Yucca walked in.

Niya stepped forward, clutching the strap of her bag. "I'm sorry I broke all your stuff," she said morosely.

"It's okay, accidents happen!" Paz said, giving her shoulder a gentle rub. "We've already got people working on repairing the fence, and we needed a new coop anyway. If you think about it, you kinda did us a favor!"

Niya managed a small smile.

"Are you sure we can't help repair the damage?" Aurelio asked.

"You can help by getting the sun back," Yucca said, tossing Teo a plastic bag full of pan. Paz was right. She was already back to her calm—but still surly—self.

He caught it and forced a smile, doing his best to ignore the queasy churning in his stomach.

Paz exhaled a laugh and thumped her fist against his shoulder. "No pressure or anything."

CHAPTER 15
TEO

With the ever-capable Aurelio leading, they entered Los Restos. Dense trees meant heavy foliage that blocked out the stars, so they relied on the lights of their suits to guide the way. Ropy vines draped across branches and snaked around trunks in suffocating loops. The semidioses trod over spongy moss and through dense green undergrowth. It was drier than the swamp, but the leaves that slid across Teo's skin were still wet from a since-passed storm.

While there were some smaller rivers that ran through the jungle, they decided to avoid all bodies of water from here on out.

Niya talked a mile a minute the whole time, hopping from one topic to the next without pause. It was something she did when she was anxious, so Teo just let her go without interruption. Listening to her ramble about the best kind of pillow—the firmer the better, according to Niya—was better than having only the sounds of the jungle.

Teo could hear slithering through creeping roots, small paws scratching at leaves, and creaking branches overhead, but he couldn't see a damn thing. It felt like forever but somehow no time at all when Aurelio decided they should make camp to rest for a while.

"It's weird we haven't run into anything, right?" Niya asked, head on a swivel. She hacked away some overgrown vegetation with her Unbreakable Blade to make room for them to set up camp. "I mean, Los Restos is supposed to be crawling with monsters—er, I mean *critters*," she corrected, adopting Paz's term.

"I think we should just be grateful that we *haven't*," Teo said. "Do you think we're close to where they set up the fifth trial?"

"That's much farther east," Aurelio told him. He crouched down to brush away jungle debris until he had a patch of naked dirt. "In Caos's territory."

A shiver tickled the back of Teo's neck. "Whose territory are we in now?" he asked, taking a seat on the ground.

"Venganza's."

"Oh." He shouldn't have been surprised since the whole point of this journey was to go to Venganza Temple and rescue everyone, but the closer they got, the more his anxiety spiked.

Teo watched Aurelio root around, picking up a log about the length of his forearm. Holding it against his chest, Aurelio dug his fingers into the rotten end. He pressed his lips into a hard line and with a flex of his biceps, he tore the log in half with his bare hands.

Niya plopped down next to Teo, startling him from his staring. "Is it getting colder or is it just me?" she asked, knees bouncing as she rubbed her bare arms.

"Might be the fact that you're barely wearing any clothes," Teo said with a pointed nod at her sports bra and shorts.

Niya scoffed and narrowed her eyes. "I'm *always* wearing barely any clothes, that's got nothing to do with it!"

Teo snorted. In truth, he *had* noticed a creeping cold settling into his bones.

"Without the sun, the temperature is dropping," Aurelio said as he dug through his backpack. "After about four weeks, everything will be covered in frost and uninhabitable."

Niya tipped her head to the side. "Seriously?"

"Yeah, how do you know that?" Teo asked.

Aurelio shrugged. "I watched a video on TúTube about hypothetical natural disasters."

Teo exhaled a short laugh. "Great." So if the Obsidians didn't destroy the world, nature would.

"Put on your jacket, Niya," he told her.

She listened and pulled it out of her bag without a fight. Niya struggled to get it on, like she'd never encountered sleeves before.

"What's that?" Teo asked when Aurelio pulled out something that was the same size and shape as a disc of hot chocolate.

"Dried manure."

Niya gasped. "POOP?!"

"Yucca gave it to me," Aurelio went on. "It makes a good fire starter."

"But it's POOP!"

"Can we help?" Teo asked.

"I could use some dried moss and dead palm leaves."

It didn't take long for Teo and Niya to find some in the underbrush. Aurelio set the two pieces of log side by side and face up to make a nice dry surface. With a snap of his gloves, he ignited the starter and used the kindling and his own breath to coax it into a proper fire. The heat wafting off the dancing flames warmed Teo up almost immediately.

"Damn, that went *way* better than last time!" Niya laughed with relief. She gave Aurelio a congratulatory thump on the back. "Good job!"

Aurelio grimaced a smile.

Teo shot her a glare—Aurelio did not need a reminder of that right now—but Niya didn't even notice.

"I'll get the food out!" she said, reaching for Aurelio's bag.

"*I've got it*," he said, snatching it away before Niya could reach it.

Niya jerked to a stop, brow furrowing. She pressed her lips between her teeth, the golden lights of her uniform illuminating the hurt in her eyes.

Teo inwardly groaned. Apparently he wasn't the only one feeling stressed out.

But, to his credit, Aurelio closed his eyes and took a breath. His shoulders drooped and his grip on the bag relaxed. "Sorry," he murmured.

"Looks like Aurelio's got fire and food covered," Teo said, taking charge. "What can Niya do to help?"

"We need more wood to keep the fire going," Aurelio said. He turned to Niya. "Could you split open some larger logs and cut out the dry wood from the center?"

Niya was already on her feet before he finished his question. "On it!" she said, the Unbreakable Blade materializing in her hand. "Aurelio, protect Teo!"

"I don't need to be protected!" Teo called after her.

"Yes, you do!" Niya called back before disappearing into the trees.

Teo rolled his eyes. "I'll put up the hammocks."

Some hours later, Teo was fast asleep when urgency pulsed through his veins, shouting at him to open his eyes. He had to drag his consciousness awake, like he was pulling himself through mud. With effort, Teo rolled over in his hammock. Squinting, he looked around with bleary eyes.

Their campfire was still smoldering in a pile of embers. Niya was asleep.

But Aurelio's hammock was empty, his bag nowhere to be seen.

Teo sat bolt upright. Panic cut right through him. His thoughts spun wildly with visions of every possible terrible scenario.

A flash of light at the corner of Teo's eye caught his attention. He froze and stared into the inky night, too afraid to blink. A warm orange light flared from between trees in the distance before fading away. Teo watched and waited, and when it happened a second time, he decided to go check it out.

He thought about waking Niya, but given how overprotective she'd been lately, he decided to let her keep sleeping. If anything went wrong, Teo knew all he had to do was shout and Niya would come running.

Quietly, he slid out of his hammock and followed the strange light. He didn't activate the lights in his suit, just in case. Each flare was bright enough for him to follow it through the maze of trees. When it went out, he stopped and waited in the dark until there was another.

It didn't take long for him to follow it to a small clearing. He peeked around a trunk just in time to see flames burst to life behind a silhouette.

Teo stepped forward. "Relio?"

Aurelio spun to face him, the fire in his hands momentarily illuminating the startled look on his face. He quickly extinguished them.

"Sol's *sake*," Teo hissed. "You nearly gave me a heart attack!" He activated the lights on his suit so he could see.

Aurelio stood there, looking exceptionally guilty.

"What are you doing out here?" Teo asked, now fully annoyed at being woken up. He noticed Aurelio's hands were behind his back. "And what are you holding?"

At first, Teo thought he was going to lie, but Aurelio folded immediately. His posture slumped, chin dipping before he presented his hands.

The Scorching Circlet rested in his palms. The coals—nestled between fire opals that probably cost more than it took to build Teo's high school—burned faintly just like the pectoral adornments Aurelio had worn to the opening ceremony of the Sunbearer Trials. Their flickering glow danced across Aurelio's warm brown skin.

Without thinking, Teo reached for the circlet. Heat prickled the tips of his fingers before Aurelio wrenched it away.

"*Careful*," he warned. "You'll get burned."

Teo frowned. "Why—"

"I was just trying it out."

Was this why he'd been acting so cagey about anyone touching his bag?

"How does it work?" Teo asked.

"She said it amplifies my abilities."

Teo didn't really trust that Lumbre had good intentions when she gave Aurelio that circlet. Judging by his obvious issues and the scars hidden under his armbands, Teo assumed not. In fact, he was pretty sure that Lumbre only ever saw Aurelio as one of Auristela's accessories.

If this circlet could enhance her son's powers, why hadn't he been training with it all along? Instead, she'd just thrown him a live grenade and waved him off to go save the world. Or, more important, save Auristela.

He thought about telling Aurelio not to use it, especially if he was iffy on his abilities. But they needed every advantage they could get.

"All right then, give me a demonstration!" Teo said.

Aurelio blinked. ". . . Right now?"

Teo chuckled. "Yeah!"

"I was just trying out some warm-up moves I learned at the Academy," Aurelio explained, clearly trying to back out, but Teo wouldn't let him.

"Great!" he said, getting comfortable on a stack of felled logs. "Don't let me stop you!"

Aurelio looked around the empty clearing. "Okay . . . Just keep back at a safe distance. It's kind of unruly, and I haven't gotten the hang of it yet."

Once Teo was an acceptable distance away, Aurelio took a deep breath and squared his shoulders. He brought his hands up to his chest and clapped them together. As they separated, small sparks danced to life between his palms. He had summoned fire—without his flint gloves on.

"Holy shit," Teo breathed.

Aurelio stayed focused, the muscles in his jaw taut. It was rare to see him so uncertain. If Teo hadn't known better, he would've thought Aurelio was scared.

With another steadying breath, Aurelio began to move. He ran through a series of basic strikes, slinging fire at a tree and leaving scorch marks on the bark. But the fire began to spread again. Flames danced up his arms, licking the shoulders of his crop top. If the Academy hadn't designed his gear specifically for him, it would've burned to ash by now.

The fire suddenly jumped, flaring in Aurelio's face.

"Watch it!" Teo warned, but Aurelio had already jerked back.

He winced and shook out his arms, extinguishing the flames.

"Shit, are you all right?"

"I'm fine," Aurelio said, checking himself. "It boosts my resistance to fire."

"Damn, that's a handy perk," Teo said, impressed.

Aurelio was too deep in his own thoughts to reply.

Teo had a funny feeling in the pit of his stomach. He wasn't sure why, but something felt off.

Aurelio went back to where he started and tried again.

Whoosh.

Teo threw up his hands to shield himself against a wall of heat. The fires in Aurelio's hands blazed three feet into the air, so bright it was like someone had turned the sun back on. Aurelio quickly put them out. Teo was left blinking spots from his vision.

"*Come on*," Aurelio muttered to himself.

He tried again but this time, the fire was smaller and he only ignited his left hand. Aurelio focused, not even blinking, as he did a twisting motion with his fingers. The fire spun and stretched into a shaky vortex about six inches tall. It shook like it was trying to escape while Aurelio fought to keep it balanced in his palm.

But it didn't last long. The fire exploded in a bright flash of light, startling Aurelio so much that he dropped it. The tiny flame tornado scurried around the clearing like a spinning trompo, igniting a few patches of dead leaves.

Teo lunged forward to stomp them out, but Aurelio was on it. With one sweep of his arm, the fires went out, leaving behind smoldering tendrils of smoke. Aurelio stood there breathing heavily, his eyes watering.

"You good?" Teo asked hesitantly.

Aurelio dragged the back of his hand across his eyes in one irritated movement. "Smoke" was all he offered before going right back to it.

This time, he summoned a much smaller blue flame. So small, in fact, that it went out as soon as he moved. Teo realized that whatever power the circlet gave, it required a degree of finesse Aurelio hadn't mastered yet. Apparently he could conjure an explosion or a matchlight, nothing in between.

Sensing that this was, perhaps, not going as well as Aurelio wanted, Teo decided he could use a rest. Sol only knew how long he had been practicing *before* Teo found him.

"Why don't you take a break," he suggested, closing the space between them. "Cool off a little."

Aurelio looked down at his hands, clearly frustrated. "I guess," he grumbled, which Teo decided was good enough.

Teo led him back to the pile of logs and took a seat, but Aurelio decided to stay standing, scowling at his hands. The Scorching

Circlet's coals glowed and flickered on Aurelio's head. Teo couldn't explain it, but it almost felt like it was taunting them.

"I thought you didn't want to use your mom's circlet?" Teo asked as nonchalantly as possible.

"I don't," Aurelio said, then released a heavy sigh. "But she was right."

Teo seriously doubted it, but he took the bait anyway. "About what?"

"Fixing my..." Aurelio squinted like he was searching for the right word. "Deficiencies."

Teo barked a sarcastic laugh. "You are *Aurelio, Son of Lumbre!*"

"A Son of Lumbre who isn't resistant to fire," Aurelio replied tiredly. "I can't even create fire without my gloves or the circlet."

Teo couldn't believe what he was hearing. He'd learned that Aurelio had a warped sense of his own worth, but was he really this oblivious to how amazing he was? "You're top of your class at the Academy!"

"Second," Aurelio corrected.

Teo ignored him. "And you've probably saved like *a billion* people! You're a famous Gold Hero! Do you know how many people would do *anything* to be you?" he demanded.

"Auristela can *breathe* fire," Aurelio pointed out.

"...Okay, that's pretty fucking cool," Teo admitted. "But you are NOT your sister."

"My mom wishes I was."

It would've been better if Aurelio were angry. It'd probably be healthy for him to throw a tantrum just to get it out of his system. Teo would've even preferred a sad Aurelio, because at least then he could cheer him up.

Instead, Aurelio was resigned to it, like he'd given up.

It pissed Teo off.

"Yeah, well, your mom's got a major attitude problem, and that's coming from *me*," he huffed, crossing his arms. "Besides, you can't be your sister. Your ass isn't thick enough to fill out her uniform."

A surprised laugh bucked in Aurelio's chest.

Teo grinned. "Hey. Look at me." When he didn't, Teo leaned forward to peer up into his face. "You are *not* deficient."

Warmth pooled low in Teo's stomach at Aurelio's shy smile. For a moment, everything else became background noise. Teo wondered how much deeper he could coax Aurelio's blush.

"I got you something," Aurelio told him. He went and retrieved something from his bag. "Here," he said, holding out his closed fist.

"From where, the swamp?" Teo teased. "If it's a leech or something, I don't want it."

That time, Aurelio actually laughed. "Just take it."

Teo held out his hand. Aurelio placed a mazapan candy in his open palm. It was badly smushed and the wrapper was loose, leaving powdery crumbs on his skin.

"Where did you get this?" Teo asked, delighted. "Have you been carrying it around this whole time?"

"Paz gave it to me," Aurelio explained. He leaned his hip against the log Teo sat on. "She'd gotten some on their supply run—"

"Definitely a necessity," Teo agreed.

"So I asked if I could have one. Because I know you like them," Aurelio added, in case that wasn't clear.

Teo stared at him.

That adorable bastard.

With a goofy smile plastered across his face, Teo's gaze dropped to Aurelio's lips and he leaned in.

"What are you doing?"

The question was so abrupt, Teo jolted to a stop. "Uh...I was going to kiss you." Damn, was his game *that* bad?

"Oh," was Aurelio's short reply. He stood there, frozen in place and eyes practically bulging from their sockets. There was a sheen of sweat on his forehead that Teo was pretty sure had nothing to do with the Scorching Circlet he still wore.

He immediately leaned back to give him space. "Do you *want* me to kiss you?"

Aurelio nodded, short and jerky.

Teo squinted at him. "Are you sure? It's okay to tell me no, I'm not—"

"I want to," Aurelio blurted out. His face and ears turned an impressive shade of plum. "But I've never kissed someone before," he confessed.

Teo's eyebrows shot up. "Seriously?"

Aurelio nodded again. "I—I'm worried I'll be bad at it . . ."

"That's what you're worried about? Being a bad kisser? Holy crap." Teo pressed a hand to his chest and laughed. "Sorry, I'm not laughing at you, I'm just relieved!" he said when confusion flickered across Aurelio's face. "I thought I had *completely* misread the situation and weirded you out!"

Poor Aurelio did not look relieved.

"So, you want me to kiss you?" Teo clarified.

"Yes."

"And *you* want to kiss *me*?"

Aurelio leveled him an annoyed look. "You're gloating."

Teo laughed. "I'm not gloating, I'm basking. And now I'm going to kiss you."

It wasn't like a kiss in the movies. It was awkward and clumsy, and Teo could feel Aurelio's tense lips tremble against his own. But it was soft and warm, and it tasted like sweet mazapan. To be honest, Aurelio could've drooled on him, stepped on his foot, or even sneezed directly into his mouth and it wouldn't have mattered because he was kissing Aurelio for the first time after dreaming about it for so painfully long.

Finally, finally, *finally.*

Aurelio pulled back and Teo didn't even have time to reopen his eyes before he asked, "Was that okay?" He looked so adorably vulnerable that Teo didn't know whether to rip his own feathers out or crush him into another kiss.

"We'll keep working on it," Teo said, grinning up at him.

Aurelio laughed. It was shaky and breathless, but it seemed to melt his tension away. He smiled, so bright and brilliant it was like he'd swallowed the sun. Teo beamed back, mesmerized by his radiance.

Aurelio stepped forward, closing the distance between them. His earlier apprehension was gone, now replaced by determination. Bracing himself against the log, Aurelio leaned down to meet him. Teo grinned, brimming with smug satisfaction as he held Aurelio's smoldering gaze.

When they kissed, a flood of sensations drowned any coherent thoughts Teo had left. The rush of heat low in his stomach. The sweltering warmth of Aurelio's body pressed against his. The feverish burn of Aurelio's skin where Teo pressed his palm against his lower back. Aurelio's sooty musk.

Teo felt the exact moment something ignited within Aurelio. Not just a want, but an all-consuming *need*. Teo's breath hitched, stealing the oxygen from his lungs and fueling Aurelio's desire.

It burned and blazed, engulfing Teo in a delicious ache.

He was too lost in kissing Aurelio to notice something was wrong. Sweat prickled all over Teo's skin. He wasn't just overheated anymore— he was *sweltering*. Smoke tickled his nose, slamming him back into reality.

Teo's eyes flew open a split second before searing heat bit into his thigh. He cried out in pain. Aurelio pulled back, horror evident on his face as he realized what he'd done. Before either of them had time to react, a fist reached out and wrapped itself around the back of

Aurelio's shirt, yanking him away from Teo and throwing him to the side.

Niya stood before him, panting. Her hair was a mess from sleep, her eyes bloodshot and afraid. Aurelio recovered first, rushing to put out the fire he'd started.

Teo stumbled away, patting out the singed material on his leg. "Holy shit," he hissed, frantically checking to make sure his wings hadn't also caught fire.

"Are you okay?!" Aurelio asked in complete shock. His cheeks were still stained red. "I'm *so* sorry, I had no idea—"

Teo put his hand up, trying to stop Aurelio before he could fall too far into a panic spiral. "I'm fine—seriously—I don't even think it got me," he told him. "Semidiose skin, remember?"

Aurelio didn't seem to believe him. Niya went into full Mama Bear mode.

"What the hell were you doing?!" she demanded, seething. "You could've roasted him like a chicken!"

"Hey!" Teo scowled, offended.

Aurelio was beside himself. "I—I didn't mean to, I didn't realize—" He shook his head, tipping the Scorching Circlet askew. Aurelio's eyes lit with realization and he ripped it off his head. The coals burned down to an ominous glow as Aurelio stared down at the circlet in disbelief.

Niya was still standing between the two of them with her arms raised, like she was ready to launch into attack mode. Hurt and anger and confusion were at war on her face, her eyes pinging back and forth between the boys.

"Niya," Teo said gently, resting a hand on her forearm.

"*No!*" she shouted, yanking free. "Stay behind me." Niya turned to Aurelio with a snarl. "Put the circlet *down.*"

Aurelio was bewildered. "Niya, you know I would never—"

"Put it *down*!" she insisted. Aurelio complied, placing it carefully on the ground. When he stood up, he lifted his hands in surrender.

Niya's chest heaved, too fast and too deep. The muscle above her left eyebrow twitched.

"*Niya*," Teo said again. "Look at me."

She tilted her face toward Teo, but her eyes remained locked on Aurelio.

"*Look at me*," Teo repeated, firm. He placed a hand on each of her shoulders, boxing her in. "It's okay! It was just an accident! Aurelio wasn't trying to hurt me—you don't need to protect me from him. We're on a team, yeah?" he asked, giving her a small shake.

"I don't *like* being on teams anymore!" Niya exclaimed, tears springing into her eyes. Teo's stomach dropped. Behind her, Aurelio's eyes grew wide.

Okay. Niya was fully in breakdown mode, but Teo could handle this.

"Relio, would you give us a sec?" he asked.

When Aurelio stared back at him with a horrified look, Teo inwardly groaned. Great. Aurelio's first kiss, and now he'd be traumatized by it for forever.

"Also—that was great," Teo told him. "And I'm looking forward to doing it again. Maybe with a little less fire next time," he added with a grin.

Aurelio blushed, which was reassuring. "Okay," he finally said, still sounding nervous. "I can. Um. Start breakfast."

"I'd love that," Teo agreed, maybe a little too enthusiastically. Aurelio slinked off, his shoulders hunched to his ears.

Once Aurelio was safely out of earshot, Teo met Niya's eyes again. "Dude, what's going on with you? I'm completely fine, not a feather out of place, okay? I'm not so fragile that a little fire is going to take me out."

"It's not that! I'm just—" Niya stopped short, pulled on her braids like that would somehow force the right words out. "I've never had to *doubt* my team before. Even at the Academy, we don't all *like* each other, but I know we've got each other's backs. I never worried about other people's intentions or—or what they might want from me, or if they were hiding some big, earth-shattering secret..."

Her words hit Teo like a kick to the chest. "You mean Xio."

"Yeah," Niya admitted, relief momentarily smoothing over her face, like she'd been holding it in for a while.

Teo reached out and pulled her hand away from her braids, stilling her fingers with his own. "Hey, I get that. What Xio did...I mean, it's not like we've had a ton of time to process it, you know? But he tricked all of us. And that's not something you just get over."

Niya nodded, but her eyes were fixed downward.

"It just has me questioning everything—every*one*," she told him. "I don't know what to believe anymore. I looked over and I saw the fire and I thought, *it's happening again*—and I know you're going to say Aurelio would never, and I know he wouldn't too but I would have said the same thing about Xio ten days ago and I'm trying so hard not to fall apart right now—" The words spilled from her lips faster and faster. "But I feel like I'm losing my grip on everything and it'sonlyamatteroftimebeforeIloseyoutooandIcan't—"

"*Breathe!*" Teo interrupted. She'd said all that without taking a single breath, and her face was starting to turn purple. "Niya, *I'm* sorry. I haven't been a very good best friend through all this—I wanted to believe that because you were acting normal about the Xio stuff, you were okay. And if you were okay, I kept telling myself that I could be okay about it, too."

"Well, that's just stupid," Niya said, dabbing at the corners of her eyes.

Teo cracked a smile. "Yeah, it was."

"I *loved* that kid," Niya said, angrily rubbing her eyes. "It doesn't make sense, but this whole time, I keep thinking, *I hope he's okay.*"

"Me too," Teo admitted, and it felt like a huge weight had been lifted off his shoulders. "I mean. Obviously what he did was not cool—"

"*So* not cool," Niya agreed, bottom lip wobbling.

"—but he's still just that wimpy little kid we snuck hot chocolate with on the first night of the trials, you know?"

Niya's lips tugged up in the corners, a not-quite smile. "He looked so lost with the rest of us. I mean, you're a Jade, too." She sniffled. "But at least you have that kind of cocky, overconfident swagger to compensate."

"I'm sorry," Teo said, "I didn't realize I came across as *cocky*—"

Niya rolled her eyes. "Oh please, you totally do it on purpose. You think it's cute," she said with a little laugh, wiping the snot from her runny nose.

"I do not!" Teo said defensively, his voice pitching into shrill territory.

"I mean, it's clearly working for you," Niya added, gesturing back toward their camp.

They stood there in silence for a moment, letting the tension left in the air fizzle out.

Finally, Niya cleared her throat. "So, uh. You guys finally kissed, huh?"

Teo's cheeks bloomed with heat. "You saw that part?"

Niya whistled. "I think all of Los Restos saw it."

"All right, all right." Teo turned around and started walking back toward the camp, trying to hide his face. "That's a little dramatic." He picked up the Scorching Circlet from the ground. It was still hot to the touch. Teo made a mental note to check in with Aurelio the next time they had some privacy.

Niya wasn't letting him get away with it, though. She jogged backward alongside him, so she could see how embarrassed he was getting. "I mean, it must have been getting *pretty* steamy for Aurelio to completely lose control like that—"

Teo forced a smile and said through his teeth, "It's not funny if he *hears you.*"

"If he hears me, what? Talking about the two of you lighting up the eternal night with your impassioned smooch—"

"—I'm going to light *myself* on fire if you don't shut up."

Niya *tsk*ed. "You were super into it, weren't you?"

Teo didn't bother holding back a smirk. He shrugged. "I mean—"

"Dirty bird!" Niya scolded.

Teo shoved her playfully.

"But seriously," she said, slowing down before they reached the camp again and Aurelio could hear them. "How was it?"

Teo hummed thoughtfully. "A little awkward, but mostly hot. Intense. Not unlike a fire, I guess," he added, letting his mind wander back to the kiss.

Niya bobbed her head. "Yeah, Stela was like that, too."

She said it so casually it took a second for Teo to register.

"Wait—*what*?!"

"It was back at the Academy after Xochi's gender confirmation ceremony," she said in an annoyed tone. "Dezi snuck in a bunch of alcohol—that's all I'm legally allowed to divulge."

"No way!" Teo grabbed her arm and tried to tug her to stop. "I want details!"

Niya ignored him and kept walking, dragging him along with her. "I've already said too much. Let's go before your boyfriend starts to worry."

"That's not fair!"

Niya shrugged, unbothered. Teo made a silent resolution to coax more information out of her once this whole *end of the world* business was over and done with. The idea of a Fire Twins double date was terrifying, but potentially entertaining enough to be worth it.

Just before they stepped into the light of the fire, Teo stopped one last time. "Hey, Niya?"

Niya turned back, confused. "Yeah?"

"*I* will always have your back. You know that, right?"

Niya's mouth pinched into something that was almost a smile. "I know, Teo."

CHAPTER 16
XIO

Xio stepped through the archway and into the tunnel where the Golds remained in their cells. They were weary and exhausted, their spirits dimmed by the oppressive darkness and isolation.

"There they are," Venganza said. "Our precious Golds, all locked away for safe-keeping." Their father looked around at the sorry states the semidioses were all in. "They look awful." Venganza's mouth curled in a smile. "Well done, Xio."

Xio did their best to smile back. "Thank you, Father." Earlier, Venganza had said he wanted to see the Golds, and that he had something important to tell Xio.

Their mind buzzed with possibilities, unsure if they should be excited or nervous. Maybe both.

"Make sure you don't get too close," Chupacabra sneered. "We wouldn't want any of them to use their powers on you—oh wait!" She broke into shrill laughter at her own bad joke.

As the Obsidians inspected each prisoner with disdain, Xio couldn't help feeling a sense of satisfaction, especially after everything that had gone down during their last visit. Marino was too weak to do more than watch as the Obsidians filed in. Xochi stepped away from the glass, frightened eyes betraying her brave posture. Ocelo bared their teeth, but even Xio could see how their anger faltered. Dezi was fast asleep, completely unaware of the dangers just beyond his cell.

Atzi was ever defiant, staring the Obsidians down. When they moved past, her eyes went to Xio, some of the fear slipping through. *What's happening?* she seemed to ask.

But Xio didn't know, so all they did was lift a shoulder and give Atzi a small shake of their head.

Auristela, on the other hand—

"ENJOY THE VIEW WHILE IT LASTS!" she shouted, straining against the ice.

Xio's heart thumped in their chest as they followed the Obsidians. They approached Auristela's frost-encrusted cell, the air growing colder with each step. Icy tendrils snaked up Xio's spine, constricting their breath.

"Ah, Auristela," Venganza purred. "Our feisty little firecracker."

Auristela glared at him from within her icy prison, her eyes blazing with defiance. "Mark my words, Obsidians," she spat, her voice shaking with fury, "once I'm free of this wretched cage, I'll tear you apart with my bare hands."

"You take after your mother, I see." Venganza chuckled. "Arrogant and egotistical, even when you're so obviously outmatched."

"Thank you," Auristela said as she flashed a venomous smile.

"You're nothing more than a child playing with matches," Chupacabra snapped.

"Matches that I'll use to burn you from the inside out," Auristela shot back. A tendril of smoke curled from her lips as she spoke.

Xio didn't know whether to be scared or impressed. Even after being locked up in ice for several days, Auristela was somehow still producing her own fire. Was it just brute strength? Or was she sustaining herself on anger alone?

"You really believe that you, a half mortal, could last more than five seconds against us?" Chupacabra laughed, a harsh and grating sound. "We are *gods*, and you are nothing!"

"Why don't you let me out and we can time it?" Auristela asked, batting her eyelashes.

Xio clenched their fists. They wanted to tell Auristela to *stop*, that she was only going to make things worse for herself. They knew what the Obsidians were capable of, and her stubbornness was going to get her into more trouble than she was already in.

"Enough of this foolishness. Let her stew in her own impotent rage," Venganza commanded, almost bored as he turned away. "She poses no threat to us."

Auristela's anger was a tangible heat radiating from her skin, melting some of the frost on the glass. The air hissed and crackled as the ice began to melt. Steam rose in ghostly wisps around her as rivulets of water ran down the sides of the icy sphere, puddling on the ground below her.

In that moment, she seemed more like a primordial force of nature than a mere demigod.

"Once my brother gets here, he'll tear you apart," Auristela snarled, her voice thick with hatred. Small tendrils of flame licked at the ice around her exposed neck. "He won't rest until he's freed us all and made you pay for what you've done."

Xio stared in shock and awe, their heart pounding in their chest as they watched Auristela's display of power. They could see the raw determination etched into every line of her face, and it stirred something deep within them—a sense of respect, perhaps, or even envy.

Venganza and Chupacabra exchanged glances, amusement dancing across their faces.

"So, the mighty Aurelio is coming to save the day?" Venganza said, his words dripping with disinterest. "Xio has done his research, and I know your own mother wouldn't trust him to be alone with a pair of scissors, let alone save anyone."

"Pathetic," Chupacabra agreed, her eyes narrowing. "He stands no chance against us."

Xio's thoughts raced and collided at the idea of Aurelio, Niya, and Teo showing up at Venganza's temple.

Because, of course, if Aurelio decided to go on a mission to take on the Obsidians and free the Golds, there was no way Teo and Niya would let him go alone. *Those idiots*, Xio hissed in their mind. They didn't stand a chance.

"Listen up, asshole," Auristela declared, looking Venganza in the eye. "My brother would do anything to save me, regardless of what our mother told him to do."

The Obsidian gods chuckled.

"Is that so?" Venganza mused thoughtfully, a wicked grin spreading across his face. "Well, then we'll just have to give him a proper welcome, won't we?" He looked to Chupacabra and Caos. "I'm sure we can come up with *something* for Aurelio and whoever else is foolish enough to help him."

"Imagine what a prize they would make," Chupacabra said, her maw hanging open and salivating.

"Why don't we send La Lechuza out to greet them?" Caos suggested, fingers fidgeting with excitement. "I'm sure she'd like to get out and stretch her wings."

Oh no, not her. The owl witch really stood out among the rest of the Celestials. She was incredibly powerful and ruthless, and she enjoyed playing with her prey before she—

"Excellent idea, Caos," Venganza said before turning to Auristela. "And what better bait than you, Auristela, to catch your foolhardy brother?"

Auristela's menacing snarl faltered. Xio watched the full weight of her mistake drop onto her shoulders. Her eyes bulged and her mouth clamped shut, but the damage was already done. She had been so consumed by anger and desperation that she had revealed Aurelio's plans, and now the Obsidians would be ready for him.

"I didn't mean it," she said, her voice trembling with fear and regret. The ice stopped melting. Frost thickened on the glass. "I was just . . . trying to scare you."

Xio winced. He'd never seen Auristela like this.

She'd fucked up and she knew it. And what was worse, Venganza knew it, too. "Scare us?" Venganza laughed, a cruel sound that echoed through the darkness. "You've done much more than that. You've given us the perfect opportunity to crush your precious brother and his little friends," he told her.

As he spoke, Xio could see Auristela's fire dimming, the cold encroaching. "If you lay a hand on him—" She thrashed against the ice. "I'll set your bone marrow on fire! I'll force flames down your throat!" Auristela's face crumpled. Tears welled in her eyes. "I'll kill you!"

Venganza gave Auristela an amused grin. "I really don't think you will."

"Don't hurt him!" Her enraged screams turned to gut-wrenching sobs. "He's only trying to protect me!" There was so much pain and anguish in her cries, it was like her soul had been torn in two.

"Ah, but that is his weakness," Venganza replied, his voice dripping with malice. "His blind loyalty will be their undoing."

Auristela stared in horror at Venganza's sinister grin as the ice pressed closer around her, creeping up her neck and spreading across her cheeks. Tears froze on her skin, her eyelashes crystallizing.

Xio felt sick.

"Please, don't do this!" she croaked as the ice overtook her cell door and sealed her away from view.

"Caos, fetch La Lechuza," Venganza said. Caos vanished in a puff of blue smoke. "She'll be able to handle the Son of Lumbre. As well as Teo and Niya. From what you've told us, Xio, I'm sure your so-called *friends* will be tagging along."

Friends. The word stuck in Xio's head, a painful reminder of what they had lost.

The Golds, except for Dezi, were all standing at attention now, concern etching their faces.

"Once this is over, the Golds will be nothing more than a distant memory." Chupacabra growled with anticipation. "Including you lot."

"Can't you see it, Xio?" Venganza said wistfully. His fingernails cut into Xio's shoulders as he gave them a conspiratorial squeeze. "This is just the beginning. Soon, we will reign supreme, and those who once mocked us, who destroyed our families and homes, will bow at our feet. Now it's time to reward you for all your hard work."

Xio's heart leapt. "Reward me?" they repeated, their voice full of hope.

Venganza nodded as he thoughtfully stroked his goat beard.

"I want you to go with La Lechuza."

Xio balked. "Me? B-but—" they stammered. "Why?" The last thing they wanted to do was go into the jungles of Los Restos in the dark.

Especially not with *her*.

Venganza chuckled. "Because she's an excellent hunter, and you've come so far with your training." He smiled fondly down at Xio. "She'll track them down, and *you*, my son"—Venganza's large hand was a heavy weight on their shoulder—"will destroy them."

Xio's lips were numb, a faint ringing in their ears. "Destroy them?" Xio repeated.

The Golds started to panic.

"You can't do that!"

"Leave them alone!"

Venganza nodded, as if the interruption hadn't happened. "What better way to exact your revenge on the dioses than taking their children from them?" he said, grinning around at the cells.

Xio felt dangerously close to passing out. They knew what their responsibilities were, that they'd eventually have to get their hands dirty, but killing Teo, Niya, and Aurelio? "I—I don't think I'm strong enough yet to take them on my own," Xio said.

"Of course you are, you're my son," Venganza said. "And if you need assistance, La Lechuza will be there to provide it.

"When the Golds have lost," Venganza continued, "there will be a whole world of humans at our disposal. We're counting on you to subjugate them while we entertain ourselves with more engaging duties."

Chupacabra cackled. "If the semidioses make it through this war, we could feed them to their parents. I always loved that one—classic."

"If the semidioses make it through this war," Venganza said, with finality, "you may do whatever you like with them."

Chupacabra squealed with delight. The sound shot ice through Xio's veins.

"You, Xio, will oversee the human labor force," Venganza continued. "We will rebuild our empire to its former glory. There will be no more Golds, no more Jades, no more Sol and Tierra with their self-righteousness. The future is for us." He smiled a wicked smile. "And *only* us."

He turned to leave, Chupacabra right behind him. "Come, my son. We have much to do."

For a moment, Xio was frozen to the spot. They clenched their hands into fists to keep them from shaking. It was time to prove themself, or suffer the consequences.

"Coming," Xio said.

Sounds of protest rose from the cells again, but Xio refused to look at the semidioses.

Until they passed Atzi's cell.

Their eyes snagged on hers as they passed. Atzi's eyes bored into theirs, round and pleading. Xio could practically hear her voice in their head.

Please, don't.

Xio looked away.

CHAPTER 17
TEO

The crackling flames of the trio's campfire cast a warm glow over the dense jungle around them. Teo stretched out against a felled tree as the tension from his recent heart-to-heart with Niya dissipated like the smoke that curled up into the canopy above them.

There seemed to be a renewed sense of purpose in the air as they prepared for the next leg of their journey—infiltrating the Obsidian temple.

Aurelio had wandered out into the jungle and returned an hour later with slabs of peccary meat, which he now busied himself with cooking using the limited ingredients they had left or had scavenged along the way. He worked the fire expertly, his fingers dancing through the flames without fear, lending a smoky richness to the improvised pozole. Teo was already salivating.

While Niya sprawled nearby, Teo moved closer to watch Aurelio cook.

"Sorry about the, uh . . ." Aurelio trailed off awkwardly as he stirred the pot.

"The kiss?" Teo guessed. He smirked at the brilliant shade of red Aurelio's cheeks turned.

He nodded, an uncertain expression on his face. "Yeah."

"Don't be," Teo said. "I liked it. A lot. In fact—" He leaned into Aurelio, bumping his shoulder against the other boy's. "I'd like to do it again. And often."

Aurelio laughed. His posture relaxed and he looked downright content. "Deal," he said.

Teo leaned in to steal a kiss. It was quick and fleeting, barely long enough for Aurelio to even pucker his lips, but it was just as satisfying as the first.

A short time later, food was ready. "Careful, it's hot," Aurelio warned as he handed Teo and Niya each a bowl.

Niya grabbed a spoon in her fist and held the bowl up to shovel the pozole into her mouth. "Oh my gods, Aurelio!" she said, staring at him in awe. "This is the best thing I've ever put in my mouth, like, ever! You're like a culinary genius! You should become a chef!" Her eyes gleamed with mischief as she grinned at him. It was good to see her back to her usual self.

Teo took a bite. "Holy Sol," he moaned. The intensely spiced bits of peccary and sweet kernels of maize were perfectly paired with the aromatic red chile broth. "All those TúTube videos really paid off, Relio."

Aurelio's cheeks flushed a deep red that brought an even wider grin to Niya's face. Teo enjoyed it, too, and let himself freely gaze up at Aurelio's adorably flustered face as he stirred the pot.

He muttered something about needing to practice more before hastily changing the subject. "We should reach the Obsidian temple soon," Aurelio said, avoiding eye contact as he served up a bowl of soup for himself.

"Really?" Niya asked, her face growing serious. It would've been nice to pretend for a little while longer. "What's our plan?" she asked before shoving another heaping spoonful into her mouth.

"We find the temple," Teo began, hoping he sounded more confident than he felt. "Sneak inside, scope out the place, and hope none of those Obsidian freaks sense us before we find where they're keeping the Golds and the Sol Stone. Then we free our friends, grab the stone, and call in the dioses."

"Sounds simple enough," Niya said between bites.

It was a bad plan. Teo knew it, and by the look Aurelio gave him, he knew it, too, but it was all Teo had. He stared into the darkness beyond the glow of the campfire, his heart heavy with anticipation. The sounds of insects and distant nocturnal creatures filled the air, so different from the familiar cityscape he'd left behind.

At any moment, the shadows could come to life as another Celestial pounced on them. But there was no sign of an approaching threat, just the weight of the unknown pressing down on him like the persistent night.

He was good at putting on a brave face, but beneath his bravado, fear gnawed at Teo's insides. He had led his friends into danger time and time again. Teo always relied on his instincts to get them through, but what if this time, it didn't work?

"Relax, Teo," Niya urged, placing a reassuring hand on his arm. "We'll be ready for whatever comes our way."

"You've got us," Aurelio agreed.

Teo managed a tired smile.

"I miss Quetzlan," Teo admitted. Homesickness gaped like an open wound in his chest. "I miss my mom, and the birds," he said. "It's so dark and quiet out here. Back home there's always *noise*." A bitter laugh escaped his lips. "I even miss the boring stuff."

Niya and Aurelio murmured in agreement.

"I miss my dads and my brothers," Niya said, staring glumly down at her nearly demolished pozole. "And I *really* miss La Cumbre," she added. "I miss feeling the volcano rumble under my feet." Niya wiggled her toes in the dirt. "I miss cooking myself in the hot springs—I would *kill* for a hot bath right about now."

"I miss the Academy," Aurelio admitted in a quiet voice.

Niya cocked an eyebrow. "Seriously?"

Teo nudged her with his foot and threw her a stern look, but Aurelio didn't seem bothered.

"Yeah, I know," he said. "But I miss being surrounded by our class-mates. It's nice being in a room full of people talking, laughing, and joking."

This surprised Teo. He'd figured based on his general demeanor that Aurelio longed for silence and solitude.

"And I really miss Auristela," he added, sadness clouding his hand-some face. "We used to sneak into the kitchens—"

Teo gasped. "Aurelio, Son of Lumbre, breaks *rules*?" he teased with a smile.

Aurelio grinned back. "Only so I could bake us sweets in the middle of the night," he said. "Buñuelos, churros, pan de canela," Aurelio listed off, smiling fondly. "Auristela loves cinnamon."

They fell into silence, each lost in their own memories.

"Thanks for dinner, Relio," Niya said eventually. She got up and yawned, stretching her arms above her head. "I'm looking forward to some sleep!" she said.

As if on cue, something rustled in the jungle behind them.

Niya turned toward the sound, braids whipping. Aurelio was imme-diately on his feet, igniting twin flames in his hands. Teo jumped up after him, his wings spreading wide, braced for a fight.

Soft cursing reached Teo's ears just before someone burst through the foliage, stumbling into their campsite. Covered in dirt with jungle debris stuck in his curly hair, he stared up at them with wild eyes.

Teo's stomach dropped, breath catching in his throat. "Xio?"

CHAPTER 18
TEO

Teo stared in disbelief. He'd run through hundreds of scenarios about seeing Xio again. None of them involved him randomly showing up in the middle of the jungle.

A thousand questions flooded his mind—Where had he come from? What was he doing here? Was he a threat? Where were the rest of the Obsidians? *What was happening?*—but Teo couldn't get his voice to work. He'd spent the journey so far trying to avoid even thinking about Xio, because when he did, it was like being stabbed in the chest. And now, Teo wasn't ready.

"Xio?" Niya asked, like she couldn't believe her eyes, either. A wide smile broke across her face. "Xio!" she cheered.

Despite everything, Xio actually smiled back. It was disarming. Now Teo *really* didn't know what to think.

But then Niya's expression darkened. "XIO," Niya snarled, hands reaching for his neck.

A wave of heat hit Teo's side.

Aurelio stood in an offensive position, a ball of fire held threateningly in his palm. Shadows caught in the angry lines of his face. "Where are they?" he demanded.

Xio threw up his hands and stumbled back. "Whoa, where's who?!"

Aurelio's eyes darted around the trees. "Did you lead them to us?"

Xio balked. "What?! No! I didn't bring anyone!" He hesitated. Teo saw the pink creep into his cheeks, the way he nervously fidgeted with his hands. "Well, I mean—"

Teo's heart lurched. Dread dropped into his stomach. "What did you do?" The words came out of his mouth before Teo even realized what he was doing.

Xio grimaced. "They sent me to find you—"

Niya stomped toward him. "I'M GONNA—"

"Wait!" Xio cried, throwing out his arms to protect himself. "I'm not here to fight!"

"You expect us to believe that?!" Niya demanded, her voice shaking. "After everything you've done?!"

"We don't have time for this!" Xio said, panic rising in his voice. "They sent me with one of the Celestials to stop you. We have to—"

"There is no *we!*" Niya snapped. "There's *us* and then *your* deceitful ass!"

Teo couldn't shake the feeling that something wasn't right.

Xio was so pale he looked sick. The way his hands trembled and his chest rose and fell in short, sharp breaths couldn't have been for show. Xio was scared, but was he scared for them, or for himself?

"Teo, *please,*" Xio begged, desperation etched into every line of his face. "You *have* to listen to me!"

Aurelio stepped forward. "Or what?" he challenged, his flames flaring with renewed intensity. "You'll take us to the Obsidians like you did with my sister?"

Xio swallowed hard. "Look, I know I messed up!" Xio began, his voice cracking. "But I swear, I'm here to help you now! The Obsidians—they're planning to destroy you!"

"Yeah, no shit!" Niya spat.

"But I'm trying to stop them!" Xio pleaded with Teo, but Aurelio and Niya closed ranks.

"Convenient," Aurelio said, anger sparking behind his copper eyes. "You've suddenly seen their true colors and now you want to stop them?"

"Well, k-kind of," Xio stammered. "Teo!" he tried again. "Listen to me! The Obsidians know you're coming!"

Teo's brain buzzed as he tried to process what Xio was saying, and whether he could believe him. The arguing was setting his teeth on edge. His wings kept twitching. He squeezed his eyes shut for a moment, trying to focus his thoughts. His head started to throb.

"More lies!" Niya snarled, her hands clenched into fists. Teo could've sworn he felt the earth tremble beneath her feet. "We're not falling for your tricks again, Xio!"

Teo couldn't take it anymore. "Enough!" he shouted, silencing them all. He turned to Xio, willing his face not to betray the hurt aching in his chest. "What Celestial did they send after us? Why are you here, Xio?"

Xio's shoulders were hunched up to his ears under their distrustful looks. "La Lechuza, the owl witch!"

Teo sucked in a breath. *Fuck.* In Quetzlan, La Lechuza was like El Cucuy—the monster his classmates told scary stories about to each other. The one parents threatened their kids with when they were misbehaving.

"She's not like the other Celestials," Xio said quickly. "She's clever, and she'll destroy you before you even make it to the temple!"

Teo shook his head, confused. "How did you—"

A branch groaned directly above their heads.

"What have we here?" The eerie, raspy voice made Teo's blood run cold. His wings trembled as his head jerked up. He searched the strange shadows cast by the looming trees, but he couldn't see anything.

Aurelio and Niya immediately pressed their backs against Teo's and squared up.

Then one of the massive shadows moved. Bark crunched under talons as a massive barn owl stepped out onto a branch nearby. It was more than seven feet tall, its feathers deep gray with a denim blue hue. Silvery spots covered its head, back, and upper wings.

But its face—

Instead of a barn owl, an old woman stared down at them.

The creature's human face was heart-shaped, fringed with small feathers. Her shiny eyes were completely black, framed by fluffy dark lashes and slender eyebrows. She had the pale, delicate upper beak of a barn owl, but the fleshy red bottom lip of a human. "Poor diositos, so far from home," she cooed. "Have you lost your way?"

"She said—" Teo started, his voice strained.

"We know what she said, Teo!" Niya barked. "We can hear her!"

This baffled Teo until he realized the Celestial hadn't spoken in bird language.

La Lechuza's voice floated around them. "Teo, Son of Quetzal," she crooned. "You finally had a chance to prove yourself. Crowned *Sunbearer* by your beloved Sol. And look what you've done with it."

A shiver zipped down Teo's spine.

Xio inched back toward the trees. Teo wasn't sure if he was hiding from the witch, or if he had just set them up. Every nerve and muscle in Teo's body screamed at him to run. But it wasn't in Niya's or Aurelio's stubborn Gold DNA to back down from a fight, so he wouldn't, either.

"I wanted to thank you," La Lechuza taunted. "It's been so long since I've been able to stretch my wings."

Niya charged forward.

"LEAVE HIM ALONE!" she shouted, raising her blade over her

head with both hands. Niya swung the blade down, but the owl woman was too fast. She took off and disappeared into the shadows, leaving Niya's blade to slice the branch clean off.

"Where did it go?!" Niya demanded as they frantically searched the trees. "What the hell is it?!"

"La Lechuza," Teo said, confirming what Xio had said. His eyes dashed from branch to branch, trying to spot her. "The owl witch."

"Another Celestial?" Niya guessed.

"Yes—well, kind of. She's not like the others," Teo tried to explain. "There's only one of her."

Niya decided this was good news. "Great! All we gotta do is kill her, then."

"I don't think *killing her* is really on the table," Xio chimed in. He was still standing at the edge of the trees, ducking under the canopy. "She's not like the other monsters—she used to be human. A witch who defied the Golds and was cast out into the wilderness. She offered herself to Caos to use as an experiment, a hybridization of beast and human with the power to fight entire armies and the intelligence to pull it off."

"How do you know all that?" Aurelio asked.

Xio gestured down at himself. "*Obsidian*, remember? They let me read all their secret books."

Teo shook his head. "So how do we stop her?"

"Decapitation!" Niya said.

Teo ignored her. "Relio? Xio?"

Before either had time to respond, a gravelly, taunting laugh echoed through the trees.

"Bruja, they called me," La Lechuza rasped. "A witch. An omen of deadly, dangerous things to come."

Teo spun to the left where her voice had come from, but when she spoke again, it came from the right.

"If only they'd known how right they were."

Aurelio shot a ball of fire, but it crashed uselessly into a trunk. "*Dammit*," he hissed. "I can't track her."

"How is she doing that?" Niya said, practically spinning in circles. "Is she teleporting?!"

"Owls fly near silently," Teo explained. "It can be almost impossible to hear them approach."

"The precious humans feared me, so the dioses chased me off into this jungle." Her voice floated through the trees. "The Obsidians found me and took me in. They helped me reach my full potential, don't you think?"

The owl witch swooped in front of them, her beaked mouth stretched into a terrible smile. No one dared to respond.

"In return, I helped them overthrow the Golds and start the war. Things didn't work out. I have your father to blame for that," she added, circling Niya.

"Come down here and say that to my face!" Niya shouted back.

"Oh, Niya, Daughter of Tierra," La Lechuza sighed, as she slid back into the shadows. "All those muscles, yet you still aren't strong enough to save anyone, let alone your friends."

Niya's lips pulled back in a vicious sneer, but Teo caught the uncertain flash in her hazel eyes. Her knuckles had gone white around the hilt of her blade.

"You're the one hiding, lady!" Niya yelled back.

"*Niya!*" Teo hissed, elbowing her in the side, but Niya was *mad* mad.

"Some big scary owl witch you are! I've never even heard of you!"

A screeching laugh filled the air.

"I was banished with the rest of them, into the stars where it was cold and dark. But now? Venganza has given me a gift: the chance to exact my revenge on the dioses. And what better way than killing their beloved children?"

Teo had a terrible vision of La Lechuza dropping their lifeless bodies at Venganza's feet.

"Yeah, well, joke's on you," Teo snapped back. "The Golds would probably *love* it if you killed me."

In spite of everything, Teo heard a laugh bubble up in Xio's throat as Niya and Aurelio protested together, "*Teo!*"

La Lechuza screeched with delight. "I could swallow you whole and spit out your bones for your parents to find!"

Pillars of flames blazed to life in Aurelio's hands, shooting into the air, bright enough to momentarily illuminate the jungle. This time, they caught a glimpse of a massive wing as La Lechuza veered away into the canopy.

"Oh yes, let's not forget Aurelio, Son of Lumbre," the witch said with a low chuckle. "No matter how forgettable you actually are."

Aurelio didn't even flinch, but red-hot anger ignited under Teo's skin. He wanted to rip La Lechuza's feathers out until she apologized to Aurelio.

"How does she know who we are?" Niya hissed at Xio, who seemed startled that she was asking him.

"Because she's basically a diosa!" Xio whisper-shouted back. "She can smell blood types, and Caos gave her—"

"And Xio, Child of Venganza. Running away again?"

"—psychic powers," Xio finished dully. He turned to Teo. "If she tells Venganza I've betrayed them, we're fucked."

Betrayed them.

The words echoed in Teo's head. This still could've been part of an elaborate lie, but right now, Teo decided to believe him. He looked at Aurelio and Niya, who stood guard nearby, anxiously waiting for Teo to say something.

"What do you need?" he asked.

"Did you bring stuff to cook with?" Xio asked out of nowhere.

Aurelio, who always maintained his composure, was obviously baffled. "*What?*"

"Do you have salt?" Xio specified.

Aurelio just stared at him, so Teo stepped in.

"Yes, we have salt," he said.

A relieved smile lit up Xio's face. "Great! Where is it?"

Teo hesitated then looked around the clearing. "There, Niya's bag," he said, nodding to where her pack lay discarded by a tree.

La Lechuza stretched, opening her fifteen-foot wingspan, feathers flaring like dozens of blades.

Teo's wings jerked, threatening to take off, but he held his ground.

Suddenly, she launched herself forward. Before Teo could register what was happening, the owl witch sank her talons into Niya's shoulders.

She cried out in pain. "*Son of a*—" Niya lurched off her feet, carried away by La Lechuza.

"Niya!" Teo threw Aurelio a panicked look before taking off into the air. "Hang on!"

Teo chased after La Lechuza while Niya swung wildly from her clutches. "LET GO OF ME!" she yelled, trying to land a kick.

The owl witch was fast, dodging and diving under branches and around tree trunks. Teo kept slamming into bark and getting smacked in the face with leaves as he tried to catch up. He turned sharply and clipped his wing, knocking him to the ground.

Luckily, the dense foliage and damp soil broke most of his landing.

Aurelio was at his side immediately, tugging him back onto his feet. "Are you okay?" he asked, frantically looking him over.

"I'm fine," Teo groaned, doing his best to ignore the aches all over his body. Niya was in trouble, and Teo couldn't get to her. "She's too fast, I can't keep up!"

"*Crap*," Xio hissed, rubbing his forehead. "Quick! We need to try knocking her out of the air without Niya getting caught in the crossfire!"

Aurelio seemed unsure, likely torn between wanting to help Niya and not trusting Xio.

"I think we should listen to him," Teo said quickly. "He knows more than we do."

Aurelio dropped his hands and let out a frustrated growl.

Xio tried again. "Listen, I get that you don't trust me, but we don't have time for this! I can help!"

Aurelio glared at Xio, but what choice did they have? "How?"

Xio squeezed his eyes shut. "C'mon," he murmured to himself.

At first, Teo thought he was trying to come up with a plan, but then he felt a strange crackle of electricity in the air.

Black veins appeared in the skin around Xio's eyes. When he opened them, his pupils had expanded, swallowing the whites whole. They looked just like Auristela's and the others' had during the trials. Xio flexed his fingers and the crackly purple and smoky black energy swirled around his hands.

"That's new," Teo said weakly. He was so used to seeing Xio as a young Jade with no real abilities. Now he was seeing who Xio truly was—a powerful Obsidian.

Aurelio stared at him for just a moment before nodding once. "Let's go."

Teo, Aurelio, and Xio chased after La Lechuza on foot. Niya continued to cuss and thrash, making plenty of noise for them to follow. "Let go of me!"

La Lechuza threw out her wings and tossed Niya away. A scream tore through her throat as she plummeted toward the ground.

Teo launched himself into the air. "I've got you!" he shouted, flying as fast as he could. He dove after her, hands outstretched, but La Lechuza darted into his path. She knocked Teo off course before catching Niya in her talons again, toying with her.

La Lechuza dropped through the air again. This time, she tossed Niya to the side before landing on the ground. Niya rolled, tumbled, and slammed into a tree with a loud *crack*.

La Lechuza shook out her feathers and let out another screeching laugh. "*This* is what the dioses have sent to save their world? Pathetic!"

"Niya!" Teo shouted, dropping to her side.

"I'm okay," Niya groaned, rolling onto her back. She was definitely in better shape than the tree, which now had a Niya-sized dent of splintered wood in its trunk.

"And won't Venganza be *grateful* when I present the corpse of his traitor spawn as well," La Lechuza added, her head swiveling in Xio's direction. His face turned gray before contorting with anger.

That confirmed it—Xio wasn't working with the Obsidians any longer.

Xio charged forward. Purple energy crackled around his hands before bolts blasted from his palms.

Teo shouted a warning. "Watch it!" But it was too late.

Aurelio, a ball of fire swelling in his hand, was also running toward the owl witch. He crossed into Xio's line of fire. Teo's heart lurched into his throat as the bolt struck the owl witch and Aurelio both, exploding in electric purple and wispy black.

Aurelio's body seized as he was blasted right off his feet. La Lechuza let out an ear-piercing shriek.

"Relio!" Teo all but screamed, already running with Niya right on his heels.

Xio got there first. "I'm so sorry!" He tried to pull Aurelio up, but the Gold had a solid foot and who knew how many pounds on him.

Teo rushed to Aurelio's side. "Are you okay?" he asked, using his hands to steady the other semidiós.

Relief crashed over Teo as Aurelio stumbled to his feet. "It's fine," Aurelio said with a grimace, one hand braced against his ribs.

Teo frowned. He didn't believe Aurelio.

"He's trying to get us killed!" Niya shouted, pointing at Xio.

"I didn't mean to!" Xio rushed to explain, his face bright red with humiliation. "It was an accident, I swear!"

"He wasn't trying to kill Aurelio!" Teo barked. "He just has bad aim!"

"I'm fine," Aurelio repeated, leaning on Teo's shoulder. "Where did La Lechuza go?"

They all looked around the clearing, but the owl witch had vanished again. Xio grabbed Teo's arm and nearly yanked it from its socket. "We need to get the salt!"

"Don't listen to him, Teo!" Niya said. "He wants to destroy all our food and *starve* us!"

Xio turned to her and shouted back, "You won't have a chance to die of starvation if you don't show me where the salt is!"

Teo lurched back a step, surprised by Xio's anger. He could practically feel it wafting off his skin.

Niya, on the other hand, squared up. "I don't *WANT* to die of starvation, Xio!"

They didn't have time for this. Before Xio could keep fighting with Niya, Teo got behind him. In one swift movement, he hooked his arms under Xio's armpits, holding him tight, and took off into the air.

Xio yelped as the ground dropped out from under him. Teo was far from steady, but it was definitely faster than running. They landed hard and stumbled over to Niya's bag. Teo wrenched it open, pushing aside clothes and empty Taki bags.

Suddenly, Aurelio screamed, "WATCH OUT!"

Teo didn't think. He just acted.

He grabbed Xio, shoved the backpack into his arms, and threw him to the side. A second later, La Lechuza was on top of Teo, knocking him onto his wings. Standing over him, she bent down, opened her terrible mouth, and *screeched*.

It was abruptly cut off when Teo slammed his foot into her throat. "Hurry, Xio!" he shouted.

Xio ripped open the bag again and searched frantically until he found it. Xio jumped to his feet and waved the plastic cylinder of salt above his head. "I got it!"

That got La Lechuza's attention. With a terrifying twist of her neck, her head swiveled a full 180 degrees toward Xio.

At first, Teo thought La Lechuza was somehow growing bigger, but then he realized she was just standing up. Scrawny feathered legs stretched out under her, nearly half the length of her entire body, as she stretched her wings out wide and screamed. In one of the most horrifying things Teo had ever witnessed, La Lechuza charged at Xio in long, lumbering steps.

Teo scrambled to his feet and launched himself forward. He dropped in front of her in an attempt to slow her down, but La Lechuza headbutted him, knocking him out of the way. Teo crashed to the ground.

Xio scrambled to get the saltshaker open, his fingers fumbling with the stopper.

Aurelio tried to intercept, but La Lechuza blocked his fire attack with her wings before sweeping him out of the way. Xio wrenched the stopper free as Niya tried to tackle the owl witch, but was flung away.

The creature was mere feet away, beaked mouth gaping open, ready to swallow Xio whole.

Horrified terror ripped through Teo. "XIO!" he yelled.

Just as Xio threw a handful of salt in her face.

La Lechuza *screamed.*

The salt sizzled and burned like acid. The owl witch stumbled back, desperately trying to wipe off her face, but it continued to scorch her. Aurelio appeared at Xio's side. He poured salt into his hand and tossed it at her, too.

La Lechuza threw up her wings to shield herself, but it just burned through her feathers, releasing puffs of smoke.

When she tried to run away, Teo called to Aurelio. "Here!" he said, taking off into the air.

Aurelio tossed the shaker into the air. Teo caught it and dumped the whole thing out over the bruja's head.

La Lechuza howled and wailed, colliding into trees and almost tripping over Niya before Teo landed next to her and pulled the battered Gold out of the way. Xio stood with Aurelio and all four watched as La Lechuza disappeared into the jungle, leaving nothing but wails and wisps of smoke in her wake.

"Holy crap, it worked!" Xio panted as he struggled to catch his breath. A delirious laugh bubbled in his chest. It was nice to hear. "It worked!" Xio repeated, like he hardly believed it.

Teo found himself grinning.

Xio turned toward them, a smile plastered across his face.

Only for a heavy golden net to knock him off his feet.

Teo jumped. "What the—"

"What the hell!" Xio shouted, thrashing and trying to free himself.

Niya stood over him, disheveled and bleeding gold, her face contorted into a snarl. "You *asshole!*"

CHAPTER 19
XIO

Xio was an expert at running away. They knew the moment you let the fear in—the second you started to question, *Should I really be doing this? What if I get myself lost and die out here?*—that was the moment you were done for. Being a runaway was 10 percent motive, 90 percent confidence that you would be okay, that things would be better on the other side.

But right now, "the other side" happened to be three disheveled semidioses, staring back at them.

This was supposed to be it—the opportunity they needed to prove to Teo, Niya, and Aurelio that they were on the same side now. Xio had been feeling confident, too.

Until they'd messed up and blasted Aurelio.

Xio had thought they'd made up for it with their salt idea. They'd changed sides, ditched the Obsidian dioses, and risked everything to save their friends.

But, judging by the fact that Xio was currently trapped under a net with a *furious* Niya stomping toward them, maybe not.

"We found the traitor!" Niya announced triumphantly.

Xio sat on the ground, scowling up at Niya through the gaps in the golden ropes. "I literally came looking for you."

"*Shut up!*"

Aurelio frowned at Xio. He didn't seem quite as distrustful as Niya, but the fire demigod was clearly still pissed, likely about his sister, which Xio couldn't blame him for.

Teo seemed like their only hope, but he just kept staring at Xio like he'd seen a ghost.

"So what do you want to do with him?" Teo asked Niya.

Xio glanced up at him. When their eyes met, Xio's chin immediately dropped to their chest, attempting to shield their red face with their hair.

"I wanna take him, and I wanna put him in a jar," Niya said, enunciating every word. "And then I wanna take that jar and *shake it.*" Niya violently pantomimed the motion for emphasis.

Xio scoffed and rolled their eyes. They knew they were supposed to be groveling at the other semidioses' feet, but time was precious. Xio let out a frustrated growl and tugged at the net again. "Look, you're not on a secret mission anymore!"

Teo turned. "What do you mean?"

"The Obsidians know you're coming!" Xio rushed while they had his attention. "That's why they sent La Lechuza! Because of how predictably *noble* you Heroes are—no offense," they added, trying to keep their anger under control. "And beyond that, Auristela telling them you were going to come kick their asses gave it away, for sure."

Aurelio surged forward. "You've seen her?" he demanded. "Is she okay?"

Xio shrank back. "Uh, yes?" they tried, not fast enough to be convincing. "I don't know—she's in a ball of ice, locked up in a prison cell! " they admitted. "I *can* tell you she's been giving me hell since she got there."

Aurelio nodded, but his mouth was pressed into a hard line, his expression tight.

"How far is the temple from here?" Teo asked.

"I'm not a GPS, but it took me like four hours to find you?" Xio guessed. "So, however far that is."

"Where are the others?"

"Also locked up in the tunnels below the temple, like I said. Caos put together cells—" Xio cut themself off. Guilt and shame soured their stomach. They couldn't work up the nerve to admit they were the one who came up with the idea. "Each cell is designed specifically to keep each of them contained," they added hesitantly.

"Are they all alive?"

"Yes."

"Is anyone hurt?"

Xio hesitated again. They thought of Auristela in her block of ice, Marino slowly dehydrating to death. It didn't seem so bad in theory, but in practice? Xio's stomach gave another churn.

"Not yet," they finally said. "Which is exactly why we need to get going. The Obsidians are keeping them alive as bait, but I don't know how long that's gonna last. Especially after La Lechuza tells them I'm a traitor."

"That's because you *are* one," Niya replied viciously, getting herself riled up again. "He's probably just *lying* to us again!"

Xio bit back a reply. Was no one going to believe them?

Teo wiped the sweat from his forehead, looking exhausted. "How did you find us?" he asked.

"Venganza sent me out with La Lechuza to find you guys," Xio explained. They left out the part where the Obsidian god wanted them to use their powers against the trio when they found them. "She came back and told me where you were, so I ran for it. I don't know how I got to you before she did. I was just—" Xio's words caught in their throat. "Lucky."

Niya took over the interrogation. "How do these Celestials keep finding us?"

"Oh, I don't know, probably because you're all cosplaying as glowsticks right now?" Xio said sarcastically.

The trio looked down at their illuminated suits, and then at one another.

"Okay," Teo sighed. "That *does* seem like an obvious one we should've considered sooner."

"He did help us get rid of La Lechuza," Aurelio said, but the look of distaste—one that was eerily similar to his sister's—made it clear he wasn't giving Xio the benefit of the doubt.

"Yeah, and he also helped us get rid of *the sun* and trigger the apocalypse, remember?" Niya pointed out. "We have no idea what he's up to, or what nasty little *scheme* he's cooking up!"

"I can hear you," Xio barked.

Niya turned and snapped at them. "Good!"

Teo stepped forward. "Why did you betray us?" Xio was surprised to hear the heavy emotion in his voice. "We were your *friends.*"

Xio stared up at him. The look on Teo's face caused them physical pain. They opened their mouth and everything came spilling out.

"Because I *hated* the Golds and how they treat anyone lower than them! They *slaughtered* my family and *whole cities,*" they stressed, pleading with Teo to understand. "My only flesh and blood was banished to the stars! The man I thought was my dad, who I *trusted*, lied to me about who I was my entire life!"

They felt tears prickle their eyes. "I was in a *dark* place. I thought I was literally a monster and if anyone else found out, they'd *kill* me! I thought the only place I was safe—the only place I could be *myself*—was with the Obsidians." Xio's shoulders slumped. "I thought I had nowhere else to go."

Xio's heart pounded in their chest as the reality of their actions crashed down on them like a tidal wave.

They had joined the Obsidians in hopes of tearing down an oppressive system, but they had only succeeded in replacing one caste of ruling gods with another, far worse one. The world they were helping the Obsidians create was not one where they fit in, either.

"Still not a good enough reason to release the Obsidians and kidnap our friends," Aurelio told them, but at least he wasn't mean about it.

Xio sniffed and rubbed their nose on their sleeve. "I know I messed up," they admitted, their voice barely audible. "But I can't change the past. All I can do is try to make things right."

"How? By doing what?" Niya demanded, determined to stay mad. "You've been working for Venganza this whole time!"

"I didn't realize how wrong I was," Xio conceded, quickly losing steam and just feeling *tired*. "But I'm not going to stand by and watch the Obsidians destroy everything. I'll do whatever it takes to stop them."

Xio's drive for vengeance had blinded them to the true nature of the Obsidians. They wanted a world where people would be captured and shackled. Where more fighting would lead to more death.

And as this thought settled in their mind, a different kind of anger ignited within them—one of defiance against the very gods Xio had risked everything to swear allegiance to. They couldn't stand idly by as the Golds suffered, not when they were responsible for trapping them there in the first place.

"Even if it means betraying your new 'family'?" Niya asked.

The word conjured up memories of laughter-filled meals, warm embraces, and whispered words of comfort. Xio thought of Teo and Niya, who had stood by them through thick and thin during the trials.

Xio knew now that Venganza, Chupacabra, and Caos weren't their family, no matter what color their blood was.

Teo and Niya were. Xio shimmied under the net to tug down their sleeve, revealing their azabache bracelet. The polished, fist-shaped obsidian charm looked out of place against the velvety jet and red coral. Without a second thought, Xio pried it off and, through the netting, flicked the piece of Venganza's gylph into the dark jungle.

"I'm not one of them," Xio said firmly, their resolve hardening. "Not anymore. I don't belong with the Obsidian dioses, and I never did."

Teo sighed. "I want to trust you so bad, Xio. But you've made it hard."

Xio nodded, blinking rapidly, willing their tears not to fall. "I know."

The four of them stood in silence for a moment, sizing one another up. In one way or another, they all felt they had failed—Teo as the Sunbearer, Aurelio as the son his mother wanted him to be, Niya's own desperate need to save everyone, and Xio, the Obsidian-blooded traitor.

"Listen," Xio said. "We really need to get going." They drew their hands together and with a crackling *snap*, a section of net disintegrated in a puff of purple.

Niya gasped, offended. "My net!"

"They're going to realize I'm missing soon," Xio continued, crawling through the hole and leaving the rest of the net in a heap. "So, let's haul ass, maybe?" they asked, dusting themself off.

Niya sniffed. "I still think you're a piece of shit."

"No, no," they said, already leading the way into the trees. "I *used* to be a piece of shit."

"You are still *acting* like a piece of shit," she slung back.

Xio stopped and spun around. "But I used to *want* to be so much worse." They huffed, exasperated. "And that should count for something." They looked at Teo, hopeful. "Right?"

Xio held their breath, waiting for him to respond. It was hard to look him in the eye.

"What are you thinking?" Aurelio asked, watching Teo carefully.

Teo's mouth twisted into a guilty smile. "I'm scared to make the wrong choice."

Aurelio nodded. "Me too. What's your gut telling you?"

"To leave him tied up to a tree," Niya grumbled, angrily fixing her braids.

"That he's probably telling the truth," Teo answered.

A wave of relief hit Xio straight in the chest, nearly buckling their knees.

"We either take a chance and bring him with us, or we risk going into Venganza's temple with no information," Teo said.

Aurelio sighed. "All right, let's do it."

Xio's brow lifted. A lot had changed since they'd parted ways. Aurelio seemed fully integrated into the unbreakable duo that was Teo and Niya. Xio was ready for Niya to put up a fight, but instead, she let out an exasperated groan. "Fine!" she growled before warning them, "But I'm gonna be a dick about it!"

All three turned back to Xio.

"We'll trust you," Teo told Xio.

Their eyes widened in surprise. "Really?"

"But if you do anything remotely suspicious," Teo said firmly, "we *will* leave you tied to a tree."

Xio nodded. "Noted."

"Just—" Teo sighed. "Don't make us regret it," he said earnestly. "Please?"

Xio grinned. "I won't! I swear!"

"And Niya gets to be your chaperone," Teo added as an after-thought.

This immediately improved Niya's mood. With a flick of her hand, her titanium bangle turned into a set of manacles—one on Niya's wrist that was attached to one on Xio's by a woven metal cord.

Niya beamed. "This makes me feel better."

Xio held it up and gave Teo a flat look. "Seriously?"

Teo nodded. "That's the deal."

Xio rolled their eyes but agreed. If it helped the trio trust them, then they'd deal with it. "Whatever. Now, let's go. The temple isn't that far," Xio said, gesturing for them to follow. "Also, turn off your glowy suits. We're trying to be *covert*, so—"

Niya yanked on the cord attached to Xio's wrist, sending them stumbling backward.

Xio turned to her and glared.

Niya grinned smugly. "Just checking!"

CHAPTER 20
TEO

"We should probably stop and rest," Xio said, glancing around the jungle. "This is our last chance before we get too close to the temple."

Niya cut them a suspicious look. "Are you lying?"

"Oh my gods," Xio grumbled, pinching the bridge of his nose. "No, I'm not lying!"

"Niya," Teo sighed. "Please?" Her constant vigilance was grating.

Thankfully, she made a disgruntled noise and plopped down against a tree. Xio joined her, close enough to Niya for the manacle not to pull, but far enough to give her some space. She seemed unable to relax, shifting restlessly as she glared at the ground.

It wasn't just Niya. Aurelio sat there, tapping on his golden armbands as he stared off into space. Teo dug in his pack and gave each of them a squished protein bar.

Aurelio pulled out a jar of instant coffee and filled a pan with the Decanter of Endless Water. His movements were slow and mechanical, controlled within an inch of his life.

Teo attempted to eat, but the protein bar stuck to his teeth and throat like cement.

"What exactly is our plan?" Xio asked Teo, fidgeting with his azabache bracelet.

Niya cut in. "First, it's *our* plan," she said, gesturing among the three of them. "Not *your* plan. And secondly"—she turned to Teo—"we shouldn't be giving *him* our secrets!"

"Actually, I'm trying out they/them pronouns," Xio said.

Teo's eyebrows lifted. "Are you?" When they nodded, Teo smiled. "Thanks for telling us. Good for you."

Xio smiled back and blushed.

"Sorry," Niya said, surprisingly sincere before going back to being angry. "*They* are the enemy and we shouldn't be giving *them* our secrets!" she corrected.

"We've committed to trusting Xio," Teo told her again. "If we're gonna pull this off, they need all the information." To her credit, Niya snapped her mouth shut and didn't argue, but she *did* shoot Xio an impressive death glare.

"We're not just rescuing the others," Teo told Xio. "We're going to resurrect Sol, take down the Obsidians, and bring back the sun."

Xio frowned like they'd heard him wrong. "Wait—what?"

"The dioses are gathering the Sun Stones from the temples," Teo went on. "It's our responsibility to get the Sol Stone and then summon the dioses so we can re-form Sol's body. Then, we'll complete the ritual to refuel the stones, resurrect Sol, and hopefully they'll banish the Obsidians back to the stars."

"So . . . we're bringing Sol back to life?" Xio said.

Teo nodded. "That's the plan."

Xio stared at him.

Teo knew it was half-baked, but what else could they do? These were three *dioses* they were going up against. Hopefully, with Xio's insider information, they could figure out a way to take them down.

"Do you know where the Sol Stone is?" Aurelio asked Xio, still working over the fire.

"Yeah, but Venganza carries it around with him all the time like some kind of trophy," Xio explained. "We can't just sneak in and steal it."

"I guess we'll have to be creative," Teo said, rubbing the back of his neck. Teo was better at thinking on his feet, anyway.

Xio grew quiet, lost in thought.

"You okay?" Teo asked, giving Xio a bump of his shoulder.

"I wanted to fit in and now I've only made things worse," Xio said miserably. "I used to just be a loser Jade Child of Mala Suerte, now I'm the evil Obsidian who released Venganza and killed the sun—"

"Actually, I did that part," Teo pointed out.

"What's Sol going to do with me?" Xio asked in a weak voice.

Teo froze. "What do you mean?"

"If Sol banishes the Obsidians back to the stars, are they going to banish me, too?" they asked.

Teo's chest ached. Suerte had basically expressed the same worry, but at this point, it didn't matter what Xio had done in the past. Teo refused to let anything happen to them.

"Though maybe banishment is better than whatever sort of punishment Lumbre and Guerrero would cook up for me when all this is over," Xio said with a shudder. "Even if we pull this off, what are people going to think of me? Or *do* to me?" they continued, their voice cracking. "How can I ever make up for ... everything?"

"By working to create a better future," Teo told them firmly, holding Xio's gaze. "You may not be able to change what you've done, but you can use it as fuel to drive you forward. You can still make a difference."

"*We* can make a difference," Niya insisted.

"I don't know if I can," Xio mumbled.

"Of course you can," Teo said with a reassuring smile. "But you have to be willing to try. So, let's do it together."

"And kick some Obsidian ass in the process!" Niya agreed.

Xio looked at them and nodded. Teo didn't know if they believed him—he wasn't even sure he believed himself—but he was going to do whatever he could.

Aurelio's voice startled Teo from his thoughts. "Here." He handed Xio a steaming cup of coffee.

"Thanks," they said, curling their hands around the warm mug. "Any chance you've got—"

Aurelio held out a small container of sugar.

Xio took it. "Wow, you'll make a great house-husband one day," they teased.

Teo chuckled. "He's an amazing cook," he confirmed. It felt so good to finally have all four of them back together again.

Niya also laughed, but when Xio grinned at her, she quickly went back to glaring. "Teasing Aurelio is a privilege, not a right," she said. "You have to earn it back." Niya plucked the sugar from their hand and dumped some into her own coffee.

Xio sank into his jacket like a turtle.

"She'll warm back up," Teo whispered to Xio. "Niya's not built to hold grudges." Xio gave him a doubtful look. "What about her feud with Auristela?"

"Umm . . . ," Teo waffled. "It's complicated."

Aurelio sat down next to Teo, close enough that their hips touched.

"Thanks," Teo said, beaming at Aurelio as he took a coffee. Aurelio flashed him a quick smile. They looked down at their cups at the same time, but Teo could see from the corner of his eye that they were wearing matching goofy grins.

Xio leaned toward Niya and whispered, "Has this been going on the whole time?"

Niya dramatically threw herself back. "Oh my *gods*, you have *no idea!*"

Aurelio blushed furiously, but Teo had no shame left. If this really was the end of the world, then he was not going to deprive himself of small pleasures. Teo ignored them and rested his hand on Aurelio's knee. It did not help the blushing.

"It's been killing me, and I—" Niya went on before cutting herself off. She scowled at Xio. "And I'm still mad at you! So stop trying to trick me into liking you again!"

"I saw you use Tierra's Unbreakable Blade back there," Xio tried. "It's super famous, one of the most powerful weapons in history. The dioses usually give their gifts to their strongest children, and you're the only one I know of he's ever given it to."

Teo had the feeling Xio was trying to butter her up. And it worked.

Niya's face lit up. She puffed out her chest with pride and flicked her wrist. The golden sword sprang to life in her hand. "Isn't she pretty?" she said, lovingly caressing the flat of the blade. "And Diose Guerrero gave me this!"

Xio ducked, narrowly avoiding decapitation as the massive shield materialized in her other hand. "Whoa," Xio breathed, gaping at the jaguar head embossed in leather. "That's Guerrero's Ring of Shielding!"

"Some of the dioses gave us presents before we left," Teo explained.

Xio's eyes grew wide. "Really?" they asked, scooting closer. "Can I see?"

"Hell yeah!" Niya put the shield away. "Diosa Agua gave us her Decanter of Endless Water," she said, pointing. "And Diosa Primavera gave us the Gem of Regeneration," Niya continued. She pulled out the brilliant green gemstone from a side pocket of her backpack.

"Damn, that's handy," Xio said.

"Aurelio's mom gave him the Scorching Circlet," Niya went on. "But he doesn't like to talk about it."

Aurelio scowled in response. Xio took the hint and didn't ask.

"Oh!" Niya went on, unfazed. "Diosa Amor gave us that little bottle of stuff—"

She went for Aurelio's bag, but he yanked it out of reach.

"Relio! I want to see it!" Niya barked.

He rolled his eyes, opened a pouch, and tossed Niya the vial.

She caught it out of the air and handed it to Xio. "This thing!"

Xio examined the metallic red liquid. "The Elixir of Charming," they said, giving it a shake. It swirled and glittered. "That's so cool!"

"And Teo got a used candle from Fantasma and a feather from his mom," Niya said flatly.

"That sounds . . . neat?" Xio offered, forcing a smile.

Teo sighed. "Pretty sure the candle is just a candle," he admitted. He would never insult Fantasma by saying it was a bad blessing, but sometimes she seemed confused by how others worked. "But the feather is like a walkie-talkie, so we can tell the dioses we've got the Sol Stone and they can come provide backup," Teo agreed, touching his earring.

"I almost forgot!" Niya dove into her pack again and handed Xio the Bag of Winds. "Tormentoso gave me this!"

"What is it?" they asked, tugging on the drawstrings.

"Be careful!" Teo shouted, lunging forward and snatching it from Xio's hands before they could release a hurricane.

Xio nearly jumped out of their skin.

"It's"—Niya paused for dramatic effect—"Tormentoso's Bag of Winds."

Xio blinked. ". . . Really?"

Niya's head bobbed in a nod, her lips pressed between her teeth.

They broke into laughter simultaneously.

Aurelio just shook his head at them, but Teo grinned.

"Hey, during the fight with La Lechuza," he said, drawing Xio's attention, "what was that stuff you shot out of your hands?"

"I didn't hurt Aurelio on purpose!" they blurted out.

Teo exhaled a surprised laugh. Poor kid. "No—I know. You were just trying to hit the owl witch."

Xio relaxed a little. "Yeah."

"Emotional energy generation?" Aurelio guessed.

They nodded with a meek smile. "Yeah—well, technically it's manipulation, not generation."

"How does it work?" Aurelio asked, leaning forward. It was nice to see him excited about something.

"I can gain power using my own vengeful energy to make me stronger, faster, more durable," they listed off. "The usual stuff. But I can also find the source of, and increase, a person's feelings of vengeance that they already have. I can't just *make* them feel vengeful."

Teo exchanged a confused look with Niya. It was a lot of words at once, but Aurelio nodded. "And you can use that energy to produce physical manifestations of vengeance?"

Xio sat up straighter. "Exactly!"

"Is that what the purple-and-black stuff is?" Teo guessed, looking between the two. He had to admit, it was a killer aesthetic.

Even Niya looked impressed. "With your mind, dude? I didn't know you could do that!"

"It's new," Xio said simply.

"Packed a punch, too," Aurelio added.

Xio's chest swelled with pride. "That's my Bolt of Vengeance! That was the first time I ever tried it!"

Teo's mouth twitched. "Bolt of Vengeance?" he asked, trying not to sound like he was laughing but he totally was.

"It's actually one of my least powerful moves," Xio told them.

"What's—" Niya cleared her throat. "What's your *most* powerful move?"

"Well, my Wave of Vengeance is stronger, but that one covers a larger area, so I have to be careful of who's around. I can do a Beam of

Vengeance, too, but it's pretty hard to aim," Xio listed enthusiastically. "I want to try making explosions—an Emotional Energy Bomb—but I definitely haven't gotten the hang of that one yet—"

A snort escaped Teo. Niya was barely holding back laughter. Aurelio glanced at them, confused.

Xio deflated. "You're making fun of me, aren't you?" they asked flatly.

"No!" Teo rushed, but now he was definitely laughing. He wasn't trying to make fun of Xio, but it was objectively both adorable and hilarious. "It's not that!" he insisted.

"I like that you've named them!" Niya said through laughter.

"You guys don't name your moves?" Xio asked.

"Usually the media comes up with the names," Niya explained.

"I'm not even cool enough to have moves," Teo confessed with a shrug. "And the media barely even knew I existed until a few weeks ago."

Xio's face was bright red. "Oh."

Niya nudged their leg with her foot. "Hey, don't be embarrassed!"

"We're just teasing you," Teo tried to reassure them. "It's our love language. Poor Aurelio's been getting the brunt of it without you. Isn't that right?"

Aurelio nodded gravely. "Yes."

"Yeah, whatever," Xio grumbled, but they did smile.

Later, when Aurelio squatted down next to Xio to take back their empty cup, he quietly admitted, "I secretly named my moves, too."

Xio looked like they felt a lot better.

Teo stood up and stretched. "Why don't we get some rest?" he suggested. "We could—"

In the distance, a branch snapped. All four of them froze.

"What was that?" Teo whispered, straining his ears.

A long, low howl echoed through the trees.

The color drained from Xio's face. "Oh no," they breathed, barely above a whisper. "She found us."

CHAPTER 21
TEO

Dread filled Teo's veins with ice as a figure slid from the trees, red-and-yellow eyes gleaming.

"Look who it is!" Chupacabra yipped, black lips peeling back to reveal rows of razor-sharp teeth.

"How did she find us?" Niya asked, her blade already out.

"La Lechuza isn't the only one who can hunt." Chupacabra snickered. "I could smell you from miles away."

"Stay focused," Aurelio urged quietly. His hands sparked with fire.

The diosa's wolfish head tilted as she eyed them hungrily. "And you've brought Junior with you!" Chupacabra cackled with delight. "Here I thought you'd run off for good, Xio!"

Xio trembled at Teo's side.

Niya's fists clenched, her eyes narrowing. Teo knew they were all thinking the same thing: It was time to fight.

"Let's do this!" Niya charged forward, her body a blur of motion. Aurelio followed close behind, his hands wreathed in flames.

"Sol's sake," Teo hissed. They needed a plan first! He expected this from Niya, but Aurelio was usually more levelheaded. Teo shot a look toward Xio, whose face had gone white. "It's all right," he said, quickly trying to reassure them before they dove headfirst into fighting a freaking diosa.

Xio nodded shakily.

Teo did his best to smile. "You've got this!"

Xio huffed a big breath and nodded again. "I've got this," they repeated.

Teo launched into the air, his wings carrying him above the fray while Xio darted after their companions.

Niya swung first, aiming a punch at Chupacabra, but the wolf-woman was faster—impossibly fast. She effortlessly dodged out of the way, leaving Niya to slam her fist into the trunk of a tree. The wood burst into splinters.

Chupacabra cackled. "This is going to be too easy."

"Oh, I can't wait to make you eat your words," Niya spat, pushing herself to her feet. "We're just getting started."

Aurelio came out of nowhere and threw himself at Chupacabra. His hands glowed with intense heat as he hurled a torrent of fire. She sidestepped out of the way before lunging for Aurelio, pushing him off-balance. Teo's breath caught in his throat as he watched Aurelio stumble back, narrowly avoiding a swipe of Chupacabra's claws.

"No wonder you're Mommy's second favorite," Chupacabra taunted, her eyes flickering maliciously. "You aren't even in the same league as your sister!"

Teo had never seen Aurelio so enraged. But before he could react, she was on him, closing the distance in a blink. His right hand ablaze, Aurelio swung at her, but Chupacabra blocked his strike, hitting his forearm to knock him off target.

Breathing heavily, Aurelio leapt back and regained his footing. He let out an angry bellow and threw another fire blast, this time hitting Chupacabra square in the chest.

The impact sent her reeling back, a pained yelp escaping her muzzle, her fur singed and smoking.

But the victory was short-lived. "Nice shot," she snarled, baring her teeth, "but you won't get another." She rushed Aurelio, claws extended, ready to tear him apart.

Aurelio ducked just in time, avoiding a potentially fatal blow. He tried to retaliate with a full-body uppercut, but Chupacabra was quicker. She kneed him in the face. Golden blood streamed from Aurelio's broken nose as he fell to the ground, dazed.

"Aw, did that hurt?" Chupacabra mocked, her laughter echoing through the trees. "You're going to have to do better than that if you want to save your precious sister."

Gritting his teeth, Aurelio wiped the blood from his face and struggled to his feet.

"Come on, fire boy," Chupacabra taunted, circling around Aurelio. "Show me that you're worth my time."

"I'm not afraid of you," Aurelio spat.

"Such confidence," Chupacabra cooed. "But can you back it up?"

"Enough!" Xio stepped out from the trees and into the clearing, drawing Chupacabra's attention. Black-and-purple energy crackled around their hands. "You're not going to hurt anyone else!"

"Really?" Chupacabra snorted, her eyes narrowing. Her wolfish grin stretched across her face. "How cute!"

While she was distracted, Teo saw his opening and banked sharply.

Xio launched an energy beam at Chupacabra just as Teo swooped in from above, aiming a kick to the back of her head. But Chupacabra dodged both Teo's dive and Xio's attack with a mocking laugh. The beam slammed into Teo, sending him tumbling through the air, breath knocked out of him.

"This is just pathetic," Chupacabra said, laughing maniacally as Teo struggled to recover.

"Ugh," Teo groaned, clutching his head as he tried to shake off the impact. He couldn't afford to make a mistake like that again.

"Are you okay?" Xio asked worriedly, quickly helping Teo to his feet.

"Yeah," Teo muttered.

"Pathetic." Chupacabra sneered, her gaze fixed on them with predatory intent.

"Why don't you take on someone in your weight class?" Niya shouted. She stomped her foot, and the earth beneath them trembled in response.

"Ooh, this should be fun!" Chupacabra said. "Let's see how a Child of Tierra measures up!

"Let's do this," Niya growled, launching herself forward with a powerful leap. The Unbreakable Blade burst to life in midair, and Niya swung it right for Chupacabra's neck.

The Obsidian diosa struck Niya's wrist, knocking the sword out of her grip. Niya let out a shout of pain as the Unbreakable Blade clattered to the ground. Now it was an all-out brawl. It was like an effortless game for her while Teo and his friends fought for their lives. They were outmatched. Four teenage semidioses were no match for an Obsidian diosa.

Chupacabra darted among them, her movements fluid and unnervingly fast. It was like an effortless game for her while Teo and his friends fought for their lives. They threw punches, kicks, fire, and vengeance, but it was like trying to hit air—the god was always one step ahead.

"Such impatience," Chupacabra sighed. "You really should learn to take your time."

"Shut up!" Niya snarled, her frustration growing with every missed blow. Behind her, Xio fired another energy beam, but Chupacabra just laughed and jumped aside. The beam sliced across multiple trees, leaving a scorched path across the bark.

"Over here!" Niya yelled. She snatched her sword up and leapt through the dust cloud, delivering a kick to Chupacabra's chest.

The impact sent the diosa skidding back but only slightly, and she quickly recovered. "Nice try," she hissed, reaching out to grab Niya by the leg.

With a vicious twist, she flung Niya toward Teo, who was unable to dodge in time. They collided, both of them tumbling to the ground in a tangle of limbs and feathers.

Teo groaned as Aurelio helped him to his feet, the weight of Niya's collision aching in his bones. "Thanks," he gasped, rubbing his bruised shoulder. He didn't know how much more he could take.

"No one worry about me, I've got it!" Niya grumbled as she struggled to her feet on her own.

"Enough games," Chupacabra hissed as she slipped behind Xio. She moved like a predator, her eyes wild and bloodthirsty, wolfish head low to the ground and teeth bared in a savage grin. "Time to end this." She slammed them to the ground, sending up a cloud of dust.

A shout lodged in Teo's throat as he watched helplessly. His heart raced, fear gripping him tightly. They had to do something, and fast.

But Niya was already in motion. She shot forward, her arm whipping out to strike Chupacabra in the throat. For a brief instant, hope bloomed in Teo's chest as Chupacabra crumpled to the ground, gasping for air.

But then, with a snarl that sent shivers down Teo's spine, she surged back to her feet, saliva dripping from her black lips. Before anyone could react, she barreled into Niya, knocking her back down and pinning her.

"Niya!" Teo shouted, racing forward, but in a flash, Chupacabra leapt off of Niya and launched herself at him. He tried to flap his wings and lift himself higher, but sharp pain tore into his wings as her claws raked across them, drawing lines of fire that made him cry out. Teo kicked out at her, desperately trying to escape her relentless pursuit.

"Slowing down already?" Chupacabra asked, her eyes gleaming with cruel delight. "I thought you were Sol's chosen one, Sunbearer!"

"Leave him alone!" Xio shouted, rage contorting their face as they fired an energy beam at Chupacabra. The force of the blast sent her flying off Teo.

Teo's heart pounded in his ears, drowning out everything but the sound of Chupacabra's snarls and his friends' ragged breaths. "Thanks," Teo panted, his wings quivering from the pain. Xio just nodded, their eyes locked on Chupacabra as she picked herself up and sprinted toward Aurelio.

Chupacabra's laughter echoed through the air as she dodged the semidiós's attacks and effortlessly knocked Aurelio down, her claws digging into his shoulders. Aurelio tried to push her off, but Chupacabra's grip only tightened. He let out an agonized shout as her claws sank deeper into his skin.

"Aw, is the little luciérnaga tired?" Chupacabra sneered into his face. "How cute."

"Get off me!" Aurelio snarled, thrashing under her.

Forcing his wings to hold steady, Teo swooped in, tackling Chupacabra off Aurelio and sending her crashing to the ground. Teo helped Aurelio to his feet, their hands lingering for a second.

"Thanks," Aurelio whispered, his cheeks flushing from both the heat of battle and the warmth of Teo's touch.

"Anytime," Teo replied with a grin, but their moment was short-lived.

With a roar, Niya appeared out of nowhere, throwing a punch that actually connected with Chupacabra's jaw. The diosa reeled, giving Teo and Aurelio the opening they needed.

"I've got an idea!" Without warning, Teo hooked his arms under

Aurelio's and took to the air, flying them above the fray. Aurelio jerked in surprise as the ground disappeared beneath him.

"Time for an aerial attack?" Teo asked. In response, Aurelio summoned a roaring ball of fire in his hands. Teo aimed for the perfect opening.

"Ready?" Teo asked, his voice tight with concentration.

"Ready," Aurelio confirmed, his eyes locked on Chupacabra below.

They struck as one, Teo diving toward the ferocious god while Aurelio unleashed a torrent of flames. But Chupacabra was cunning. She dodged their strike, leaving Teo and Aurelio to crash-land into the hard dirt.

"Pathetic!" Chupacabra laughed, sprinting toward them with murderous glee.

"Niya, now!" Teo shouted, coughing through the dust. Niya responded with a fierce battle cry, her earth powers surging as she threw up a wall of stone to protect them from Chupacabra's relentless assault.

"Xio! Here!" Niya called out, sprinting toward Teo and Aurelio, bare hands glowing in a way Teo had never seen before.

Xio didn't need to be told twice. They collided into a huddle as Chupacabra rolled to her feet. Teo latched on to Niya's waist, Aurelio behind him while Xio tucked into her other side, covering his head with his arms.

Niya slammed her fists onto the ground. Slabs of limestone erupted from under her feet, folding over the four to shelter them from Chupacabra's relentless assault.

"Knock, knock! Let me in!" Chupacabra sang, her claws digging against the stone barrier. Sweat beaded on Niya's brow as she strained to maintain it.

"Why are you hiding?" Chupacabra hissed through the cracks. "Auristela was much braver. It took much longer for her to break—"

"Shut up!" Aurelio roared.

Before anyone could do anything to stop him, Aurelio broke through the stone. He summoned a massive fireball and hurled it at Chupacabra with all his strength. But even that was not enough—she merely laughed off the flames, unfazed by his fury.

"Enough talking, time for some screaming," Chupacabra taunted in sadistic delight. "The world will suffer slowly at our hands, but I will make sure your deaths are much slower."

"I'm not afraid of you or death," Aurelio spat, his voice shaking.

"Then you're just as foolish as you are brave," Chupacabra shrieked.

"Teo," Aurelio called, desperation creeping into his voice. "Give me the Scorching Circlet."

Teo hesitated. "Are you sure?"

"We don't have a choice," Aurelio insisted. "Do it!"

There was no time for him to think.

A huge chunk of limestone soared by. It slammed into Chupacabra, sending her flying. Niya breathed heavily, her brown skin covered in dirt and golden cuts. "Go!" she told Teo. "I've got this!" With that, she went after Chupacabra, her shield and blade in hand.

Teo's heart hammered in his chest as he raced for Aurelio's pack, abandoned by the tree line. His shaky fingers fumbled with the straps. "Where is it," Teo muttered, his heart pounding as he dug through the bag. The sound of Chupacabra's laughter echoed through the air, mingling with the clash of metal and shouts from his friends.

His fingers touched something smooth and warm. "Got it!" He wrenched out the Scorching Circlet, its velvety coals glittering in the starlight. But as he pulled it out, a glint caught his eye as something slipped from the pack and clattered to the ground.

Teo stared for a moment, unable to process what he was seeing. It was a dagger. But not just any dagger.

It was the sacrificial obsidian dagger. The one Teo had held in his hands the night of the Sunbearer ceremony. The one he had been supposed to use to carve out Auristela's heart. The one he'd lost after the Obsidians' attack.

What was it doing in Aurelio's bag?

"Teo!" Aurelio shouted, snapping him out of his thoughts. "The circlet!"

Teo turned to him, the circlet in one hand and the dagger in the other. Teo looked at Aurelio, confused. His mind raced, the pieces falling into place like a horrifying puzzle.

Aurelio met Teo's gaze, his eyes widening in understanding.

The gravity of his intentions weighed on his face, as Aurelio reached out and took the circlet from Teo's unresisting hand. Something heavy settled in the pit of Teo's stomach. The realization hit him like a punch to the gut—

Aurelio was going to sacrifice himself.

Before Teo could say anything, the Scorching Circlet sparked to life on Aurelio's head. With the powerful artifact in place, a surge of power flowed through Aurelio, like a shock wave of golden light glowing under his skin. "Stand back," Aurelio warned his friends, turning to face Chupacabra, his fiery resolve burning brighter than ever.

"Aurelio," Teo said, stepping forward. His feathers were on edge, every fiber of his being screaming at him to stop Aurelio.

"Ah, so you've decided to show your true strength, little fire godling," Chupacabra taunted, her voice dripping with malice. "I must say, I'm quite eager to taste Auristela's fear when I devour her whole." She chuckled, licking her lips. "Most find the smell of fear off-putting, but I find it *delectable*."

Aurelio roared, his voice filled with pain and fury. The air around him shimmered with heat, the ground beneath him smoldering. His body convulsed with the intensity of it all, transforming him into a living torch. Flames erupted around him, wild and uncontrollable, lashing out at everything within reach.

Teo had never seen Aurelio like this—so consumed by anger that his rationality had been burned away along with any regard for his own safety, or that of his friends.

"Teo! Get back!" Niya shouted, grabbing his arm and pulling him away from the searing heat radiating off Aurelio. Xio followed suit, their face etched with concern. But Teo couldn't tear his gaze away from the raging inferno, his heart aching.

"Aurelio, stop!" Teo shouted.

But Aurelio seemed beyond reason, only focused on annihilating Chupacabra. He charged at her, a blazing meteor of wrath.

The air crackled with the heat of his passage. Chupacabra cackled with glee, flames sparking in the reflection of her wild eyes. "You're nothing but a puppet, dancing on the strings of your own anger! You think you can save your sister? You can't even save yourself!"

"Stop talking!" Aurelio screamed, the sound barely audible over the roar of the firestorm he had become.

"Such anger, such power!" she exclaimed. "But you're going to destroy everything around you, including your precious friends."

"Leave them out of this!" Aurelio snarled, his eyes wild and unfocused.

"Is this truly what you want?" Chupacabra asked, a twisted smile splitting her face open. "To burn so brightly that you destroy everything you hold dear?"

"*Aurelio!*" Teo shouted from a safe distance, but his words seemed lost in the chaos. How could he reach Aurelio when even his voice was swallowed by the flames?

"Teo," Niya said, her voice urgent. "We need to find a way to help him. If we don't, we'll all be toast."

Teo watched in horror as Aurelio, consumed by rage and fire, became a living inferno. Chupacabra's taunts echoed in his ears, but it was the look of desperation in Niya's eyes that spurred him into action. He *had* to stop Aurelio from hurting them and himself.

"Niya, Xio! Keep Chupacabra busy!" Teo shouted, taking flight. As he flew through the heat haze, the air scorched his lungs, but he forced himself to keep going. This was for Aurelio, and he couldn't let fear hold him back.

"Hey, Chupacabra!" Xio yelled. "Over here!" They threw a rock and hit her in the back. Chupacabra flinched and spun toward Xio, but it wasn't enough to hold her attention.

When Chupacabra turned back to Aurelio, Niya hefted a boulder the size of a donkey over her head.

"THEY SAID, 'OVER HERE'!" Niya shouted. She tossed the boulder, and it crashed into Chupacabra, slamming her into a tree.

With Chupacabra busy—for now—Teo zeroed in on the Scorching Circlet on Aurelio's head.

The searing heat intensified as Teo closed in. It was unbearable, searing his flesh, but he refused to relent. With a final surge of determination, he reached out with trembling hands and ripped the circlet off Aurelio's head.

"No!" Aurelio roared, the flames around him flaring wildly. Teo's wings and hands were scorched, the pain shooting through him like a thousand claws. But just as suddenly, the fire and Aurelio's anger began to recede.

Aurelio's eyes snapped open, flickering back to their warm copper hue. The firestorm was extinguished, the weight of what he'd done crashing down like a tidal wave.

But he was okay, and that was what mattered.

Teo's wings faltered, the pain overwhelming him. His vision blurred as he tumbled from the sky, landing with a bone-rattling *thud*.

CHAPTER 22
XIO

Niya screamed. Xio's blood ran cold.

Niya abandoned what she was doing and sprinted to Teo's side. She yelled his name, hands hovering over Teo's unmoving body as she hyperventilated.

Xio started to panic. Teo was in trouble, Niya was losing it, and Aurelio was in a pale-faced daze after his inferno.

Chupacabra stood in the clearing, rattling the trees with her malevolent laughter.

They had to think, and they had to think *fast*.

Xio lunged for Aurelio's bag, fingers digging until they found what they were looking for—the Elixir of Charming.

"Here goes nothing," Xio muttered, uncorking the bottle and downing its contents. The taste of sweet oranges tickled their tongue as a warm sensation spread through their veins, followed by a swell of confidence.

"Chupacabra!" Xio shouted, stepping forward. They tried to infuse their voice with charm—the way Teo did sometimes when he was talking to Aurelio. "Why don't you just let us go? We're not worth your time."

Chupacabra froze midlunge, narrowing her red-and-yellow

eyes as she assessed Xio. She shook her head with a low growl, like she was trying to clear her head. She snarled in annoyance. "You can't fool me with your pathetic attempts, Junior! I am a god, not a weak-minded mortal! Your little magic spells won't work on me!"

Xio started to panic as Chupacabra stalked forward. "Shit."

"It's an Elixir of Charming, which you are not!" Niya hissed angrily behind them, tears streaming down her cheeks as she clutched a still-unconscious Teo.

She was right. Xio wasn't charming.

But they were a master manipulator.

"You're right, you are a god," Xio said, trying their best to sound casual even though their heart was thundering in their chest. "So, why does Venganza act like you're his lapdog?"

"LAPDOG?" Chupacabra bellowed.

"He does, doesn't he?" Xio rushed to add, not wanting to be the focus of her rage. They chose their words carefully, poking and prodding at the aura of vengeance surrounding her. She reeked of it. "You could be doing so much more than chasing after us like some errand girl for Venganza!" they said, playing into her ego.

"I mean, why do you always do what Venganza says, anyway?" Xio asked with their best attempt at sounding innocently curious. "He needs you to do all his dirty work—like chasing us through the jungle," they pointed out.

Chupacabra frowned. "His dirty work . . ." she repeated, mulling it over.

Xio saw a thread and grabbed it. "You're Chupacabra," they stressed. "The most feared diosa in all of Reino del Sol! You don't need Venganza—Venganza needs you!"

"He does need me," the diosa agreed, anger edging her voice the longer she thought about it. Her eyes were distant, lost in thought.

Xio licked their dry lips before speaking. "Imagine how powerful you could be if you took control, stood up to Venganza. You could be the most powerful Obsidian there is. You should be the one giving orders, not acting as his mindless puppet."

Chupacabra's eyes flickered with interest—she was clearly tempted by the notion of power. She growled, her rage directed at Venganza now. "I'm out here doing his dirty work, fighting you demigods, while he sits in his temple!"

"Exactly," Xio agreed, planting the seeds of rebellion. "Why share power with Venganza and Caos? You could rule over Reino del Sol without them."

"I should!" Chupacabra agreed, clawed hands clenched into fists.

Holy shit, Xio thought, *this might actually work.*

Now was the tricky part.

"You should refuse to take his orders," they suggested slowly, carefully. For a moment, it seemed like Chupacabra might actually be convinced. "And you could start by letting us go . . ."

Too far.

Recognition lit Chupacabra's eyes.

She shook her head furiously, snapping herself out of Xio's trance.

Chupacabra let out a sharp laugh. "Oh, Daddy Dearest has taught you new tricks!" Her hackles raised, she opened her mouth to reveal rows of jagged teeth and a scarlet tongue. She took slow, deliberate steps toward Xio. "Now it's time for me to teach you some discipline."

Xio didn't have time to move.

She lunged at them, claws reaching for their throat—

WHOOSH.

Aurelio's fireball exploded inside her gaping maw. The diosa screeched and reared back, pawing at her mouth. The stink of singed fur burned Xio's nose.

In a blink, Niya was at Xio's side. She dug her fingers into the dirt and ripped large chunks of stone from the earth, throwing them on top of Chupacabra.

The diosa howled, claws scrabbling at the boulder, but Niya was relentless. In a matter of moments, Niya had Chupacabra buried under a heap of rocks.

"Go!" Aurelio shouted, grabbing their packs and herding them into the jungle.

Xio didn't need to be told twice.

Niya scooped Teo up in her arms and ran for it, Xio right behind her and Aurelio taking up the back.

"Giving up already?" Chupacabra jeered from behind them. "I thought you were supposed to be Heroes!"

"Keep going!" Aurelio snapped, giving Xio a shove when they tried to look back.

"You can't hide from me, diositos!" Chupacabra called through the darkness. "I'll chase you to the ends of the earth!"

They ran for their lives.

Once they were hidden deep within the jungle, darkness shrouded the group. Xio stood frozen, staring down at Teo, who lay unconscious on the damp forest floor, jade blood oozing from his wounds. Niya and Aurelio crouched over him.

"Shit, shit, shit!" Niya fumbled with her bag, panic lacing her voice. Her hands shook as she searched for something— anything—to help.

"Is he——?" Xio choked.

"He's alive but hurt," Aurelio said, his voice shaking with fear. "We need to do something."

"R-right," Niya stuttered, her breaths coming in ragged gasps. Aurelio's hands shook as he reached for Teo. "I'm so sorry," he choked out. "I didn't——"

"Stop!" Niya snapped, face pale as she smacked his hands away. "Where's Primavera's gem?! I can't fucking *see anything!*"

Aurelio raised his hands, sparks dancing between his fingers, illuminating the area for a quick moment before Xio grabbed his arm.

"That's too bright, Chupacabra will find us!" they warned him.

"Here, light this!" Niya exclaimed, finding the half-used candle Fantasma had given them. Aurelio's fingertips ignited, and he lit the candle. The small flame cast a warm, flickering glow over their terrified faces.

"We need to——" Niya didn't finish her sentence.

Suddenly, the ground beneath them trembled violently. Without warning, they were swallowed up by the earth.

Xio fell through the air and plummeted into icy water, the shock stealing their breath. Desperation filled them as they kicked to the surface. They broke through first, gasping for air, followed by Aurelio and then Niya, who managed to keep Teo afloat.

"Are you guys okay?!" Xio asked, bewildered and disoriented.

"I think so," Aurelio said, eyes wide. "Where's Teo?!"

"I've got him," Niya grunted through clenched teeth as she held Teo against her, keeping his head above water.

Xio looked around, confused and treading water. "Where the hell are we?"

"Cenote," Aurelio said, swimming for shore.

High, high above them, a circle of darkness opened up into the jungle above. The roots of ancient trees hung over the edge, reaching all the way down. Tiny black catfish darted through the luminous blue waters. Deep below, objects glittered that Xio couldn't quite see, even through the crystal clear water. Cobalt blue motmots flitted around, their vibrant plumage a stark contrast with the stone walls they nested in.

After Niya dragged Teo to shore, she looked around in a daze. "How did we—HOLY GODS!"

Xio whipped around, expecting to see another Celestial, or even Chupacabra.

Instead, they found a familiar figure.

"Fantasma!" Niya barked. "You scared the heck out of me!"

Fantasma stood at the edge of the water, waving at them with a cheerful smile. When she caught sight of Teo, her expression shifted to concern and she hurried over to help.

Xio grabbed their bags bobbing in the water and swam after them. Aurelio and Niya, who still held Teo, carefully made their way out of the water and onto land.

The area surrounding the water was littered with offerings— jade, gold, obsidian, crocodile teeth carved from green stone, and crystal eyes that stared back at Xio as they stumbled onto land. Beetle wings and large spiral shells crunched beneath their careful steps, forcing them to watch their footing.

"Did your candle bring us here?" Xio asked, still reeling.

Fantasma nodded, her monarch butterfly companions fluttering around her like an extension of her lace mantle.

Xio let out a relieved laugh. "You saved our asses!"

Fantasma gestured for them to follow her.

As they walked farther in, Xio noticed a cozy seating area,

decorated with a peculiar mix of items that only a goddess of death could find comforting. There were a couple of moth-eaten couches around a coffee table and a small fire nearby. Xio wondered what kind of company Fantasma had over to use them.

The goddess motioned Niya to one of the couches. She laid Teo down with tender care.

"Fantasma, can this help?" Aurelio asked, holding out the Gem of Regeneration. Fantasma's eyes widened in surprise as she took it from him, nodding gratefully.

Much to Xio's surprise, she pulled out a simple obsidian knife that honestly looked more like a letter opener and sliced her palm open. Xio watched, transfixed, as red blood welled up.

"Red?" Niya said, confused.

Aurelio shook his head like he didn't get it, either.

Xio was just as perplexed. Red was the color of *mortal* blood. As Fantasma's blood mixed with the gem's power, she gently applied it to Teo's wings. The effect was almost immediate. The pain seemed to ebb from his face as he relaxed into a deep sleep.

Niya huffed a big sigh. "Thank Sol—or, thank Fantasma!" she corrected.

Fantasma smiled sheepishly.

Even Aurelio seemed to relax a bit, but he was clearly still messed up from what had just happened. His nose was very obviously broken, and there were golden stains down the front of his shirt.

Xio yelped and scrambled back as a skeleton hand popped out of the ground, holding a stack of towels.

"Oh yeah, she does that," Niya said, taking one for herself as Fantasma handed another to Aurelio.

Aurelio mumbled his thanks and gingerly mopped up his face and dried himself off. Much to Xio's horror, Aurelio grabbed his own nose, squeezed his eyes shut, and with a grunt, reset it before it healed all the way.

Xio nearly gagged.

Fantasma held up the Gem of Regeneration in her bloody hand and glanced at all the golden cuts covering Niya's skin before giving her a questioning look.

"Thanks, but no thanks," Niya said with a grin, squeezing the water from her braids. "These are gonna make awesome scars."

Xio couldn't help grinning. They were bruised and battered, but they were alive, and right now that was all that mattered. "Is this where you live?" they asked Fantasma as she puttered around, fluffing pillows and smacking dust off couch cushions.

Fantasma nodded enthusiastically.

"That explains all the offerings," Xio mused, looking around at the discarded artifacts and trinkets. Death was the only diose who didn't have a city or temple. Instead, any offerings that were made to Muerte and Fantasma were sent through cenotes, the portals to the underworld. And, apparently, they all ended up here.

While Fantasma busied herself tending to Teo's injuries, some helpful skeleton hands popped up, offering the trio cups of steaming hot coffee. It was, shockingly, some of the most delicious dark roast Xio had ever tasted. Both they and Niya loaded their cups with cream and sugar.

They settled in to take a much-needed rest. While Niya regaled

Fantasma with stories of their battle with Chupacabra—and everything else they'd been through before that—Xio noticed Aurelio standing pensively by the edge of the cenote.

The flickering light from the blue water cast strange shadows over his face, making him appear even more solemn and enigmatic than usual. Xio approached him cautiously.

"Hey," Xio said softly, holding out the Scorching Circlet they grabbed before fleeing Chupacabra. "Thought you might want this."

Aurelio looked at the circlet with a mixture of surprise and dread. He took it from Xio, his fingers tracing the intricate patterns of coals. They glowed a deep, sleepy red at his touch. For a moment, he seemed lost in thought, staring at the circlet as if the answers to all his problems were carved into it, if only he could see them.

"Thanks," Aurelio murmured. Then, without a word, he hurled the circlet into the cenote. It sank beneath the surface with a soft splash, disappearing among the other offerings that lay hidden in its depths.

Xio smiled. They thumped Aurelio on the back and he grinned tiredly in response.

"Teo's waking up!" Niya exclaimed, her voice filled with relief.

Everyone gathered around Teo as he stirred, blinking groggily.

"Teo, you're a fucking badass," Xio said, looking at him with newfound respect.

"Did we win?" Teo asked, trying to drag himself back into consciousness.

Xio hesitated. "Well, we didn't *lose*—"

"Chupacabra's gone for now," Niya replied, gripping Teo's

hand gently. "But we need to regroup and figure out our next move."

"Good," Teo sighed, sinking back into the cushions with an exhausted grin. "I could use a break." But then he noticed the goddess perched on the couch next to him and jumped. "Fantasma?"

She beamed at him.

"Wait—" Teo blinked and frowned. "Where are we?"

"Fantasma's clubhouse!" Niya said cheerily.

"In a cenote," Xio clarified. "Somewhere. Turns out that candle she gave you wasn't just a candle."

Teo laughed and shook his head. "Thank you, Fantasma," he said, reaching for her hand. She blushed and gave his hand a gentle squeeze before abruptly standing up and hurrying through a crevice in the stone wall.

Aurelio stood nearby, his gaze locked on Teo's burnt hands and wings. Guilt and gratitude seemed to war inside him. The price Teo had paid to protect him obviously weighed heavily on his heart.

He crouched at Teo's side. "I'm so sorry," he said, his voice barely audible. "I didn't mean . . . I never meant—"

"Hand it over," Teo said, suddenly much more alert with his gaze fixed on Aurelio.

"Hand what over?" Xio asked, puzzled. Niya shrugged, equally confused.

Without a word, Aurelio reached into his bag and pulled out a dagger.

The group went silent.

Teo and Aurelio just stared at each other, wearing matching sorrowful expressions.

Xio tugged on Niya's arm. "Let's go," they whispered.

Niya frowned, confused. "But—"

Xio tugged her harder. "Let's go look for stuff in the water," they prompted.

Niya finally got the hint. She looked irritated but stood up to follow Xio, and they left Teo and Aurelio to have their privacy.

CHAPTER 23
TEO

Teo stared at the dagger.

The dagger.

He took it from Aurelio, wincing as he sat up, and tucked it into his bag.

Teo turned to look at Aurelio again, his expression a mix of concern and understanding. "You were planning to use it on yourself when we fight the Obsidians, weren't you?"

Aurelio stared at the ground, unable to meet Teo's gaze.

In that moment, Teo realized just how much his friends had been put through, and just how far they were willing to go to protect one another. They all had a burning desire to see this battle through to the end—even if it meant sacrificing themselves for the greater good.

But Teo wouldn't let that happen. He couldn't bear to lose his friends. To lose Aurelio.

Teo took a deep breath before turning to Aurelio. "So, let's talk," he said, his voice just above a whisper.

Aurelio winced and looked down at his hands.

"Are you really willing to die?" Teo asked, his voice trembling. "To leave us all behind?" *To leave* me *behind?* he wanted to say.

"Sometimes sacrifices must be made," Aurelio replied. "And I would do anything for my sister."

Teo refused to let the tears welling up fall. "What if there's another option?"

"Teo," Aurelio said, his tone firm but gentle, finally meeting his gaze. "We can't risk any more lives. We have to stop the Obsidians at all costs."

"Even if it means losing you?" Teo choked out, his heart aching.

"Especially then," Aurelio replied softly, and before Teo could say anything else, he added, "Auristela shouldn't have to be the one to die. She's destined for greatness—everyone knows it, especially my mother." The words seemed to cause him physical pain.

Anger burned in Teo's chest. "Your mother sucks," he said flatly. "And I think you are worth a hundred Auristelas."

Aurelio released a surprised laugh. "You are a good person who cares a lot about people," Teo told him. "You're kind, smart, and brave to the point of being stupid. You're an excellent cook, and you always put others before yourself, and sometimes it really pisses me off! But that's just part of what makes you *you*. Who cares that you aren't fire-proof, or that you're not the strongest semidiose of all time? You don't have to be a Hero! You could become a baker, or whatever!

"Not being a famous Hero doesn't mean you're not important, or that your life is expendable," Teo insisted, holding Aurelio's uncertain gaze. "There *has* to be another way. We didn't come all this way to still sacrifice your sister, *or* you."

Aurelio hesitated, fidgeting with his golden armbands. "But we could be together in the next world," he suggested, a devastatingly shy blush blooming across his cheeks. "I'd wait for you."

Teo couldn't take another word. He grabbed Aurelio's hand and squeezed it hard. "We could be together *now*."

A small, sad laugh escaped Aurelio's lips. "My sister always made me brave," he confessed, looking into Teo's eyes. "But you, Teo . . . you make me fearless."

Teo wanted to scream.

"This isn't sad," Aurelio tried to explain. "I'll be taken care of in the afterlife—Muerte and Fantasma make sure of that. I'm making this choice for the good of everyone, just as every other sacrifice has before me." He sat up straighter, his conviction clear. "It's an honor for me to give up this life in order to ensure the safety of Reino del Sol, and everyone who lives in it."

Aurelio gently pulled his hand away from Teo's and stood up. "I'm going to get more salve for your wings," he said. But then he paused and bent down, pressing a small kiss to Teo's temple, the warmth of his lips lingering on Teo's skin.

As Aurelio walked over to Fantasma, Niya slunk over to Teo's side. "Not that I was eavesdropping," she said, perching on the armrest of the couch.

Teo exhaled a bitter laugh. "Weren't you?"

Niya nodded. "I was," she confessed without remorse before going on. "He's always protecting everyone," she said thoughtfully, watching Aurelio. "But I think you're the only one who's ever thought to protect *him.*"

Teo watched as Aurelio carefully measured out the salve with Fantasma's help. He marveled at how someone could be so beaten up by the world and yet still willing to do everything in their power to protect it.

The recent trials had exposed the cracks in their world, the suffering of people on the borders, and the darkness lurking beneath the surface. Aurelio, the very embodiment of the Gold standard, had suffered greatly under the dioses' governance. And what about everyone else? The Jades, the mortals, even the unlucky souls seeking refuge with

Suerte—they were all at the mercy of the gods. Who, exactly, did the system serve? Certainly not the mortals they were meant to protect.

His thoughts racing, Teo felt an overwhelming sense of responsibility for not just Aurelio, but Niya and Xio as well. They were a team, bound together by fate or circumstance, and it was this understanding that made him realize they didn't need to throw themselves on the altar.

What had brought them this far was their ability to work together, care for one another, and *never* give up on each other. He knew they not only had the power to challenge the gods' flawed system, but the responsibility.

Aurelio kept saying it was an honor to sacrifice himself, but the same question still kept nagging at the back of Teo's mind: If being the sacrifice was such an honor, why was it given to the semidiose who came *last* in the trials?

He remembered being at the fountain in the Laberinto town square with the other semidioses. How Marino felt like he was cracking under the pressure. How tired Xochi was and how Atzi was homesick.

What was the point of it all? What was Sol's plan?

And why did they choose Xio to compete in the trials?

As stars peeked through the opening of the cenote, Teo and his friends settled down to sleep. They'd gathered all the cushions, pillows, and blankets Fantasma had fetched for them on the floor to sleep on, but heaviness hung in the air. They all knew these were their last moments of peace before the impending battle.

Niya was asleep immediately. Xio curled up in a ball, tucked between her and Teo. All he could see of them was their mass of black curls peeking above the edge of the blanket.

Aurelio was on his other side. Teo could feel the subtle tension that ran through his body like an electric current.

"Tell me about Quetzlan," Aurelio whispered, breaking the silence between them. His voice was soft, almost hesitant, as if he feared saying the words out loud might shatter the fragile quiet.

Teo was surprised by the request but grateful for the distraction. He began to paint a picture of his home with words, describing the bustling food carts that lined the streets, their tantalizing aromas. The vibrant colors of tropical birds flitted through his memories as Teo spoke, their songs echoing in his ears as if they were there with them in the cenote.

Aurelio listened intently, his eyes shining with longing. As Teo spoke, he felt the tension between them slowly dissipate, replaced by a sense of comfort that made his heart swell.

"Sometimes after detention I'd get fried potatoes to go from Lisa-Marie's and bring it to Lorenzo's food cart," Teo continued, his voice tinged with nostalgia. "He'd shave off pieces of al pastor straight from the trompo and onto the potatoes for dirt cheap. Then I'd sit under this enormous white sapote tree, watching the birds darting through the branches and picking at the fruit. It was the most peaceful place I knew."

"I wish you could show me," Aurelio said quietly.

"I will show you," Teo promised, his voice catching in his throat. "We'll go there together, and we'll get potatoes from Lisa-Marie, al pastor from Lorenzo, and a shit ton of candy from Chavo, and we'll eat until we can't move. Then I'll take you to the top of my mom's temple and we'll watch the sunset over the ocean."

Aurelio's lips curved into a small, bittersweet smile. "I'd like that," he murmured, resting his head against Teo's shoulder.

As they lay there entwined, Teo couldn't help letting his thoughts drift to the uncertain future. He knew the odds were stacked against them, but he refused to allow despair to take root. Instead, he clung to the image of Quetzlan, the promise of a sunset shared together in a better world.

"Aurelio," Teo whispered, his heartbeat as unsteady as his words, "promise me that, no matter what happens, we'll find our way back to each other. Wherever that is."

"We will," Aurelio replied softly, his grip tightening around Teo just a little bit more. "I believe in us."

And with that simple affirmation, their hearts took solace in each other as sleep fell over them, like a curtain drawing closed. But that moment, bathed in the glow of the shimmering pool and the warmth of their devotion, didn't feel like an ending.

Together, they drifted off to sleep, their dreams intertwined like the roots that grew along the walls of the cenote, reaching for the stars like the canopy of trees stretched above.

CHAPTER 24
TEO

W hen Teo woke up, the sounds of his friends talking and the soft crackling of fire filled the cavernous space around him. He couldn't help feeling a strange sense of warmth despite their precarious situation. The flickering flames cast dancing shadows on the ancient walls of the cenote, and the water's surface shimmered with reflections like tiny stars.

Fantasma emerged from a crevice in the craggy stone wall, laden with plates of food. Teo sat up straighter. The aroma of spices filled the air, making his stomach growl in anticipation.

"That smells so freaking good!" Niya crowed. Xio and Aurelio joined her, sitting on the ground around the coffee table by Teo's spot on the couch.

Fantasma beamed, her marigold earrings swaying gently as she walked over, her monarch butterfly companions fluttering about. She set down several platters and little helping hands popped out of the ground, handing out plates and utensils. There were blue corn tortillas, chile tamulado, chicken mole, slices of avocado, fresh mamey sapote, and a large clay jug of warm atole.

She had even made one of Teo's personal favorites, papadzules—a dish of hard-boiled egg–filled tortillas smothered in a smooth, rich pumpkin-seed-and-epazote broth.

"Wow, it all looks amazing," Teo said, unable to tear his eyes away from the array of food. There was one thing he didn't recognize, though. "Uh, what is this?" he asked, pointing to a bowl of tiny morsels that resembled white corn kernels. Although they looked harmless enough, he couldn't shake the feeling that there was something unusual about them.

Niya gasped. "Escamol!" She and Aurelio dove in without hesitation, spooning it onto the tortillas with avocado and chile tamulado.

Teo gave Xio a confused look, and they just shrugged in response.

"But what is it?" Teo asked again.

Aurelio opened his mouth, but Niya threw out her hand, cutting him off.

"Aurelio, don't tell him," she warned, then turned to Teo. "You don't wanna know. The only thing that matters is that it's delicious!" She took a big bite and added through a mouthful of food, "Trust me, you're gonna especially love it!"

Teo looked to Aurelio for answers, but he just nodded. "She's right," he said before taking a large bite himself.

"Just eat and don't think about it!" Niya told him, waving him on.

Teo hesitated, but then, with a deep breath, he decided to take their advice. Xio watched him as he reached out for a forkful and took a bite. It had a strange texture. The kernels were slightly crunchy and they burst between his teeth, but they had a nutty, buttery taste and had been cooked with onion and chili.

"Mmm," Teo hummed in appreciation.

With Teo's confirmation, Xio dug in. Their dark eyes grew wide. "Wow, that is really good."

Niya grinned, her cheeks full.

"Thank you, Fantasma," Aurelio said.

The diosa's smile was bigger than Teo had ever seen it.

As they continued to enjoy their meal, Teo's eyes landed on something that warmed his heart—the Chupa Chups he'd given her over the years, decorating every available surface. Shelves, her desk, even an ornate bowl, each lollipop still in its colorful wrapper.

"Hey, Fantasma," Teo began, grinning as he plucked one of the colorful lollipops from the coffee table. "Do you know that these are candy?"

The goddess tilted her head quizzically, her butterfly companions fluttering about her lace mantle. With a flick of her wrist, she summoned one of the Chupa Chups to her hand, examining it closely.

"Chupa Chups are lollipops," Teo explained, chuckling. "You're supposed to eat them."

A look of realization crossed Fantasma's face, and she hesitantly unwrapped the candy, popping it into her mouth. Her eyes widened in delight, and Teo couldn't help laughing.

"I'm glad you like them!" he said, feeling a warm sense of affection for his diosa friend.

"Teo, did you see the cool birds?" Niya asked, pointing to the dark blue motmots flitting across the cenote and perching in the cracks of the walls.

Teo grinned. "Yeah, they're—"

"Blue-crowned motmots," Aurelio said idly as he wiped up the last bit of sauce on his plate with a tortilla.

Teo blinked in surprise. "How do you know that?"

Aurelio looked up like he hadn't noticed he'd said anything. He shrugged. "I watch the Quetzlan bird show every year on TúTube."

Teo's brain short-circuited for a moment, the realization hitting him like a ton of bricks. He always judged that show with his mom—did Aurelio watch it because of him? The urge to grab Aurelio and drag him across the table to kiss his painfully handsome face was overwhelming.

"Hey there!" Teo called up to the motmots. Their excited chatter filled his ears. They seemed to have been waiting for Teo to notice them.

They congregated around him, vying for his attention with cheerful trills. Their bright colors dazzled, the refracted lights from the pool sparkling on their blue and green feathers. Despite their small size, they took up a lot of space around Teo's feet as they fluttered about him in excitement.

Son of Quetzal! they chirped happily. *We're so relieved that you're safe!*

Their genuine concern filled Teo's heart with gratitude.

Each bird vied for his attention as they presented their best selves, singing out in sweet melodies that made the cave echo with music.

They reminded Teo of home. Of everything that was at stake, of what he was so desperate to get back to.

With newfound determination, Teo stood up—releasing a groan from his battered body—and approached Xio, who was sifting through the artifacts they'd found along the edge of the pool. They looked up expectantly from a collection of crystal eyeballs.

"What if... what if all of this was part of Sol's plan from the beginning?" Teo asked, his voice steady despite his uncertainty.

Xio raised an eyebrow, intrigued. "What do you mean?"

Teo's thoughts churned as Niya and Aurelio joined them. "Maybe Sol chose you for the trials to force us to question everything."

Xio stared at Teo. Their face remained carefully nuetral as the weight of his words slowly sank in. "I don't know about that . . ."

"What if you needed to bring the Obsidians back so the gods would be forced to resurrect Sol properly? To put an end to the trials, the sacrifices, our dependence on them? Think about it," he insisted, looking at each of his friends in turn. "Is this the way Sol intended the world to work? Is all this suffering really necessary?"

Xio, Niya, and Aurelio exchanged uncertain looks.

Aurelio's gaze shifted to meet Teo's. "That's hard to imagine. We've been raised to believe that this is the only way—"

"But what if it isn't?" Teo pressed, his heart pounding. "What if we could find a better way, one that doesn't involve sacrificing ourselves or the people we love?"

"Teo's right," Xio suddenly chimed in, their eyes full of determination. "We've seen how the gods' ways have hurt people. It's time we tried something different."

"Let's make a pact!" Niya announced, extending her hand. "We can work together to create a better world for everyone, semidioses and mortals alike."

"Maybe we can," Aurelio replied, always the practical one. "But first, we have to stop the Obsidians."

"Then let's do it together," Teo vowed, reaching out to clasp Niya's outstretched hand. "We'll face whatever challenges come our way, and we'll keep fighting until we change the world for the better."

"I'm in!" Xio said, throwing out their hand as well.

Aurelio sighed and gave Teo a look—the same one he'd given Teo dozens of times, when he was hell-bent on achieving the impossible. "You're not going to give up on this, are you?"

Teo shook his head. "Nope."

Aurelio exhaled a laugh. "All right, I'm in, too," he said, adding his hand to the pile.

As the four of them stood there, hands entwined, Teo felt a spark of hope ignite within him. It wouldn't be easy, but with his friends by his side, he knew they stood a fighting chance, and that was all he needed.

CHAPTER 25
XIO

A soft breeze rustled through the vines hanging from the cenote walls as Teo and Xio sat side by side on the couch. Teo's wounds were healing, even quicker with Fantasma's help. The jade blood had been washed from his skin and the burns had turned purple. There were patches of feathers still missing, but Teo seemed confident that they would regrow soon.

The others had decided to rest for a while, leaving the two of them alone with their thoughts. The quiet was comforting, but also unnerving—forcing them to confront the feelings they'd been trying to ignore.

"Hey, Xio," Teo began, his voice barely audible over the gentle lapping of water against the edge of the pool. "I've been thinking about your dad."

Xio tensed.

"Suerte, I mean," Teo rushed to clarify.

Xio blinked, surprised by the topic, but remained silent, prompting Teo to continue.

"I never knew—I never *realized* how different he ran things in Afortunada, compared to the rest of Reino del Sol." Teo paused, searching for the right words. "The people there take care of one another. They don't rely on the gods for protection or safety the way they have to in the other cities. Suerte built it that way on purpose, didn't he? So that they would be able to defend themselves, if another war ever came. He gave them the tools and the resources to protect their own, the way the mortals in the Obsidian cities—your ancestors—couldn't."

Xio stared at their hands, fingers fidgeting with a loose thread on their pants. Hearing Teo speak so highly of Suerte left them feeling overwhelmed. They hadn't expected this kind of praise for the man—the dios—who'd raised them.

But deep down, they knew Teo was right. During the trials, Xio had been surprised to see how reliant the other Jade and Gold cities were on the dioses who ran them. Suerte was always adamant that his role as patron of the city had boundaries. The people were responsible for their own governance, for the most part. Suerte even sat on an annual council of elected leaders, giving them the opportunity to speak their concerns for the city to him face-to-face.

They couldn't imagine something like that happening in the other cities they'd seen—especially not under the Golds.

At the time, that had only strengthened Xio's resolve that the Golds were corrupt, that the system was broken. But they'd never stopped to appreciate how much work Suerte had already done to change things.

"Growing up," Xio admitted quietly, "I never really understood all the tiny ways he protected me. But now . . . I'm starting to see it."

Teo nodded. An uncomfortable silence settled between them, threatening to swallow them whole. It was Xio who broke it first, their voice shaky but determined.

"The Obsidians . . . they're filled with vengeance. Consumed by it. And I think we can use that against them.

"I know what it feels like," they continued, unable to meet Teo's eyes. "To be so . . . *obsessed* with getting revenge. It stops you from seeing things that should be obvious."

Teo gently placed his hand on Xio's shoulder, and the small gesture made their chest swell with warmth. Teo got up and Xio sunk into their jacket, stuffing their hands deep into their pockets. They were so lost in their own thoughts, it took a moment for them to realize they were touching something. From their pocket, Xio withdrew an azabache charm. It was the original azabache Suerte had given them all those years ago. Xio rubbed it between their fingers. The jet was warm and velvety. They didn't remember packing it—they didn't even remember what they'd done with it after swapping it with a piece of Venganza's obsidian glyph. How did it end up in their pocket? That was— Xio let out a weak laugh. "Lucky." With fumbling fingers, they reattached it to their bracelet.

On the opposite side of the room, something shimmered in the candlelight. Squinting, Xio recognized the obsidian dagger poking out of Teo's bag—not hidden, but clearly reclaimed to keep Aurelio honest. An idea scratched at the back of Xio's head.

To lock the Obsidians up the first time, Sol had to sacrifice themself. To keep them locked up, someone had to recreate that sacrifice.

But what if the Obsidians were sealed by a sacrifice from one of their own? What if there was a new source of power that could keep them sealed away, forever this time?

In the quiet of Fantasma's cave, Xio could practically hear their heart beating, pumping obsidian blood through their veins.

Xio had let their own anger and pain dictate their actions for so long, but now the possibility of change lay before them like an uncharted path. It wasn't going to be easy, but with every step forward, they could redefine themself—not as the monster others thought they were, but as someone who would fight for a better world.

Maybe Sol *had* spared Xio for a reason all those years ago.

Maybe this was what they were always meant to do.

Some things couldn't be forgiven, Xio understood that now. But they'd be damned if they wouldn't try everything in their power to make amends.

Even if it meant being the sacrifice themself.

CHAPTER 26
TEO

Fantasma's kind face was seared into Teo's mind as they were sent back to the aboveground world. She couldn't accompany them and risk Venganza and the other Obsidians sensing her presence—they needed any advantage they could get at this point. But it was hard to say goodbye to the small diosa. Being in Fantasma's cenote was the safest Teo had felt in a long time.

Now they were back in the darkness of the jungle. Teo blinked, adjusting to the sudden change in light. His heart raced with a mix of fear and hope. They moved through the jungle, trying to be as silent as possible, keeping their eyes and ears sharp in case they came upon Chupacabra again.

Finally, Venganza's temple came into view.

Teo's eyes scanned the imposing structure looming over them like an ancient beast. It was unlike any other Teo had seen. This was not a cozy home, and, even in its state of disrepair, Teo found it hard to believe that it once had been a city's epicenter. It was brutalist and unwelcoming, its walls covered in vines that obscured the grotesque faces of stone goats.

"I feel like they're watching us," Niya whispered. Her bangles clinked together as she fidgeted with them anxiously.

"You're making too much noise," Aurelio warned.

"I can't help it, I'm nervous!" she hissed back.

As they approached Venganza's temple, Aurelio's brow furrowed in confusion. "Still no sign of Chupacabra," he said, his copper eyes skimming their surroundings. "Where is she?"

"Probably up there with Caos and Venganza, plotting and being terrible," Xio replied, jerking their chin to the top of the temple and forcing a smirk. "Venganza loves sitting on his fancy throne and talking about how great he is while the other two grovel at his feet."

Teo paused before the large stone steps of the temple, glancing back at the others. "All right," he said with a huff, looking at each of his friends in turn. "Here's the plan. You two need to break into the prison cells," he said to Xio and Niya. "Xio, you still think you can manage that?"

They nodded, sweat clinging to their curly hair. "Caos's barriers are only meant to keep the semidioses in. I don't think they ever thought about Obsidian magic being used against them."

"Wait," Niya interrupted, her face pale. Her gaze darted nervously among her friends, her fingers worrying at her braids. "Can't I go with you, Teo?" she asked. "What if something goes wrong? What if—"

"Niya, it's going to be fine," Teo reassured her, placing a hand on her shoulder. "Me and Aurelio will keep the Obsidians busy while you and Xio break out the Golds."

"Right," Xio chimed in. "We've got this, Niya!"

Niya hesitated but then nodded. "Okay."

"Ready?" Aurelio asked in a low voice.

She bounced on her bare feet and shook out her arms like a boxer before a match. "Let's do it."

"Aurelio and I will buy you as much time as we can," Teo continued. "Once the others are free, we'll fight the Obsidians together."

Together, the group stood at the entrance of the temple, staring up at the seemingly endless stairs to the top. Teo's heart raced, his hands clenched into tight fists.

"Three Obsidian gods against a group of teenage semidioses," Aurelio said, a muscle in his jaw flexing.

"Pretty bad odds," Xio muttered.

"Yeah," Niya agreed. But then she smirked and thumped her hand against Xio's back. "They don't stand a chance."

"Damn right," Teo chimed in, grinning at Xio. "We're troublemakers, right? So let's make some fucking trouble."

Teo and Aurelio took their time creeping up the long steps that led to the throne room. Many were broken, and if someone stepped on them wrong, it'd send a cascade of rocks tripping down the steps. The temple was practically falling apart beneath their feet.

They needed to be quiet, so they needed to be slow.

Up and up the stairs stretched until they were at the same level as the jungle canopy. Trees stretched out around Teo in all directions, as far as he could see in the fathomless night.

As they continued to climb, a rustling noise sounded.

Teo paused. "Did you hear that?" he whispered, tugging on Aurelio's arm to stop him.

Aurelio listened for a moment. The rustling happened again. "The trees?"

Teo frowned. "No, not that—"

Teo.

He jumped. "That!" He jerked his head around, trying to figure out where the voice had come from.

"I don't hear anything," Aurelio said, a concerned look on his face.

Psst, Teo! the voice said a little louder. *Over here!*

Suddenly, two *somethings* flew from the trees.

At first, panic shot through Teo. But then two caiques swooped down, landing on the steps above them.

Holding cans of spray paint in their beaks.

Hello, Son of Quetzal! one of them greeted, immediately dropping their can on the stone steps with a metallic *thunk.*

"Pico! Peri!" Teo was so happy to see them, he forgot he needed to be quiet until Aurelio shushed him, looking down at the caiques in confusion.

"They're friends of mine from back home," Teo whispered. The smile plastered across his face was so big that it hurt his cheeks. "What are you doing here?!"

We've come to help! Pico sang loudly.

Shh, Pico! Peri hushed, nipping at her best friend's wing.

Oh, right! Pico ducked his head bashfully and added in a much quieter tone, *I forgot!*

The news of what you and your human friends have to do got back to us aaaaall the way back in Quetzlan, Peri explained. *Your mom asked us to look after you!*

Yes, and we couldn't let you face those big nasty dioses on your own! Pico agreed, shaking out his feathers. *We brought weapons!* he said, bonking his head on the nozzle of his can, releasing a spray of jade green paint.

"Oh, uh, thanks," Teo said. He didn't want to sound rude, but he didn't know how much help two caiques could be against three Obsidian gods. "That's—that's really nice of you, but—"

And backup! Peri added before he could finish.

The sound of rustling leaves pulled Teo's attention. Hundreds of birds in all colors and shapes peeked out from their hiding places within the canopy of leaves. They hopped around on branches, singing to Teo in greeting.

Hello, Son of Quetzal!

We're here to help!

We've got your back! said Macho, Chavo's companion from back home.

He recognized more of them, too. There were quetzals and parrots from his mother's temple. There were the toucans that had helped him prank Ocelo during the trials, the curve-billed thrasher they'd met in the desert, and even the hummingbird who'd helped them along the way.

It was like every bird Teo had ever met had shown up to help him, along with ten of their friends.

"Whoa," Aurelio breathed next to him, looking more shocked than Teo had ever seen him.

"Holy shit," Teo laughed quietly.

The birds exploded into excited chatter and Teo had to quickly hush them again. "We have to be quiet! If the Obsidians catch us before we get the jump on them, we're fucked," he explained.

The birds did their best to quiet down, whistling their apologies.

How can we help? Peri asked.

Yeah, we're ready to take on the bad guys! Macho chirped.

Where do you need us? Pico said, fluffing out his feathered chest.

An idea flared to life in Teo's head.

"What are they saying?" Aurelio asked. Teo couldn't even imagine how strange this probably was for him to witness, especially when he couldn't understand bird.

Teo grinned. "We've got reinforcements."

CHAPTER 27
TEO

After getting their asses handed to them by Chupacabra on her own, Teo knew he and Aurelio alone wouldn't stand a chance against all three of the Obsidian dioses. If they wanted to live long enough for backup to arrive, they'd have to be clever.

Teo made sure the lights on his and Aurelio's suits were turned off before they reached the top of the temple. He slowly crept toward the large doors that stood ajar, using the night and shadows to hide. With Aurelio at his side, Teo peeked through the crack.

It was just like Xio had described it—big, cold, and dark. Shadows danced across the towering stone walls. Massive obsidian statues of Venganza, Caos, and Chupacabra stood like sentries.

In the back of the room, Caos and Chupacabra stood before Venganza, seated on his raised throne. They were too far away for Teo to make out their murmuring, but—

"*Look!*" Teo whispered, jabbing his elbow into Aurelio's side.

Venganza sat lounging on his throne, rapping his fingernails on the Sol Stone balanced on the armrest.

It was going to take a lot of luck to get it back from the dios, but at least they knew where it was.

Carefully, Teo pulled the door open wide enough for them to slip through. Using the darkness to their advantage, Teo and Aurelio hid behind the obsidian statue closest to them. It was a particularly garish one of Venganza in dark, flowing robes, his arms held out at his sides and a vicious grin on his polished face.

"You ready?" Teo asked Aurelio.

Aurelio nodded, copper eyes blazing.

Teo drew in a deep breath and let out a long, sharp whistle.

There was one beat of silent confusion, the Obsidians tossing one another uncertain looks before Venganza stood. "What—"

Before he could finish, the door burst open, letting in a flood of birds.

FOR QUETZAL! Peri proclaimed, leading the flock.

Pico was right behind her, screeching a battle cry and banging his head on the spray can in his talons. Puffs of jade green paint were left in his wake.

The temple exploded into a cacophony of birdsong and vibrant feathers as birds mobbed the Obsidians.

Macaws streaked through the air in shades of scarlet, yellow, blue, and green. Teo had to cover his ears against their window-shattering, psychosis-inducing shrieks.

Toucans harassed Caos, snapping their vibrant lime green and ruby red bills as they used their talons to pull and rip at the diose's robes. Caos cowered, grabbing their hood to keep the toucans from pulling it off, but the birds just went for their fingers.

The aggressive curve-billed thrashers dashed through the air, cussing up a storm as they yanked out chunks of Chupacabra's fur. She shrieked and slashed wildly at them with her claws, but the birds were too small and too fast for her to catch.

Tiny gem-colored hummingbirds dive-bombed Venganza, striking him in the back of his head with needle-sharp beaks. Even the regal quetzals, who were usually pacifists, pummeled the dioses relentlessly with their beaks and talons, scratching faces and tearing at flesh, their long tail feathers streaming behind them.

As Venganza snarled and swiped at his attackers, Pico and Peri swooped in.

Pico—still shouting incoherently—blasted Venganza in the face with spray paint. The dios roared, confused and frantic as he tried to wipe the jade green paint from his eyes.

This is for Son of Quetzal! Peri shouted as she flew in and scratched at Venganza's face with her talons before diving out of his reach.

The two friends circled each other.

Excellent job, Pico! Peri said.

Thank you, Peri! said Pico before starting up his battle cry and diving back into the fray.

On their own, birds were small and fragile—certainly no match for a god. But they were fierce, determined, and protective of Teo. And together, they were bringing the Obsidians to their knees.

Teo was so proud of them he felt like his heart would burst.

"Quick!" Teo said to Aurelio. "While they're distracted!"

He grabbed Aurelio under his arms and launched into the air, making a beeline for the Sol Stone perched on the throne. Teo urged himself to go faster, dodging birds and flapping his wings as fast as he could. They were closing in on the Sol Stone, it was *right there—*

BANG.

Black electricity slammed into Teo and Aurelio, exploding on impact. Teo's body seized and they crashed to the ground, landing in a heap. Teo groaned. It was a thousand times worse than being struck by Atzi's lightning. This pain was sharp and lingering, digging into his bones.

Son of Quetzal! The birds' panicked cries tumbled over one another. They hesitated and turned, distracted.

Venganza roared with rage. "ENOUGH."

The god of vengeance released a powerful blast that exploded through the room.

Several birds were thrown into the walls and crashed to the floor.

"NO!" The word seared through Teo's throat.

Pico and Peri swooped down to him.

Are you okay?!

Are you hurt?!

"Get out of here!" Teo said, pushing himself up onto his knees.

We'll protect you!

We won't let you face them on your own!

Across the room, the Obsidians stalked toward him.

There wasn't time to be polite. "I'm the Son of Quetzal, and I'm ordering you all to leave *now*!"

Pico and Peri looked hurt and confused.

Panic clawed under Teo's skin. He couldn't stand the thought of them all being slaughtered because of him. "Just—just keep out of the way! If any of you get killed, I'll—I'll—" He couldn't think straight. "I'll tell my mom!"

Peri gasped. Pico dropped his spray paint.

"*Please!*" Teo begged, his voice breaking.

That seemed to get through to them.

Pico and Peri took off again.

You heard Son of Quetzal!

Evasive maneuvers!

Before Teo could even breathe a sigh of relief, Aurelio was at his side, pulling him to his feet. "Are you all right?" he demanded, his grip on Teo's arms hard and trembling.

"I nearly pissed my pants, but yeah," Teo said.

There was no time to say anything else. The Obsidians had arrived.

"You semidioses must have a death wish," Chupacabra sneered. Her fur was missing chunks and streaked with paint.

Venganza smirked as he looked down at them with bloodshot eyes, his goat face covered in green. "Where's the rest of you? Did Xio already betray you *again*?" His voice was like gravel, harsh and unforgiving. "That spineless coward probably ran away."

If Venganza didn't think Xio was with them, then they could use that to their advantage. The less Venganza knew, the better.

Teo rolled his eyes, trying to ignore the pain all over his body. "Oh, please," he panted. "We don't need the help of a traitor with daddy issues."

A cackle erupted from Venganza's mouth, as his thin lips formed into a twisted sneer. "You are an arrogant child," he hissed, staring at Teo with pure contempt. "You're just a nothing Jade. You have no talent or skill. You don't even possess any power."

"I'm flunking math, too," Teo spat.

Venganza chuckled, amused. "But you defied the Golds, something no one has had the gall to do in thousands of years. The world you knew is gone now, because of *your* actions." He paused to stroke the fur on his chin thoughtfully. "And yet you refuse to give up, even though it's pointless. I have to admit, your determination is impressive— a trait I'd value in one of my own children—"

Teo pretended to gag loudly.

Venganza's face contorted in anger. "You have no idea what you are up against," he hissed. "What chance do a Son of Quetzal, the useless diosa of birds, and the talentless Son of Lumbre have against us?"

Anger swelled under Teo's skin. He could feel the enraged heat wafting off Aurelio.

"You couldn't even beat the Golds last time," Aurelio shot back.

Venganza paused, narrowing his eyes as he considered Aurelio's words. "If you know your history, then you know there is nothing that can be done to stop us. You should have known better than to cross me, diositos . . ."

The air around Venganza crackled, a black aura seeped around him. "But now it is too late. And we do not show mercy."

Teo locked eyes with Venganza. "Neither do we."

Caos stepped forward, their voice booming as they spoke. "You may have courage, little mortals," they said in a deep baritone, "but do not think that bravery alone is enough to save you."

"We're going to stop you," Aurelio said, fire engulfing his fists.

"Ha!" Venganza jeered, the sound echoing throughout the chamber. "You're nothing but insects trying to crawl out of my web." He strode toward Teo and Aurelio with predatory steps, looming over them. "I will devour you piece by piece until there's nothing left."

"I do enjoy playing with my food before I eat it!" Chupacabra happily sang. She gave them a wicked smile, showing off her rows of jagged teeth. Her venomous eyes shone, wild and hungry.

Teo glanced at Aurelio. He nodded, ready to fight.

"Do give my regards to Muerte when you meet her," Venganza growled.

"You'll have to catch us first," Teo replied, grabbing Aurelio under his arms.

With a powerful flap of his wings, they shot into the air. They swooped down over the Obsidian gods, diving toward their heads.

"You might want to get that fur groomed!" Teo called out as they flew overhead. "You're starting to look like a dog with mange!"

Chupacabra roared in anger, swiping at them with razor-sharp claws, but Teo's agile flying kept them just out of reach. Teo used everything he'd learned since embracing his wings, dropping down on the Obsidians for Aurelio to chuck fireballs at them before banking out of their reach again. The two continued their onslaught until Venganza stepped up and conjured chunks of obsidian, creating a wall of polished black glass between them. "Caos, do something about these pests!" he snarled.

"Gladly," Caos uttered, their voice slithering through the air like a snake, raising goose bumps on Teo's skin. Colors shifted and twisted, distorting the throne room into an unrecognizable landscape. Teo was hit with a wave of vertigo as he struggled to tell up from down. The two demigods struggled against the bizarre display of power as reality unraveled around them.

"Teo, what's happening?!" Aurelio called out.

"Caos is playing games with us." Teo gritted his teeth, struggling to maintain focus as the world warped before his eyes. "We have to keep moving!"

Navigating the chaos-laden room was like trying to find solid footing on a storm-tossed ship. Teo fought against the disorientation, wings beating furiously to correct their course.

"We need to stop Caos!" Teo said.

"There!" Aurelio shouted, pointing to where Caos stood, fractals of their reflection spreading out around them like a horrible kaleidoscope. Teo banked to the left, but Chupacabra was on them, feral eyes flashing as she snapped her powerful jaws. She lunged at Teo, her claws slashing through his uniform, dragging across the skin covering his ribs. Teo cried out in pain as hot, jade green blood bloomed on his skin.

Aurelio launched himself from Teo's faltering grasp and shot a blast of fire at Caos's head. The impact reverberated through the air, momentarily disrupting the illusions.

Everything around them shuddered back into place as Caos clutched their head.

"Nice hit!" Teo shouted, as together, he and Aurelio crash-landed on the ground, the impact jarring but not enough to keep them down. Teo winced as pain shot through his body, but he refused to let it slow him down.

If they stopped, they were dead.

Aurelio launched himself at Chupacabra, his foot connecting squarely with the wolf-headed god's temple. The impact sent Chupacabra stumbling back.

"You really need to stop chasing your tail!" Teo said, dodging her claws by mere inches as he maneuvered around her to grab Aurelio again. "It's making you look desperate!"

"Laugh all you want," Chupacabra snapped, lunging again. "Your time is running out!"

Teo's heart thudded in his chest, but he refused to give in to fear. With a burst of speed, he carried Aurelio higher into the air.

"Now, Relio!"

Aurelio shot balls of fire in rapid succession, barely keeping the Obsidians at bay as Teo carried him around the room, dodging attacks with acrobatic fumbling. They crashed and slammed into the obsidian walls, which splintered easily. The temple shook and groaned as the blasts opened large holes in the glossy black walls.

They couldn't keep up this dance forever. The relentless barrage of strikes from the gods was wearing them down. Aurelio was dripping with sweat, his flames becoming smaller and smaller with each throw.

Then, faster than Teo could clock, Chupacabra grabbed Aurelio's leg out of the air.

Before Teo could even gasp, she yanked both of them down with brute force. They crash-landed on the cold stone floor again, the breath knocked out of them.

"Teo, you okay?" Aurelio asked, gritting his teeth against the pain.

"Never better," Teo grumbled, forcing himself back onto his feet. They took a defensive stance, back-to-back, relying on each other for support, as the Obsidian gods converged.

"Where's your bravado now?!" Venganza roared, his black energy crackling around him.

"Still here!" Teo shot back, though he knew they were hanging on by a thread. Teo sent a silent prayer to Sol, begging Xio and Niya to hurry.

"Teo, I don't know how much longer we can do this," Aurelio panted, fear creeping into his voice.

Venganza laughed, a terrible, cavernous sound. "Your time is up, diositos!"

Aurelio was right. They needed help.

CHAPTER 28
XIO

Xio couldn't deny the thrill that coursed through them as they led Niya through the maze of decrepit corridors and dark halls, down, down, down into the tunnels below, using the glow of Niya's suit to guide their way. It cast eerie shadows on the walls, making the ancient carvings seem alive.

"Stay close," Xio whispered.

Niya nodded and followed closely behind them. They had to admit, it was reassuring to be teamed up with her. Xio had seen what she was capable of during the trials, had done hours of research on her and knew how talented she was. Teo and Aurelio were brilliant, but Niya was *strong*.

As they ventured deeper into the temple, Xio led her through intricate passageways and hidden tunnels that only someone who'd spent considerable time here could navigate.

"Down this way," Xio said, moving through a narrow gap in the wall, barely visible beneath a veil of twisted roots. The tunnel was damp and musty, the walls unnervingly close.

Finally, they reached the archway at the entrance to where the Gold demigods were held. Xio entered with Niya right behind them. The light drew the attention of the semidioses.

Xio glimpsed them stirring in their cells to get a better look, but there was no time to waste.

"Everyone, stand back," Xio warned, concentrating their power until they could feel the familiar hum of vengeance energy coursing through them. They released a blast of black-and-purple energy that shattered the first cell's barrier.

Atzi, her lightning powers crackling around her, leapt out. "Traitor!" she shouted, eyes blazing. She sent a bolt of lightning hurtling toward Xio, cracking like a whip.

Xio had to throw themself onto the dirt floor, narrowly avoiding the attack. They could only gape up at her as Atzi advanced, white-hot lightning wreathing her hands.

"Wait!" Niya shouted, jumping between them. "The little shit's on our side! They led us here to break you all out!"

Atzi paused, her hand raised above her head. "Really?" she asked skeptically, her lightning flickering as she looked between Niya and Xio.

"I know I messed up, but I'm done with the Obsidians," Xio replied weakly as they slowly got up. "I want to help."

Her stance relaxed. She lowered her hand, a smug smirk settling on her pretty face. "Wow, sometimes bullying works."

"I—I thought—" Xio stuttered. This was going a lot differently than how they'd imagined coming to Atzi's rescue. "I thought that we—that you—"

"That I what?" Atzi demanded, her eyebrow arched. "I was going to *swoon* at your feet because you broke me out of a prison cell? You're the one who put me in here to begin with!"

Xio's cheeks flushed with embarrassment. "Yeah, that's a good point."

Atzi sighed, the tension in her shoulders easing slightly. "Sorry for trying to kill you," she said, offering a small, wry smile.

Xio's heart pounded in their chest as they risked a glance at Atzi. Maybe things could be different between them after all.

Ocelo and Xochi pressed themselves against their barriers, trying to see what all the commotion was about.

"Who's there?!"

"What's going on?!"

"Atzi, are you okay?!"

"Yeah!" Atzi called back. "The rescue party finally decided to show up!"

Xio blew open Xochi's cell next, quickly followed by Marino's and Dezi's.

Xochi and Atzi crashed into a tight hug.

"Thank Sol!" Xochi nearly cried.

The sound of shuffling feet drew their attention to Dezi, who stepped out of his cell looking lost. He caught sight of Marino, weak and unable to move from the sweltering heat of his own cell across the way, and immediately rushed over to him.

"Drink this!" Niya barked, joining Dezi in pulling Marino out of the cell and into the cooler tunnel.

She unscrewed the lid of the Decanter of Endless Water, revealing the Gem of Regeneration inside. Dezi propped Marino's head in his lap. The larger boy's gaze was unfocused as he looked up at Dezi, as if he couldn't believe his own eyes.

Niya tipped the decanter against Marino's dry, cracked lips and let the water trickle into his mouth. The first drop hit Marino's tongue and his eyes sprang open and he was suddenly wide awake. He sat up and chugged it down. His ashy skin returned to its usual ochre luster, healthy and glowing.

"Thank you," Marino said, gasping for air. Dezi threw his arms around Marino in a tight embrace and smothered him in kisses.

Marino squeezed him tight, a wide smile illuminating his face as he held Dezi close, rubbing his back.

The sight of their reunion warmed Xio's heart.

"Everyone else drink, too!" Niya said, passing the water to Xochi.

She gasped and snatched the decanter from Niya. "That's my mom's gem!" Xochi said, gazing at the glowing stone.

"What is it?" Atzi asked, crinkling her nose as Xochi took a long drink.

"Gem of Regeneration!" Niya announced. "She gave it to us!"

Xochi sighed and smiled. "It's delicious!"

As the Golds passed the decanter around, Xio could already see the color returning to their flawless skin.

"What the hell is going on out there?" Auristela's voice echoed through the dungeon, catching everyone's attention. Her breath fogged against the glass as she glared at Xio angrily. "What are you doing here?" she demanded.

"Helping," Xio said before blasting the barrier open.

Auristela could only give them a bewildered look before they smashed apart the block of ice she was trapped in. Chunks of ice skittered across the ground as Auristela dropped to the floor.

Immediately, fire roared to life in her hands. Auristela seethed, eyes blazing. "I'm gonna *kill you*—"

Xio recoiled, a shout lodging in their throat, but before Auristela could turn them into a pile of ash, Niya stepped in, knocking Auristela's arm away with the edge of the shield. The fire exploded against a tunnel wall.

Xio stood there, frozen to the spot and breathing heavily. *"Holy shit."*

Auristela advanced on Xio, and again, Niya stepped in the way.

"LET ME THROUGH," Auristela snarled.

"No!" Niya shouted back.

Auristela growled through her teeth. "WHY?"

"BECAUSE! XIO SUCKS!" Niya shot back.

Xio flinched, but they understood.

"But they're also the reason you all won't be rotting away in these nasty-ass cells!" Niya said.

"They put us here to begin with!" Auristela said, pointing an accusing finger at Xio.

"Yeah!" Ocelo echoed in agreement, copying Auristela's posture.

"Again, *Xio sucks*," Niya clarified. "But without them, we'd all be fucked!" She glared at the rest of the Golds.

Auristela opened her mouth to argue further, but Niya cut her off. "I'm serious! Xio found us in Los Restos and told us where you were! They helped us fight off this scary-as-*shit* owl lady and Chupacabra! They've got these badass vengeance blasts and they know their way around this stinky temple! We only stand a chance against the Obsidians *with* Xio's help!"

Xio was actually touched. Even though she was angrily yelling, and most of her compliments were half insults, Xio was touched that she was sticking up for them. *Praising* them, even.

"So can we just get over this for now and deal with it later?" she demanded, looking between the Golds. "If we don't hurry, Teo and Aurelio—"

Auristela's eyes grew wide. "Relio? Where is he?"

Niya huffed. "I'm *trying* to tell you! He and Teo are distracting the Obsidians while me and Xio break you out—"

"*Where?!*" Auristela repeated.

"At the top of the temple in Venganza's stupid little throne room!"

Auristela was stomping down the tunnel before she even finished her sentence.

"Where are you going?" Atzi called after her.

"To find my brother!"

"Do you even know where you're going?" Marino asked.

"Nope!" Auristela called back, her voice echoing as she stomped up the stairs.

"Sol's *sake*," Xochi groaned.

"C'mon, Xio, before she does something stupid," Atzi said, pulling on their arm to follow.

Xio nodded, tripping over themself to keep up.

Ocelo fell into step next to Xio momentarily as they rushed after Auristela. "So, you're good now?" they demanded, muscles bulging and jaguar eyes flashing dangerously.

"Uh, yeah—I mean, I'm trying to be," they replied with a nervous laugh.

Ocelo narrowed their yellow eyes at Xio for a moment longer before nodding their approval. "Nice."

CHAPTER 29
TEO

Teo could feel his strength waning, but he refused to give up. Despite his earlier orders, the birds were fighting as best they could, but their numbers were dwindling.

With a victorious roar, Venganza launched a massive blast of black vengeance energy directly at Aurelio.

In that instant, everything seemed to slow down. Aurelio, still slinging fire at Chupacabra, didn't even have time to react. But Teo, driven by an unshakable determination to protect him, dug deep, summoning whatever strength he had left. He lunged forward, spreading his wings wide, and shielded Aurelio just as the blast hit.

A shout ripped through Aurelio's throat. "*Teo!*"

The force of the blast sent them both crashing to the ground, panting and weak, gold and jade blood trickling from various wounds. "You shouldn't have done that!" Aurelio said. "I'm supposed to protect you!"

"Yeah," Teo replied with a weak laugh. "Niya's gonna kill you."

Aurelio laughed despite himself, even though he looked on the verge of tears.

Teo forced a weak smile despite the pain. "We're in this together, remember? That means we look out for each other."

"Pitiful," Venganza sneered, striding toward them with an air of cruel triumph. "You thought you could stand against the Obsidians? We are power incarnate, while you are nothing but frightened children playing at being Heroes."

As Venganza loomed over them, Teo could feel the blood trickling down his face, the pain from his battered wings growing more insistent with each passing second. He glanced at Aurelio, who glared up at the god. His body was bruised and battered, but his spirit was still defiant. Teo knew they were in deep trouble.

Just as Venganza raised his hand to deliver the final blow, the throne room doors burst open with a resounding crash.

"Sorry we're late!" Xio's voice rang out clear and confident. Teo's heart leapt.

"*Xio*," Venganza sneered. "You—"

"OH MY GODS, SHUT UP."

Teo twisted to find Niya holding the carved obsidian head from one of Venganza's statues. Her hair was wild, loose strands sticking out of her braids and a snarl twisting her features.

Before Venganza could react, Niya planted her bare feet, heaved the obsidian over her head, and chucked it. Everyone watched as it shot through the air and slammed into the ceiling.

The obsidian exploded on impact. Teo and Aurelio threw themselves out of the way as tiny, razor-sharp pieces of the brittle glass rained down. Venganza, Chupacabra, and Caos ducked to protect themselves as the roof broke apart and collapsed, burying them in slabs of smoky glass.

Niya stood there for a moment, sweat glistening on her skin and chest heaving. But then she turned to Teo, a wide smile plastered across her bruised and grimy face. "That was awesome!"

A relieved laugh broke the tension in Teo's chest.

At his side, a gasp caught in Aurelio's throat. "Stela?"

Auristela's eyes widened. "Relio?" she said, as if she couldn't believe it, as if it were a trick. The way her face crumpled made Teo's heart ache. "Relio!" she cried, sprinting to him.

She threw herself onto him and Aurelio held her tight, tears streaming down his face as they embraced.

"Thank the gods you're safe," he choked, voice raw.

Auristela sobbed and grinned, pulling back to look at him. "Of course I am!" she said stubbornly, angrily wiping the tears on her cheeks. "I knew you'd come for me!" They crushed into another hug.

Niya grabbed Teo and easily pulled him upright with one hand. "Drink up!" she said, giving him the decanter. He took a long swig and a shiver tingled over his skin. Renewed energy flowed through him.

"All right—" Teo began, handing the decanter to Aurelio so he could also take a drink.

"We've got one shot at this, so let's make it count." Teo looked around at the group, his gaze settling on each and every determined face. "We have a chance to stop the Obsidians—" When Aurelio arched an eyebrow at him, he clarified, "I mean, Venganza, Caos, and Chupacabra, not Xio."

"Thanks, man," Xio said at his side.

"Count me in," Xochi said, her eyes shining with excitement. Atzi, Ocelo, Marino, and Dezi all nodded in agreement.

"Whatever," Auristela sighed.

"We need to work together and get the Sol Stone by any means necessary," Teo told them.

"Then Teo will call the dioses," Aurelio said and signed. "And while we all fight off the Obsidians, Tierra will resurrect Sol."

"*Resurrect Sol?*" Marino balked.

Dezi looked less than convinced as he signed.

Ocelo nodded in agreement. "Is that even possible?"

"Hopefully," Teo said. "It's kind of the only plan we've got."

Xochi rubbed her temples, but Auristela was surprisingly unaffected.

"Dezi, Marino, you good?" Teo asked, watching as Marino signed the question to Dezi, who nodded vigorously.

"Of course," Marino replied confidently. "We won't let you down."

Teo looked over at Xochi, Atzi, and Ocelo. "And you three? Ready to show those gods who's boss?"

"More than ready!" Xochi exclaimed. "We're gonna make them regret ever messing with us!"

"Agreed," Atzi chimed in as electricity crackled between her fingers. "They won't know what hit them."

"It's a good thing you came and got us," Auristela said, pulling her hair back into its knot, her cheekbones sharp as glass. "There's no way you could pull this off without us."

"Are you guys good to go then?" Teo asked.

"Absolutely," Ocelo growled. "Let's make those assholes wish they'd never stepped foot back in Reino del Sol."

"Damn straight," Auristela agreed, her voice fierce as she met Teo's gaze.

Suddenly, the pile of obsidian burst into tiny pieces, flying through the air like sand. The Obsidians emerged, their skin torn and clothes ripped. Venganza's face—covered in several gashes that glistened with black blood—twisted with fury.

The semidioses stood in formation, each of them poised to strike. Teo's pulse raced. "Work together," he told them, his wings outstretched and ready for flight. "We need to be smart about this. Use your powers strategically."

Xio, determined and crackling with purple electricity. Atzi, fingers sparking as lightning danced around her. Aurelio and Auristela, flames flickering from their hands. Niya, crouched low, blade and shield ready. Ocelo, their yellow eyes glowing with jaguar fierceness. Marino, ribbons of water swirling around him. And Dezi, looking strong and focused.

"Time for a slaughter," Venganza sneered.

Teo launched himself into the air. The battle began in earnest, semidioses and Obsidians clashing amidst the chaos.

"Push them back!" Xio yelled, sending an energy blast toward Venganza. Niya followed up with a wall of stone, while Dezi threw punches with speed that rivaled Chupacabra's.

Venganza laughed, brushing off their assault as if it were nothing. "This is child's play."

"Shut up!" Auristela roared, her fireballs blazing like miniature suns. Marino sent a wave of water crashing down on the Obsidian gods, forcing them to scatter momentarily.

"Keep going!" Ocelo encouraged, their jaguar claws outstretched and muscles bulging as they leapt into the fray.

The Obsidians seemed to grow more powerful with every passing moment, dark energy swirling around them. The semidioses fought valiantly, but it was clear they were overwhelmed. Teo's breath came in ragged gasps as he tried to keep up with the relentless pace.

But things were getting messy. Teo could see the cloud of vengeance threatening to consume his friends. He felt it in himself, growing and stretching, affecting his ability to focus. They'd started out as a team, but now they were falling apart. The semidioses were beginning to act out of rage instead of with clear minds and strategy.

"Stay focused!" Teo reminded them, even though he was struggling to keep his own anger in check.

"Venganza is using his powers on you guys!" Xio shouted, confirming Teo's suspicions. Sweat was trickling down the younger kid's face, panic rising in their voice. "We have to fight through it!"

"Fall back!" Teo shouted over the din, his voice strained.

With a heave of her arms, Niya ripped up slabs of the stone floor and threw them up into a massive wall. Xochi followed up by weaving her vines between them, strengthening the barrier for temporary protection.

"Is everyone okay?" Ocelo panted, their feline eyes scanning the group.

"More or less," Atzi grumbled, nursing a painful-looking welt on her arm.

"Listen up," Teo said, trying to mask the fear in his voice. He looked around at his fellow semidioses—beaten, bruised, but still determined. He took a deep breath. "I know things look bad right now, but we can't lose hope. And we can't give in to our rage. If we are smart we can do this together."

He's right, Dezi signed. *We're stronger together. Let me help.*

He stepped forward, arms outstretched, and pulled them into a tight huddle. Teo didn't understand what was happening, but he hooked his arms around Xio and Aurelio as they all closed in together.

As Dezi's warm touch enveloped them, Teo felt a swell of determination flood his veins. Renewed energy shot through the group as Dezi worked his magic. Love, unity, and strength. It washed away their fatigue and fear. One by one, the semidioses leaned into Dezi's embrace, absorbing the powerful inspiration and fortitude that surged through them like a tide.

"Wow," Niya breathed. "That's some strong shit, Dezi!"

Ocelo flexed, their muscles bulging. "I feel like I could kill a god!"

"Good," Auristela said, her voice deadly as she grinned, cruel and terrifying. Everyone leapt back as flames ignited across her bare arm. "Because that's what we're going to do."

Teo grinned. "Let's go get that Sol Stone."

With renewed vigor, the semidioses charged the Obsidians again, their combined abilities creating a dazzling spectacle of elemental prowess. The Obsidians faltered under their onslaught, but Teo knew it wouldn't last. He had to hurry.

Aurelio hurled a torrent of flame toward Venganza and Chupacabra, momentarily distracting them before Caos snapped their fingers. Aurelio was yanked off his feet and suddenly he was hanging upside down in the air, as if an invisible hand had grabbed him by the ankle.

Atzi and Xochi moved in next, lightning crackling around Atzi's hands while Xochi's vines twisted and grew, creating a tangled snare. But when they got too close, Chupacabra charged like a bull, crashing into them and sending the girls sprawling.

"Keep fighting!" Teo yelled. "We can do this!"

The battle raged on, a tempest of fire and fury.

"Come on!" Auristela yelled, summoning a wall of fire to hold back Chupacabra's relentless advance. Caos conjured up a wave of water, extinguishing the flames as Chupacabra leapt forward and kicked Auristela square in the chest. She flew back, careening into the wall.

Marino took control of the water. It flew to him and morphed into ribbons, twisting around his arms. He and Ocelo moved in sync, taking turns as Marino slung the water like whips at Venganza and Ocelo pounced forward to rip and tear at the dios with their claws before retreating back for Marino to have another go.

"Teo, now!" Xio shouted, launching another emotional energy blast at Caos. Teo swooped down from above, his wings slicing through the air as he aimed for the Sol Stone.

But Venganza was faster. He blasted Marino and Ocelo before turning to Teo. "Nice try!" Venganza sneered, swatting Teo away with a dark burst of power.

It hurt like a son of a bitch, but he regained his balance in time.

Teo's mind raced, searching for a way to tip the scales in their favor.

"Is this what you want?" Venganza taunted, holding up the Sol Stone as he dodged Dezi's powerful blows with ease. "Sol can't help you now!"

But then Dezi feinted to the left. Venganza went right and Dezi smiled. He darted forward, tagging Venganza's chest.

The god stuttered to a stop. He looked around, confused and blinking rapidly. Teo held his breath.

Venganza's eyes unfocused. He turned to Dezi and—

Smiled.

Not an evil, toothy smile, either. A genuine one that was so out of place and *wrong* on Venganza's terrible face, it made Teo's skin crawl.

Dezi smiled back, maintaining eye contact with Venganza as he gently patted the monstrous god's chest. In response, Venganza's shoulders slumped and he let out a long, deep sigh.

"Holy shit," Teo breathed. Everyone was right—Dezi was scary powerful.

Teo saw his chance. With Venganza momentarily occupied with Dezi, he lunged forward, fingers outstretched toward the Sol Stone.

But when his fingertips grazed its warm surface, Venganza snapped out of it.

He struck Dezi and sent him flying out of the way. With violent speed, the dios swung his arm and sent Teo crashing to the ground.

Pain exploded in his body, jarring his neck.

Venganza snarled, towering over Teo. The other semidioses lay scattered around him, bruised and exhausted. "There is only darkness for you, and only death for your people. Our monsters are just the beginning. Mountains will shake. Cities will crumble. The skies will be ripped apart. We will ravage this world until every light has been extinguished. Your will is strong, child, but I am beyond strength. I am the end, and I have come for you. You are alone."

Teo stared up at Venganza, fear curdling in his gut.

"No, he's not!" Xio appeared, planting themself between Teo and Venganza.

Don't! Teo tried to say, but he could barely move.

"And we're not giving up," Xio said, gritting their teeth. Teo could see the way their knees shook and their hands trembled, but they didn't back down. Venganza's eyes flashed with fury as he raised his hand to unleash his vengeance upon Xio. But, in a daring move, Xio reached out. Teo watched as the black energy in Venganza's hand flowed into Xio. They gasped as brilliant purple swirls of energy surrounded them.

"Big mistake," Venganza sneered, expecting Xio to crumble under the weight of his power.

Instead, Xio's eyes shone with determination. Their purple-and-black aura exploded around them, crackling and twisting.

"I am a Child of Suerte," they said, a brilliant violet ball of energy growing at their chest. "And you're all out of luck," Xio continued, hands glowing. "I'm not letting you hurt anyone else."

"Impossible!" snarled Venganza, releasing another wave of darkness toward Xio.

But Xio stood firm, absorbing the onslaught. With a fierce battle cry, they turned the power against its source, unleashing a torrent of energy that slammed into Venganza and his fellow Obsidians, shoving them back against the temple wall.

"NO!" Venganza screamed as the Sol Stone slipped from his grasp, skidding across the floor. Aurelio dove forward, seizing the stone.

"NOW, TEO!" Aurelio shouted.

Teo pulled the feather from his ear and held it aloft, sweat beading on his forehead.

Please work, Teo thought desperately.

The feather began to vibrate in his hand.

CHAPTER 30
TEO

The feather emitted a soft light that grew brighter and brighter until it engulfed the entire room. A shining portal opened.

Fire exploded as Lumbre appeared, engulfed in flames. Eyes blazing, the diosa tore into the Obsidians without pause. They fell back, scrambling to defend themselves against Lumbre's ruthless inferno while the other dioses rushed in.

As if answering Teo's prayers, the gods materialized before them, radiant and powerful, bearing the Sun Stones from all the temples.

Dios Tierra was the last to walk through the portal with an armful of Sun Stones.

"PAPI!" Niya tackled her father, knocking the stones from his hands as he scrambled to catch her, squeezing her tight. "I made the whole roof collapse!" she said, bouncing excitedly as she beamed up at her dad. "Did you see how good I kicked their asses?! Did you see it?!"

"About time you showed up," quipped Teo through shaky laughs.

"I'm so proud of you all," Diosa Amor said and signed, her warm voice brimming with pride. Her eyes glistened with tears, clutching Dezi to her chest.

"Let me take that from you," Tierra said from behind his golden mask, gingerly accepting the Sol Stone from Aurelio.

"Thank you," Aurelio said, climbing to his feet. Teo slumped in relief, feeling the weight of responsibility lifting from his shoulders for a brief moment.

"Teo!"

In her beautiful dress, her feathers draped behind her, Teo's mom appeared. Quetzal immediately swept him into her arms, her soft wings encircling him in an embrace. Teo let himself fall into it, squeezing her tight. "You're so brave, mijo," she cooed, pulling back to look her son in the face. Her eyes shone with tears, and it surprised Teo to realize some were spilling down his own cheeks as well.

Teo's remaining avian comrades flocked to Quetzal. They dived and tumbled through the air, singing for their diosa. She laughed and smiled as the birds landed on her shoulders, trilling and preening her feathers.

Pico and Peri landed on top of Teo's head. "Ouch!" Teo hissed as their talons pricked his scalp.

We protected your fledgling, Diosa Quetzal! Peri said, flapping her wings.

We kicked their butts! Pico added.

Peri gasped. *Pico!* she chided, nipping at his wing.

Pico squealed and ducked his head in embarrassment. *Forgive me, Diosa! I didn't mean to curse!*

Quetzal let out a melodic laugh. "My dear friends," she said, her voice like a song. "You have fought so hard and I owe you my deepest gratitude." She reached out and gently scratched them both on the head.

Pico's feathers ruffled, eyelids fluttering as he nearly fainted.

"But now, I need you—all of you—to leave this place," she said in a solemn tone. "You have done more than enough, and I would never forgive myself if further harm fell upon you."

Teo expected them to put up a fuss or ask questions, like they always did with him, but instead, they listened without question.

Yes, Diosa!

Call us if you need us!

We won't go far!

We are at your service! Peri chirped before giving Quetzal a deep bow.

YOU HEARD HER! Pico shrieked, taking off into the air. *RETREAT!*

In a flock, the birds left through the gaping holes of the throne room and into the night.

Quetzal straightened and smoothed her hands down her dress. "Now it's our turn to fight," she announced, turning to the gathered dioses. "For our people, our children, and our home."

"IT'S TIME FOR A BRAWL!" Diose Guerrero crowed with what Teo could only describe as unbridled joy, leaping over Lumbre's fire and onto Chupacabra's back.

With renewed vigor, the deities took over fighting the Obsidians alongside their children.

Teo could hardly believe his eyes as he watched Ocelo fight alongside Guerrero, who resembled a fierce jaguar ready for war. Atzi's lightning crackled through the air as she fought beside her father, Tormentoso. Dezi communicated with his mother, Amor, through sign language, their love and unity making them a formidable force against their enemies. Xochi and Primavera weaved a deadly snarl of plants and vines, entangling and immobilizing the Obsidians as Marino and Agua created tidal waves to pummel them. Auristela and Aurelio fought side by side with their mother, their combined fire burning brighter than anything Teo had ever seen.

Tierra worked diligently on melting the Sun Stones and the Sol Stone, their molten form beginning to take shape. But something was missing.

"We need a sacrifice to complete the ritual!" Tierra called urgently.

Teo's heart stopped. "No!" There was no way in hell he had risked *everything*, gone through *all of this* just for a semidiose still to be sacrificed—

"Auristela!" Diosa Lumbre barked at her daughter. The diosa snapped her fingers and the ceremonial dagger appeared in her hand. She marched right up to Auristela, pushing it into her hands. "Do it!"

Dioses and semidioses alike stared at Lumbre, shocked by her callousness.

Auristela froze and stared at the dagger before blinking up at her mom. She was obviously terrified, and Teo didn't know what it was— blind loyalty, or that duty had just been beaten into her by Lumbre her whole life—but Auristela nodded.

"DON'T, Stela!" Aurelio bellowed from across the room. His eyes were wild, panicked as he pleaded with his sister. "We shouldn't be forced to give up our lives!"

That snapped her out of it. "If I don't, everyone in Reino del Sol will suffer!" Auristela's eyes blazed with determination as she held the dagger to her chest, like she was afraid Aurelio would take it. "I won't let that happen!"

It was the most selfless thing Teo had ever heard her say. He was surprised, but maybe he shouldn't have been. Maybe this had been Auristela's character the whole time, but he just didn't see it through her arrogance and anger.

"It's my responsibility—I'll do it!" she said, her voice rising above the clatter of battle.

"Wait, stop!" Teo shouted, but his words were lost in the sudden uproar as the other semidioses converged and began arguing, each volunteering to take Auristela's place. The room echoed with their bickering, creating a cacophony that almost drowned out the sounds of the dioses fighting the Obsidians.

"Let me do it!" Ocelo yelled, their jaguar eyes fierce. "I want to be the one who saves the world!"

Teo felt a surge of frustration well up inside him. He launched into the air, propelling himself as fast as he could, and snatched the dagger away from them all, gripping it tightly in his hand.

"Enough!" he shouted, his voice hoarse. "No one is being sacrificed! Can everyone stop trying to kill themselves for *five godsdamn minutes?!*"

The semidioses fell silent, staring at Teo with a mix of shock and confusion. But then, the obsidian blade suddenly flew out of his hand.

Teo turned to find Xio standing in the middle of the room, reaching out for the dagger floating in front of them. They were obviously using their control over obsidian, and the look of determination on their face filled Teo with fear.

This wasn't the same Xio he had known before. This Xio was different. Stronger.

"Teo," Xio said softly, their voice carrying across the hushed room. "I'm sorry, but I have to do this."

Teo felt his heart shatter. "You don't—"

Xio shook their head. With a final glance at Teo, they turned toward Tierra, the dagger held firmly in their hand. "I'm going to make things right."

CHAPTER 31
XIO

The obsidian dagger gleamed wickedly in Xio's hand, heavy with the weight of their decision. Tierra watched them with apprehension.

Xio hesitated for a moment, their heart racing. They had betrayed everyone, releasing the Obsidian gods upon the world, and this was the only way they knew to make amends. Determination etched across their face, Xio said, "This is my sacrifice to make."

Across the room, Venganza roared with fury. He charged like a wild beast, closing the distance between him and Xio in seconds, ready to rip them apart, dark energy crackling around him.

As they looked back, Xio knew there would be no mercy.

Venganza raised his hand high above his head. Xio clutched the obsidian dagger to their chest and threw up their free arm to shield themself.

Xio heard Teo scream, "*NO!*"

Venganza's hand came crashing down, then there was a sudden explosion of light.

Venganza was thrown back by the force of the blast.

Squinting through the brilliance, Xio saw their azabache bracelet had created a shield around them. It was a barrier of pure, shimmering energy. The jet charm Suerte had given them as a child was protecting them, just as he'd promised it would.

Suerte appeared between Xio and Venganza, clothed in radiant white.

"STAY AWAY FROM MY CHILD," Suerte roared, his voice booming with the force of a thousand storms.

Xio's heart hammered in their chest as they stared up at Suerte.

"Dad?" they croaked. A torrent of emotions surged through Xio—relief, gratitude, confusion. They had been so certain that Suerte wouldn't show up. That he hated Xio and never wanted to see them again.

Their eyes flicked between Venganza, staring in disbelief, and the steady figure of Suerte. In that moment, the difference between the two dioses could not have been more stark. Venganza was chaos and destruction. Suerte, love and protection.

He turned to Xio and knelt. "Xio, my child," Suerte said softly, his voice tinged with both sorrow and pride. "I am so sorry."

Xio shook their head, swallowing hard against the sudden lump in their throat. "No—I'm the one who's sorry! I ran away. I did terrible things—I released the Obsidians—"

"None of that matters now," Suerte said, his gaze locked on Xio's face, filled with unwavering love. "We're here, together, and we can make things right. All that matters is that you're safe."

Xio felt a strange sense of calm wash over them. For the first time in their life, they truly understood what it meant to be loved unconditionally. Suerte's presence was like a beacon of hope, cutting through the darkness that they'd been trapped in for so long.

All this time, they had felt like an outsider, like they didn't belong anywhere and had no real family. But blood had little to do with kinship. Suerte was their dad. Teo, Niya, and Aurelio were their family.

"Xio," Suerte murmured, cupping Xio's face in his large hands. He looked older to Xio, tired and sadder than they'd ever seen him. "I'm so sorry. I thought I was doing the right thing. All I ever wanted was to keep you safe."

Xio nodded, tears prickling at the corners of their eyes. "I know you did," they said through sniffles.

Suerte's expression darkened into fierce determination. "Now it's time for me to end this," he said grimly.

Xio blinked, confused. Fear choked Xio as they saw the obsidian dagger in Suerte's hand.

"NO!" Venganza howled from across the room. He tried to surge forward, but the dioses moved in, blocking his way.

Suerte raised the dagger high above his head.

Xio's eyes widened in horror as they realized what he was about to do. "No!" they screamed, reaching out to stop him.

But it was too late.

The obsidian dagger plunged into the dios's chest with ease.

Jade blood spilled from the wound. Suerte's face contorted in pain. His legs crumpled. Fantasma appeared. Gently, she caught his head in her lap when he collapsed.

"*Dad!*" Xio cried out, their voice breaking as they fell to their knees beside Suerte. They clutched his large hand between their small, trembling ones. "*Why did you do that?*" they shouted, hot angry tears on their cheeks.

"*Xio,*" Suerte sighed, his voice the same soft velvet as when he'd comfort Xio after a bad dream. Suerte smiled weakly, reaching up to brush away their tears. "My brave, stubborn child," he said with a small laugh.

"Please don't leave me here alone," Xio managed to choke. "I need you."

"Xio," Suerte whispered, his breaths growing shallow and weak. "You're not alone." His dark eyes slid past them.

Xio followed his gaze.

Teo, Niya, and Aurelio stood over them in a tight half circle.

Niya's broad shoulders were slumped, her arms hanging limp at her sides with her blade and shield still in hand. Her chin was lowered to her chest, dimpled as her bottom lip quaked. Aurelio stood tall but very still. His steady gaze was comforting.

Teo was between them, his hands clenched into fists at his sides, his body rigid. There was a fierce look of determination on Teo's face, betrayed by his frantic eyes. They darted between Xio and his dad.

Teo was still trying to come up with a plan, but Xio knew not even he could solve this one.

"That won't change when I'm gone," his father rasped.

Fantasma gave Xio a sad smile, a reassuring nod.

"My love for you is eternal," Suerte told them. "And I will watch over you, *always.*"

Xio threw themself onto Suerte, gripping him tight. They sobbed into Suerte's shoulder, trying to memorize the way his arms felt around them, the smokiness of his voice, and the itchy stubble of his cheek.

As they embraced, Suerte's body began to fade, dissolving into brilliant jade green stardust. It shimmered and twisted, drifting upward and disappearing into the night sky. Fantasma left with him, leaving Xio grasping at air.

Quetzal appeared by their side. She placed a soft hand on Xio's curls, eyes shining with grief, and swept them into a hug with her wings. She leaned her forehead against Xio's, her soft skin warm against the cold numbness of their own.

Xio's heart was a gaping chasm, threatening to swallow them whole.

"Xio," a voice murmured gently.

Teo slid between his mother's wings and wrapped his arms around Xio from behind. Niya joined them, her embrace fierce and protective as she added her own strength to theirs, closely followed by Aurelio's strong, reassuring hands on their shoulders. Atzi gently placed her hand on Xio's, her eyes full of understanding and empathy.

As the pain threatened to overwhelm them, Xio found solace in the love of their friends and clung to the hope that somewhere out there, Suerte still watched over them, as he'd promised.

CHAPTER 32
TEO

Breaths sawed in and out of Teo's lungs as he stood there, desperately trying to think of a way to fix this, but there was nothing. No amount of quick thinking or cleverness would bring Suerte back.

The god of fortune was gone.

Anger and grief warred in Teo's chest. Everything he had done was to protect not just the people he cared about—it was to protect *everyone*. He hadn't wanted Auristela to die. He hadn't wanted Aurelio to take her place. He hadn't wanted Xio to suffer. And he hadn't wanted to lose Suerte.

The dioses had allowed the Sunbearer Trials to continue, placing the fate of the world on their children's shoulders, when all this time any one of them could have made the same sacrifice as Suerte.

The last remnants of Suerte's jade stardust still lingered on the floor. Tierra scooped up a handful, his eyes fixed on Sol's golden skeleton, then tipped the stardust into Sol's open jaw.

For a moment, nothing happened. Then, like a spark igniting a flame, golden light rushed through the bones, spreading and intensifying until it exploded in a burst of radiance. The sudden, dazzling brilliance forced Teo to shield his eyes as Sol's body began to take shape.

Venganza's face contorted with terror, Sol's light flashing in his wide eyes. Caos and Chupacabra cowered, retreating behind Venganza.

As the light began to settle, Sol rose, their form shimmering like the sun, too bright to look at directly.

Sol turned to face the Obsidian gods.

"No!" Venganza shouted. The defiant snarl contorting his face was betrayed by the fear in his eyes and the strangled desperation of his voice.

The once terrifying Chupacabra rolled onto her back, exposing her belly. Her eyes were wild and frantic as she panted and whimpered. Caos sank into the folds of their robe, nothing more than a quivering heap of laundry.

With a simple lift of their hand, Sol blasted the Obsidian gods with a torrent of brilliant, burning light. Venganza, Caos, and Chupacabra screamed and howled as they incinerated before Teo's eyes, bursting into stardust.

The particles trembled before streaking up, up, up into the night. With a flicker, their constellations reappeared among the stars.

Teo's knees shook as he stared at the scorch marks left behind, nothing more than smudges of ash on the stone floor. Sol remained in the center of the room, a body of undulating light. They were the same height as the other dioses, but standing this close to them was like standing in the shadow of a skyscraper—overwhelming and dizzying.

"Are they gone?" Teo asked, doing his best to keep his voice from shaking.

His mother nodded. "Sol has banished them back to the stars," Quetzal confirmed, resting her hand on Teo's arm. "The Obsidians are gone."

"Except for one."

Diosa Lumbre stepped forward. She stared down at Xio, lip curled in disdain. He'd seen that same expression reflected on Auristela's face more times than he could count.

Xio scrambled back, running into Teo. A violent anger unlike any Teo had ever felt tore through his veins. Without thinking, he surged toward the diosa.

"*If you think*—"

Before he could do something incredibly stupid, like throw hands with a goddess, his mother stepped between them. She flung out her wings, blocking Lumbre's path.

"We have killed enough of our children," Quetzal said, quiet but firm.

Fury burned in Lumbre's fiery gaze. "That is *not* one of our children," she seethed through her perfect teeth. Lumbre jabbed her manicured finger at Xio. "That is a *monstrosity*. If this has taught us anything, it's that Obsidians will keep coming back unless we exterminate *all of them* like the vermin they are—"

Sol exploded with light like a solar flare. A hum filled the air so loud that Teo had to clamp his hands over his ears.

Dios and semidiose alike shrank back from Sol as they floated forward. But Quetzal didn't budge.

Teo's blood turned cold as Sol stared down at her. For a moment, they silently regarded each other. The humming started again, but this time it was quiet and warm. When it faded, his mother's eyebrows drew together.

Then she lowered her wings and stepped aside.

Slowly, Sol approached Xio.

Teo rushed forward. Niya immediately appeared at his side, weapons drawn but looking terrified as she stared up at Sol.

"*Wait*—" Teo started to plead, terror thick in his throat. He didn't know what he was going to do, or what he was going to say, but he couldn't let Sol banish Xio.

He stepped forward, but his mom caught his arm. Teo's panic sky-rocketed. He tried to pull away, but Quetzal's grip didn't budge. Sol stopped before Xio, looming over them. Xio stared up at Sol with dark, glistening eyes. The young Obsidian had no fight left. Xio was so small and tired, stricken with grief.

Teo could hardly breathe as he watched, every fiber of his being screaming at him to *do something*—

But then Sol sank to their knees. The sun god and Xio were mirrors of each other, their gazes locked. Slowly, Sol bowed their head, touching their forehead to Xio's. Xio's eyes slid shut.

A melodious hum grew. Sol's glow burned brighter, radiating warmth and engulfing them both in brilliant light.

Teo had to look away until it receded. When he looked again, Xio had slumped into Sol, their face hidden in the diose's chest as small sobs shook their body. Sol's sunlight arms wrapped around them, their hand resting on Xio's black curls.

Teo's legs nearly collapsed under him.

The humming faded and Sol stood.

Teo, Niya, and Aurelio were immediately at Xio's side.

"Are you okay?" Teo asked, giving Xio's shoulders a squeeze. It was a stupid question—of course they weren't okay—but he was too light-headed from the relief of Xio not getting blasted into stardust to think of anything better.

Xio only nodded and dragged their fist across their damp eyelashes.

Sol crossed the room to Tierra. The earth god's eyes glistened behind his golden mask. Sol gently cupped Tierra's face in their hands. Light danced and melodic humming filled the air as the two gods embraced, reunited after being apart for so long.

Niya looked on with a crumpled smile, holding back tears.

With Tierra at their side, Sol turned to face the others.

Sol's voice hummed, "These wars between the gods have gone on long enough."

The room broke out into chatter.

Lumbre's voice rose above the rest. "See? It's as Sol says! We must deal with this final Obsidian threat!"

Guerrero nodded their jaguar head solemnly. "We must do as Sol says," they agreed.

"Nini," Ocelo said, tugging on their parent's red cape. A deep frown settled onto their strong features. "I'm not sure that's what Sol meant. They spared Xio."

Guerrero's head tipped to the side, betraying their confusion.

"The war has been between *us* gods," Quetzal said. "*Our* meddling, *our* fighting, and *our* egos."

"Our children were only ever dragged into it after the fact," Amor agreed. "We should be protecting them, not—"

Lumbre snarled. "*That* child freed the Obsidians from their prison of a thousand years! Obsidian blood runs through his veins and he will betray us again! There needs to be order and punishment for our world to survive!"

"Perhaps it is time we took a step back," Tormentoso said thoughtfully. "Let Reino del Sol recover from the destruction we've brought—"

"And *continue* to bring," Quetzal added, gesturing around them.

"Reino del Sol cannot function without the guidance of the dioses! The humans are *human*," Lumbre boomed with distaste. "They are flawed and they are stupid. Without us, they would fall to their own ruin! They do not know what is best for them—"

"They know better than you do!" Teo cut in.

The dioses turned to Teo, stunned—except for Quetzal, who beamed at him.

"This is the problem!" he shouted, looking around at the gathered gods. "You all think you know what's best for everyone in Reino del Sol, when you don't know *anything*!" The angry words spilled from his mouth. "You just make up rules for the world, interpreting Sol's intentions in the most fucked-up way possible! You've spent *centuries* letting your own children get murdered when any one of you could've put a stop to this at any time!" he accused them.

Most of the dioses at least had the decency to look ashamed.

Except for Lumbre.

"You think *you* know better than the gods, boy?" she snarled.

"Yeah, I do, actually!" he spat back. "You all are too busy being fancy and self-important in your temples! Most of you don't even hand out your own blessings—you leave it for your priests to do, like it's a chore!"

The dioses exchanged guilty looks.

"When was the last time one of you even *talked* to a human?" Teo demanded.

None of them spoke.

Teo threw up his hands. "Exactly! You don't know anything about them, including what they need!" He thought of Yucca, Paz, and the other villagers. They'd seen how irresponsible and dangerous the gods were, and had created their own haven.

"You should be turning to the members of your communities to figure out what the people of Reino del Sol need, and how to provide for them," Teo continued. "Not making all these decisions without a single thought for how it could affect them!

"The view from your golden temples will never be the same as the view from your city streets!" Teo told them angrily. He took a deep breath, dropping his arms to his sides. "*Suerte* understood that."

Sol turned to Tierra, who sighed deeply and offered them his hand. Light sparked where their fingertips met. A long moment stretched as the two communed.

Teo noticed the dioses looking on, shocked, as Sol hummed to his partner. He remembered how so many of the Golds looked down on Tierra, believing that losing Sol had been the earth god's fault to begin with.

The light faded and Sol's hums quieted. Tierra nodded in understanding.

Sol regarded the crowd. "We will join Luna," they said, their thrumming voice echoing in the broken room.

The dioses immediately broke out into chatter again.

Teo frowned. What did that mean? He looked at his mom.

Quetzal's eyes popped in surprise. But then she exhaled, a soft, resigned sound.

It made Teo's chest clench. "Mom?"

She gave him a somber smile and pushed his hair from his eyes. "It's okay, Pajarito," Quetzal said.

Icy-cold dread dropped into Teo's stomach.

"Sol has spoken," Tierra said, his raspy voice louder than Teo had ever heard it. He waited for the dioses to quiet. "We are going to join Luna on the other side. All of us," Tierra said.

"*What?*" Teo said, but no one heard him.

"The other side?"

"You mean leave?"

"We can't leave!"

"Papi?" Niya stepped forward, her breathing strained. "What do you mean? You're not gonna *leave* leave, right?"

Tierra sighed, absently tucking one of Niya's messy braids behind her ear. "We have failed those we were created to protect," he said, as if they were the only two in the room.

"No!" Xochi cried out, clinging to Primavera.

"We just got you back!" Atzi said angrily, looking to Tormentoso for backup.

"That's not fair!" Ocelo said, retreating to Guerrero's side.

The jaguar-headed god placed their hands on Ocelo's shoulders. "You are a Child of Guerrero," the diose reminded them, looking down at Ocelo with a stern look. "You are a warrior, and a good warrior follows the orders of their leader. Isn't that right?"

Ocelo nodded, their face contorted as they fought to hold back their own tears. "Y-yes, Nini."

Guerrero smiled, flashing their sharp white teeth. "Ocelo," they purred before crushing them in a bone-cracking hug.

Teo's heartbeat thudded in his ears. He grabbed his mom's hand and searched her face, trying to form a sentence. "But you didn't do anything!" he blurted. Why did *all* the gods have to be punished?

"I didn't," Quetzal agreed, doing her best to smile. "But I didn't speak up, and I didn't stop it, either."

Teo was furious with her for being so calm.

"But you have to stay and take care of *me*!" Niya insisted, tears streaming down her cheeks.

Tierra's eyes were pained behind his mask. "I'm so sorry, mija," he said softly. "But the rule of dioses is over." He looked at the others. "It's time for the humans to decide for themselves."

Niya turned to Teo, her eyes frantic and desperate. He was the plan guy, after all.

Teo's thoughts spiraled as he raced to think of a solution. He thought of Suerte's sacrifice—the god of fortune giving his life to save them all. It was a heavy burden to bear, knowing that he had died for them, and Teo knew they could not let that sacrifice be for nothing.

He thought of brave Paloma standing at the sacrificial table in the old video.

Xio had already lost their dad. Teo didn't want anyone else to suffer the same fate. Including himself.

"Can't we negotiate?" Teo blurted out.

Sol and Tierra turned to him, surprised.

"Negotiate?" Tierra repeated, like he wasn't sure if it was a joke or not.

"Can we get weekends and evenings?" he asked, looking between the two creator gods.

Sol regarded him silently, so he rushed on.

"Or—or—" Teo stammered, wracking his brain as his heart hammered in his chest. "Once a month?"

Sol made a low, rumbly sound that might've been a chuckle. They hummed, and Tierra nodded.

"We will all convene at Sol Temple every ten years to commemorate the sacrifices made to protect Reino del Sol," Tierra announced.

Teo's fingers twitched at his sides. It was good, but they could do better.

"Can you throw in holidays?" he asked with a hopeful lift of his eyebrows.

That time, Tierra was the one who laughed. Sol hummed and Tierra confirmed. "The dioses may return every year on their personal holy days," he agreed.

Teo breathed a sigh of relief. His heart was still heavy, but at least he was comforted by the promise of not losing his mom completely. The semidioses murmured amongst themselves, their fear slowly dissipating as they clung to the thought of reuniting with their parents.

"My dad, too?" Xio asked in a small, hopeful voice.

Tierra gave a slow shake of his head. "I'm so sorry, Xio," he told them. "But Suerte is with Muerte now."

Xio's eyes fell to the ground.

"He can't return physically, but he's still around, looking after you from afar, just as he promised," Tierra reassured them. "You will be able to commune with him at his altar, as with all the dioses. And you have others to look out for you, too," he added, nodding to Teo and Niya.

As if on cue, Fantasma appeared at Xio's side in a shower of marigold petals and golden butterflies.

Tierra chuckled. "Including the little lady," he said as Fantasma squeezed Xio into a hug. When she pulled back, a skeletal hand popped up from the ground, holding a grape Chupa Chup. Fantasma handed it to Xio.

They took it and did their best to smile.

"Fantasma will continue to traverse both worlds," Tierra explained. "She will look after you all and the humans. She still has a very important job to do here."

Fantasma nodded solemnly, her eyes meeting Teo's with an unspoken promise. Sol bowed his head to her, and as he did, her appearance changed.

Her skin took on the smoothness of stone, milky white and translucent, revealing a golden skeleton beneath. Her dress turned white, billowing out around her like a cloud, and a crown of marigolds adorned her dark hair. Her eyes became molten gold, reflecting Sol's light that bathed them all.

"Smash," Niya whispered to Teo. Despite everything, he couldn't help cracking a small smile.

The air grew heavy with the weight of goodbyes. The gods and their children embraced, tears flowing freely as they exchanged heartfelt farewells.

Teo clung to his mom. When he looked up, Quetzal's eyes filled with a sadness he had never seen before.

"It's time for the semidioses and the people of Reino del Sol to take control and make change without the dioses standing in your way," she said. She sniffled and smiled down at Teo. "I can't wait to see what you do next."

With a flash of sunlight, Sol and the other dioses ascended into the sky, leaving the demigods and Fantasma behind in the destroyed temple.

The sun finally rose once again. Warmth seeped into every corner of the room, chasing away a cold that had burrowed deep into Teo's bones barely two weeks ago. Its rays spilled across the endless jungle, the golden light filtering through the leaves, dancing upon the ground, and warming Teo's cheeks.

In the distance, the moon's crescent smile kissed the horizon.

As the sun continued to climb, its warm embrace enveloping them all, Teo couldn't help feeling the bittersweet victory settling in his chest.

"Wow, I can't believe we pulled it off," Teo said, his voice wavering. "We actually stopped the apocalypse."

Aurelio turned to him, his serious expression softening. "We couldn't have done it without you."

Teo snorted. "You could've, but you would've really sucked at it."

"Okay, to be fair," Niya chimed in, "you literally started this whole mess to begin with!"

Teo bumped his shoulder into Xio's, grinning mischievously. "Actually, that was Xio." At this, Xio looked stricken for a moment, but Teo's grin only widened. "And thank Sol they did."

Teo wrapped his arms around Aurelio's middle, his fingers tracing patterns on the warm skin beneath the fabric of the taller boy's shirt.

"Can we please do something normal when we get back, like go on a date?" Teo asked.

Aurelio's face turned a beautiful shade of red. He tentatively caressed the feathers just below Teo's shoulder blades. "That sounds . . ." Aurelio trailed off, looking for the word.

"Nice?" Teo guessed.

"Normal," Aurelio finished.

Teo laughed and crushed him into a kiss.

"Ew," Auristela cut in, angrily wiping tears from her cheeks. "I leave you alone for, like, two weeks and you're dating a *Jade*?"

Niya rolled her eyes, grabbing Auristela's hand and threading their fingers. "Oh, shut up. You're so annoying."

Auristela scowled up at her, but left her hand where it was.

Together, the group of semidioses stood amidst the ruins of the temple, surrounded by the aftermath of their battle. The air somehow felt lighter now.

They stood together in the growing light, their hearts full of hope and dreams of the future. They were the architects of a new era, the ones who would help shape Reino del Sol into a land of peace and prosperity, with the guidance and help of everyone else. And as the sun crested in the sky, they knew that whatever challenges lay ahead, they would face them head-on, united as one.

"I have a question," Atzi said, speaking up. "How exactly are we getting home?"

The semidioses looked around.

Teo blinked. "Oh . . . I hadn't thought about it."

"Kinda rude to just ditch us here," Marino agreed.

A thought popped into Teo's head. "I think we've got some friends nearby that might be able to help," he said.

Niya giggled. "Yucca's gonna be *pissed* when we all show up."

"Who are they talking about, Relio?" Auristela asked.

Aurelio sighed and draped his arm across her shoulders. "It's a long story."

EPILOGUE

The Quetzlan bird show was only a week away, and there was still so much to do. Teo had been staying late at school for days, helping to organize every detail, from the choreography of the performances to the design of the elaborate costumes.

"What do you think about using these golden threads to accentuate the tail feathers?" called out Chela, one of his classmates who had volunteered to help with the event. They'd set up a work area in the auditorium, where the bird show was held every year.

"Perfect!" Teo replied, examining the shimmering strands in her hand. "That'll make them stand out even more when they catch the sunlight!"

As he spoke, Teo glanced over at the window and noticed that the sun was indeed beginning to dip toward the horizon. Its golden rays streamed through the glass, casting long shadows across the room—

"Shit!" Teo hissed, jumping to his feet. "It's almost sunset, I'm late!"

"Late?" Chela asked as Teo sprinted for the door. "Hey—where are you going?"

"I've got a date!" Teo called back. "Thanks for all your help today, Chela!" he added before running out the door.

"Have fun!"

Down the hall and through the courtyard, Teo unfurled his wings as soon as he stepped outside and took flight. As he sped through the bustling city of Quetzlan, he could feel the anticipation that had been growing since the Obsidians were banished and the dioses left six months ago. Golds mingled with Jades and mortals, working side by side to rebuild their world after the recent chaos and destruction.

Teo's wings beat furiously against the warm evening air as he raced against the setting sun, weaving through the colorful streets and passing by familiar faces.

"Teo! A moment of your time?" called out a priest from the street, waving him over. In the absence of the gods, the priests had become their voices, guiding the people and maintaining order. Teo had been instrumental in this transition, working closely with Huemac to keep things running smoothly.

"Sorry, I can't stop right now!" Teo replied hurriedly, his voice laced with regret and a hint of frustration. He knew his responsibilities were important, but all he could think about was Aurelio waiting for him.

Reino del Sol was being rebuilt. With their sense of faith in the dioses deeply shaken, humans wanted to have as much say in their destinies as possible. Many people no longer believed in their priests. The fear of backsliding into the old ways was ever present, so life in Reino del Sol had to change.

Newly elected officials included trusted priests, semidioses who used their powers to fight the Celestials, and humans who organized to defend others when the world was on the verge of collapse. People questioned themselves and how to exist in a world not governed by dioses. Their determination to make things work was already an act of rebellion against their former society. No one was giving up.

Semidioses like Teo now had unprecedented freedom to shape their own destinies. While any semidiose was welcome to join the

Academy and start their journey to become a Hero, Teo had taken a different route.

With his mom gone, Teo decided to learn how to help run the logistics of Quetzlan under Huemac's tutelage. The priest had been voted onto the city's council, along with other human citizens.

The sun cast a warm golden hue over the streets. Teo couldn't help smiling as he watched people pass by, their wrists adorned with azabaches. It was a small yet poignant tribute to Suerte, to honor the dios who had made the ultimate sacrifice to save everyone in Reino del Sol.

"Teo, do you have a minute?" Yami asked, holding out a stack of papers.

"Can it wait until tomorrow?" he called down. "I've got somewhere I really need to be!"

She hesitated, then nodded. "All right, tomorrow it is! Have a good evening, Teo!"

"Thanks!" Teo shouted as he flew by, the wind whipping through his hair and rustling his feathers. He knew he needed to reach Aurelio before the sun dipped completely below the horizon—they had been planning this rendezvous for weeks, and he didn't want to miss a single second of it.

With each beat of his powerful wings, he propelled himself faster, determined not to let anything stand in his way. Finally, he landed at the entrance to the temple.

"Almost there," Teo whispered to himself, glancing anxiously at the fading light. "Just a little bit farther..."

As he approached the temple, the bane of Teo's existence came into view. A colossal golden statue depicting himself, Pico, and Peri towered above the entrance. Teo's statue gazed down at the people below while Pico and Peri were midflight at his sides.

Heat crept into Teo's cheeks, embarrassment washing over him as he took in the monument dedicated to their efforts. It was flattering, sure, but, gods, did he hate those garish statues.

Huemac was waiting for him at the entrance, eyebrows raised. "You missed the council meeting" was all he said, though there was a hint of amusement in his tone.

Teo ducked his head sheepishly. "I know, I know!" he said, rushing right past him. "I'm sorry—it won't happen again!"

Huemac's lips twitched. "I'm sure it will," he said, though there was no real admonishment in his words. "Your boyfriend is waiting for you in the courtyard," he added, his expression softening ever so slightly. "Don't keep him waiting any longer."

"Right, thanks!" Teo said, already turning on his heel and rushing toward the courtyard. His heart raced as he thought about seeing Aurelio again—it had been too long since they'd spent time together, and he was eager to make up for lost moments.

When Teo finally burst into the courtyard, it was alive with the vibrant colors of birds flitting about, their iridescent feathers glinting in the sun. The scent of blooming flowers filled his nose, and the soft rustle of leaves whispered in his ears as a gentle breeze danced through the foliage.

But all these sensory delights paled in comparison to what he truly sought.

There, squatting by the pond and watching the birds play, was Aurelio. His silky black hair cascaded down his back like a waterfall, catching the sunlight. Peaceful, radiant, and utterly captivating.

"Hey!" Teo said as he approached. "Sorry I'm late!"

Aurelio looked up. A smile lit his face, his eyes crinkling at the corners. "It's all right," he said, getting to his feet. "I know you've been busy helping Huemac and the others."

Unable to contain his excitement any longer, Teo broke into a run, covering the distance between them in a matter of seconds. As he reached Aurelio, he wrapped his arms around him and pressed a smooch onto his lips. "I've been dying to see you all freaking day!"

Aurelio's cheeks flushed a deep shade of rose as he pulled back slightly, a satisfied grin playing on his lips. "You have?"

Teo grinned back, the joy bubbling up inside him like champagne. He loved seeing this side of Aurelio—more open, more emotive, and definitely more talkative.

"Of course! I mean, who wouldn't want to spend time with their favorite fire-controlling demigod?" Teo teased, giving Aurelio's hand a playful squeeze.

"How's the planning going?" Aurelio asked.

Teo groaned, thumping his forehead against Aurelio's chest. "It's going to be a nightmare," he grumbled. "We have twice as many birds as last year, and the aviary is already bursting at the seams."

"I'm sure you'll figure it out. You always do." Aurelio patted his shoulder. "And now I'm here to help out."

"A whole weekend of you to myself!" Teo sang. "If I can survive the stress, anyway."

Aurelio pulled Teo in and pressed a kiss to the top of his head. "It's going to be great. I can't wait."

Teo smirked up at him. "Ready for our date?"

Aurelio tilted his head, eyes glinting with humor. "I've been ready for the past hour."

Teo laughed. "All right, all right. Let's go before someone asks me to do something else."

"First," Aurelio said, "I got something for you." He went digging into the tote slung over his shoulder and pulled out a brown paper bag. "I made this for Paloma," Aurelio said, his voice gentle yet proud. "It's a seed loaf. I thought we could put it on her altar."

Teo's heart swelled with warmth at the sight, and he couldn't help smiling as the scent of freshly baked bread filled the air. But before he could say anything, the birds around them seemed to catch wind of the enticing aroma, their beady eyes zeroing in on the loaf in Aurelio's hands.

"Hey, back off!" Teo barked, waving his arms to shoo the excited birds away. They squawked in protest, flapping their wings as they begrudgingly retreated.

"Persistent little shits, aren't they?" Teo muttered under his breath, shaking his head in amusement as he watched the birds regroup a safe distance away.

Aurelio chuckled, his eyes softening with fondness. "They just know good food when they smell it."

Teo inhaled deeply, the scent of freshly baked seed bread filling his senses. "This smells amazing!" he exclaimed.

Aurelio frowned, knitting his eyebrows together as he stared at the loaf in his hands. "I messed it up," he admitted, his tone tinged with disappointment. "The crust should be crunchier. I must've taken it out too early or not kneaded the dough enough."

"Are you kidding me?" Teo playfully nudged Aurelio's shoulder. "It's perfect! Even the birds think so!"

As if on cue, a flock of colorful birds swooped down from the nearby trees, their excited chatter filling the air. They fluttered around the couple, eyeing the seed bread hungrily. Teo couldn't help laughing as he juggled shooing away the persistent birds and holding on to Aurelio's hand.

Teo glanced at Aurelio, taking in the hint of a smile that played at the corners of his lips and the way his copper-brown eyes sparkled with happiness. It was moments like this that reminded him just how far they had come—how they'd found stability and comfort with each other after the chaos and destruction.

"Thank you, Aurelio," Teo said, his voice full of gratitude. "Paloma will love it."

Aurelio simply nodded, his expression serene as he held the bread protectively. He knew how much Paloma meant to Teo, and Teo couldn't help feeling an overwhelming sense of appreciation for the way Aurelio continually supported him, even in the smallest gestures.

"Hurry up!" Teo said, grabbing Aurelio's arm and dragging him toward the stairs. "Before we miss the sunset!"

They fell into step next to each other and began to climb the stairs to the temple's observatory.

"How's pastry school?" Teo asked.

"It's good. Fun but challenging." After a moment, Aurelio added, "I'm happy there. I don't need to be a Hero or even Aurelio, Son of Lumbre, I can just exist and bake." His voice was soft, content.

"Good." Teo smiled, a genuine warmth spreading across his face. "The world needs pastry chefs just as much as Heroes."

Teo listened as Aurelio told him about the classes he was taking at the culinary institute in Pan Dulce's city. He asked questions when prompted, but mostly he was just content to listen and enjoy Aurelio's enthusiasm.

When he asked how the others were, Aurelio scrolled through his phone, pausing at a picture of Marino and Dezi, their arms around each other as they stood on the steps of a temple. Their smiles seemed to light up the screen, radiating happiness and contentment in their new roles. They'd decided to take Teo's route and serve their own home cities.

Aurelio's thumb swiped to the next image, revealing Xochi standing in front of a breathtaking quinceañera gown, its layers of shimmering fabric and fresh flowers cascading down like a waterfall of color. The intricate floral embroidery that adorned the bodice was unmistakably her handiwork.

"Wow, can you believe Xochi did this?" Teo asked, unable to keep the awe out of his voice.

"Believe it? I'm still trying to wrap my head around how she managed to become the top quince dress designer in Reino del Sol so quickly," Aurelio replied fondly. "It's incredible."

"I've been getting nonstop complaints from Niya about your sister and Ocelo," Teo said.

"That doesn't surprise me," Aurelio replied.

Niya had decided to return to the Academy and—along with Auristela and Ocelo—was a brand-new rookie Hero. The three were being trained together, which Niya claimed to hate, but Teo was pretty sure she secretly liked both of them.

"Niya mentioned something about La Cumbre and primordial gods?" Teo said before shrugging. "I don't know, she was too excited and talking too fast for me to understand."

"Are they coming to the bird show?" Aurelio asked.

Teo nodded with a smile. "All eight of them!"

Atzi was at the Academy, quickly rising through the ranks as one of the most promising semidioses of her time. According to Xio, who spoke to Atzi on a regular basis, she'd even taken some of the newly admitted Jades under her wing.

"I'm surprised you talked Xio into it," Aurelio admitted.

Xio had been learning about the Obsidian cities, their family, and the people who'd once lived in Los Restos. They had recruited professional archaeologists to go with them into Los Restos and excavate the sites of the destroyed cities in order to learn more about who they were.

Xio had told Teo they wanted people to know about the Obsidian mortals, who they were, what they loved, what they believed in before they were wiped out, so they weren't forgotten to time and were no longer seen as evil.

"Yeah, well, they owed me one," Teo said with a laugh.

Teo led Aurelio up the final steps of the observatory. He couldn't help feeling a sense of awe at the sight that greeted them.

The temple was bathed in the warm glow of the setting sun, casting long shadows across the polished floors. His mother's jade glyph remained in the center dais, but now it was surrounded by an array of altars, each one lovingly crafted and adorned with offerings.

Teo's eyes swept over the rows of ofrendas, each one dedicated to a fallen semidiose. Their names and pictures were displayed prominently, a reminder of the sacrifices they had made during the course of the Sunbearer Trials. The scent of incense hung heavy in the air, mingling with the fragrances of fresh flowers that adorned the altars.

"Wow," Aurelio murmured, following Teo's gaze. "I didn't realize there would be so many."

"Neither did I," Teo admitted, his voice barely more than a whisper. "And that's not even all of them." There had been many sacrifices over the course of thousands of years, so the cities all shared the responsibility of honoring every single one.

Teo could feel the weight of their sacrifices pressing down on him every time he went to the observatory now, a tangible reminder of the lives that had been lost in the Sunbearer Trials. He took a deep breath, forcing himself to focus on the task at hand. "Come on, let's pay our respects."

As they approached the altars, Teo noticed how each one seemed to have its own unique personality. Some were covered in candles and flowers, while others held personal items—tokens of love and loss passed down for generations through their families. He felt a pang of sadness as he realized just how many people had been affected by the trials, but also a fierce determination to make sure their deaths hadn't been in vain.

Teo led Aurelio to Paloma's altar, hand in hand. Teo couldn't help thinking about how life had changed since the gods' absence, and how he and Aurelio were now part of a new mythos—one that was being written by their own hands.

"This is Paloma's," Teo said, drawing Aurelio's attention to an altar covered in carefully arranged feathers. An old picture of Paloma sat in the middle, surrounded by candles. She and Teo had the same wavy hair, the same big dark eyes, and even the same dimples.

"It's beautiful," Aurelio said.

"It is," Teo agreed, feeling a lump forming in his throat. He reached out to touch one of the feathers, tracing its delicate contours with his fingertips. "They deserve to be remembered like this. All of them."

Aurelio nodded solemnly, placing the loaf of seed bread on Paloma's altar. "We'll make sure of it."

He glanced at Aurelio to find his eyes soft with warmth. Teo smiled and raised their joined hands, pressing a kiss to Aurelio's knuckles. "Thank you for this," he said quietly.

A faint blush stained Aurelio's cheeks, but he held Teo's gaze steadily. "You're welcome," he said, voice just as soft.

Teo felt his own face heat at Aurelio's words. He ducked his head, embarrassed at being caught out in a moment of sentimentality but pleased all the same.

When he looked up again, Aurelio was watching him with a small, private smile, the one that never failed to make Teo's heart skip a beat. He leaned in for a quick kiss, unable to resist.

"Come on, before we miss it!" Teo urged, grabbing Aurelio's hand and leading him out of the observatory and into the open air.

Teo paused for a moment, allowing Aurelio to take in the scene before them. Above, the sky was ablaze with brilliant hues of pink, orange, and violet as the sun dipped closer to the horizon. The vibrant colors reflected off the surface of the ocean, creating a mesmerizing dance of light on the water.

Teo glanced over at Aurelio, noticing the way the dying sunlight brought out the gold in his eyes.

"Wow," Aurelio murmured, his eyes wide with wonder. "This really is incredible."

"See?" Teo teased, nudging him playfully. "I told you so."

"All right, you win this time," Aurelio conceded with a small smile, his gaze still fixed on the vibrant sky.

Standing at the edge of the platform, Teo unfurled his wings, feeling the warm breeze rustle through his feathers.

"I brought you something, too," Aurelio said, reaching into his bag once more.

"Ooh, did you get me a present?" he asked.

"Maybe," Aurelio teased, a playful glint in his eyes. He pulled out a perfect piece of homemade mazapan wrapped in red cellophane. "Here," he said, handing the treat to Teo, "I made this for you."

"Really?" Teo's voice rose with surprise and delight as he accepted the gift. The scent of almonds and sugar filled his nose. Teo's heart swelled with affection for the quiet, thoughtful young man beside him. As he carefully peeled back the red cellophane wrapper, he marveled at the skill and care that had gone into making it.

It was just like Aurelio—subtle, yet sweet and full of heart.

"Thank you," Teo said. "It's perfect!"

Before Aurelio could object and point out all the ways he *hadn't* made it perfectly, Teo silenced him with a kiss.

Together, they sat down on a bench to enjoy the mazapan, their fingers intertwining as they watched the sun dip below the horizon, painting the sky in breathtaking shades of orange and pink. The sounds of Quetzlan drifted up to them—laughter and chatter from those who had come together to rebuild and grow after the dangers that had once threatened their world.

They watched as the sun dipped lower and lower, casting ever-changing patterns of light and shadow across the landscape below.

"Thank you for bringing me here," Aurelio said softly, turning to look at Teo.

"It's my favorite spot with my favorite person," Teo replied, squeezing him gently. "We've been through a lot together, and I just really wanted to share this with you."

There was still beauty in the world, even after everything they'd seen.

Aurelio nodded, his eyes never leaving Teo's as they sat on the edge of the world, the sun sinking into the sea before them. In that moment, the weight of their shared past seemed to lift, if only for a little while, as they found solace in each other's presence and the breathtaking scene that lay before them.

"Promise me we'll have lots of moments like this," Teo murmured, his voice barely audible over the gentle breeze rustling through the trees below.

"Always," Aurelio vowed, kissing the top of his head.

In the fading light of the day, Teo knew he could trust that promise with every fiber of his being.

ACKNOWLEDGMENTS

With the Sunbearer Trial duology coming to a close, there's several people I'd like to thank who made this story possible.

The first person I want to thank is my dear friend, Alex Abraham. You helped me create this story, survive multiple drafts, and while many times I wanted to cry like a big baby, you got me through it with a lot of laughs. Your voice, humor, and talent echo throughout this book, and especially in Xio's voice. I don't think I could ever express how much your help has meant to me, not only as an author developing their skills, but as a friend. This book literally would not exist without you.

The second person that needs to be recognized is my incredible editor, Holly West. I am so beyond thankful to have you as my editor. I've gone through this whole author journey with you as not only my guide, but as my storytelling companion and friend. I love our brainstorming sessions so much! You make me a better writer and I am *so proud* of everything we've achieved together.

HUGE thanks to my incredible agent, Jennifer March Soloway. I can't believe how lucky I am to have you in my life and guiding my career! Thank you for all of your constant support, encouragement, and for reassuring me when I'm being harsh on myself. You always know how to make me feel better and I'm constantly blown away by what an incredible advocate you are for me. Thank you for being my partner on this wild journey!

I wouldn't be the person—or writer—that I am today without my incredibly talented friends! Max, thank you for everything you do to support and take care of me, especially when I'm at my lowest. At the risk of constantly repeating myself, I'd be lost without you!

My loves and my muses—Anda, Katie, Mik, Ezrael, Bird, and Raviv. Thanks for all the love, laughs, and support! Your friendships have changed my life.

I'd also like to thank my dear friend, Teddy Adelberg, for their help with fleshing out our good, sweet boy Aurelio. You're the best! I also owe a HUGE thanks to Matthew Colston who helped me come up with what Reino del Sol would look like after this story ended.

I need to shout out my INCREDIBLE publishing team: publisher Jean Feiwel, managing editor Dawn Ryan, production manager Raymond Ernesto Colón, Kristin Delaney and Kaitlin Loss in subrights, designer L. Whitt, publicists Kelsey Marrujo and Sara Elroubi, Elysse Villalobos and Teresa Ferraiolo in marketing, and the entire sales team. I constantly brag about you guys to everyone! When I say I can't imagine working with a better team, I mean it! Most of us have been together for my entire publishing journey, and your support and care has made me feel so safe and happy at Feiwel & Friends—I ADORE YOU ALL SO FREAKING MUCH!

I obviously have to thank Mars Lauderbaugh, my obscenely talented friend. LOOK AT US! LOOK HOW FAR WE'VE COME!!!

My copy editor, Melanie Sanders, and my production editor, Starr Baer, also need some serious recognition. Y'all don't understand how much work they do to make my writing legible and decipher my malaprops—thank you both SO much!

Special thanks to Madaz Di Pinza for coming up with the brilliant idea of Teo's top surgery scars being jade green, and to Clara M.G., Alexander, Karma, and Jeimy for coining the term "Quetzaldeanos" for people who live in Quetzlan. Y'all are amazing!

I'd like to thank my family—De Anna, Christine, Chris, and Gramps. You guys have always been there for me, through thick and thin. Thank you for always believing in me.

And to Grammy, I miss you so much.

Last but certainly not least, I'd like to thank you, my dear reader! Thank you for coming on this journey with me. I'm so excited for the adventures we have next.

Thank you for reading this Feiwel & Friends book. The
friends who made *Celestial Monsters* possible are:

Jean Feiwel, Publisher
Liz Szabla, VP, Associate Publisher
Rich Deas, Senior Creative Director
Anna Roberto, Executive Editor
Holly West, Senior Editor
Kat Brzozowski, Senior Editor
Dawn Ryan, Executive Managing Editor
Raymond Ernesto Colón, Senior Director of Production
Foyinsi Adegbonmire, Editor
Rachel Diebel, Editor
Emily Settle, Editor
Brittany Groves, Assistant Editor
L. Whitt, Designer
Starr Baer, Production Editor

Follow us on Facebook or visit us online at mackids.com.
Our books are friends for life.